Date Due

DARK AS DAY

TOR BOOKS BY CHARLES SHEFFIELD

Cold as Ice
Dark as Day
The Ganymede Club
Georgia on My Mind and Other Places
Godspeed
How to Save the World (editor)
One Man's Universe

JUPITER™ NOVELS
Higher Education (with Jerry Pournelle)
The Billion Dollar Boy
Putting Up Roots
The Cyborg from Earth

DARK AS DAY

CHARLES SHEFFIELD

TOR®

A TOM DOHERTY ASSOCIATES BOOK ■ NEW YORK

DARK AS DAY

Copyright © 2002 by Charles Sheffield

This book is printed on acid-free paper.

Edited by Beth Meacham

A Tor Book
Published by Tom Doherty Associates, LLC
175 Fifth Avenue
New York, NY 10010

www.tor.com

Tor® is a registered trademark of Tom Doherty Associates, LLC.

ISBN 0-312-87634-3

First Edition: March 2002

Printed in the United States of America

0 9 8 7 6 5 4 3 2 1

To Kit and Karen

LIST OF MAJOR CHARACTERS
(IN ALPHABETICAL ORDER)

RUSTUM BATTACHARIYA:
aka Bat, aka *Megachirops*, the Great Bat, reclusive problem-solver and Master of the Puzzle Network.

JACK BESTON:
the Ogre, head of SETI Project Argus.

PHILIP BESTON:
the Bastard, head of SETI Project Odin.

SEBASTIAN BIRCH:
displaced person after the Great War, with obsessive interest in outer planet cloud systems.

DR. VALNIA BLOOM:
head of the Ganymede Department of Scientific Research.

JANEED JANNEX:
displaced person after the Great War, and would-be Outer System colonist.

MAGRIT KNUDSEN:
senior member of the Jovian Worlds cabinet, and former boss of Rustum Battachariya.

CAPTAIN ERIC KONDO:
captain of the *Outer System Liner Achilles*.

HANNAH KRAUSS:
senior SETI analyst, and boss of Milly Wu.

HAROLD (HAL) LAUNIUS:
a leading nanotech designer.

AGATHA LIGON:
a Commensal, great-aunt to Alex Ligon and a member of Ligon Industries' board of directors.

ALEX LIGON:
  predictive modeler and junior member of the Ligon family.

CORA LIGON:
  great-aunt to Alex Ligon and a member of Ligon Industries' board of directors.

HECTOR LIGON:
  cousin to Alex Ligon.

JULIANA LIGON:
  cousin to Alex Ligon and a Commensal.

KAROLUS LIGON:
  uncle to Alex Ligon, and Ligon Industries' senior "fix-it" specialist.

LENA LIGON:
  mother of Alex Ligon and a Commensal.

PROSPER LIGON:
  great-uncle to Alex Ligon and the head of Ligon Industries.

TANYA AND REZEL LIGON:
  cousins to Alex Ligon.

KATE LONAKER:
  division chief for advanced planning and predictive modeling on Ganymede, and Alex Ligon's immediate superior and lover.

PAUL MARR:
  first officer of the *Outer System Liner Achilles.*

CHRISTA MATLOFF:
  director of Earth's orbiting medical facility.

CYRUS MOBARAK:
  the "Sun King," inventor of the Moby fusion drive, and head of Mobarak Enterprises.

LUCY-MARIA MOBARAK:
  daughter of Cyrus Mobarak.

MORD:

the idiosyncratic high-level Fax of the late Mordecai Perlman.

PACK RAT:

senior member and Master of the Puzzle Network.

OLE PEDERSEN:

the capable but paranoid head of a predictive group competing with Alex Ligon and Kate Lonaker.

THE SEINE:

the integrated quantum-entangled computer system that extends all through the solar system.

NADEEN SELASSIE:

legendary developer of a lost "dark as day" doomsday weapon, presumed killed at the end of the Great War.

BENGT SUOMI:

chief scientist for Ligon Industries.

MILLY WU:

SETI analyst, and former junior champion of the Puzzle Network.

ZETTER:

security chief for Project Argus.

PROLOG
2071 A.D.

The Great War was over. It ended four months after it began, when the leaders of the Belt—crushed, humiliated, drained, and defenseless—agreed to an unconditional surrender.

And yet the Great War did not end. It could not end. It had swept like a gigantic storm across the face of the solar system, and like any storm it left behind its own trail of destruction, invisible eddies of unspent energy, whirlpools of hatred, and cluttered heaps of flotsam: people, weapons, and secret knowledge thrown together and abandoned.

Mars was not aware of the fact, but although hard-hit it had been doubly blessed. True, over half of its people had died. But life could still continue far below the surface, and the same infernal forces that swept clear the northern hemisphere had set in motion the melting of the permafrost. Two thousand years later, humans would walk unaided on the surface and breathe the clear Mars air.

But that was far off, in a remote and unimaginable future. Today a gummy slick of microphages covered the land from equator to poles, waiting for anything with a GACT sequence that invited disassembly.

Night fell, for the seven hundred and fiftieth time since the end of the Great War. The stars came out, bright and steady in the black sky. Phobos raced across the heavens, west to east. The purblind phages were unaware of its presence, or of the rising of Jupiter and Saturn.

But others on Mars knew. Three hundred kilometers from the barren equator, in the dead center of a low, flat valley, a ten-meter circle of surface released into the thin air a mist of chemicals. Any GACT or GACU form would have died within milliseconds. The disassemblers were made of sterner stuff, but they knew enough to recognize danger. A wave of microphages surged backward, clearing an annulus of bare gray scree around the misted ring. Those disassembler phages unlucky enough to be caught within the ring writhed, retreated toward the middle, and withered to a small heap of desiccated powder.

A puff of warmer air from below dispersed their dust. In the center of the ring a black dot had appeared. The dot widened into a dark open disk, through which a flat circular platform slowly rose. The microphages retreated farther, recoiling from the blown spray at the platform's perimeter.

Two suited figures stood at the center of the platform. The woman was holding the hand of the little boy, and pointing upward. He was about four years old, and showed far more interest in the writhing circle of microphages and the bleak landscape beyond than in the starry sky.

"Do you see it?" The woman's voice was wheezing and husky, and her back was oddly twisted. She shook the child's hand impatiently. "You're looking the wrong way. Over there. The brightest one."

The boy was tall for his age, and sturdily built. He followed her pointing arm to the place where rising Jupiter hung above the eastern horizon. Dark eyes gleamed behind the suit's visor, but his scowl was invisible in the dim light. "It's not big. You said it would be big."

"Jupiter *is* big. Huge. A lot bigger than this whole world. It only looks small because it's so far away."

"I could squash it in my fingers, it's so little. It can't hurt us."

"It *did* hurt us. Jupiter looks tiny, but it's really so big there are whole worlds, worlds nearly as big as this one, that circle around it. The people who live on them started the war. They were monsters. They killed your mother and father, and they killed your baby sister. They would have killed us, too, if we had stayed in the Belt. They are the reason we have to hide away here."

It was an oft-told story, but the boy stared at Jupiter with greater interest. "I don't see the other worlds at all."

"They are there, just so far away you can't see them. You've heard their names often. Ganymede, and Europa, and old Callisto."

"And smoky smirky Io. You missed one. In the Gali-lo song there are four."

"You're right. And there really are four. But nobody lives on Io."

"Why not? Does it have lots of these?" The boy's arm waved toward the ring of microphages, standing like the curled lip of a breaking wave just beyond the protective spray.

"No. Io has lightning and burning hot and other bad things. Nobody can live there. You wouldn't want to go there."

"If Jupiter is so big, I'd like to live there."

"You can't do that, either. Jupiter is *too* big. It would crush you flat."

"I bet it wouldn't crush me. I'm strong. I'm stronger than you."

"You are." The woman tried to laugh, and it came out as a weak-lunged cough. "My dear, everyone is stronger than I am. The people up there who started the war didn't kill me, but they certainly did their best. I used to be strong, too."

A warning chime sounded in the suit helmets on her final words. The spray that held the phages at bay was thinning. The woman stared around her at the barren landscape, seeing changes there invisible to the boy.

She took his hand. "You can't stay here much longer, things are getting worse. We have to make plans. No, not for Jupiter. Jupiter is a giant, it would crush even you. Come on. We have to go back down."

"In a minute." He turned his head, to scan the whole sky. "Where's the other one? I can't see it."

"Because it's not so bright as Jupiter." She pointed to a star whose light had a leaden gleam compared with its neighbors. "There you are. That's Saturn. It's big, but not so big as Jupiter."

"But I can go there?"

"You can go. There, or maybe Jupiter." She laughed again, at some secret joke. The platform was beginning its slow descent into the dark shaft. The circle of microphages began to creep in. She painfully straightened her rachitic spine. "Oh, yes, you can go. And one day, my dear, you *will* go to one or the other. And then they'll pay, all of them, for what they've done to us."

It was hard to say which was worse: waiting for Seine-Day to arrive, or enduring the torrent of hype that preceded the event.

Alex Ligon stared at the output that filled the two-meter display volume of his Ganymede office. In that display the solar system was evolving before his eyes. The year showed as 2098, ticking along a steady daily tally of status: population, economic activity, material and energy production and use, and transportation and information flow between worlds. Any statistic was available for the asking. And every statistic, he knew from past experience, was likely to be wrong. For anything beyond a week, the predictions steadily diverged from reality.

It was not the fault of his models, he felt sure of that. It was simply that he was forced to run them with too-high levels of aggregation. Otherwise, a one-day prediction would be slower than real-time and take more than a day to run.

The Seine, once it came into operation, would cure that completely. He would be able to model each individual human unit, all five billion of them, together with data bank details from everywhere in the System. He would also, if the Seine's performances matched the promises made for it, be able to run at a million times real-time. He could sit back and watch his models blur through a century of solar system development in an hour.

"*When I dipped into the future, far as human eye can see.*" Or well beyond, with a little help from the right computer. More than that, with the Seine's quantum parallelism you could vary any parameter and observe the effect of changes.

If the Seine's performance matched the promises.

Alex glanced at the bottom left-hand corner of the display, where media inputs were displayed. He had the sound level damped way down, but the picture was enough to tell him what was going on. It was another puff piece about the Seine, set against a background of a high-level entangling unit. A smiling woman with an unnatural number of teeth was doing the talking; a portly older man beside her was nodding confidently; and a thin woman with worry lines marking her forehead stood in the background—probably one of the engineers, poor bastard, who actually had to *deliver* the Seine's entangling and instantaneous data transfer across the whole System.

Alex turned his attention back to the main display. It was chugging along toward the end of 2099, almost two years from now, and the model showed a million tons of materials were being shipped daily between Ganymede and Rhea, Saturn's second largest moon. And if you believed *that* figure you would believe anything. Present shipping was less than a hundred tons a day. The model was diverging again. Higher resolution was a must if the results were to mean anything.

Alex swore and glanced back to the media corner. They were handling the return of the Seine as the event of the century, bigger even than the war that had disrupted and dispersed the original Seine. Maybe they were right. The original pre-war version of the Seine had linked the System, but it was primitive compared with its quantum logic successor. And Alex needed every bit of computing power he could lay his hands on.

The media corner switched without warning from a shot of the worried computer engineer. Kate Lonaker's face appeared, and the sound level changed. "Sorry to pull an override on you." She grimaced out at Alex. "But Mrs. Ligon is on the line."

"Shit. Will you tell her that I'm not—"

"No, I won't. She knows that you're here."

"Tell her I'm working."

"You're always working. Come on, sweetheart, you can't refuse to talk to your dear old mother."

"But I'm right in the middle of running the model—"

"Right. And from the look on your face it's going nowhere, so you can afford to take a break. Here she comes. Be nice to her."

Kate vanished. In her place appeared a woman whose vitality and beauty seemed to burst out of the display. She smiled at Alex. "There you are."

"Hello, Mother."

"The young woman who put me through to you seems like a sweet little thing. Is she your assistant?"

"No, Mother." Alex checked that they were on Record. He wanted to watch Kate's expression when she learned that she was a *sweet little thing*. She would hate it. "Ms. Lonaker is my boss."

"Boss?" Lena Ligon's perfect face took on a startled look.

"Boss. I report to her."

"But that's ridiculous. No one in our family needs to report to anybody. Who is she?"

"She's division chief for Advanced Planning in the Outer System. She works for the government. Like me."

"Doing what?"

"The same as the last time you asked me. I build predictive models for the whole solar system—Inner and Outer." Alex glanced at the big display, where the simulation was still rolling along. Estimated shipping tonnages for 2101 had exceeded fixed-point range and were being reported as floating-point, with ridiculously large exponents. "Not very good models, I'm afraid."

"If that's what interests you, you could do it just as well by yourself without reporting to anybody. We're not exactly paupers."

"I know."

"And you wouldn't have to work in a place like *that*." The single word covered all of Alex's spartan office, where the display volume left space for only a single chair and a small desk. The walls were neutral pale yellow, with no pictures or decorations.

"I know. Let me think about it. Maybe we can discuss this after the family meeting." Alex knew he was committing to something else he didn't want to do, but it was the easiest way to avoid an argument he couldn't win.

"That's why I called, Alex, to make sure you will be there. And don't forget about the *other* thing. I can make arrangements whenever you are ready."

"I won't forget." Alex studied his mother's image, seeking the invisible. "I've been considering it."

"Good. We'll talk about that, too. Tomorrow, then. At four."

"Yes, Mother."

Lena Ligon nodded. "Try not to be late, as you usually are." To Alex's relief she vanished from the display. He glanced at the main simulation, where half the variables now showed overflow. Gibberish. He touched the pad to terminate the run, at the same time as he heard the door behind him slide open.

It was Kate, he knew without looking. He could smell her perfume, which always made him think of oranges and lemons.

"Got a minute?" she said.

"The model run—"

"Is garbage." She took his arm. "I've been keeping an eye on it. Come on, sweetie, let's go to my office."

"I should change parameters and do another case."

"It can wait. Me, I think we could easily take the rest of the day off." Kate was leading the way along a narrow, dingy corridor. "If the Seine performs as advertised, tomorrow everything changes."

"The run results can't be any better than the models. The Seine won't change them."

"Runs also can't be better than their inputs. The Seine will draw from every data bank in the System, no matter where it is. At the moment we're starved for Belt data. Suppose that's the missing ingredient?"

They had reached Kate's office. It was twice the size of Alex's, and as cluttered as his was empty. In pride of place on one wall, where Kate would see it whenever she looked up from her work, was a hand-embroidered cloth. Within an elaborate floral border were the words, *"Prediction is difficult, especially of the future."*

Alex slumped into the chair opposite Kate, accepted a tumbler of her made-to-order carbonated drink, and said abruptly, "What do you want to talk about?"

"You. How are you feeling?"

"I'm fine."

"Lie Number One. Every time you meet your mother or

anybody in your immediate family, you can't think straight for hours. No, make that days."

"So why did you insist that I talk with her?"

"Suppose I'd put her off until later. Would you have been able to work, or would you have worried all the time until she did reach you?"

When Alex said nothing, Kate went on, "You know, your mother just offered you what most people who work here would die for."

"You tapped in to a private conversation!"

"I might have. Most of it I knew already. Anyway, you were talking in working hours, so I could claim the right. But don't let's get sidetracked. Me, I need to earn a living. I have to work, and I have to put up with bureaucratic bullshit. I even generate some myself, though I try to keep it down. But you don't. You could walk out tomorrow. You'd have the freedom to work on what you want, when you want, where you want. There'd be nobody like me to pester you for reports."

"You don't understand."

"Probably not. But I really want to. I'm a relatively recent arrival, but you've been here for over three years. Why do you stay?"

"You have the reason sitting right there on your wall." He pointed to the hand-embroidered sign. "I agree with Niels Bohr, prediction is difficult. What will happen in the next ten years, or the next fifty? We don't know. I just happen to think that it's the most important question in the solar system."

"I'm with you. And maybe the hardest."

Kate said nothing more, but sat waiting patiently until Alex at last took a huge gulp from the tumbler, swallowed hard, and burst out, "The models in use when I came here were useless. They couldn't even predict the *past*. They'd been run over and over for the years leading up to the Great War, and they never saw it coming until the Armageddon Defense Line was gone and Oberth City was destroyed, and by then it was too late."

"What about your models?"

"You saw today's run. You said the right word: garbage."

"But isn't that a problem of inputs, and of computer limitations? You designed the models to run with more than ten billion Faxes. That should be enough to include a simulation of every individual in the System, even if you let the prediction run for a whole century. You've always been forced to aggregate to a million or less. What do you think of the models themselves?"

"They're pretty good."

"I think I ought to call that Lie Number Two. I'm not able to judge what you're doing, but before I took this job I talked to people whose judgment I respect. I also love modest men, but tell me true. Don't you have an entirely new theoretical basis for predictive modeling?"

"I believe I do." Alex could feel the knot inside him starting to dissolve. Was it something in the drink, or something in Kate Lonaker? "At least, no one seems to have run across it before."

"That's what I've heard. Look, you must know by now that I'm not much of a techie. I've looked at your papers, and didn't get diddly-squat out of them. Can you describe what your models do in words of one syllable, so I'll understand?"

"I don't think so. Not unless you have a few hours to spare."

"I don't. But your models did predict the Great War?"

"Sort of. When I ran from 2030 on, they reached a singularity in 2067. That was the correct year, but of course you can't compute past a singularity of the time line. So there was no way of knowing the war's outcome."

"You predicted a cataclysm. That's good enough for me. Let's go on. I asked you to tell me true, now it's my turn to do the same. My worry list has three items at the top of it. First, I'm worried that you'll take your mother's offer, leave, and set up your own research shop."

"Not a chance."

"Why not—and don't tell me it's because your mother makes you nervous."

"She does, but that's got nothing to do with it." Alex paused. "You said you love modest men. This is going to sound anything but."

"I didn't say I didn't like immodest men. I've certainly met enough of them. Go on."

"All right. My models may be producing garbage, but every other long-range predictive model that I've ever seen, here or elsewhere, *is* garbage. My models have the potential to *get it right*. You say you don't understand what I do, but in a way you don't have to. Because if you approve my results, they go up the line, and with any luck they'll keep on going up to the point where the results lead to action."

"I hope so. Otherwise there's no point in either of us working here."

"Now suppose that I go off and do what my mother suggests. I'd have plenty of research funds—Ligon Industries is huge, and it's all in the family. Vast available assets."

"Richer than God, if you believe the media."

"So I run my models, and suppose they produce surprising results. I come here, and say, look what I've discovered. What happens next?"

"We'd have to verify them before we could act." Kate nodded. "Go on. I think I see where you're leading."

"You'd verify them. Of course. And verify with what? The other models you have floating around here, that I know are crap? No agreement, we can pretty much guarantee that. And it would be NIH for me—Not Invented Here. I could come in showing that the Sun would go supernova, and I wouldn't be heard. I'm working on the most important question in the solar system, but what's the point if I'm not taken seriously? And for that, I must be an insider. Does that take care of your first worry? I'm not going to leave, unless somebody higher up comes along and throws me out."

"Which conveniently leads me to my second worry. You told me that you can't easily describe your models in a way that I can understand."

"It would take hours."

"I believe you. But I can't accept that answer. Because I have faith in you and your models, and I assume that soon— maybe starting tomorrow—they will start producing meaningful predictions, results that we really believe. So I take them up the line to Mischa Glaub. And the first thing I'm asked to do is explain what's going on in a way that *he* can understand—and he has a lot less time to spend on this than I do. Then he has to brief his boss, Tomas De Mises. And *he* has to explain to anyone on the Council who shows interest."

"You make it sound impossible."

"If you talk about 'iterated multiple convolution kernels,' which is a snappy phrase I remember from your last paper, it is impossible. I want you do to something for me, and put it as high on your priority list as anything in your models. I want you to find a way to *explain the models* in a way that someone with no special training will understand."

"How can I do that?"

"Your problem. Use analogies, use pictures, use metaphors,

I don't mind if you have to try poetry and dancing. But we really need this—or all your work will be ignored, just as surely as if it came from outside the organization."

Alex stared at her. He was feeling like a fool. She was right, and so obviously right that he should have thought of it for himself. "I'll do my best. But how will I know when I have what you want?"

"We use the Napoleonic principle." At Alex's raised eyebrows, she went on, "You'll brief Macanelly, from Pedersen's group. Do you know him?"

"No. But I've heard about him."

"Heard *what* about him?"

"That nobody likes to work with him. That he's conceited, and also that he's close to being a moron."

"That's what I've heard, too. He'll be perfect. Napoleon used to have a special officer, a very dim one, who read all outgoing dispatches. Unless a dispatch was clear even to that man, it didn't go out. Loring Macanelly will be our dispatch reader. When we have an explanation of what you're doing that he can understand and repeat back to me, we'll be happy. Won't we? You don't *look* happy."

"Kate, I want to work on theory, and I want to develop analytic models. I consider what we are doing supremely important. But I *hate* this other sort of stuff, simplifying work to the point where it's more misleading than informative, and then feeding it to half-wits."

"You know what they say: God must be specially fond of half-wits, because he made so many of them. Will you do it?"

"I told you, I'll do my best."

"When you get something halfway ready, I'll be your first half-wit." Kate leaned back in her seat. "All right. That takes care of worries one and two. I'm not sure I have any right to ask you about worry three."

"But you're going to." Alex had been vaguely upset when Kate Lonaker was appointed as his boss. She was two years younger than he, and before the end of their first brief meeting he knew she had little technical talent. Now, bit by bit, he was realizing what she had instead. More nerve than he would ever possess, and an inexplicable charm that took the edge off whatever she said.

And one other talent. How could a person do that, make you feel that they liked you and found you fascinating, without saying a single word? She was sitting there now, smiling at Alex as though he was the most interesting person in the System. And Kate could do it with *anybody*.

"If you're going to ask me, then ask."

"I will." Kate glanced at her watch. "But I'm getting hungry. Can we talk and eat at the same time?"

"That's fine with me." Was she stalling? "What's the third worry?"

"I was watching your face when your mother said that you mustn't forget about the *other* thing, and she would make arrangements whenever you were ready." Kate's gaze, blue-eyed and sympathetic, was again fixed on Alex's face. "As I said, it's really none of my business, but I don't believe that people I'm fond of should ever have to look like you looked. What is the *other* thing that you said you'd consider?"

2 THE TROJAN L-4 POINT, YEAR 2097, SEINE-DAY MINUS ONE

Alex Ligon and Kate Lonaker held their meeting in one of the "low-rent" levels of the Ganymede interior, where most government offices are located.

Draw a line that joins Alex and Kate to the Sun. It's a straight line, a long line, and a line of variable length, because Kate and Alex rotate with Ganymede, and Ganymede revolves around Jupiter, and Jupiter itself circles the Sun. But to one significant figure none of that matters. The distance is seven hundred and seventy million kilometers, give or take thirty million. Using that Sun-Jupiter line as base, draw two equilateral triangles in the same plane as Jupiter's orbit. The apex of one of those triangles, trailing Jupiter in its orbit, is known as the Jovian L-4 point. The apex leading Jupiter is the Jovian L-5 point.

Both these locations are gravitationally stable. An object placed at one will remain there, co-orbiting with Jupiter. Nature long ago discovered this, and the group known as the Trojan asteroids reside there. The mathematician Lagrange proved the existence of such stable points in the eighteenth

century. Humans only found a way to get there a good deal
later.

Milly Wu arrived at the Jovian L-4 station most recently
of all. She had flown out in an economy 0.2 Earth-gee ship,
on a flight of two weeks duration; long enough to worry to
excess about the adequacy of her talents, but not long enough
to learn all she felt she needed to know about the Argus
Project. Now, only six days after arrival, Milly was sitting in
her first staff meeting and wondering how long it would take
her stomach to adjust to a micro-gravity environment.

The good news was that she was not expected to do anything. "Just sit in the back and keep quiet," her supervisor,
Hannah Krauss, had said. "Answer a direct question if the
Ogre addresses one to you, of course. But I don't think that's
likely. JB is going to talk more than listen."

The Ogre. Hannah was about twenty-four, just a couple of
years older than Milly. She was alert and attractive, with a
wild mop of dark curly hair, a slim figure, and a mobile face
that could take on a huge variety of expressions. When she
said, "the Ogre," her whole countenance somehow adopted a
look of menace and malevolence. Milly had heard bad things
about Jack Beston, even back on Ganymede. But could he
really be as ogre-ish as he was painted?

Milly looked, and decided that maybe he could. JB, Jack
Beston, was standing in front of the group now. He was tall,
red-headed, and skinny as a stim-stick. Not bad looking, if
you liked skinny guys, as Milly did. But his expression can-
celled any possible attraction. He was glowering at everyone
and everything before a word was spoken. It made Milly wonder why she had struggled through all the horrendous apti-
tude tests in cryptanalysis and pattern analysis needed to

bring her here. Was she all that keen to be part of the Argus Project?

She decided that she was. If anyone made contact with aliens, Milly wanted to be in the front row. But for the moment she was quite happy to follow Hannah Krauss's advice and sit at the back. She scanned the windowless room. Minimal furnishings. Twenty-one people, fourteen women, seven men; three empty seats in her row. *Sit tight, keep quiet, and try to be invisible.* She placed the rectangle of the scribe plate flat on her knees, where she could make unobtrusive condensed Post-logic notes on whatever she felt needed recording.

"You've heard the crap the media are putting out." Jack Beston made no introductory remarks. "The Seine is going to link everything to everything and solve every problem in the solar system. I turn that around. When the Seine is up and running—and that's less than a day from now—nobody will be safe. Nobody will have secrets. People will use the Seine to wander all over the System and stick their nose in where it's got no right to be. We can't have that. I want to review where we stand on battening down on Argus information. Druse?"

A small man with a wizened face and a shaved scalp stood up. "The incoming signals all come in from open space, and we can't do anything about that. Anyone with the right receiving equipment will get exactly what we get. But so far as we know, no one else in the System has our sensitivity, or our modulated neutrino beam detector. Except—" Druse hesitated.

"Except the Bastard." Beston scowled. "He's got Odin working different targets and a different set of neutrino energies, but his equipment's as good as ours. No point in worrying about the security of incoming signals. What about the rest of it?"

"We propose to use the Seine's computer power only for raw data reduction and for first frequency scan. We don't give much away there, even if someone taps our whole feed. That's all that the Seine will do for us. Our private crypto programs and results will be completely caged, so no electromagnetic signals of any kind can get out. If we find a SETI signal—"

"*When* we find the SETI signal."

"Right. When we find an unambiguous SETI signal, everything switches from search to analysis. We have to make a choice there. If we use the Seine for decrypt, we lose secrecy. If we don't use the Seine and stay caged, we limit our computer power."

"That's not your department. I'll make that decision when the time comes. Just make sure I have a copy of the cage specs." Beston turned to a woman just a couple of seats along from Milly. "Zetter. Any progress?"

The woman had a thin vulpine face with a sharp nose. She must have slipped in late, and very quietly, because Milly had surveyed everyone in the room when she first arrived.

Zetter—first name? last name?—did not stand up. She leaned forward, so that Milly was presented with only a quarter profile, and shook her head in a slow, reptilian manner. "Not as of four hours ago. I received a report from—"

"No names. You know the rules."

"I wasn't about to." The woman sniffed. "I received a report from our source at L-5 four hours ago. Odin is tightening security on all fronts."

"Of course. The Bastard is as worried about leaks as we are. Any peepholes?"

"Too soon to say. Maybe one weak point—human, not equipment."

"Better. You can't buy a machine. How much?"

"I don't know yet. Pricey. You get what you pay for."

"Or less. Get onto it again. Tell our source we don't want general information. If it's not decrypt methods—" Jack Beston stopped in mid-sentence. His green eyes, apparently staring at nothing, had suddenly focused their glare on Milly. "You in the back. What the hell do you think you're doing?"

It was a direct question, the kind that supervisor Hannah Krauss had told her to answer. But it wasn't one that Milly understood. She sat frozen.

"Who are you?" Beston barked. "What's your name?"

"Milton Wu."

"Milton?" Beston moved to peer at her body. "What sort of a fucking name is that? You're no man."

"No." Milly, as always since the age of thirteen, was conscious of her too-large breasts. "Milton is my real name, a family name. But everyone calls me Milly."

"She's new. Only been here six days." Hannah Krauss was trying to divert Jack Beston's anger. It didn't work.

"I don't give a flying fuck if she's been here just six minutes. And I'm not talking to you, Krauss." He pointed straight at Milly's crotch. "What's that?"

He meant the scribe plate sitting on her lap. He had to mean the scribe plate. They had already established that she was a woman. Milly felt herself blushing. "I thought I ought to make notes. I have a lot to learn."

"You can say that again. Tell me this, Milly Wu. Are we safe inside a cage, so no E/M signals get out?"

"No. I mean, I don't think so."

"I'll tell you. We are not. You've been writing on that thing?"

"Yes, sir. Just notes. Squiggles. In condensed Post notation."

"Which are converted to words for storage. Converted *elec-*

tromagnetically." Jack Beston turned to the woman on Milly's right. "Zetter? Are you on?"

"Yes." She opened her jacket, peered at something inside, and the thin nose twitched. "So is she. I'm picking up and recording. Not interpreting, but that's an easy piece of processing. Unless we're shielded, the reception range for that strength of signal will be at least five kilometers."

"Which might as well be infinity. Look around you, Milly Wu. Do you see anybody else making electronic notes?"

Milly looked. Neutral stares, except for Hannah's rueful rubber-lipped quirk. *Sorry. I ought to have warned you.*

"No, sir."

"And you won't. This is a maximum security installation. We don't let *anybody* know how we're doing. We are going to be the first to pick up and decipher an alien signal, and nothing is going to stop us. Understand?"

"Yes, sir." Milly, greatly daring, added, "I want to be part of the team that gets there first. That's why I came here."

"Damn right. Can you do hand-writing, on paper?"

"Yes, sir, I can." *Thank heaven for Uncle Edgar, and his insistence on an old-fashioned education.*

"Then that's what you do, if you want notes. Hand that thing over."

He took the scribe plate and casually erased everything on it—including all that Milly had noted about the geography and operations of the L-4 Argus Station.

"You want notes," Beston repeated, "you write 'em on paper."

"Yes, sir." He was turning away as she added, "But that's a permanent record, too. What do I do with paper notes?"

He swung back to her. "You learn what's there, or you put what you have on e-file inside the cage. Either way, you destroy your original notes. Burn 'em, eat 'em, swallow 'em, stick 'em up your ass, I don't care. Just get rid of them—fast. I'm giving you one chance, Milly Wu. That's all you'll get."

He turned away. "Poldish. Yesterday was your deadline for the 'promising patterns' analysis. I've not seen anything on my desk."

Poldish, red-faced and pudgy, turned an even brighter red. "It's not quite finished. You see, the diversion of my group's resources to Seine protection—"

"I don't give a rat's left testicle for your reasons. You tell me *before* if a piece of work is going to be late, not after. You're a horse's ass, Poldish. I'll meet with you separately."

Milly thought, *Right. But first I have to humiliate you in public with a bit of animal imagery.* Hannah had turned her way, and when no one was looking she gave Milly a quick wink. If it was designed to say, *There, that wasn't too bad, was it?*, Milly wasn't sure she could agree. For this, she had left Ganymede? For this, she had given up her three-year championship on the Puzzle Network, and the chance to ascend from Journeyman to Masters' level? She must be crazy.

Hannah mouthed at her. *Talk later.*

Jack Beston was an equal opportunity employer. Milly didn't make an exact count, but so far as she could tell everyone in the room came in for a personal roasting before the meeting was over. Hannah was chewed out for failing to give new staff an adequate briefing. Even Zetter, who seemed to have no first name and with whom Milly would certainly not like to argue, was blasted for her failure to scan the room for electronic devices, and so eliminate Milly's scribe unit before it was ever turned on. The woman said nothing in response to Beston's tirade, but her face turned pale and her dark eyes promised murder.

"Don't let it worry you," Hannah said, as she led Milly away at the end of the meeting. "That was a perfectly normal start to the week's work. Come on, let's go see if the arrays are picking up anything new."

"He's a bastard."

"He is, but I'd suggest you don't say so. Around here the word bastard is reserved for the distinguished leader of Project Odin, over at L-5."

"When I was sitting in that meeting I thought I should have applied there, instead of here."

"Not a good idea. You'd be no better off. Philip the Bastard is supposed to be more cunning than Jack the Ogre, but from what I've heard he's an even bigger shit to work with."

"Then they deserve each other. They ought to work *together*."

"They once did. From what I've heard they were a perfect combination, Philip extremely sneaky and better on theory, Jack with the edge when it came to design of detection equipment. But Jack was two years younger, and you know how it is with brothers. Philip had been used to bossing Jack around when they were kids, but by the time Jack was nineteen he wouldn't take it anymore."

"He decided he'd rather dish it out."

"Maybe. But you're just pissed right now because of what he said to you. Don't let it bother you. Didn't you hear how he spoke to everybody?"

"I don't care. Nobody has the right to talk to people like that."

"Jack thinks he does."

They were about to enter the main chamber for signal reception and initial scanning, and Hannah paused on the threshold. "Milly, there's one other thing I want to say before we get to where others can hear. You look young enough to pass for a fresh-faced kid, but that won't save you. Jack Beston finds you attractive—yes he does, don't argue with me. I know the signs. And so far as I can tell his only two interests in life are the search for extraterrestrial intelligence and the seduction of new female workers. You can feel free to refuse—"

"I damned well will!"

"—although he won't easily take no for an answer. Also, if you do decide that he's attractive, and sleep with him, you'll find that it doesn't bring any special out-of-bed privileges. Don't look for special favors from Jack Beston. He'll still be the Ogre when it comes to work."

"You know all this, for a fact?"

The corners of Hannah's ultra-mobile mouth turned up and down again in a fraction of a second. "Believe me, Milly, I know. And don't bother to tell me I was stupid, because I don't think I was. There's not too many things to do around here apart from work, and JB doesn't hold grudges when it's all over. Nor do I. I'm just saying to you, watch it. He'll come sniffing, sure as Sunday. Keep hating him, and that's fine. It's when you feel sympathy for the Devil that you're in trouble."

Hannah didn't offer a chance for more questions, but stepped through into the great cube of the signal reception room. At first, Milly did not follow her. She had been here before, but again she wanted to feel the thrill, the prickle of awe creeping along her spinal column and up into her hind brain.

This was *it*. Here, in this room, thirty-four billion separate signals, culled from narrow parts of the neutrino and electromagnetic energy spectrum, and from all parts of the heavens, came into convergence. Here, the myriad signals were sifted and sorted and searched, in the quest for anomalies that stood out from the rest, the deviation from random noise that cried out, "Look, look at me. I am a message!"

Six years ago, when she was seventeen, Milly had encountered another message, one passed down from the very dawn of SETI. A century and a half ago, Frank Drake had sent a string of 1's and 0's to his colleagues, inviting them to decipher its meaning. Not one of them had succeeded.

But Milly had, proceeding from prime factors of an array of numbers, then to a picture, then to an interpretation. She could trace her presence here directly to the emotional rush of that day. It had been a fork in her personal road, the moment when the pleasures of mastering the Puzzle Network faded before the challenge of messages from the stars.

Now there was no guaranteed signal, but in its place a near-infinity of possible ones. The distributed observing system around the L-4 Argus Station still explored the ancient waterhole of the early investigators, between the spectral lines of neutral hydrogen and the hydroxyl radical, and to that they had added the preferred zone of neutrino resonance capture, a region undreamed of in early SETI work.

The work took on new complexity when you could not be sure that a possible signal *was* a signal, and all the time the detection equipment became more sensitive and sophisticated. *Is something there?* That question was harder to answer than ever. Milly wondered about the comparison. Which was more difficult to decipher: A signal sent by humans to humans, deliberately obscure and challenging their ingenuity, but with a promise that it was a signal? Or a message from aliens, designed to be clear, struggling to be heard, wanting to be transparent in meaning, and sent to any life form who might be listening?

What would Frank Drake say now, if he could be here to

regard his legacy? The original listening had been done for just two stars, Tau Ceti and Epsilon Eridani, on a minimum of radio frequencies, for a period that was no more than one tick on the great celestial clock. Drake would probably just shake his head and smile a secret little smile. He was a scientist and a realist, but he had an element of fey, deep inside, that led him to label his project *Ozma*, a name with more than a touch of magic and a hint of exotic mystery. Maybe more than surprised he would be disappointed, that they had looked so long and so hard and found nothing.

Nothing yet. Where are they? Be patient, Frank, and old Enrico Fermi. They are there. We are going to find them.

The smaller room beyond, in contrast to the one where Milly stood, was completely shielded from external signals. Within it the anomalies, the potential messages, the scores or hundreds daily culled from raw inputs, were sent to be analyzed. It is one of the curious results of information theory that the possible information carried within a signal is proportional to its randomness, to its *unpredictability*. If something is totally predictable, then by definition you know its content exactly and it can tell you nothing new. If the incoming signal is totally unpredictable, on the other hand, then in principle every single bit of data is a potential message. There had to be a fine line: enough regularities to announce intelligent design (a sequence of prime numbers, the Pythagorean theorem, a sequence of squares, the digits of pi), yet enough variation to offer information. How would an alien intelligence draw the line?

Milly crossed the big receiving chamber and stood on the threshold of the inner sanctum. Hannah had vanished. Milly had not been looking for her for minutes, and did not know where she had gone. That was all right. For the moment there was neither need nor desire for company. She was at a nexus, the focus of a torrent of information streaming in from every direction and distance in space, from everywhere in the galaxy and beyond it. The chamber was silent, but her inner ear discerned a mighty rushing river of data, rain-fed by the whole universe.

And the Ogre, with his insults and his coarse manners? Screw Jack Beston. She had not come here for him, she was here for *this*.

Milly was starting toward one of the work stations, where she could grab a batch of anomalies and analyze them to see if anything there spoke of purposive signal, when at that moment she saw him. He was standing in the center of the room, no more than ten meters away. Clearly, he had no idea that she was there. His head was tilted to one side, looking slightly up. The green eyes were slitted half shut. The expression on his face was nothing like the one she had seen and hated in the review meeting. It was rapt, it was concentrated, it was yearning.

Strangest of all, Milly could read that look. Jack Beston heard the cosmic roar of the swirling galaxy, beating in from all around them. But he was not listening for that. He was listening, with all his heart and soul, for something that he could not hear. *Within the whirlwind, a still small voice.*

Jack Beston wanted to hear the message, the one that would tell him that all this dedication of spirit and mighty labor was not in vain.

Milly could suddenly see inside him, as clearly as if Jack were lit from within by lightning. She looked, she understood, she yearned in just the same way to hear that same small voice. She felt *connected*.

And, like it or hate it, she felt a first faint stirring of sympathy for the Devil.

3 EARTH, YEAR 2097, SEINE-DAY MINUS ONE

Seine-Day would be huge in the Jovian system, perhaps bigger yet at the L-4 and L-5 Trojan locations, and most important of all as a unifying influence on the expanding Outer System.

On Earth, however, huddled in close to the Sun and with old war wounds still unhealed even after thirty years, Seine-Day could not compete with other worries.

Worries such as the application. The written part had been submitted three weeks earlier. The oral examination would be held one hour from now, by an interviewer who had ridden a high-gee vessel all the way from Ganymede. Janeed Jannex stared east toward the rising sun and wondered if it would be worth showing up to meet the man. There must be tens or hundreds of thousands of applicants. Less than one thousand would pass the test and be allowed to head away from Earth for training in the Outer System. And most of those would be youngsters, early twenties or less, whereas Janeed and Sebastian were already well over thirty.

She was sitting at the extreme eastern edge of the GM platform, as far down its side as she could get without falling in. Her feet dangled in the cold salt water of the eastern Malvinas' shelf. Behind her she could hear the gentle *thrum-thrum-thrum* of the great extractor. Its upper portion curved away to become a one-meter pipeline that headed arrow-straight south and west, past the Falkland Islands, across the full width of the Malvinas' shelf, all the way to landfall at Punta Arenas.

The spine of the extractor plunged down through the middle of the Global Minerals' platform and continued all the way to the seabed. Janeed and Sebastian were, according to their job description, "in charge" of the extractor operation during the remaining hour of the dawn shift. What that meant in practice was that any change in extractor performance, gas leak, or reduction in methane flow through the pipeline would be signaled by a klaxon loud enough to wake the dead. At that point the problem rose by definition above Jan and Sebastian's authority and responsibility level. They would run at once to alert a more senior member of the GMS operations' staff, assuming that by some miracle that person had slept through the din and was not already on deck.

The sun was well above the horizon, but here, in July at fifty degrees south, the wind off the winter ocean of the South Atlantic would remain brisk all day. Jan lifted her bare feet from the icy water, examined her long, near-prehensile toes that had chilled to a bluish-red, and dried them on the lower edge of her sweater. She had been sitting far too long, introspective and brooding in the glimmer of pre-dawn. She was supposed to be the optimist, the initiator, the "can-do" queen. But it was hard to be all those things when you felt sure that the next few hours would bring only disappointment. And if she reacted like this, how must Sebastian be feeling?

She put on her shoes, stood up stiffly, and climbed the ten-meter ladder to the main surface of the platform. Finding him should be no problem. He lacked her taste for minor masochism, and would be tucked in the warmest and most protected spot of the deck that still offered a broad-angled upward view.

This morning she found him on the western side of the extractor, well shielded from the breeze. He had spread an air mattress there—no hardships for Sebastian—and lay on his back, staring upward.

Janeed said, "Well?"

Without looking at her, or seeming in any way to acknowledge her presence, he said softly, "Formation to the northeast. Triple layer, alto-cumulus over strato-cumulus over cumulo-nimbus, all moving in different directions. Wind vectors different at each height. We'll see rain within the hour, I'll make bet."

Jan didn't want to bet, or look north-east or in any other direction. Clouds were clouds, and that was all. She moved to lean over him. "Not the *weather*, Sebastian. The *interview*."

"What about the interview?"

"It's less than an hour away. I'm nervous."

He sat up, slowly. Sebastian did everything slowly, so slowly that Janeed often felt ready to scream at him. Sometimes she did. It made no difference.

"Jan, you're nervous because you care." His round moon face was smiling. "If we fail, we still have jobs."

Jobs that could be done as well or better by machinery. Jobs that needed so little of your skills and energy that someone like Sebastian could spend all his days happily dreaming and staring at the ever-changing cloud formations of the South Atlantic, without any question from their superiors. Dead-end jobs for all of them, while the Outer System was desperately short of people, even if beyond the Belt they were so picky in their choosing from Earth that an applicant who lived here felt like a resident of an old leper colony applying for a position as a masseuse.

Jan didn't say any of that. In fairness, she couldn't. She had been the one who insisted, who did all the pushing and coaxing and persuading until Sebastian agreed that they would apply as a team. They were the same age, but ever since their rescue in the ruined northern hemisphere and transfer to a displaced persons' camp, she had felt like his mother. Her chances would be better if she had applied alone, but she couldn't do it. Who would look after Sebastian then? He was not stupid, no matter what others said, but he was undeniably strange. He had been rescued as a young child, and even at thirty-five he remained in many ways childlike.

She said carefully, "They'll interview us together, as a team. Promise me one thing."

"I promise."

"You don't know what it is yet. Promise me that you'll *talk*. When we applied for these jobs you just sat there like a big dead fish."

"But we got jobs." He was smiling again, serene and gentle. "I'll talk. Or try to."

"Come on, then. Let's at least try to make ourselves look presentable." Janeed smiled back and reached out a hand to help him to his feet. She loved Sebastian, and she always would. Not in any sexual way, of course—she recoiled at the thought—but as the closest thing to family that she had ever known. Her parents, like Sebastian's, were faceless and nameless, among the seventy percent of Earth's eleven billion people who had died in the first few minutes of the Great War. Janeed should have been old enough to remember what her mother and father looked like, but her first memory was of a terrifying airplane ride followed by a hot meal at a displaced persons' camp in Arenas. Before that: nothing.

* * *

The interviewer was a woman, not a man. She was a bone-thin redhead, with thin, tight lips. She wore the dark-green uniform of Outer System civilian government, and she appeared as confused by them as Janeed was nervous of her.

"Janeed Jannex and Sebastian Birch," the interviewer said. *"Miners."* She gave the word great emphasis. She frowned at the screen of her personal, and then peered around her at the hundred-meter floating platform of Global Minerals and the endless water beyond. She had chosen to sit out on deck for the interview, although the sky was growing darker and Sebastian's prophecy of rain appeared more and more plausible. "You described your jobs as miners?"

"That's right." Janeed glared at Sebastian. Beyond a muttered greeting he had so far said not a word.

The woman, who had introduced herself as Dr. Valnia Bloom—Dr. *Director* Valnia Bloom, head of the Department of Scientific Research on Ganymede—said, "Would you care to explain that?"

"Certainly." Jan looked at Sebastian, waiting. He said not a word, and finally she went on, "This will take a few minutes."

Sebastian said, "It will rain hard in a few minutes."

Valnia Bloom seemed skeptical, and looked up at the cloud-barred sky. Janeed wondered, had the woman ever seen rain? It certainly didn't rain water on Ganymede, or anywhere else in the Outer System. On Venus it rained sulfuric acid, and on Titan it rained droplets of hydrocarbons. On Triton, Janeed had read, there were geysers of liquid nitrogen, but they hardly counted as rain. Sebastian was staring vacantly at Valnia Bloom, who finally said, "We'll see about the rain. Go ahead. Keep it short."

Jan stared daggers at Sebastian. Her look said, *Talk!* After a long silence, she felt that she had to go on. "Well, most of the onshore fossil fuels of Earth were always in the northern hemisphere, which is still uninhabitable. The coal under the Antarctic ice-cap is inaccessible, too. But the southern hemisphere is booming, and there's a big need for energy and plastics, and no way to satisfy it."

"I thought that Cyrus Mobarak had solved your energy problem, with the Moby Midget fusion reactors."

"He did, for anything that can handle eight megawatts and up. But there's a need all over the developing southern regions for small, portable units that generate only a few kilowatts. That's what *that* provides."

Jan gestured to the extractor, sticking up from the middle of the GM platform, and the pipeline running away to the southwest. Dr. Bloom stared at it uncomprehendingly.

"Methane," Sebastian said, a split-second before Janeed felt she would be obliged to jump in again. Thank God, a word at last! But apparently that one word was all they would get. Jan finally added, "Methane down on the seabed. Trillions and trillions of tons of it."

"But methane is lighter than water. In fact"—Valnia Bloom was frowning, in the effort of recollection—"the atmosphere of Earth is mainly oxygen and nitrogen. Methane is a lighter gas than either one of those. It can't possibly be found down on your ocean floor."

"Oh, it's not. I mean, it is, but it's not stored in gaseous form. It's stored as methane clathrates—a structure that has four molecules of methane locked into a stable form with twenty-three molecules of water. At the temperatures of the deep ocean, around four Celsius, methane clathrates are solids. And they're denser than water, so if they form on the ocean bed they won't float up to the surface. And everything that sinks down from the surface of the sea decays and rots, and produces methane."

Dr. Bloom looked less than thrilled by that vision of universal rot and corruption, a phenomenon unique to Earth. Other worlds, her expression suggested, kept their decay and recycling well away from civilized life; but she nodded and Jan went on, "So with all that methane from decomposition, plus naturally upwelling primordial methane, the seabed contains enormous amounts of it. And of course there's loads of water. So we have these enormous clathrate beds, hundreds of kilometers across and tens of meters deep. All we do—all *that* does"—she pointed to the extractor—"is run the spine down to the clathrate beds and warm them up a bit. The methane is released in the higher temperatures, and rises to the surface, and flows away through the pipeline."

Their interviewer was pleased. For the first time she was smiling. Dr. Bloom said, "So you're miners. Yes, I guess that you are."

"And you know," Jan went on, "now that I think of it, I bet the same method would work for the Europan ocean. There's life, there's decomposition, there's plenty of water."

That was less of a success. The smile became a fixed and very starchy frown. "I thought that it was well-known, even in the Inner System"—her tone implied, the *primitive* Inner System—"that Europa is off-limits. Native life was discovered there five years ago. We do not care to have the only other known life form in the Universe contaminated for minor industrial gain."

Sebastian opened his mouth. He was going to choose this worst moment to argue with the interviewer, Janeed felt sure of it. That would cancel out any good impression they had made. She could think of no way to cut him off, until like a gift from Heaven she felt two heavy raindrops strike her on the left cheek and square on the nose.

"Here it comes," she said, "just the way Sebastian said it would. Let's get below, before we're all soaked."

And maybe on the way I'll have a chance to get you to one side, you moon-faced lump, and say that talking about the wrong things is worse than not talking at all.

The best-laid plans . . .

Dr. Valnia Bloom stuck to Sebastian, tight as a vacuum seal, all the way below until the three of them were packed into the tiny room that served as the junior crew hideaway.

Apparently the interviewer had reached a new point on her agenda, because she listened in silence to an internal prompt, opened a file, and pushed it forward.

"These yours?"

"Yes." Janeed recognized her own test answers, to both the standardized question set and the free-form invitation to pick a subject and work it through. She had taken a chance, reviewing the growth of the economy of the Jovian moons since first colonization, then using that to make projections on Saturn and Uranus system development.

She expected at least a comment, but Dr. Bloom merely grunted, picked up a second file, and laid it in front of Sebastian.

"And this is yours?"

He peered, as though he had never seen the file in his life, then nodded. "Yep. That's mine."

Sebastian nodded. Janeed winced, she hoped invisibly. It was the standard question set, and a quick glance was enough to show that at least half had been left blank.

"How about these?"

This time it was half a dozen sheets. They showed not writing or numbers but drawings, black-and-white sketches with the unfinished look of something done at high speed. They were—Janeed ought to have guessed it—cloud formations, whorls and bars and herringbone patterns, mixed together with no apparent logic.

Sebastian took his time, stared, and at last said, "Yep. Didn't have time to finish this one." He pointed at a swirl like the image of a moving hurricane, spinning off smaller whorls from its trailing edge.

"They resemble storms on the face of the planet Saturn. Did you base what you drew on something you had seen?"

"Yep. There's a regular vid feed, images from Mars and Jupiter and Saturn. I watch them. Uranus, too, though there's nothing to see there."

"You mean no cloud patterns."

"Smooth as a billiard ball."

"But you didn't just copy these from the latest video feed."

Sebastian frowned. "No. Didn't copy them."

"So where did you get them? I assume that you took the tests under controlled conditions."

"We did." Jan was not being spoken to, but she couldn't keep quiet. "No one could come or go, no one could look at what anybody else was doing."

Valnia Bloom ignored her. "Where did you get these drawings, Mr. Birch?"

Sebastian cleared his throat. "Well, I seen Saturn pictures on the vid feed. And these ones, I like *dreamed*, the way you do when drawing goes good."

If Janeed's wince had been invisible before, she was sure it wasn't now. Fortunately, Dr. Valnia Bloom seemed to be taking no interest at all in what Janeed did—until she raised her head and speared both Sebastian and Janeed with a single glance.

"Your application was a rather unusual one. You are both over thirty, much older than our norm. Also, you asked to be considered as a team, but not singly."

Jan nodded. "Yes, ma'am."

"And that is still your position?"

Jan nodded again and glared at Sebastian, who said, "Yep."

"Very well. So be it." Dr. Bloom collected the files and stood up. "That will be all."

"Thank you." The words stuck in Janeed's throat, and she had to swallow and start over. "Thank you for letting us try. Will we be allowed to try again?"

"I think not." Maybe Dr. Valnia Bloom was a sadist, or maybe she had been trained not to show feelings, because she had an odd little smile on her face. "There will be no second try."

"Yes, ma'am."

"However, as I understand it, you are both required to give two weeks notice for service with General Minerals. I suggest that you do so immediately. Two and a half weeks from now there will be places reserved for you on a passenger shuttle. Once in a micro-gravity environment you will undergo complete physical examinations, after which a high-acceleration transit vessel will take you to Ganymede. Formal indoctrination will begin there."

She was heading up the steep ladder that led back to the main platform. Halfway up, she ducked her head and turned to where Janeed and Sebastian sat stunned at the little table.

"I should mention one other thing of interest. You took the test three weeks ago. Correct?"

"Yes, ma'am."

"Those sketches that Sebastian made at that time. They closely resemble actual storms on Saturn. But you did not copy them."

"No, *sir*." Sebastian spoke firmly for the first time. "I mean, no, ma'am. I said already, I didn't copy them."

"My last remark was not a question but a statement. I know that you did not copy images forwarded to Earth, for the best of all possible reasons." Valnia Bloom was at the top of the stairs when she added, "You could not have. The storm system that you drew did not appear on the face of Saturn until ten days ago."

THE BAT CAVE,
PANDORA, YEAR
2097, SEINE-DAY
MINUS ONE

At about the time when Dr. Valnia Bloom spread before
Sebastian Birch his sketches of Saturnian clouds and asked
about their origins, Rustum Battachariya was in a position to
take a look at the real thing. All he had to do was walk twenty
paces to the end of the Bat Cave. Then he could ride an
ascending elevator to an observation chamber on Pandora's
surface, float forward in the negligible gravity of the tidally-
locked little moon, and stare down on the vast rings and broad
face of Saturn itself.

Not, of course, that Bat had the least intention of doing
any such thing. He never went near the surface, and anyway
he was busy. He and his software tools were locked in combat
with one of the most formidable intelligences in the Solar
System, and if things went well the fight would continue for
the next ten or twelve hours. The nearest actual humans were
maybe a million kilometers away, observing the Von Neumanns at work on Saturn's giant moon, Titan. That suited
Bat fine. He neither needed help, nor wanted it.

The decision to move the Bat Cave from Ganymede's deep
interior had not been made lightly. Bat had worked there,

productively and misanthropically and generally ignored, for more than fifteen years. Then, four years ago, the worst thing possible had happened: he had made a trip to Europa to resolve a mystery, and in the course of his visit the existence of an alien life form in Europa's deep ocean had been revealed. It was nothing like the distant intelligences sought by Jack and Philip Beston in their SETI projects, merely a curious aperiodic crystal with the ability to reproduce and with a minimum of internal metabolism. But it was enough. Enough to have Europa placed off-limits for development, and enough for something else. A member of the media—the invasive, intrusive, inquisitive, insatiable, intolerable media—had been present on Europa, and Nell Cotter in her report had fingered Bat as the hero of the whole incident. The name, shaved black cannonball head, and three-hundred-kilo body of Rustum Battachariya became famous throughout the Solar System. All hope of privacy was lost.

After that, almost daily, some media wretch would employ a combination of bribery and bare-faced lies to discover the location of the Bat Cave. They would then seek out Bat and plead for exclusive interviews.

Four months of this was more than Bat could stand. He began the search. Where to go?

At first there was a temptation to move inward. Following the ending of the Great War, Earth had become the Sol-ward limit of human existence. The research station on Mercury and the research domes on Venus had been utterly destroyed. Bat could have gone there. But both Mercury and Venus had substantial surface gravity, and Bat, although tolerant of Ganymede's weaker pull, wanted less weight rather than more. As bad or worse, as the System steadily recovered, so the urge to rebuild lost resources grew. Scientific pressure was increasing for a station on Venus and Mercury. If that happened, in the whole Inner System there was nowhere else to go. You had four planets and three moons, and no wiggle room.

Bat turned his analytical eye outward. The habitable Jovian satellites thrummed with life and daily became more crowded. You had to look farther, recognizing that no matter what you did today, at some time in the future you might have to make another change. He expected to live a long time. The lesser satellites of Uranus or even of Neptune were not beyond consideration.

He made his decision, he made his plans, and when all was ready he resigned his position as head of Passenger Transport Schedules for the Outer System. He revealed where he was going only to his boss, Magrit Knudsen, first obliging her to swear that she would never contact him, visit him, or reveal his whereabouts to any living soul. And then he relented. Magrit Knudsen had provided protective cover for Bat for more than a dozen years. She could, he said, contact him if she was in personal difficulty. *Or*—an afterthought—if someone came to her with an intellectual problem that she deemed worthy of Bat's powers. He was still a senior member of the Puzzle Network, and he had no intention of abandoning that activity.

Bat arranged to move the whole Bat Cave, complete with its unique contents, to a natural chamber deep within one of Saturn's minor satellites, Pandora. Everything was handled by machines controlled by Bat alone, and when the operation was finished he used his knowledge of the Ganymede computer systems to erase all records. Then it was time for the final step. Bat had to conquer his own agoraphobia enough to suffer the long journey through open space.

He did it the easy way. He imbibed a carefully mixed combination of hypnagogic drugs, closed his eyes, and opened them to find himself on Pandora.

The moon was an irregular rock splinter fifty kilometers long and thirty across. Compared with Saturn's nine major moons it was a flyspeck, skimming along underneath them and orbiting the planet in less than a day. Since it was above the great ring systems and had a downward view partly blocked by them, no one would choose it as a preferred site for planetary surveillance. It had no atmosphere, no mineral resources, no natural water or other volatiles. It should have no interest to anyone.

For Bat, however, Pandora seemed perfect. He had no desire for a window seat to examine Saturn, and he would bring his own self-contained habitat, together with ample volatiles to last a century. After that, if necessary, he would review his options.

And so far Pandora had lived up to all of Bat's expectations. In three full years, he had been plagued by not a single visitor. Magrit Knudsen had contacted him exactly once, when she was faced with a transportation requirement involving an apparently impossible scheduling conflict. Bat embedded the structure within a more general class of problem, provided an algorithm for the whole set, and sent a complete answer to Magrit two days later. He had allowed himself the indulgence of one major gloat before returning to his studies of lost artifacts of the Great War.

Today, however, gloating and Great War relics were an indulgence that he could not afford. The clock was ticking. In one more day, the Seine would be activated. This must be a final test.

Bat sat on a specially-made seat at the "thinking" end of the Bat Cave, his black-clad bulk ballooning out in a way impossible in higher gravity. He had sent out his software probes, and now he was patiently awaiting their return. The system that he had established was designed to mimic, so far as any entity can mimic something larger than itself, the functions of the whole, quantum-entangled Seine. Bat was on the attack with it, working his way inward past the invisible and dynamic defenses of his antagonist. So far, the probes of his Seine-simulators had been thoroughly balked.

"Forty minutes since anything happened," said a rasping voice from close by his side. "Are you stuck?"

Bat turned. "Let us say that we are temporarily halted. Two firewalls have been negotiated, but the third provides great resistance." He did not seem surprised by the sudden voice. The image in the display volume at his side showed the face of a balding, squint-eyed man in late middle age. The newcomer seemed to be staring at the screens, too, but Bat knew that was just for show. Mord received all his inputs in real-time. That gave him a definite advantage, because he knew what Bat's programs were reporting before Bat did.

"It's taking longer than ever before." It was hard to tell from Mord's tone if he thought that good or bad.

Bat nodded. "When did you enter?"

"Right at the beginning. I noticed the changes in resource allocation." Mord's eyes narrowed as he peered at the latest outputs. "I was wrong last time, when I thought you'd never get in. Want to go double or quits? I say, this time you definitely won't break the defenses within twelve hours."

Bat closed his eyes and settled back in his chair to ponder the question. He glanced at the clock. Five hours had already elapsed since his first onslaught. His foe's defenses showed no sign of weakening. But with seven hours to go, and at least one line of attack still held in reserve . . .

"Forget the double-or-quits offer," Mord said abruptly. "Bet's off."

Bat blinked his eyes open and stared at his banked displays. He could see no change. And then, suddenly, he could. A fixed loop of instructions was being run, hundreds of millions of times a second, and sections of the displays were slowly changing color.

"Ahhhh." His long exhalation slowly faded. "There is penetration of the third firewall."

"Is there another one behind it?"

"I am afraid not. Complete access can be only moments away."

"That's it, then." Mord leered out of the display. "All right, fat boy. Back to the drawing board."

Bat nodded, but his mind was already beginning the curious change needed to move perspective from attacker to defender. He had spent a whole year building what he hoped was an impenetrable series of shields, traps, blind ends, and firewalls designed to thwart something—even a something with the full power of the Seine—from entering his private computer system.

And he had failed. He had just proved that at least one individual in the Solar System, Rustum Battachariya, could mount an external attack able to squirm and worm and drill past that same Rustum Battachariya's best computer defenses. He had, in a very literal sense, just defeated himself.

Mord added, "Unless you think you're safe enough with the system the way it is, because you believe nobody else could do what you just did. I mean, you do have the arrogance."

Bat said mildly, "Mord, this is no time for goading. Nor is such goading necessary. I have sufficient incentive to work further on my defenses, and I will do so. But first, I must have sustenance. Join me if you wish."

The offer was genuine. Bat would welcome Mord's company. He rose from his seat and headed along the Bat Cave toward the "eating end" with its elaborate and splendidly furnished kitchen. That kitchen was well-provided with display units, on any of which Mord would be able to appear.

Mord could not, of course, eat, any more than Bat could have tolerated Mord's insults from any human. Mord, however, was not human. Mordecai Perlman had been; but he had died more than twenty years ago, his body cremated and his ashes sent at his own request into the Sun.

Perlman had been involved in the early development of Faxes, the expert systems that simulated humans and fulfilled many of their simpler functions. You could buy everything from a Level One Fax, which could answer only the simplest questions about you, such as your name, all the way to a Level Five, which managed a fair conversation on your behalf and was smart enough to know when it was out of its depth and call for help.

None of that was enough for Perlman. He was a maverick, an outsider who disagreed with everyone on the way to do simulations. To the others, a Fax was a body of logical rules and a neural network that allowed a computer to mimic the thought patterns and responses of a particular human being.

Wrong approach, declared Mordecai Perlman. That's all crap. A human isn't a set of logical rules. A human is a mixture of thoughts and glands and general confusion, and what goes on in a person's subconscious mind is more important than any A implies B predicate calculus of the conscious mind. We spend half our time trying to produce explanations for the fuck-up messes that our glands lead us into.

Perlman had been ignored. The need was for simple Faxes, ones whose responses to a given situation would always be the same. No one wanted Faxes with moods, passions, senior moments, PMS, or temper tantrums.

No one but Mordecai Perlman. Convinced that he was right, he had set out to produce his kind of Fax. When the work had gone as far as he could take it, he gave the final proof that he believed in what he was doing: he constructed a Fax that mimicked the worldview, knowledge base, and gut reactions of Mordecai Perlman. He did not claim that what lay within the computer was a Fax. It was something new. It was a *Mord*. The image that appeared on displays was of Mordecai Perlman, as he had been at the time when Mord was implemented.

Bat had discovered Mord hiding away on the Ceres computer system. He was intrigued by what he saw, and asked for a version of his own. Mord had come right back with an answer: no cloning. Would *you* want to be cloned? But Mord was willing to make a deal: he would agree to being transferred into Bat's system, and erased on Ceres, in return for certain guarantees. All that Mord wanted was system-wide input data, with access to the news feeds.

Bat had considered, and agreed. For one thing, Mordecai Perlman had lived through the Great War as an inquisitive, observant adult. Mord must be a treasure-house of information about those times, and there was much still to be discovered about the war, particularly the past weapons. The Bat Cave held a unique collection, but Bat always wanted more. The Mother Lode, a complete listing of all Belt weapons developed and intentionally destroyed, might be no more than legend. So might the "ultimate weapon," the unspecified device that post-war lore insisted would make the whole solar system "dark as day," whatever that self-contradictory phrase might mean. On the other hand, these things just might be real. So many improbable Great War weapons had turned out to be far from imaginary.

Bat drifted along the length of the Cave, admiring and appreciating its contents. Without the real estate constraints of Ganymede's interior, he had made the Cave ten times its old size. Its contents were expanding to fill the space available. So, according to Mord, was Bat.

He moved slowly. The aroma of food, an *olla podrida* that had been cooking all day, drew him on, but at the same time he wished to savor and even touch items of his collection. Women had no aesthetic appeal for Bat, nor had men; but each item arrayed in its case or hung along the wall possessed, to the connoisseur, its own strange beauty.

Here was a rare infrared communications beacon, developed on Pallas and one of only four known copies. Next to it, the little antique Von Neumann was a true original, used in the preliminary mining of the Trojan asteroids before Fishel's Law and Epitaph—*Smart is dumb; it is unwise to put too much intelligence into a self-reproducing machine*—became System-wide wisdom. The Von Neumann now sat confined by a magnetic field within a triple-sealed chamber. Without raw materials, it was not dangerous.

Bat loved them all, the brain-gutted Seeker, the mesh-caged Purcell invertor, the Palladian genome stripper.

He might have lingered longer, but Mord's impatient voice rang out from the kitchen ahead of him. "Hey, Mega-chops, I'm sitting here doing nothing. You gone to sleep out there? Soup's on."

Bat moved a little faster. Mord was also a relic of the war, perhaps the oddest one of all. What else could explain why Bat found Mord's company more congenial than that of any human?

▭ 5 SEINE-DAY!

SEINE-DAY! SEINE-DAY! SEINE-DAY!

The signs blared out at Alex on every level as he made the long trip from the depths of the government offices to the near-surface levels where Lena Ligon made her home, and Ligon Industries kept its corporate offices.

He wondered, who was *paying* for all this Seine-Day publicity? And why? It wasn't as though you had a choice, and could accept the use of the Seine or opt out of it, just as you chose. In two hours time, the ceremonial "golden spike" would be driven, in the form of a final connection linking the Ganymede, Callisto, Earth, Mars, and Belt main databases. A thousand others would come on-line later in the day, but those first five were the biggest. By this time tomorrow, every shred of data anywhere in the solar system should be available for general use. Unless you had taken measures ahead of time, privacy would be more difficult than ever before.

And maybe impossible, at least during the shake-out period. But along with wider data availability came a massive increase in computational power, and Kate had cursed about Alex's absence at the very time when they were in a position to run his models with adequate computer resources.

Alex had disagreed. "You have a million different systems and databases out there, scientific and financial and personal and institutional. If you expect to be able to join them all together and have everything run correctly the first time, you're more of an optimist than I am."

He had phrased that badly. Kate *was* more of an optimist than he was. She said, "So what will happen when they switch on?"

"I don't know, but I'll tell you what I expect. We'll see transients through the whole Seine for the first few hours, maybe longer. Any results for a day or so will be suspect."

Kate had wrinkled her nose. She was a risk-taker. Left to herself she would have run the models at once, even in his absence. But they were Alex's models. She had agreed to wait until Seine-Day Plus One. But then, she said, they would make the runs no matter what transients were bouncing around the extended Seine network.

A day's delay sounded about right to Alex. He actually thought that the system would settle down in the first few hours. On the other hand, family meetings could take forever. Kate might then execute runs without him, and he was beginning to understand her personality. If the results showed problems, he didn't want her fiddling around inside his models, changing parameters she didn't understand. He wanted to be back to keep an eye on Kate, long before Seine-Day was over.

He glanced at his watch. Like all Jovian timekeeping systems, it kept Standard Decimal Time. SDT had retained the length of the twenty-four-hour Earth day but divided it into ten hours, each of one hundred decimal minutes, each minute a hundred decimal seconds. The decimal second was a little bit shorter than the Earth-second, 100,000 of them in an Earth day, rather than the usual 86,400.

Now it was three-ninety-six. The morning meeting was scheduled for four. Alex had three more ascending levels to go, and he would be a little late. Already the wealth was beginning to show. You could see it in the elegance of the bioluminescent inlays illuminating the corridors with muted blue and white, the custom-designed murals and statues that lined the walls, and the carpets that swallowed up every sound. Alex's yearly stipend would not cover a month of rent at these levels.

Money, however, was not an issue. If he chose, he could build a complete lab here, with resources that dwarfed everything available to Kate Lonaker's whole division. His mother was going to pressure him to do that. And, of course, they were all going to push him on the *other* thing, the matter he had intended to explain to Kate days ago but had evaded yet again.

He didn't think she would understand—*could* understand. He had to live with it all the time, two hundred and fifty years of family tradition and obligation, invisible to anyone but pressing down on Alex's shoulders far harder than Ganymede's gravity.

Ligon Industries dated back to Alonzo Ligon, the nineteenth-century tyrant who had built some of the first iron-hulled ships that sailed the oceans of Earth. Alex was a direct descendant, nine generations removed from Alonzo.

And that might not be the worst of it. Since setting off for the meeting, Alex had been cursed with another thought. He had been reviewing in his mind's eye yesterday's image of his mother as it had appeared in the display, and thought he could detect some troubling elements.

He came to the bronzed double doors with the discreet brass plate, LIGON INDUSTRIES; BY APPOINTMENT ONLY, and peered into the eye-level camera above the plate. His retinal pattern was recognized, and the great doors swung silently open. The Level Three Fax on duty said, "Welcome, Mr. Alex. The meeting has already begun, and it is in the chamber to your right."

Alex steeled himself and went straight in. The marble-topped oval table had sixteen positions, each with its own work station. Eleven seats were occupied. Alex stepped quietly across a deep carpet of living purple and green and sat down next to his mother. Lena Ligon nodded a greeting. The man at the end of the table did not nod, or change for a moment his tone of voice.

"That phase of the work is concluded," he said. "The *Starseed* is on its way, and a financial accounting must be made. The details are available to anyone here who wishes to examine them, but my summary is simple: Ligon Industries took a calculated risk in accepting a contract to mine helium-three from the atmosphere of Jupiter and deliver it into rendezvous orbit with the *Starseed* vessel. We also took a bath. At the time, I recommended against signing the contract, and it proves to have been a financial disaster."

Alex glanced around the table. Prosper Ligon was the ranking family member by virtue of seniority. No matter who was senior, however, Prosper Ligon's conclusions on questions like this were not likely to be challenged. Alex's great-uncle was the chief financial analyst and *de facto* head of the company, a lifelong bachelor and a celibate, slow, deliberate, and precise in thought and deed. Those thoughts and deeds excluded sexual activities of any kind. Although only in his mid-sixties, with his long face and yellowed teeth Prosper was easy to imagine in old age as a skinny and weathered donkey.

His lifestyle and work habits were legendary. Rising at three, he ate a simple breakfast and proceeded at once to his office in a dark corner of the company's corporate facility. There he sat at a cluttered desk and worked, through the day, through the evening, and on late into the night. No task appeared boring to him when it involved financial elements. Numbers were the donkey's passion, and apparently numbers alone. It was rumored—and probably no more than rumor— that he disliked computers, and performed his voluminous calculations by hand. When he ate it was infrequently, alone, and in random amounts.

"The contract provides an option," Prosper went on, "to continue the work and collect the helium-3 needed to fuel *Starseed-Two*. That leaves us with a difficult decision."

Alex did his survey of the family members present. Around the table, to his left, were his mother Lena, then the two childless great-aunts, Cora and Agatha, and then Cousin Hector Ligon, with two empty chairs between him and Prosper Ligon. Two more empty seats lay on Prosper's left. The other four places were occupied by girl cousins Juliana, Rezel, and Tanya, and in the place to Alex's right Uncle Karolus sat scowling down at the table.

"It's obvious what we do," Karolus growled. "We get out now, and cut our losses. We should never have taken that bloody contract. I was against it."

As Alex recalled, his uncle had been the one who pushed hardest for taking on the *Starseed* contract. However, Prosper Ligon did not choose to argue. "Perhaps you were opposed," he said. "So was I. And if, five years ago, we had known about the difficulty of mining Jupiter's atmosphere, even with the best Von Neumanns available, then everyone at this table would surely have sided with us. That, however, is history. The number of Von Neumanns lost during ascent from Jupiter wrote red all over our balance sheet."

Cousin Juliana was interested only in certain things, but company finance was one of them. If Uncle Prosper ever retired—or, more likely, his dead body was dragged away from his desk to the knacker's yard—then she was a logical candidate to take over. She said, "The Von Neumanns are not much better today than they were three years ago. If it was a loss operation then, it will still be one. *How much* of a disaster?"

Prosper Ligon's voice did not waver. "We sacrificed approximately twenty percent of Ligon Industries' total assets."

Cousin Hector said, "Wow!"

"Wow, indeed." Prosper Ligon nodded slowly. His head seemed a size too large for his skinny neck. "However, I am in favor of accepting the contract option to provide helium-3 for *Starseed-Two*."

Eyebrows were raised all around the table.

Hector had his brow furrowed in obvious thought. He glanced at his cousins, but his comment was directed to his great-uncle. "You're going to lose *all* our money!"

"Thank you, Hector, for that acute observation. Such, however, is not my intention."

Cousin Juliana, as usual, came in on Hector's behalf. "Do you think that our learning curve on the first contract was steep enough to turn another one profitable?"

"We are certainly more familiar with the Von Neumanns' performance, and with other risk factors. But the big changes are elsewhere." At Prosper Ligon's gesture, the lights in the room dimmed. In the display volume behind him appeared an image of Jupiter with its train of satellites.

"Mine Jupiter for helium-3," he said softly, as though talking to himself in the dim light. "It seemed like the right decision at the time. The isotope is more abundant there than anywhere else in the System. We could construct Hebe Station, for docking of the loaded Von Neumanns and their general service. Ganymede was close enough for overall command and control. We could see acceptable profit margins. There was one great problem, and it was an invisible one." He swiveled to point at the display. "Jupiter itself. Or rather, Jupiter's gravity field. The escape velocity from the upper atmosphere is sixty kilometers a second. The Von Neumanns were strained to the limit, and in many cases past the limit. Their loss and the accompanying delays were largely responsible for our financial losses."

"Hmm." Karolus snorted from the other end of the table. If Prosper Ligon was a donkey, Karolus was a bull. "The Von Neumanns are no better than they were, you just admitted that. And Jupiter was still the same size, last time I looked. I haven't noticed any change."

"Nor have I. But there have been other changes." Prosper Ligon made some unseen gesture, and the glowing image of the Jovian system vanished. "Every year," he said in the darkness, "human civilization advances a little farther outward. Every year, the available resources beyond Jupiter increase."

The room brightened again with light from the display volume, but it had changed. Now it showed another planet, recognizable as Saturn from the flattened disk, complex ring system, and attendant moons.

"The atmosphere of Saturn also contains an abundance of helium-3," Prosper went on. "The escape velocity is thirty-six kilometers a second—substantial, but little more than half that of Jupiter. This difference creates a vast change in the economics. I have performed a financial assessment. If we switch to Saturn as the source of fuel for *Starseed-Two* and move the ship itself and our own operations there, we will recoup all the losses suffered on the contract to date."

The rest of the room went dead silent. At last Lena Ligon ventured, "You mean—leave Ganymede?"

The last upheaval had been close to half a century ago, when Gonville Ligon had moved family and empire from the bustling metropolis of Buenos Aires to the stark caverns of Ganymede. That transition had taken place over the strenuous objections of everyone. Gonville, a true descendant of iron-man Alonzo Ligon, had refused to listen. He simply said, "The future of industrial development isn't on Earth, or even on Mars. It's in the Outer System. That's where we're going. Anybody who doesn't want to come along, bugger them. They can stay behind and try to scratch out a living on Earth."

The Great War had proved Gonville right in a way that he had never anticipated. Now Prosper allowed himself a dry little neigh of amusement. "No, no, not at all. I am not proposing relocation. Most of us will remain here. The *Starseed* operation will move out. As to our base there, I have examined the choices."

His display control marked out the nine major Saturnian moons, ranging from Mimas to far-out Phoebe. "None of these. They are all, together with the co-orbiting companions of Tethys and Dione, either under development or subject to lease arrangements. They are also inconveniently distant from Saturn. My own first choice is *this* one. Its period is about half as long again as a Saturnian day, which will make for easy rendezvous with Von Neumanns arriving with helium-3 cargo." The marker flashed onto a bright point that showed as the middle in distance of five small satellites. "The moon currently has a leaseholder, but every previous assay has indicated no useful resources. We should be able to make a tempting offer."

So far as Alex knew, no member of his family had ever taken the slightest interest in the sprawl of the Outer System beyond Jupiter. That idea was confirmed when Great-aunt Cora glared at the illuminated point and said, "No offer for that thing could tempt me. What's it called, and why do we need it? Why not build our own base of operations?"

"*It* is known as Pandora. As to why we need it, that is a most astute question." The long donkey-head nodded appreciation at Great-aunt Cora. "We need Pandora because the current leaseholder is apparently a misanthrope of the most extreme kind, who has been dealing with a government official who is either a buffoon or a hater of corporate activity. The lease permits *government* activity closer to Saturn than Pandora, but the leaseholder has the right to prohibit industrial operations. Operations which are, of course, for us an absolute necessity."

Lena Ligon smiled brightly at Alex, and said to the table at large, "Surely we're not going to let some government pipsqueak stand in our way?"

"It is, Lena, a signed lease."

"Breaking it—"

"Would be difficult, and at the very least time-consuming." Prosper glanced along the table to his left. "I think that we must proceed otherwise. It is my thought that if the current leaseholder is a man, then you, Rezel and Tanya, have the perfect combination of talents to assure his compliance. I also expect every family member to do whatever is asked. Alex, for instance—"

* * *

"—stop right there." Kate held up her hand. It was seven o'clock, and thinking that Alex might be back from his meeting she had dropped in on his tiny apartment. He, more nervous than he wanted to admit, had made strong drinks for both of them. They were sitting now at the little table in the bedroom alcove, while he tried to explain why he might need to make a quick trip out to the Saturn system. So far he was not doing well.

"Too many names," Kate complained. She was wearing a low-cut dress that showed off her shoulders and breasts, and she tugged at it now as it slipped lower. "Too many names, and too fast. I can't keep them straight. Weasel and who are supposed to meet with this leaseholder?"

"Rezel and Tanya. Second cousins of mine, a couple of years younger than me. They're real party types."

"Yet Uncle Prosper is willing to send them to negotiate a deal with someone nobody in the family has ever met? From what you've said I thought Prosper sounded like he knew where he was going, even if he's a dried-out bag of bones. Now he sounds like he's crazy."

"Oh, Prosper knows what he's doing. Rezel and Tanya have had diplomatic and psychosexual training, and in the past they've been very successful. They're smart, they work as a team, and they'll do absolutely anything to get results."

"Anything?"

"Pretty much. Uncle Karolus calls Rezel and Tanya the nympho twins."

"But you wouldn't know about that? Never mind. Prosper said they might need you, too. Why not Cousin Hector, he sounds like he doesn't do much."

"He doesn't. People won't let him. He looks like a berserker hero, tall and blond and with a profile like a Viking. That's where it stops. He's Uncle Karolus's son, but even Karolus says Hector would be better off with his brain removed and replaced with a bowl of fruit."

"I still don't see why they want you involved. You're busy here."

"I'm just backup. Uncle Prosper doesn't know who the leaseholder is, but he asked around and got word from somewhere that it's a kind of freak recluse computer-modeling type."

"Just like you. But uphill work for Weasel and Stoaty."

"I think that's what's worrying Prosper. No one else in the family will put their lily-white hands anywhere near a computer, so he sees me as a default option. That's why I may have to hop out to Saturn." Alex paused, stared at the table, then took in half of his drink in a single swallow. "But I haven't got to the other part of the meeting—"

" 'The old order changeth.' " With phase two of the *Starseed* contract voted on and accepted, Prosper was moving on to new business. He was handing out printed sheets for distribution around the table. "With or without the effects of the *Starseed* contract, Ligon Industries has been losing ground. The printed columns summarize the combined assets for each of the top ten commercial enterprises in the solar system, as they were a decade ago and as they are today. You will observe that two of the current top ten were not present on the earlier list. Delop SA and Sylva Commensals are new entries, replacing Global Minerals and Turbide. Delop are engaged primarily in Saturn system development, and I do not have to describe Sylva Commensals to some of those here." His eye glanced briefly at Lena Ligon as he went on, "We, I am happy to say, are still in the top ten. I am less happy to note that we have slipped from third to ninth place."

Great-aunt Agatha Ligon, her hundred and ten years impossible to guess from the trim, youthful body and lively gray eyes, said sharply, "Ninth! Pah! I remember when we were number one."

"So do several others present."

"We should never have left Earth! It was a ridiculous decision. I told Gonville so at the time."

"Possibly. But I would have you note that Global Minerals, which was formerly a top ten enterprise, elected to remain on Earth. It now occupies the thirty-fourth position on the list. Permit me to continue. My analysis suggests two possible futures for Ligon Industries. We can continue as we are, watching our relative size and influence decline over the next decade. Or we can seek merger with some other group, preferably one of the rising powers in the solar system. You may have your own suggestions. I, of course, also have my preference." Prosper Ligon's bony finger stabbed at the sheet. "I propose that we pursue alliance and merger with the burgeoning empire of Cyrus Mobarak."

Alex was surprised, but less so than others around the table. Hector sat with his mouth open. Cora and Agatha muttered, "Upstart," and "Charlatan," in unison. Alex's mother whispered, "The Sun King!" as though the phrase was original with her. Alex knew that it wasn't. But his mother's words were echoed in awed tones by Cousins Juliana, Rezel, and Tanya. Uncle Karolus gave a short bark of laughter and said, "Full marks for nerve, Prosper. But Cyrus Mobarak is riding high. Give me one sound reason why he would have the slightest interest in merger."

"I propose to do exactly that. Cyrus Mobarak has indeed been successful—"

"Damn right."

"—and he is ambitious. At the same time, he is a self-made

man who, although he would never admit it, yearns to be associated with old money and influence. Who, thirty years ago, had heard of the controlled-fusion Mobies, or of Cyrus Mobarak? Did someone here utter the word *upstart* when I mentioned his name?"

Karolus nodded across the table. "I think that was Agatha. But you're missing the point, Prosper. Merging Mobarak's operation with Ligon wouldn't give Mobarak himself any status with the Inner Circle."

"A simple business merger would not. But what if it was a union of the two families, through shared children? Cyrus Mobarak has two offspring of his own. The elder, his son David, is already committed to a union. However, his daughter Lucy-Maria is young, unattached, and eligible. Lena, we have already had discussions on this matter. If you would like to summarize—"

"Let me get this straight." Kate had stopped fiddling with the top of her dress as Alex went on with his description of the meeting. Now she was sitting totally still. "All this talk about a 'family union.' Do they mean marriage?"

"I guess so." When Kate stared at him, he added, "That is what they mean."

Alex had been told a hundred times that he was the System's least perceptive man when it came to reading women's feelings. But when Kate still said nothing, he went on, "Are you against marriage?"

"No, no." Kate's blue eyes looked away. "I think that the whole marriage business is a bit, well, *old-fashioned*, especially if people haven't lived together. But if someone wants to get married, it's up to them. Maybe Mobarak's daughter feels like that. But in *your* family—is this your mother again?"

"Of *course* it's my mother again." And then he was forced to make a correction. "No, it's not just mother. It's the whole damned family."

"But what right have *they* to decide?" Now Kate could not sit still. She was rubbing her hand along the tabletop, spreading a ring of condensation from her glass. "It would be an *arranged* marriage. You'd think we were in India or Persia, a thousand years ago. Have you seen pictures of this Lucy woman?"

"Yes."

"Well?"

"She looks nice."

"Nice? That's the best you can come up with? Strawberries and cream are *nice*. Is she pretty?"

"Yes, but I think she's been worked over quite a bit."

"I'll bet. Mobarak can afford the best surgeons and splices. Have you met her?"

"Not yet. But Hector has, and he says she's stunning."

"Is Hector a candidate to marry her? Isn't he the cousin with a turnip where his brain should be?"

"No one is talking about Hector."

"They are talking about *you*. Right?"

"They want me to meet with her."

"And are you *going* to meet her?"

"I don't see that I have much choice." Alex realized that wasn't enough. "It's hard to describe what the situation is like to somebody who has never been in one of the meetings. Family needs take precedence over everything."

"Like hell they do. Family needs weren't considered when your cousin Juliana opted to become a Commensal, with permanent sterility. Suppose that Mobarak's second child had been a boy? Family needs didn't make your mother become a Commensal, either."

"I wish she hadn't. I worry about that. Nobody really knows what being a Commensal can do in the long run."

"But she did it anyway. And so did one of your great-aunts."

"Agatha."

"So they are allowed to choose multi-organism symbiosis and sterility, in exchange for guaranteed health and beauty. But you can't. Let's get back to the subject. To be a negotiable asset with Cyrus Mobarak, you have to be young, male, of adequate intelligence, and able to *breed*. Like you. It's a miracle they let you come and work here in the first place. Who knows who you might sleep with? Who knows what diseases you might pick up? And there's another thing."

Here it came, the moment Alex had been dreading. Kate held her glass in front of her face, so he couldn't see her mouth and chin as she said, "What about us?"

"Us?"

"Us. Do you want it spelled? U-S. You and me. I suppose all this pressure of important family business has made it escape your attention, but you and I have been sharing a bed for the past two months. I had the illusion that you were enjoying it. What happens if the great family union is achieved, you are the popular choice, and Lucy becomes Mrs. Alex Ligon?"

"I don't know."

"Well, I do." Kate slammed her glass down hard, so that the sweet and sticky liquor splashed out onto the table. "I'm not a possessive person, but sharing a dick with somebody else—even if she's the heir to the whole Mobarak fortune—isn't my idea of a good time. You go fuck Lucy if you want to. And while you're at it you can go fuck yourself."

Kate stared at Alex, her eyes blinking rapidly. Then she

stood up, tugged her dress higher so that it covered her to the neck, turned, and was gone.

Alex sat alone. He had hoped to share with Kate his concerns over his mother. He had examined Lena Ligon closely during the meeting at family headquarters, and believed he saw evidence that the Commensal his mother had become was profoundly different from the original person.

He wasn't going to be able to talk about those worries tonight; nor would any bed he slept in have Kate Lonaker by his side. The evening stretched out in front of him, empty and barren.

He stood up and headed for his office. Should he run his computer models now, rather than waiting for the morning? Maybe not. So far, the glories of Seine-Day had not lived up to their billing.

6

Humans had been listening for messages from the stars for a hundred and fifty years. What were the chances that you, Milly Wu, would here-and-now discover the first one ever?

Milly told herself, all the time, that the odds were enormously against her; and yet, every morning, as she sat down in her little cubicle she felt an odd *frisson* of expectation.

It was her third week of work, and the routine was already familiar. Incoming signals from all wavelengths went first to the central "mill" of the station, for basic processing and reduction to a standard format. The mill was fully automated, and no human played any part in the operation.

Next came a series of computations and tests, again without human involvement, designed to discover deviations from randomness. There is a fine line between a signal that is unpredictable but well-determined, and one that is totally random. For example, the digits of such numbers as π or e or Euler's constant, γ, form an infinite sequence in any number base you care to choose. You can calculate each element of that sequence, such as the number-string that begins π's base-10 representation, 3.14159265358979323846 . . . for as long as you have time and patience. No matter where you stop, at the millionth or the billionth or the trillionth digit, there will always be a specific and unique next digit. The number π is therefore well-determined, with absolutely nothing random about it. At the same time, no matter how far you go, the next digit cannot be predicted from what you have already.

Of course, if you were to discover the first thousand or ten thousand digits of π, to any number base, in a signal received from space, that would be another matter. It would provide proof, without doubt and without the need for any other information, that an alien intelligence was broadcasting to the universe.

Milly had known all that, long before she applied for a position with Project Argus. It was also a safe bet that the Argus computers, billions of times faster and more accurate than any human, were screening for untold millions of digit sequences drawn from pure mathematics and physics.

So what did this leave for humans to do? Exactly what Milly was doing now: using the human ability, so far unmatched by any machine, to see *patterns*.

Every morning, the mill produced a variable number of signals with some element of strangeness. Every morning, eighteen humans in their separate cubicles were provided a quota of data sets for individual examination. No one in the analysis group knew how many signals the mill produced on any particular day for human inspection, and all assumed that on some occasions two or more people would be given the same data. In principle no data set was more than one day old, but Hannah Krauss had told Milly that new arrivals would often in their first weeks be given an old anomaly, to see what they made of it. Jack Beston calibrated and compared the quality of people as well as signals.

He was more than an Ogre, he was a paranoid Ogre. Milly

and her fellow-workers at the Argus Station could eat together if they wished and interact socially as much as they liked. What they were not supposed to do, ever, was compare notes about their work. Anomalies were not to be advertised, nor were they a subject for group discussion. They were to be reported directly to Jack Beston.

The data for individual analysis were divided into what on the L-4 station were known as "cells." As Milly pulled in the first cell of the day, she reflected that she too might as well be in a cell. Worse than that, she was in solitary confinement. The cubicle to her left was occupied by a mournful-faced woman in her middle fifties who apparently had no other existence than work. Lota Danes was never in the dining area, and no matter how early Milly came to her cubicle, the door of the neighboring cubicle was always closed and the red sign outside showed that it was occupied. The hyperactive man who sat on Milly's other side was at the other extreme of behavior. Simon Bitters kept random hours, popped in and out of his cubicle all the time, stuck his head now and again into Milly's own little partition, placed his right index finger on the end of his nose, then ducked out again without a word. He apparently spent the whole of his working days wandering the station. Milly wondered how he ever fulfilled his daily quota. But apparently he did, otherwise Jack Beston would have shredded him at the weekly review meetings.

"You'll be a long way from home," her stepfather had said, just before Milly left Ganymede. "Make friends there, so you won't feel lonely."

Sure. But how, with eccentrics like these?

Maybe Milly was one herself. This wasn't what she had expected when she signed up to come to the L-4 location and the Argus Project, but Hannah Krauss's warning after her first couple of weeks in some ways matched her stepfather's. "The work here is challenging and interesting, but it's lonely. Try to make friends, and find activities outside your work. Do you know the occupational hazards of mathematicians, logicians, and cryptanalysts?"

"Depression?"

"Depression, yes. Also insanity, paranoia, and suicide. And isolation increases the odds."

Now they warned you, when you were already here. Milly examined the screen in front of her. She could process the cell that she had just loaded in endless different ways. It came in as a long string of binary digits, anything from a million to billions of 1's and 0's. She could transform that to any number base, introduce any breaks that she liked, look for repeating strings, present the data factored into two- or three-dimensional arrays, transform the results to polar or cylindrical or any other orthogonal set of coordinates, examine the Fourier transforms and power spectra of the result, cross-correlate any section with any other, compute the sequence or image entropy, seek size or shape invariants, and display any or all of those results in a wide variety of formats. In the first few days she had developed her own preferred suite of processes, with a shell of operations to run their sequence automatically. All she had to do was sit, observe the results, and allow her imagination to run free in its search for oddities, or—there was always hope—*meaningful* patterns.

While she worked, spectral figures from the past wandered through Milly's mind. They were her heroes and heroines. Here was Thomas Young, the universally gifted nineteenth-century Englishman who moved so easily from medicine to physics to linguistics. He had taken the multi-language inscriptions on the Rosetta Stone to gain a first handle on interpreting Egyptian hieroglyphics. The polymath Young had dismissed his work casually, as "the amusement of a few leisure hours." Here was the Frenchman, Jean-François Champollion, finishing the work that Young had begun, and writing his book on the subject that had so fascinated Milly at seventeen—the same age at which Champollion had been made a full professor at Grenoble.

A century later than Champollion, the quiet American classicist Alice Kober had patiently begun to unravel the mysteries of the Cretan language, Linear B, work that after her early death was completed by Michael Ventris and John Chadwick. By Chadwick's side, as a fellow worker at an English classified facility during wartime, stood the enigmatic and tragic figure of Alan Turing. Turing, with his rumpled clothes, dirty nails, and unshaven face, had been a nonpareil cryptanalyst, as well as the godfather of all the computers that now surrounded Milly. His life had ended with the suicide that Hannah Krauss warned of for workers in cryptanalysis. Behind Turing, a century earlier, stood another computer godfather, Charles Babbage, himself a noted cryptanalyst who had cracked the "unbreakable" Vigenère cipher and who straddled the line between genius and eccentricity.

The godmother for Milly's own field, the interpretation of signals from the stars, had been born a generation later than Turing. Jocelyn Bell, when she was no older than Milly herself, sat alone day after day and night after night studying radio telescope signals, until one day she came across curious repeating patterns of electronic noise that she had named "scruff." For a time, Jocelyn Bell and her research supervisor believed that what she had found was what Milly now longed so desperately to see: synthetic signals from far across the galaxy, sent by intelligent beings. They even—in private if not in public—called them "LGM objects," the initials standing for Little Green Men. Jocelyn Bell's actual discovery, of natural signals sent out by the rapidly rotating neutron stars known as pulsars, was a great surprise and a great event in the history of astrophysics; but it must also have been, in some ways, a disappointment.

And that, Milly reflected, was both the promise and the curse of SETI. If you did discover a pattern, the odds were long against it being what you hoped. Far more likely, you had accidentally come across a natural phenomenon. Nature had a thousand ways of producing a signal with some repeating pattern. Almost everything in space—planets, moons, stars, galaxies—rotated, and each had its own magnetic field. The combination of field and spin could spit pulses of electromagnetic energy in any direction, across thousands or millions of light-years. Discovery of a new such phenomenon might be a great scientific event, but it was not a message from intelligent aliens.

And if what you saw was not natural, then it was most likely a man-made signal, thrown out casually and carelessly by some human activity within the solar system.

Like now. Milly had on her screen a power spectrum with well-defined peaks. Something was generating blips of energy at regular intervals, and it certainly looked like a signal. It also came from a definite direction in space.

She skipped back a day to examine earlier data from the same direction. The pattern vanished. However, observations were made in all directions, through the full 4π of solid angle around the station. She asked the computers to seek a match in a widening cone around the direction of the signal. It took maybe thirty seconds, and there it was: two almost identical power spectra, one day apart, and from directions three degrees apart in the sky. Conclusion: the source, whatever it was, lay within the solar system. No signal source at interstellar distances could move through three degrees of arc in one day, unless it was traveling at least a hundred times as fast as light.

Curse that one, cross it off, note it in the log, and pull in the next data cell. Like everything presented to the eighteen analysts, this one had been flagged by the computers for special treatment. However, it was contrary to Jack Beston's policy to pass onto the analyst the nature of the computer report. He argued that such information encouraged mindless agreement, and inhibited free association and pattern recognition.

Milly activated her program suite, to see what it could do with this one. It had just begun to run when she heard a jingling sound from behind her. It made her feel very uncomfortable. Jack Beston was standing outside the open door of her cubicle. He moved very quietly, but he had the habit of jingling whatever was in his pocket, coins or keys, so you could not accuse him of creeping up on you.

She swiveled her chair around. He was there, his head to one side, watching her displays. He had a little half-smile on his face and his green eyes were closed to slits. Without saying a word he stepped inside her cubicle and stood staring at the screen.

Didn't the man have any manners? No wonder everyone on the Argus Project was so rude, when its leader set the tone for the whole place.

"Hm—hm." Milly coughed, deliberately drawing his attention to her. "I'm trying to work in here, sir. You're interfering with that. I would prefer that you leave." She didn't insert the customary "respectfully" but if that got her fired, what the hell. Jack Beston looked too much like Aly Blanes for comfort, and sexy Aly was half the reason she had left Ganymede.

If Beston heard her, he didn't show any sign of it. His eyes were still fixed on the screen, although there was no way that the display could be intelligible to him. This was Milly's own set of program protocols, their outputs tuned to her way of thinking.

If Jack Beston understood that, he gave no sign of it. He watched the outputs parade across the screen, the input data transformed in a thousand separate ways.

"It's inside the solar system," he said at last. "A long way out of the ecliptic, though, so my guess is we've got some joy-riding clowns waltzing around the Egyptian Cluster at high solar latitude. Illegal, and they're bound to be caught, but they never learn." He checked a device on his wrist. "Recent, too. Nothing there two days ago."

He turned away from the display, as though suddenly it had lost all interest, and went on, "You're working very hard, Milly Wu. Also, you know what you're doing."

It was a compliment, but not much of one. She burst out, "How can you possibly know what the data show? The analysis isn't halfway finished."

"Experience, and a thousand disappointments. I've been working on this for all my adult life. Sometimes I think I've seen everything that humans and the galaxy have to offer. Except what we're looking for. A real SETI signal."

"It's there." Milly wouldn't stand for that style of negative thinking. "It's there, and we'll find it."

"Good for you, Milly Wu." Finally, he was looking right into her eyes. "Look, I told you you're working hard, and I think you're working too hard. I can see it in the bags under your eyes, and in your hands. You need a break. Would you care to have dinner with me tonight?"

A great compliment, to tell her how battered she was looking. Would she like a break? Of course she would. But there was Hannah, sitting on her shoulder and warning: "His two interests in life are the search for extraterrestrial intelligence and the seduction of new female workers. You can feel free to refuse—"

"I don't think I can go to dinner, thank you. I have too much work to do."

It didn't faze him at all. He stood, one hand in his pocket jingling keys or coins, the other touched to his brow. The little smile was still on his face. "That's up to you. But if you care to change your mind, I'll be in my quarters until six. You know where they are. Keep up the good work, Milly Wu."

The sheer *presumption* of the man. He *assumed* that she would know where his quarters were. She did, of course, because Hannah had given her the complete tour. But what an arrogant bastard.

Milly turned back to her work. She was trembling and her mind felt fuzzy. She ought to eat. A couple more cells, and then she would take a rest. The results of the latest data cell were appearing, and the most damnable thing about them was that Jack Beston had called it exactly right. Some ship was bouncing around in the Egyptian Cluster, far out of the ecliptic, with no more idea of radio silence than an interplanetary call girl. The final evidence was unmistakable. But how had Jack Beston, with nothing but a few fragments of information, *known?*

Experience, he had said. Well, all the rumors confirmed that he had plenty of that, and in more areas than one. Lecherous creep. *I should have stayed on Ganymede.*

Milly had always prided herself on her power of concentration, but the effort to turn her attention back to her work took all her willpower.

The next cell was simple and should have been caught by the computer. The SETI array had picked up signals from a vessel in transit from Dione to Hyperion. All the clues were there—orbit close to the ecliptic, moving source, standard frequencies. It made you wonder just how much you could rely on the pre-screening programs. Maybe that's the place where someone ought to tell Jack Beston to invest some effort. Not that the Ogre was likely to listen.

Milly rolled in the data for the next cell. Last one, then something to eat. This one looked different, so different that she ran her entire shell of standard programs without gaining any feel for the reason it had come through as an anomaly. The evidence accumulated slowly, and it was all indirect. First, the source was again far out of the ecliptic, and this time it came from nowhere near the Egyptian Cluster. That reduced the chance of accidental shipping signals by a factor of hundreds. Signal frequency and signal type were equally odd. Rather than being in the "water hole" between the neutral hydrogen and hydroxyl ion emissions, this was at dizzyingly high neutrino energies, where the resonance capture probability was correspondingly high. The trouble was, no human-made generator could fire a modulated neutrino beam at those energies.

Something was there. The question was, message or mirage? The universe was quite capable of producing energies so far beyond human ranges that the mechanisms themselves were still in debate.

Thoughts of food forgotten, Milly settled down to work harder than she had ever worked. It was an axiom of SETI: no matter what you think you've found, you haven't. Go back, take another look at the data, and see what you've been doing wrong.

Milly transformed, inverted, deleted, amplified, and computed cross-correlations until her head spun. The anomaly persisted. It seemed to be outside the solar system, though there was inadequate parallax from recent motion to determine just how far outside. The signal also provided repetitive sequences. One of those, factored from a one-dimensional input data stream to a 2-D array using a product of primes, revealed a pattern of 1's and 0's that hinted at the outline of a circle. Deviations were so small that they looked like signal discretization error. Milly could imagine no natural process that would lead to that result. And the imagined circle had strings attached to it, filaments of binary digits which hinted at an internal structure of their own.

It was close to midnight when she gave up. She could make no sense of what she was seeing; or rather, she could make sense in exactly one way, and it was the one that all her instincts and knowledge of history told her was too good to be true.

What now? Should she do something with what she had found, or ought she let it simmer in her brain and take another look at everything in the morning, when she was less tired? The whole history of SETI was riddled with peaks of excitement, followed a few hours or days later by troughs of disappointment when a signal was not repeated, proved to have arisen within the solar system, or had some natural explanation. It was known as the "Wow effect," named after a famous incident in the first decades of SETI when an impressive but fleeting anomaly was seen once—and never again.

Jack Beston's own words from one of the weekly review meetings finally convinced her. He had offered a warning. "We operate here in the classic 'hurry up and wait' mode. I've been working the Argus Project for ten years. I expect I'll be running it ten, twenty, thirty, forty years more—maybe until they drag me out of here feet-first. But don't let that fool you into thinking that anything we find isn't *urgent*. There's no prize in this game for coming second. If you think you're working hard, you can bet somebody on the Odin Project is matching you, hour for hour. They are a competent group, they're well-funded, and they are well-organized."

It showed respect for Philip Beston, the first time that Milly had ever heard Jack say anything positive about the Bastard.

"Don't come to me with every half-assed idea or suspicion," Jack had continued. "Check it out six ways forward, then six ways backward. But if it still checks out—almost everything won't, I'll guarantee that—you bring it to me, and only to me. It doesn't matter what I'm doing, night or day, sleeping or waking, taking a bath or taking a crap, you come get me at once."

At once.

Milly fixed her outputs in their final form and exited her cubicle. She did have the sense to close the door after her. If others at the Argus Station learned how far out on a limb she was going, she would be a laughing stock.

The station corridors were silent and dimly lit, powered down for what was by convention the sleeping period. Milly slowed her pace as she came closer to her destination. She felt sure she was going to look like a fool, if not to the whole station then at least to one person.

She knocked and pushed the door open. Jack Beston was inside, and he was not asleep. Wearing loose pants and an undershirt that revealed just how thin he was, he was sitting bolt upright at a small desk and staring at a large sheet of paper that seemed all mathematical symbols. He looked up, startled by Milly's entry. His initial look of annoyance was replaced by a smile.

"Well, this is a surprise. It's a bit late for dinner, but there are other diversions even at this hour. Why don't we—"

"I want you to come with me. You have to look at something."

An ogre he might be, but he was no fool. He caught the edge in Milly's tone and stood up at once. "Lead the way."

In his undershirt, with no shoes?

"I think I've found something," Milly said. "If I'm reading it right—"

"Ssh. First rule of SETI, you can lead the way but you can't lead the witness. Show me what you have. Don't talk about it."

He was, thank God, taking her seriously. There was no hint of mockery or derision in his tone. Milly hurried back through the quiet corridors, using her hands and feet to increase her speed in the low-gravity environment of the Argus Station. She could sense Jack right behind her, probably skeptical but still impatient.

"There." Milly, opening the door to her cubicle to reveal the display, felt that she was allowed at least one word. He nodded, pushed past her—and closed the door before she could follow him in.

What was she supposed to do now? Milly stood and waited, simmering with anger and frustration. He didn't know how to run the suite of programs that she had developed. He had no idea what tests she had performed. He had no notion of the combination of factors that suggested to Milly an extra-solar signal of non-natural origin. So what the devil was he doing?

She waited, eyes tired and stomach growling. She had eaten nothing since discerning the first hint of the anomaly, and that had been before midday. Her last meal had been breakfast. No wonder she felt dizzy and hollow.

How long was she supposed to stand and do nothing? The hell with the man, it was *her* anomaly. She reached out, opened the door, and stepped into the little cubicle. Jack Beston was sitting rigid in front of the display. The results that Milly had left on it had disappeared. In their place was an unintelligible image—not numbers or graphs, but swirls of color.

He had heard the door open, and he turned. Milly stood her ground, half expecting a curse. Then she saw his face. For the first time since she had met him, his green eyes were fully open, and they were looking through her and beyond her.

"Well?" Her own voice sounded as weak and nervous as she felt.

Gradually, his eyes focused. He nodded. "It's possible. My own tests are . . . interesting. We may have found something." He frowned. "Credit where credit is due. *You* may have found something. But don't get your hopes up high. I put the chance at one percent. I've felt this close before, a dozen and more times, and it never held up. This one seems to be extra-solar, but we need a history and a parallax to give us a distance estimate. Did you run a historical search?"

"Partial. I looked back three months, and I couldn't find any trace of it."

Milly understood the significance of Jack's question. The multiple receivers at Argus Station could pinpoint the direction in space from which a signal was coming, and if that direction was changing rapidly then the source had to be inside the solar system. However, a slow-moving signal source was not sufficient evidence to prove that it was of extra-solar origin. To determine the distance of something many light-years away, you needed to look at it from two directions. That implied at least two different observations, taken from locations far enough apart in space to provide adequate parallax. The movement of the Argus Station itself, as it orbited in the same plane as Jupiter, would eventually provide that separation. But one full revolution of the station around the Sun, like one revolution of Jupiter itself, took a full twelve years.

Milly felt her spirits drop. She knew the three stages of

SETI as well as anyone: D-V-I—Detect, Verify, Interpret. What she had done was, at best, Stage 1. Did that mean they would have to wait years and years, to obtain a long enough baseline for verification that this was truly at stellar distance?

Jack's face betrayed his own mix of emotions. He acted casual, but she could see that he was enormously excited. After a few moments he said, "Damnation." And then, "Tonight we say nothing to anybody. Tomorrow we show this to the second-tier analysis group"—Milly didn't know there *was* a second-tier analysis group—"and see what they decide."

Milly said, "And then? The long baseline observation . . ."

"And then," Jack stood up. "And *then*, if we're all agreed on a probable detection, we have no choice. We'll need verification. You and I will have to make a trip."

"To Ganymede?" Milly had in mind some vague notion of establishing their priority—her priority?—proving that she and the Argus Station were the first to discover a signal from the stars. But couldn't such a claim be made simply by sending a signal? She said again, "Do we actually need to go to Ganymede?"

Jack was shaking his head. "Forget Ganymede. Unless all this falls apart when we take a closer look, tomorrow we head for the Odin Station at Jovian L-5." He gave Milly a grim smile. "A treat for you. You get to meet the Bastard."

7

You couldn't prowl in zero-gee. If you could, Janeed would have been doing it. She was alone in the twenty-meter emergency room of the big orbital platform, with nothing to do but wait and worry.

The platform was designed to handle arrivals with space-sickness, everything from food poisoning to pure-oxy flash fires to cerebral edemas caused by too-low pressures or vacuum blow-out. Today, however, there had been no emergencies. The center was busy with routine physical examinations, for Janeed and Sebastian and a score of other people preparing themselves for a high-acceleration run from Earth to Ganymede.

Janeed's physical exam had seemed like no physical at all. A battery of machines had clicked and clucked at her while she stood in front of them. That took maybe ten minutes. Then there was the pill. It was round and the size of her thumbnail, and she had swallowed it only on her third try. Even then she needed the assistance of a gulp of water.

The technician, a cheerful blond man whose delicate bones suggested that he spent most of his days in micro-gee environments, had apologized. "The PO used to be quite a bit smaller."

"PO?"

"Peristaltic Observer—the pill. It used to be only as big as a pea, but they just put in a whole new suite of sensors to monitor liver enzymes and perform real-time blood chemistry. I've complained about the size, and they've promised a version half as big in maybe a month. But for now . . ."

But for now, the natural peristalsis of Jan's alimentary canal was transporting the marble-sized pill, with its formidable suite of sensors, along the length of her digestive tract. Tomorrow the PO would be naturally excreted, bearing a complete record (including color images) of every inch of her from throat to anus.

Even with the pill, the physical was quicker and simpler than Jan had expected. She was in and out in less than half an hour. So were the others. They had emerged from the medical center and headed off to their own quarters to prepare for the flight out.

All except Sebastian. He had gone into the medical center at the same time as Janeed, two and a half hours ago. He had not, to her certain knowledge, come out.

Where was he? Should she go back to their own quarters, and wait? But if she did, all she would do was sit and worry.

Finally she went back in, through the sliding door from which she had come out. It was marked NO ENTRANCE, but not locked.

The blond technician who had tested Jan was standing by what looked like an ultra-centrifuge, peering into a binocular microscope. He glanced up as the door closed behind Jan, and said, "The place where you go for the tests—oh, it's you." He grinned at her. "Have you been waiting around all this time? I'm sorry, I thought you knew that you were done for the day. You just come in tomorrow, so we can recover the PO if that hasn't happened naturally."

"It's not me. I'm worried about somebody else who came in at the same time as I did, and he hasn't come out."

"Is he your—"

"He's a close friend. We're flying out together."

"I'm sorry, if he isn't a relative or partner we're not supposed to give out medical information."

"I just want to be sure that there's no problem."

He looked at Jan, hesitated, and said, "Oh, all right. You know what they say, rules are made to be broken. Wait here for a minute."

"I really appreciate this."

"But don't follow me in, or I'll get into real trouble."

He vanished through another door, again labeled NO EN-TRANCE. Jan was left waiting again, but not for long. The blond man reappeared, together with a woman in a blue uniform.

The woman said, "I'm Christa Matloff, and I'm the director of this facility. Fritz says that you are a close friend of Mr. Sebastian Birch?"

"Yes. Is he all right?"

"He's fine, so far as we can tell, but we're still doing tests on him. How long have you known Mr. Birch?"

"Just about all my life."

"Good. Do you have a few minutes?"

"As much time as you want."

"Wonderful. If you would just come with me." Christa Matloff led the way through the NO ENTRANCE door. Jan followed, wondering why they bothered to put up signs if everyone ignored them. She had rather expected to see Sebastian, but once through the door the other woman turned left and led the way to a private office whose walls carried an odd mixture of pre-war artwork and detailed color diagrams of the human anatomy. She gestured to Jan to take a seat.

"Let me repeat what I said earlier. Mr. Birch is all right. In fact, unless the Peristaltic Observer finds a problem, I'd say he's in excellent health."

"But we came in this morning. I was finished ages ago."

"I'm sure. Normally, the tests take less than half an hour. In Mr. Birch's case, we discovered something rather odd—not an illness, let me reassure you of that. But something. That's why I want to ask you about Mr. Birch's background. Where did you first meet, and how often have you seen him since then?"

Something, but not an illness? Then what? Something to do with Sebastian's ability to imagine cloud patterns that had not yet happened?

Christa Matloff seemed like a down-to-earth type, not somebody who enjoyed mystery for its own sake. Jan did her best to give a concise but full answer. She suspected that it would not be enough.

Jan and Sebastian were probably not the same age, but in a sense they had been born on the same day. There must have been years of life that preceded that, two or three of them before Jan's first memory. But for her, life began with a ride in a low-flying aircraft, cradled by a dark-skinned woman who stroked her hair and told her that everything was all right now. Sebastian was on the woman's other side, snuggled close.

The aircraft flew in long, slow circles. Jan, staring out of the window, saw dark, cindered land and still waters. Once she caught sight of something moving, a brown-and-white form that slithered and lurched toward a rounded heap of earth. The aircraft banked, Jan saw a flash of flame, and the mottled object was gone. On the ground where the creature had been lay a black outline of ash. The woman hugged her closer. She said, to herself or to Jan or to someone else in the aircraft—Jan would never know which—"Another damned teratoma. How many of them can they be?"

Teratoma. *The word meant nothing. It was not until years later that Jan understood the term and realized what must have happened. The aircraft that had rescued her and Sebastian was based at Husvik, on South Georgia Island. It had flown many thousands of kilometers, up across the equator from latitude 55 degrees south, to take part in the first post-war survey of Earth's northern hemisphere. At the time no one in the south expected to find humans alive beyond the equator. What they feared and what they sought were the teratomas, genetically modified and monstrous forms created in the Belt and seeded on Earth by Belt ships during the final days of the Great War. Whatever they found, the survey craft were to destroy.*

They had found and killed teratomas by the thousands. They had also found, and rescued, a fair number of people. The adults were left with their memories intact. Small children found alone were treated as soon as they were picked up, to obliterate their earlier memories.

It was done as an act of kindness. The months before rescue were of terror and of deadly raids from the sky. That was followed by the agonizing death of parents and siblings from drinking poisoned water, or by near-starvation and sometimes by cannibalism. Before their memories were wiped, the woman on the aircraft had asked Jan and Sebastian their names. She wrote them on tags and placed them around their wrists; then she touched the Lethe spray to their temples.

That was all they had, all they kept from the past. They were logged in upon arrival at the displaced persons' camp in Husvik as Janeed Jannex and Sebastian Birch. It took a month to learn to respond to them.

"After that we spent just about every day together." Jan felt cold and clammy as she recalled the time of rescue and rebirth.

It was a relief to move on to the normal days of schooling and training and planning a future. She had always taken the lead in that. Sebastian seemed happy to sit and dream. If he went along with her plans, it was only because she coaxed and persuaded him.

"No long periods of separation?" Christa Matloff had listened in sympathetic silence. "What you've described was more than thirty years ago. You had no individual training since then, or different schools? I'm thinking of art courses, say, that he took and you didn't."

"None." That last comment sounded as though Sebastian's cloud drawings must be involved. Jan glanced at the clock. She had talked for close to a quarter of an hour, and there was still no sign of him. "If you think that he might have picked up a disease, I'm sure I would have been exposed to it, too."

She was really asking a question, and the other woman was smart enough to see it that way.

"It's not a disease. In fact, I'll be honest with you, and admit we don't know quite what it is. I don't want you to feel we're making a big mystery out of nothing. Come on, and I'll show you."

She led Jan back the way they had come, through another door and into a room filled with CAT and PET scanners and SQUID sensors, flanked by rows of monitors. Jan, to her great relief, saw Sebastian sitting down at the far end. He was fully dressed and—typical Sebastian—quite relaxed. He caught sight of Jan and gave her a nonchalant wave.

"You're feeling all right?" she called.

He frowned. "All right? Yeah. Getting hungry, is all. We about done?"

He addressed his question to a blue-uniformed man who was fine-tuning an image on a monitor.

"Done as we're likely to get." The man turned to Christa Matloff. "We've scanned, analyzed, recorded, and tagged. What now?"

"Did you perform the search?"

"Long ago. I can show you the structures, and I can assure you that there's nothing like it in the data banks."

"Did you search the full Seine?"

"No. We'd have to get special authorization, and I didn't think I needed to." The man turned to Sebastian. "You said you've never been off-Earth before?"

"Nah."

"So it's down on Earth, if it's anywhere. And it's definitely not in the Earth data banks. Do you want me to set up a full Seine search?"

"I don't think so, not at the moment." Christa Matloff stepped toward the monitor. "Let's have another look at it."

It! They kept saying "it," but what was it?

Uninvited, Jan followed the other woman. Sebastian, uninhibited as ever, crowded forward and pushed his moon face close to the display.

"Something in the white cells," the man said. "This is at one to a hundred thousand. See the little round structure, a tiny nodule in with the other organelles? There's one or two of 'em in every couple of thousand white blood cells."

The screen showed a single irregular oval. Within it, close to the cell wall, two dark spherical objects were clearly visible.

Christa Matloff stared in silence for a few seconds. "In other types of cells, too?"

"I haven't found any."

"Did you do DNA and RNA checks?"

"Sure. Not a sign of either one. We're not dealing with anything bacterial or viral. There's also no sign of interaction with the rest of the cell. They just sit there."

"Chemical analysis?"

"Yes. That's another reason I'm sure they're not alive. An ultimate analysis showed eight elements present: hydrogen, nitrogen, oxygen, magnesium, silicon, potassium, manganese, and zinc. But no you-know-what."

"No carbon?"

"Not a trace. They're inorganic."

"So what are they?" Christa Matloff addressed the question to everyone, but it was clear that she was not expecting an answer.

"Beats me." The blue-uniformed man shrugged. "But we have plenty of samples, and we'll go on looking. I can tell you one thing, nothing I've seen could possibly be interpreted as a carrier of disease. That's my job, to make sure that we're not sending dangerous pathogens to the Outer System. And of course, we had to confirm that Mr. Birch is in good health. He is. Remarkable health, considering his age is thirty-five and he says he never takes any exercise. Dr. Matloff, as far as I'm concerned he's cleared to go."

"I'm glad to hear that. Valnia Bloom would never have forgiven me if I'd said he couldn't go. She's itching to get at him. But I just hate to leave dangling mysteries." She turned to Sebastian. "There's something peculiar inside your white blood cells, and your brain functions and scans are also quite unusual—did you know you have variable neurotransmitter take-up rates?"

"Never knew I had them. Is that good?"

"Not good, not bad. Do you ever feel inexplicable fits of weariness, or rage?"

Jan laughed. "Sebastian never gets mad at *anything*, ever."

"Then I wouldn't worry about the neurotransmitter variations, because they're not doing any harm. We'll put all this into the official report, of course. Meanwhile, there's nothing to stop you leaving."

"Leaving the lab?"

"Leaving the Earth-Moon system." Christa Matloff turned, to include Jan as well as Sebastian. "Congratulations, both of you. Pretty soon you'll be on your way to Ganymede, then I gather you'll be heading for Saturn."

8

Five more minutes, and Alex must leave. He had to go, but he was so excited that he didn't know if he could bear to. His feet, in their clumsy formal shoes, felt rooted to the floor of his office. He had been standing, fully dressed and motionless, for over two hours.

At last! At last his programs were able to employ the full power of the Seine, and the difference between this and all pre-Seine runs was awesome. If only he could stay until the end of the first run . . .

The racing clock already showed 2136—three decades beyond the point where all earlier efforts had degenerated to meaningless overflow and massive exponents. On the displays he could now *watch* the outward wave, as humanity expanded faster and faster through the solar system. Total population had climbed steadily to almost ten billion. Outward Bound was busy with the major satellites of Uranus and had a firm toehold on Triton, Neptune's giant moon. A manned expedition was on the way to the inner edge of the Oort Cloud. The seventh unmanned interstellar ship was on its way. A *manned* interstellar ship was on the drawing boards.

Alex could also zoom the model in to examine in more detail the prediction for any chosen location; detail enough, if he so chose, to examine the actions of an individual program element. That element was a person, or at least the Fax of a person. And the Fax could be selected as anything from a crude Level One to the most complex of the Level Fives.

The last digits of the clock were changing too fast to be more than a blur. Already the prediction had advanced to 2140. All parameters showed only orderly change, with no wild swings or uncontrolled growth. He had set the run for a full century ahead. Another hour—even another half-hour . . .

He became aware of Kate standing by his side. She had certainly not been there thirty seconds ago. He felt like turning, reaching his arms wide, and embracing her. Kate was the one who had coaxed and argued and finessed and finagled, until the complete Seine resources were made available to Alex's computer models. This was her moment as much as his, it should be a shared pleasure and excitement.

Alex was smart enough not to offer Kate even his little finger. She'd probably bite it off. She was his boss, so they had no choice but to continue to work together ever since he told her that he had agreed to meet with Lucy-Maria Mobarak. It was necessary, he had explained, because of "family pressure." Kate had nodded, but from that moment everything between them had been on a cool and strictly professional basis. He did not recall that their hands had touched once. As for the idea of sleeping together . . .

He could see from the corner of his eye that she was looking him up and down with disapproval. He agreed with her completely. It was not from choice that he wore clothing so outmoded and uncomfortable.

Prosper and Karolus Ligon had laid down the rules. "It is

nowhere a written requirement, Alex, but it will be expected of you. We realize that there is no commitment at this moment, on our side or Mobarak's. However, your meeting with Lucy-Maria Mobarak is the first encounter between potential heirs of two of the System's wealthiest families. You must dress in accordance with tradition. We refer, of course, to *Ligon* tradition."

Ligon tradition stretched back more than two centuries. Which was why Alex, who normally worked in a sloppy jumpsuit and more often than not went barefoot, now stood attired in a stiff and starchy suit of gleaming white, a canary-yellow shirt fronted with jeweled ruby studs that had taken half an hour to fasten, and ancient two-toned shoes of yellow and white. They were a size too small and cramped his toes. Forcing those objects onto his feet, he had wondered about *Mobarak* tradition. Since Cyrus Mobarak was by Ligon standards an "upstart" and a "charlatan," was there any such thing? What would Lucy-Maria be wearing?

Kate's disgusted glance at Alex's clothing said everything. Her only comment, however, was, "Your mother is outside. I don't think you should keep her waiting."

The model's internal clock had reached 2143. Soon they would be at the half-century projection mark. "Will you keep an eye on this run?"

"I've been watching it closely since the moment it started. Don't worry, Alex. It will not lack my attention."

No enthusiasm in Kate's tone, no suggestion that this could be an historic event in the field of predictive modeling. Alex nodded, swiveled on his heel, and squeaked out.

Lena Ligon was indeed waiting, with an expression more of curiosity than impatience. "So you actually *work* here. In an office."

"Yes, Mother. Is there anything wrong with that?"

"Oh, no. If that is what amuses you." Her glance took in and rejected the metal walls, harsh lighting, and worn floor tiles. "And that was the famous Kate Lonaker. She is taller and better-looking in person than her video would suggest. Interesting, if it is all-natural and without modifications."

It was not an actual question. Alex remained silent. He allowed his mother to lead the way, through the labyrinthine inner tunnels of Ganymede, then onto an elevator that ascended rapidly more than four hundred kilometers. By the time they reached their destination level, the effective gravity had increased appreciably.

Alex assumed that his mother had dropped the subject of Kate, as beneath consideration. But Lena said suddenly, "She does not talk about you in a typical supervisor-employee way."

"Oh?"

"No. I sensed that she was angry with you about something. She has airs above her station."

"I had to leave for this meeting, right when I was in the middle of making computer runs of my prediction models."

"This meeting is important. Anyway, not that sort of anger. Something more personal." His mother flashed a glance at Alex from clear gray eyes, their whites almost luminous with health. "Are you two doing what these days is known as co-orbiting, but in my simpler youth was known as fucking each other?"

"No." That was currently a true statement. Fortunately Lena did not go on to more detailed questioning.

"Good," she said. "Keep it that way. One of your problems, Alex, is that you do not appreciate the vast gulf between you and the Kate Lonakers of the world. Ever since the time of your late great-uncle Sanford, we Ligons have followed a strict selection procedure for child-bearing. The genetic material brought into the mating from outside the family comes not from a single individual, but is a carefully-chosen chromosomal synthesis from several donors. Kate Lonaker is, I feel sure, the product of some indiscriminate, one-Y, single-father breeding. To her and to women like her—females with no family, pedigree, property, or prospects—you represent a catch of almost unimaginable value. It would not be necessary for her to extort promises from you. She could merely beguile you into ignoring all precautions, allowing her to become pregnant with your child with or without your knowledge . . . I assume that you remain on long-term prophylaxis? There is, after all, such a thing as loyalty to family tradition."

Alex felt a brief uneasiness. He had asked Kate at the outset if she was fertile, and she had replied that at the moment she preferred not to be. He had believed her implicitly, and still did; but he had not asked her recently.

His stronger emotion, however, was disgust at his mother's hypocrisy. How dare she lecture *him* about family tradition, when her own decision to become a Commensal, like that of Great-aunt Agatha and Cousin Juliana, had been made without regard to family needs? Commensality conferred, along with health and protection from almost every disease, an irreversible sterility. Alex, walking a pace behind his mother, surveyed her slender form. She had made the choice and now had the appearance and energy of a twenty year old, combined with a formidable libido. Her features and figure were perfection.

Lena Ligon was also, in specific ways that made Alex nervous but apparently worried Lena not a bit, no longer quite human.

It made Alex's own skin crawl to think what lay underneath his mother's epidermis. A hundred tailored organisms shared space in the interior of a Commensal. The one that Alex found most disgusting was the giant schistosome, a mature and genetically-enhanced worm that lay alongside and within Lena Ligon's liver. The original parasite had been the source of weakness and debility for hundreds of millions of people. This one now guarded its terrain, the lower intestines, against all infestations. A lung fluke did the same for the chest and upper body cavity, a third genemod parasite inhabited one of the larger *sulci* of the brain and warded off tumor growth, Parkinson's, and Alzheimer's. These were just the three big ones, many centimeters long. Scores of other body-dwellers in a Commensal ranged in size from a millimeter or two down to a handful of specialized cells. Put them all together, with their own needs and priorities, and it was no longer clear who or what controlled the agenda of Lena Ligon's life.

It was not even clear that the changes to Lena were safe. The technology in its present form had been applied for less than three years. If the methods had been developed in a Ganymede or Mars medical research center, that would have been some reassurance; but the Commensals were leftover Great War technology, discovered in the drifting remains of a Belt weapons shop. Reputable rejuvenators hesitated to use it. Who knew the original objectives? Who knew the undocumented long-term side effects? But Lena Ligon's feelings were fairly typical. "My dear, long-term effects are who-cares effects. We want to look good and feel good *now.*"

The worst thing of all, from Alex's point of view, was Lena's new smell. It was not exactly unpleasant, rather the opposite. His mother's body and breath exuded a subtle, musky perfume of modified pheromones. But the odor was *different.* A kiss on the cheek from Lena Ligon was now a creepy experience for Alex, to be avoided whenever possible.

"Remember," his mother said, as though reading Alex's thoughts, "even if you find the sight, sound, and smell of this young woman rather strange, you must behave properly. If she smiles at you, smile back. If she offers you her hand, kiss it. If a subject seems distasteful to her, drop it at once. We can discuss any problems later, within the family. During the meeting, take your cues from me."

Was his mother suggesting that Lucy-Maria Mobarak might also have become a Commensal?

It was a bit late to discuss the point. They were there. They had risen and risen, to a level of Ganymede higher than Alex had ever been except on obligatory school trips to see the stars at first-hand. This was the very highest level, with the actual surface no more than twenty meters above their heads. Alex's first thought, that Cyrus Mobarak must have odd tastes to live in such a place, changed after a moment's thought. The principal business of Mobarak Enterprises was fusion plants, and in the Outer System the fastest-growing use of fusion plants lay in transportation. While the number of colonized worlds grew linearly, transportation needs grew quadratically. The production of the Mobies had to be at the surface, or out in space itself.

As they stepped out onto the final level, the light changed. Alex instinctively looked up. Above his head, no more than ten meters away, stood a window with a glittering starscape beyond. His first thought—*this is dangerous!*—lasted only a split second. He realized that whatever the material of that window, it would be designed to withstand anything that hit it. The new Mobarak synthetics could supposedly tolerate a direct whack from a meteorite traveling at thirty kilometers a second. They could also dissipate impact energy so fast that only the top few centimeters of material were vaporized, while at the same time they photo-darkened so rapidly that the flash of light was no more than startling even from as close as ten meters.

The double doors in front of Lena and Alex were a fair copy

of the ones that fronted the corporate offices of Ligon Industries. The metal plate with the sign, MOBARAK ENTERPRISES, was just as discreet. Imitation is one of the more reliable forms of flattery. Alex had secretly questioned Prosper Ligon's assertion that Cyrus Mobarak yearned to join the Inner Circle of old money and influence. Now he was not so sure.

He was also beginning to wonder what he would find on the other side of those great double doors. Somehow, his agreement to have a simple meeting with Mobarak's daughter had escalated. He had imagined maybe a drink together, or a quiet meal in an informal setting. Instead it had become an official family affair, with parents as chaperons. Alex was not sure he liked the idea of Cyrus Mobarak as a chaperon. The man's reputation made anything said about Uncle Karolus or Great-aunt Agatha seem tame by comparison.

Meanwhile, the Fax who served as automatic doorkeeper had apparently satisfied itself as to their identity. The doors quietly swung open. Alex followed his mother into a huge room whose whole ceiling was a continuous window, with the naked heavens beyond. Again, Lena took no notice. Alex wondered if she knew what Nature was doing, less than twenty meters above their heads. He did, and didn't like the thought.

It was not the mixture of rock and water-ice that made up most of Ganymede's surface, that was no danger. The problem lay a little higher. Jupiter loomed in the sky, a million kilometers away. It gathered from the solar wind an endless supply of high-energy protons, accelerated them with its monstrous magnetic field, and delivered them as a murderous hail onto Ganymede's frozen surface. A human in an ordinary spacesuit would cook and die within hours. The only safe way to wander the surface was in suits bearing in-woven threads of high-temperature superconductors. Charged particles followed the magnetic field lines, harmlessly around and past the suit's surface. The human inside remained safe and snug.

Alex felt sure that his mother neither knew nor cared. Certainly, she seemed at ease as she advanced steadily toward the man standing on the richly-decorated carpet that covered the central fifteen meters of the room. The whole chamber was a recreation of some ancient Earth style, with pillars shaped as carved odalisques, red-lipped, full-bodied, and diaphanously clad, set at intervals around the walls. The furniture was all armchairs, dark and massive, with a low rectangular glass-topped table set in front of each.

The man in the middle of the ornately-furnished room was Cyrus Mobarak, known to Alex in appearance and reputation from media descriptions. Mobarak was in his fifties, shorter and more strongly-built than the video images would suggest, with a thick neck that bulged against a blue-and-white wing collar half a size too small. If Mobarak Enterprises had a "traditional" uniform for meetings like this, you would never discover it by looking at Mobarak himself. His suit was plain gray, lacking medals, decorations, or jewelry. His nose was prominent, he wore a thick shock of hair that he had allowed to gray naturally, and his brow ridges overhung pale, unreadable eyes.

Was this the famous "Sun King," the powerhouse whose inventions had transformed energy generation and transportation systems from Mercury to the Oort Cloud? It hardly seemed possible.

And then Mobarak spoke. His voice was deep, his words quiet and conventional; no more than, "Hello, I am Cyrus Mobarak. Welcome to Mobarak Enterprises. I hope that before you leave you will have an opportunity to tour my home and workplace, and see what we do here."

The man seemed to expand and glow as he spoke, investing

simple words with warmth and pleasure and just a hint of humor.

Alex felt his own positive response as he said a polite greeting and shook Mobarak's hand. His mother, so far as he could see, melted, crashed, and burned on first contact. When it was her turn to take Mobarak's hand she seemed ready to have an orgasm on the spot.

"This is *such* a thrill. Of course, I've heard about the Sun King for years and years, and longed to meet you. Unless you have other plans, you and I and Alex and Lucy-Maria could go off together and have a meal. I thought, maybe a quiet place where we could begin to get to know each other."

"That's a splendid idea, and I wish it were possible. But I just can't." No one, listening to Mobarak, could doubt for a moment that his regret was genuine. "It's my own stupid fault, arranging too many meetings in too short a time. I have to leave very soon. But there's nothing to prevent the three of you from going off together—I know a perfect place, exclusive and quiet. Why don't the three of you go? Unless, of course, you feel that the youngsters would be better left to themselves, just the two of them. I suspect that they might enjoy that."

In half a dozen sentences, Cyrus Mobarak convinced Alex of three things. First, Mobarak was a master at dealing with people. He had implied that Lena Ligon would be about as necessary to the forthcoming meeting as breasts on a spaceship, but he had done it in such a way that Lena was nodding agreement at the notion that the younger generation should be left alone. Second, Mobarak had decided to take a look at Alex before he introduced Lucy-Maria. Apparently Alex had passed that test. And third, Mobarak was as interested in a union of the two families as Prosper Ligon or anyone else in

Ligon Industries. Suddenly, Alex wondered what he was about to meet. He had seen pictures of Lucy-Maria, but you could fix a picture to look like almost anything. A king of ancient England had agreed to marry on the strength of an inaccurate picture (and had later executed the man who arranged the whole thing).

Mobarak led the way to a half-open door. Alex, prepared for the worst, followed.

The room beyond was furnished and decorated in the same lush style of a departed era. By contrast, the young woman seated on a two-person love seat defined personal rebellion and a clash of times and cultures. Her dark hair was cut in the absolute latest style, straight across her low forehead with framing curves around her cheeks and shaped to touch below her chin. Her arms, shoulders, and bosom were bare, her breasts exposed almost to the nipples. Every square inch of that glowing, dusky skin was covered with the iridescent glitter points that Alex had never seen before except on entertainment stars. She sat cross-legged, so that a split skirt showed bare leg and more star glitter all the way to her upper thigh. The overall effect was stunning. What had Hector said? That she looked terrific? For once in his life, Hector was right.

Mobarak said, "Lucy, I would like to introduce you to Alex Ligon, and to his mother, Lena."

The young woman nodded at Mobarak's words but made no attempt to stand or speak. Which left it up to Alex. Running on shocked autopilot, he followed his mother's earlier suggestion. He stepped forward, lifted Lucy-Maria's hand to his lips, and kissed it.

That produced a frown, followed by an unreadable little smile.

"Sit down, Alex," Mobarak said. And then, as Alex did so, on a chair facing Lucy-Maria, Mobarak turned to Lena. "I wonder if you might like to see a little more of Mobarak Enterprises. If so, I would be delighted to give you a guided tour."

He didn't wait for an answer, but turned at once toward a smaller door set between two marble statues of winged lions. Lena didn't even glance toward Alex as she followed.

So much for support and guidance, or any idea that Alex might receive helpful cues from his mother. He placed his hands on his knees and wondered how his computer run was going, back in the plain surroundings of the government offices. He wished he were there.

As an innocuous opening remark, he said, "Your father seems like a most impressive man."

There was a long and empty silence. The great antiquated room lacked even the normal hiss of an air supply system. Alex wondered if Lucy-Maria had some kind of hearing problem that no one had bothered to mention. Looking into her eyes, big and dark, was like looking into space. There seemed to be nothing behind them.

At last she said, "Impressive? Not if you talk to my mother."

"She's here?"

"Good God, no. She's back on Earth in Punta Arenas. He pays to keep her there. I visit a couple of times a year. She tells me he's a real shit."

As a line of conversation this one didn't seem promising. Alex, after a few dead seconds, said, "I didn't have a father in the usual sense. My mother preferred an *in vitro* development. The genetic material on the paternal side came from a combination of nine different males that she selected, providing a variety of different potentials."

Lucy-Maria raised iridescent eyebrows and stared at him. He finally read an expression—"What went wrong, if you're the result?"—in her dark eyes. She finally said, "You mother looks real good. Is she a Commensal?"

"I'm afraid so."

"Afraid? Afraid of what? I'd be one, too, if they'd let me. But it's supposed to make you sterile, and I'm the Mobarak prize cow. Breed if you want to feed. You, too?"

"I suppose so."

She examined him from head to toe. Finally she said, "Do you usually dress like that?"

"No. I *never* dress like this. My family put pressure on me to wear these clothes, because they're supposed to show our family tradition."

"You look like a Husvik whore-master." She leaned forward confidentially. "I had to meet with you, or get chopped. But I didn't want to. I'll bet you were the same."

"I was." It might not be polite, but it was the truth.

"So we're supposed to sit here and imitate armchairs, and bore each other to death. But we don't have to. They said get to know each other. They didn't say we have to stay here."

"I'm not sure that my mother—"

"I saw the way my father looked at her, and she looked at him. They're probably climbing all over each other. Talk about a family merger. I'll bet there's one going on right now."

"Well, I don't know—"

"I do." She stood up, in a fluid swirl of movement and a flash of long leg. She was taller than he had realized, eye to eye with him. "Come on. You just follow me, there's a way out of here that the security Faxes monitor but don't record."

She was off, toward a wall panel that swiveled as they approached. Alex—had he gone crazy?—followed Lucy-Maria through into a darkening corridor. Twenty paces. He counted them. He was ready to stop and ask her where they were going when his next step found nothing and he fell face-forward.

It was a drop chute. They riddled Ganymede's interior, and Alex was used to them. The difference was that this one had no trace of lighting and he was falling through blackness and accelerating at a steady sixth of a gee. That was fine—until you reached the bottom.

"Lucy-Maria?"

He heard her laugh from below him. "Relax, I've done this a hundred times and I'm navigating for both of us. We have to pass through seventeen branch points. Ten minutes freefall, then we reach the arrest phase. Lie back and enjoy. And call me Lucy. I'm only Lucy-Maria for official family business."

But this *was* family business—or supposed to be. And enjoying was one thing that Alex couldn't do. What would his mother do and say when she found that he and Lucy had disappeared together?

The descent chute went on forever. Ten minutes! That would take them down hundreds of kilometers, far below all residential levels, far below the government office levels, below the agricultural levels, closing in on the deep interior where the blue-green prokaryotes produced the oxygen for all of Ganymede.

Where could she be taking him?

They had long ago reached terminal velocity. The wind whistled past Alex's ears and tousled his hair. His hat, that silly conical family-tradition white hat with its stiff peak, had vanished long since into the darkness. And now, finally, Alex felt the arrest field. He was no longer falling at constant speed. A gentle hand, the same one that had held him clear of the walls of the chute, turned him upright. Now he was falling feet-first, and far below him he saw a small circle of light.

As he slowed, his surroundings became steadily brighter. The walls of the tunnel carried a faint green luminescence. By that light he caught his first sight of Lucy since they had left Mobarak headquarters. She was maybe thirty meters below him. On the way down she had somehow transformed her long green skirt into a rainbow version that ended at mid-thigh.

She landed lightly, and was waiting for him barefoot when he arrived. She held her shoes and skirt in one hand, but dropped them to the floor as she came close to Alex.

"All right, let's take another look at you. Stand up straighter."

Alex stood up straight and stared around him, wondering where his hat had landed. He was on a level he did not recognize and had surely never been before. The lower end of the chute formed a chamber with walls so luridly painted that he suspected that the finishing Von Neumanns had never been brought in. Three openings big enough to admit a human stood equally spaced around the walls, each one shimmering with the Moiré patterns that indicated the presence of metal detectors and sonic inhibitors.

"These have to go." Lucy was stooped at his feet, loosening the buckles on his two-toned yellow-and-white shoes.

"Because they contain metal?"

"Because they're extremely hideous." As Alex stepped out of his shoes to reveal canary-yellow socks, she felt the fabric of his jacket. "This, too. It feels like it's made of hardboard and the style is pure geeker. It has to go. I have a reputation to protect."

"What *is* this place?"

"Holy Rollers. *The* place to be. I knew you'd led a sheltered life, just from one look at you. What do you do when you're not taking orders from Mummy?"

"I build predictive computer models for solar system simulation. I don't take orders from my mother." *But he did.* Alex glanced at the despised jacket, which had joined the crumpled mess of clothes on the floor. "I should be running my predictive model now."

"Computer models. Boring. Boring beyond death." Lucy rubbed at the ruby studs on his shirt. "These, on the other hand, are pretty damned fine. Rubies are right in this season, and bright yellow is daring." She surveyed him again. "You'll do, especially those socks. When we get inside and meet my friends, tell them that you're Alex Ligon, of Ligon Industries. Nothing about models, and for God's sake nothing about computers. I don't want to have to disown you. Let's see, where shall we go?"

She glanced at the three shimmering openings. "Not Hispano-Suizas, because apparently it's doing virtuals tonight. And it's a bit early for Bugattis, they do a slow first few laps. So it has to be Lagondas. You're not certified, are you?"

"I don't think so."

"Of course you're not. Hold tight to my hand, or it won't pass you."

She grabbed Alex's hand in her own—it was warm and surprisingly strong—and pulled him toward one of the openings. There was a tingle over his whole body, then he stepped through into a roar of sound and a flicker of colored lights.

"You wait right here," Lucy shouted in his ear. "If someone asks you to dance, don't accept. Don't speak. Just shake your head."

She eeled away to the left. Alex stood rigid, wondering how he had ever been so stupid as to come with her in the first place. Lagondas—if that was the right name—was packed with people, some slowly moving together in couples and trios and quartets, some leaning against counters along the sides of the big octagonal room, others sitting on isolated round objects like giant mushrooms. In four of the corners stood square columns about two meters high, from which long hoses pro-truded ending in some kind of shiny guns. The columns were labeled: 87, 89, 91, 93. A dozen people clustered around each one. Judging from the elaborate dress and jewelry, everyone was rich. The wall paintings showed ancient forms of personal transportation that had dominated Earth in previous centuries.

The level of noise was astonishing. Everyone seemed to be talking against a background of recorded sound, rhythmic dance music overlain with the whine and roar of high-revving engines and the scream of over-stressed tires. Alex smelled fumes, like incompletely-burned hydrocarbons. He wondered why Lucy Mobarak had worried about someone asking him to dance. Unless they screamed right into his ear, he would never hear the invitation.

And then someone *was* at his side, and shouting at him. It was a short blonde girl. He felt a touch on his foot, and looked down. She was wearing a scanty halter top, long pants of faded blue, and what seemed to be heavy boots. But those boots had to be fake, because the touch on the top of his own stock-inged foot was soft and light.

"Hot socks!" She had to stand on tiptoe to get her mouth close to his ear. "I saw you arrive at the same time as Lucy Mondeo. Does she have your starting handle?"

Don't speak. Just shake your head. Alex could have used more guidance.

He leaned down and shouted, "I came here with Lucy Mo-barak."

"Lucky Lucy." She took his hand in both of hers and put her mouth so close to his left ear that her lips brushed it as she spoke. "What's your name?"

"Alex Ligon."

"Ligon?" She frowned. "I don't know that one. Are you one of the custom-builts?" She didn't wait for an answer, but went on, "I'm Suky Studebaker, except outside when I'm Suky Sylva. Wait and see how the Mondeo works out. If it doesn't, look me up."

She plunged into a knot of people in front of Alex, but he didn't have much time to ponder what that had been all about, because Lucy was at his side again.

"Didn't I tell you not to talk to anyone while I was gone? *Especially* Suky Stu. She's Lagondas' hottest tailpipe, and she claims she's done more laps than anyone. What did she say to you?"

"She asked me my name, and I said Alex Ligon."

"That's all right, but you'll need another one. Let me think. You can be Alex Lotus, I don't think that's in use. And here, take this."

Lucy was holding two tall glasses shaped like vertical trumpet horns with round balls at the lower end. She thrust one into Alex's hand. It was filled with a pale pink liquid. Alex sniffed at it suspiciously. Bubbles rose lazily through the drink in response to Ganymede's low gravity and burst to tickle his nose.

She laughed at him. "You don't need to worry, I wouldn't start us on high octane. Perfectly safe. Here's to Ligons and Mobaraks."

She raised her glass and took a long drink. Alex, more cautiously, did the same. The flavor was pleasant and he tasted no intoxicants or fizzes.

"What's in this?"

Lucy shrugged. "Who bothers to ask? It's called a Sebring Special, and it tastes right. That's all I need to know. Like it?"

"It's very good." Alex took a second gulp, and bubbles tickled his mouth and throat. "Really good."

"One of these, and maybe a Daytona Swizzle, then I'll introduce you to a couple of friends. Do you dance?"

"I can." One of the miseries of Alex's youth had been dance lessons. *For formal occasions, Alex, any Ligon must be able to give an adequate account of himself on a dance floor.* "I'm not very good."

"Nor am I. You don't have to be." Lucy gestured to the swaying groups of people. "You can do that, can't you?"

"I guess I can." Alex wouldn't have called it dancing. There was everything from close body contact to couples gesturing to each other from two or three meters apart.

He followed Lucy's lead and tilted his glass up again. This time the level was low enough for liquid to flow from the round ball at the lower end. He felt a tingle start on his tongue and follow the drink all the way down to his stomach. And suddenly the glass was empty.

Lucy was laughing at him. "Afterburner." She drained her own glass. "Time to fill the tank. That's Deirdre de Soto and her brother over by the ninety-one octane. We'll go there, I'll show you how to work a pump, then if you like we can all dance."

Alex followed her around the perimeter of the octagonal room. He was becoming used to the noise, but the lurid colors of clothes and walls seemed to be brightening. He stood beside Lucy, waiting their turn at the pump. The shouted introductions to Deirdre and Dafyd de Soto were unintelligible, but Deirdre touched his foot with hers, which seemed to be some sort of custom in this place, and Lucy shouted at her, "Go easy. This is his first circuit, and he's not ready for the pole position," which made even less sense.

Deirdre, like Lucy, was barefoot. It seemed to Alex that she was close to bare-everything. She wore a thin halter and a miniskirt, and had a ruby set in her navel. She touched that stone, put her finger on one of the studs of Alex's shirt, and said, "Snap!" Everyone around the pump except Alex burst out laughing.

The front of the square column contained a complex menu of options. Dafyd de Soto pressed a series of commands that charged his glass with fluid that changed color as the ball was filled, then showed Alex how to do the same thing. Apparently Alex did not get the combination exactly right, because the other three laughed again and Deirdre called out, "Hi-test already! Lucy, are you *sure* it's his first circuit?"

Alex tasted what he had produced. It was different from the Sebring Special, slightly less sweet and with a subtle, bitter aftertaste. He preferred it. He moved along the room with the other three, listening but not saying anything. If they noticed that he was quiet, no one commented on it.

They came to the edge of the dance area. No one mentioned dancing, but Deirdre de Soto stood in front of Alex and began to sway in time to the music. He looked, fascinated, because no matter how she moved her body the level of the drink in her glass remained exactly level. He tried to match her movements, and slopped liquid onto his own hand. Before he could do anything Deirdre had dipped her head forward and licked it off.

Lucy said, "You did that on purpose!" But whether she was accusing him or Deirdre, he could not tell. Now Lucy and Dafyd were also moving, following the pulse of the background music. He felt an increasing urge to do the same, but that would spill the drink that he was holding.

There was an obvious solution to that problem. Alex drained the remaining three-quarters of the drink in one long gulp, then walked across to one of the counters to set down the glass. He stared up at the mural beyond the counter. Four brightly-colored race cars hurtled along a straight track toward a tight corner. He heard the whine of engines as the drivers changed down to lower gears and accelerated into the banked curve. He could actually see the cars moving, jockeying for position. In the foreground, a car that had spun out of control on the curve was facing the wrong way and lying on its side. Black smoke rose from its engine. Alex could see that it was about to burst into flames. The driver was already out of his cramped seat and rolling clear on the grass.

Hands took Alex and turned him. Lucy was on his right, Deirdre de Soto on his left. "A couple of dances here, then over to Bugattis where we can sit down," one of them said. Which one? Alex was not sure. He was back on the dance floor, and either he was dancing or doing some close enough equivalent. He looked around, but everything more than three meters away was a blur. Lucy, two meters away, was dancing with Dafyd de Soto and so close to him that she might as well be surgically attached.

Deirdre moved to stand and sway right in front of Alex, blocking his view of Lucy and Dafyd. As he watched, Deirdre magically grew taller and taller, until the ruby in her navel glimmered hypnotically at eye-level. After a few moments Alex realized that he was somehow on his knees, his hands grasping Deirdre's bare thighs.

She reached down and helped him to stand up. Alex wanted to apologize, but before he could do it she draped his arms around her neck and then grabbed him at the waist. "Makes it easier to stand up." She was nuzzling his neck. "Are you going to be all right?"

It sounded to Alex like a rhetorical question, and he decided not to answer. He danced with Deirdre, and then he danced with Lucy, and when someone put another drink into his hand, he drank it. When Deirdre tugged at Lucy, and said, "Bugattis?" he drifted along with them, out through one shimmering door and into another. It was cooler here, quiet and darkness and private rooms instead of bright lights, public drinks, and a crowded dance floor.

Was this Bugattis? It must be. Alex found himself sitting on a long, wide couch. He was chewing on a square of something sweet and tangy. A soft thigh pressed against his. He liked Bugattis. He liked it even better than Lagondas.

Alex closed his eyes. He felt great.

Alex opened his eyes. He felt great, but instead of sitting on a couch he was lying in bed. Judging from the ceiling and the piece of the wall that he could see, it was his own bed.

A voice from a few feet away said, "Good evening, Alex. Welcome to the real world."

It was Kate. She was sitting on a chair by the far wall of his cramped bedroom, staring at him intently.

He sat up. "What happened?"

"I was rather hoping you might tell me that." Her voice would freeze methane. "I'll take it from where I became involved. At three o'clock this morning I was called by Wholeworld Services to take delivery of a package. They tried the office, using an ID in the pocket of your pants, and fortunately for you I was still there. The package was you. You were unconscious. When I saw you, I became worried. I ran a medical scan, and found that you had imbibed at least twenty units of tanadril."

"That's a lot." Alex by this time had noticed his bare chest. "Are you sure? That much tanadril ought to make me feel terrible, and I don't."

"Because we put you under and flushed your whole system, then kept you under."

"What time is it now?"

"After six."

"You let me sleep all day?"

"I did. And I won't tell you how much self-control that took. You told me you were going to a family meeting."

"That's where I went."

"Right. A family meeting way down on Level two-twenty, at the Holy Rollers Club. That's where Wholeworld Services picked you up. A family meeting where you have sex with people."

"I don't think I did." But Alex had a hazy memory of fumblings and the intimate touch of warm, bare bodies.

"You'd better hope you did. There was semen on the front of your pants, and it was either yours or that of a dear friend of yours."

Alex looked under the cover. He was naked.

"That's right," Kate went on. "I took them off and I sent them for analysis. *Pathogen* analysis. I don't want you diseased and sick."

"Thanks, Kate."

"Not for the reason you're thinking, you self-centered imbecile. If you imagine that I care what specimens, sexes, or even species you choose to screw, or how many of them, there're other organs of yours that need inspection worse than your genitals. Why do you think I was still at the office at three o'clock this morning? What do you think I was doing while you were using your dipstick at the Holy Rollers Club?—yes, I found out all about *that* place while you were asleep. And I still haven't slept. I've been working all day, right until I came here ten minutes ago to see if you were awake yet."

Alex examined Kate more closely. He had noticed that she was pale, and assumed that it was anger. Now he could see the tight mouth and dark-smudged eyes of exhaustion.

"You've been working right through, from yesterday morning until tonight?"

"I have. And guess what I've been working on? Your damned model."

"Has it been failing?"

"No. It's been working. That's the trouble. I must have made over a hundred runs. Nothing blew up, nothing went out of range."

The model was working! Alex started to climb out of bed, then paused when he realized that he was naked.

"Oh, don't be a fool." Kate's laugh emerged as a bitter and humorless snort. "Do you think you've got something there that I haven't seen and touched—along with plenty of other people, I guess. The models didn't fall, not in the way that they had been failing. They work. We have just one problem."

Alex, one leg into his pants, paused and glanced up at Kate's change of tone.

Kate went on, "You and I have to brief Mischa Glaub and the review committee on our status, later today. I suppose that slipped your mind, you were having so much fun."

It had. "I don't mind briefing them, or anyone else. I know the model cold."

"Maybe." She was sitting, blonde head bowed. "What you don't know are the results. I tried every variation I could think of, and each time human civilization expanded steadily through the solar system for about fifty years. It was beautiful. But then, no matter what I did, things started to fall apart. According to your model, long before the year 2200 the population of every world in the System will fall to zero.

"What are you going to tell Mischa, Alex? That humans are going to become extinct? Or that your precious infallible model is all screwed up."

Bat had made himself clear to the point of rudeness: "In or out. You make a choice right now."

And Mord, no stranger to rudeness, made his decision and replied in an instant. "Then it's gotta be out. There could be all sorts of goodies in the Seine that no one's ever looked at. We're talking about access to a million separate databases, everything from gigabyte tiddlers on rocks in the Belt to the Great White Whale at Earth Data Central. And nobody's ever looked at most of the little 'uns—they were uploaded from their original source location by automatic data scanner. *Adios, amigo.* I'm going a-wandering."

And Mord vanished, disappearing into the tangled maze of the Seine.

Bat checked that Mord was nowhere inside the Keep. It would be quite like Mord to pretend to be outside, then pop up somewhere within when Bat was least expecting it. However, a complete scan of the Keep's components indicated that Mord was nowhere to be found.

Bat grunted, reached out with one fat finger, and delicately tapped a key. That severed the final link. Now he had access on Pandora to two powerful computer systems. One was a Seine-link, coupling him to the dispersed and infinitely interconnected set of information processors that stretched through and served the whole System and in their whole comprised the Seine; the other was the Keep, existing on Pandora alone and under Bat's absolute control. Unless Bat had erred badly, the separation of the two was complete. Nothing in the Seine had access to anything in the Keep, and the Keep in turn depended on nothing from the Seine that had not been filtered through Bat personally.

Bat examined the results of a suite of test programs, and nodded his approval. The Keep, although it was just one system in a single location, could out-perform almost every pre-Seine processor. As it should. Large amounts of Bat's personal time and assets had gone into it. Only food, isolation, and Great War relics were as important as computer power.

As for the Seine . . .

Bat swiveled his great chair to face the other console. He was impressed by the validity of Mord's last words to him. The Seine was indeed a wondrous new resource, and he had every intention of probing it to the full; he just didn't want it probing *him* by invading his private data banks.

First he examined the console for new incoming messages. He found four of them and scanned the sources rather than the messages themselves. The senders were all well-known to him. Pack Rat, Ghost Boy, The Joker and Attoboy were each at the Master level in the Puzzle Network. There was no hurry reading those messages. A good challenge could take anything from a week to forever to solve. Bat had once spent a month trying to crack a puzzle from Claudius, a woman (Bat was convinced that it *was* a woman, in spite of the name), until finally he realized that he was dealing with a transformed version of the most famous unproven conjecture in mathematics.

On the Puzzle Network, that was quite legitimate. The puzzle was solved when you caught on to what Claudius had done. Of course, there was also the possibility that some puzzle master would actually prove (or disprove) the Riemann conjecture—and thereby become a major name in the history of mathematics.

Instead of reading the waiting messages, Bat began his own exploration of the Seine. It was something he had been itching to do since Seine Day, but he had deferred action until he was sure that the Keep was as secure as he could possibly make it.

Within minutes, he knew that his and Mord's instincts had been correct. Data banks were now available that had been lost or hidden since the time of the Great War. They might point to treasures of long-gone weaponry that he had never suspected existed. But he had to be careful. His lines of communication had been set in place years ago, making him the master spider at the center of his own information web. Without stirring from the Bat Cave, he could in the past be sensitive to every trend and initiative within the System.

Not anymore. The Seine was a new factor whose effects he could not begin to calculate. He suspected that it was powerful enough to destroy his web and the work of many years.

Slowly, warily, Bat allowed selected programs to reach into the depths of the Seine. As a first exercise he asked for a listing of all Great War databases available today but unknown or unavailable one month ago. He hoped for at least a handful. Within minutes he knew that he had been too conservative. The count was over seventy and showed no signs of slowing when his attention was distracted by a communications alert.

A message was coming in: a real-time message, with someone waiting at the other end.

One great side benefit, or if you were Bat one great possible side nuisance, of the Seine was instant access to the whole solar system. In the past, light-speed signals from Pandora to Ganymede or anywhere else of significance took many minutes, even with optimal orbital geometry. Now the Seine contained fully entangled quantum computers scattered all across the solar system. Messages and video could be digitized, sent computer-to-computer in no time at all, and reconstructed at their destination. Which meant, of course, that any fool in the System could try to reach you and demand real-time response.

The trick was not to let any fool in the System know of your existence or whereabouts.

So who was calling?

Bat glanced at the ID, and closed his eyes in resignation. The caller was Magrit Knudsen, one of the few people outside the Puzzle Network with permission to contact Bat. And Magrit's message was simple and information-free: "Bat, are you there? If you are, please come on-line." Magrit never called with trivia. Either she was in trouble, or she had run across a mystery sufficiently odd to intrigue him.

He glanced around the Bat Cave. The level of messiness of the floor was tolerable—Magrit would nag him if it were not. He looked down at himself. He had washed and changed clothing in the not-too-distant past.

He triggered the video link.

Magrit Knudsen appeared at once, her expression anxious.

This was a bad sign. Bat, who abhorred all human confrontations, knew that Magrit thrived on conflict. If she was anxious, then he was worried.

* * *

Magrit had put this off for as long as she could. Conversations with Rustum Battachariya were never easy, and this one promised to be a stinker.

"Bat." She didn't try for her usual smile of greeting. "Are you alone? Of course you are, what a stupid question. Bat, we've got problems. And I don't mean any of your puzzle stuff."

The face that stared at her from the display remained expressionless. Bat, if Magrit were any judge, had added at least fifty pounds since she had last seen him. He sat like a giant Buddha on his special chair, arms folded across his chest. As usual, his black clothes were three sizes too small.

The round head nodded, and Bat finally spoke. "I hear you. However, unless the difficulty that you face is of a purely intellectual nature, it seems unlikely that I will be able to assist you."

"You heard me, but you didn't hear me right. When I said that we've got problems, actually I meant that you do. I had a call four hours ago. Somebody found out that I have access to you. They said they want a meeting."

"Which you, I trust, told them was out of the question."

"I said I would get back to them. Bat, it's not that simple."

"I do not see how it could be simpler. I have no need to meet with anyone. I have no *desire* to meet with anyone. And I most certainly have no desire to *travel* in order to meet with anyone."

Magrit had been Bat's immediate superior for more than a decade. Looking back, she sometimes wondered how she had stood it for so long.

"Bat, they don't want a meeting just for the hell of it, or to admire your sunny smile. They want a meeting to persuade you to share your lease on Pandora."

"Then they are certifiably insane. Four years ago I made a major investment in money and effort to conform elements of this planetoid to my needs."

"I don't think money is an issue. They can pay anything you ask."

"You are correct. Money is not an issue, since no matter what they offer I will refuse. I also, as I am sure you recall, paid in full and in advance for a long-term lease on Pandora, approved by the Outer Planet Authority. That lease has ninety-six years to run."

"I know that. It makes no difference." Magrit stared at Bat's black and impassive face. No one she knew was as smart and as stubborn—or in some ways as innocent. "Let me put it this way. When I became your supervisor, it took me a little while to realize how valuable and talented you were. But after that, I shielded you from all the crap that was thrown at you. And there was plenty."

"This is well known to me. Your protection was, and is, much appreciated."

"Then you understand that I wouldn't bother to call you at all if it was something as simple as pointing out to a caller that you have a lease on Pandora. They checked that out long before they contacted me."

"Then they must also have learned that it is a valid lease."

"Bat, we aren't playing in a league where 'valid' means much. The call to me came from Ligon Industries. They are one of the top five industrial powerhouses in the System."

"Not so. They are currently number nine in total revenues."

"You're splitting hairs. Let's just say they're big. You know the saying, there's no such thing as an unbreakable contract. Well, with the clout that they have, there's no such thing as a guaranteed lease, either. You are an individual. They are a quarter of a million employees, a hundred lobbyists, and a thousand attorneys."

Bat did not move, but Magrit knew from experience that he heard, understood, and evaluated every word spoken to him. At last he said, "Why Pandora?"

"I asked the Ligon representatives the same question. Sorting through the bullshit, it's not hard to understand. Ligon won't admit it, but they lost a fortune on the initial *Starseed* contract because the Jupiter gravity well was too much for the Von Neumanns. They've accepted the Phase Two option, but they intend to mine helium-three for *Starseed-Two* from Saturn. For that, they need a base of operations. You can imagine how their thinking went. The nine major moons all play roles in general Outer System development. Not even Ligon has the clout to over-rule that, and anyway all those moons are inconveniently far from Saturn. They need a base outside the rings, but not too far out.

"So they said to themselves, what about the lesser satellites? There are five attractive possibilities: Atlas, Prometheus, Pandora, Epimetheus, and Janus. The last two are already locked up by Ex-Im Mining, who have as much money and influence as Ligon. Ex-Im also has a lease on Prometheus and all the co-orbiters. That leaves just Atlas and Pandora. But Atlas serves as a government-controlled Saturn observation and weather station, and the red tape to do anything to change that would take years. So we are down to Pandora. All they need to do there is put enough pressure on one defenseless and small—I use the term figuratively—individual."

Bat shrugged. "Assume that I stand firm. What can they do?"

"Let's begin with the legal options. They can try to persuade Outer System authorities that Pandora access is essential to the success of *Starseed-Two*, and that *Starseed-Two* is at the highest priority level for the human expansion imperative."

"Could they succeed?"

"They might. There's centuries of legal precedent for that sort of thing. It's called *eminent domain*. Using it, authorities back on Earth were permitted to make forced purchase of properties that happened to be in the way of a planned road or airport. But we're just getting started. They could make personal attacks on your character and competence. They would argue that no one of sound mind would choose to live alone on Pandora, avoiding all human contact."

"The attack *ad hominem* was tried against me many years ago. You will recall that the team of psychologists engaged to probe my rationality was utterly routed."

"It doesn't mean it can't be tried again; and last time, no one was angling the case toward a judge who could be bribed."

"This is intolerable." Bat sat up and inflated his chest, so that the fabric of his too-small shirt stretched balloon-tight. "Are you telling me that such tactics might succeed?"

"Those tactics, or others." Magrit knew her man. Bluster and threat would never work with Bat. Logic would never fail. "I said I would start with the legal methods they might use. But the Ligon people have a reputation for playing hardball. They'll get impatient pretty quick if you won't cooperate. Forget leases, here's another fact of life: there's no such thing as an unbreakable *head*. Maybe they'll decide that it's easier and cheaper to kill you. You know from past experience that paid assassins are not hard to find. And *you* are even easier to find, because you never go anywhere. You would only be safe if you went into hiding."

Magrit watched the fat cheeks puff out. Finally Bat nodded. "Let me summarize what you have told me. Ligon Industries want access to Pandora, badly enough to do whatever they decide is necessary. In order for them to have my home, in any negotiation with them I must agree to leave Pandora. On the other hand, if I refuse to deal with them, my life will be in danger. In order to enjoy any measure of safety it would be necessary for me to hide away. Which means I would have to leave Pandora. Since either cooperation or defiance involves my leaving here, the former is clearly the preferred option. This, I assume, is the deduction toward which you have carefully been leading me."

"Maybe. Do you see any other options?"

"No. On the other hand, I have had scant opportunity to seek them. What promises did you make to the person who contacted you from Ligon?"

"Persons. There were two of them. I promised only to get back to them. I said I could not make a decision for you."

"Very well. Tell them that you have spoken with me, and that I have authorized you to open negotiations on my behalf."

Magrit couldn't believe agreement had come so easily. "You just want me to make the best deal I can, and you'll sign off on it?"

"If you choose to think of it that way. I have only one other request, and then I must attend to important work which cannot be delayed." Bat's dark eyes almost closed, so that Magrit could read no expression there. "I know that you have both the talent and the temperament for hard negotiation. Make this a tough one."

"Bat, do you think it's just *you* who hates people pushing you around? Come take a look at the color of my guts. I hate these bastards, and I don't even know them. Trust me, I'll give them a tough negotiation. And if you can find anything to give me leverage, don't wait. I'll have your call as top priority."

* * *

Bat's early employment evaluations had been replete with terms such as "dirty," "gluttonous," "arrogant," "slovenly," "disobedient," and "indolent." Bat regarded those evaluations as unjust and scurrilous. He was not indolent.

As soon as Magrit was gone, he went through to the kitchen stores and returned with loaded dishes of peppermint candy, orange jujubes, marzipan, and Turkish delight. This was sure to be a long session.

He set parameters, provided the authorization for unlimited expenditures, and initiated a search of the Seine.

Before a man could fight back, he needed weapons. Long before Magrit concluded any negotiation, Bat intended to know more about Ligon Industries than any other human in the solar system. A large organization, like any other large structure, possessed a weakest point. Bat intended to find that point for Ligon Industries.

And what would he do then? Bat did not know. He operated using an ancient dictum: *It is a capital mistake to theorize before one has data.* But he was going to do *something*.

D-V-I. Detect, Verify, Interpret. Those were the three legs on which SETI rested. Without all three, any effort was flawed. Fail to detect, and you had nothing. Fail to verify what you thought you had found, and you still had nothing.

The most galling experience, however, would be success at detection and verification, followed by a long-term failure to interpret. You knew you had a signal, you knew it was artificial, you knew it came from far outside the solar system. But what, for Heaven's sake, did it *mean*? If you couldn't answer that question, you had better be ready for a lot of skepticism.

"We've detected a signal from the stars."

"Really? What does it say?"

"We have no idea."

"Oh. Thank you. Let us know when you do."

That was *interpretation*, something far in the future. Milly, in her first rush of innocent enthusiasm, had believed that great future might not be far away, since detection was over and done with. Now she was learning the extent of her error.

Jack Beston had assembled five people for the meeting. One was the enigmatic Zetter, who as usual seemed to prefer silence to speech. Milly had seen the others around the L-4 Station, but had never been introduced to them. In fact, in her absorption with her own work she had barely noticed them. She was certainly noticing them now. She also wished that she had thought to go to the bathroom before the session started. Maybe it was nervousness, maybe it was anticipation, but she felt a growing internal discomfort.

"Salisbury." Jack addressed a thin man with a black, drooping mustache and liquid dark eyes. "Is it there in the analog?"

The Ogre was more polite than Milly had ever seen him. He seemed cool, almost abstracted, until you noticed the left hand in the pocket and heard the constant jingle of keys or coins.

Salisbury nodded. "If it's there in the digital, it's there in the analog."

That was a guarded, conservative answer. It represented an approach that Milly was learning to appreciate. The basic signals from space, either radio waves or neutrino pulses, arrived in analog form. They went through an analog-to-digital conversion before computer analysis and display. All the usual problems of A-to-D might be introduced in the process. You could get clipping effects from using an insufficient number of digital bits, or you could get aliasing, a frequency shift caused by the use of the wrong sampling rate. You could lose information, or you could create spurious "information" when none was present. Tim Salisbury was not saying there was or was not a signal—that was not his area of expertise. He was merely saying that the presence or absence of a signal was not the consequence of analog/digital conversion.

"Right." Jack didn't offer his usual third-degree interrogation, but turned to the woman on Milly's right. "Tankard?"

Milly decided that rank had its privileges, even here. Hannah Krauss, Milly's usual supervisor, was noticeable by her absence. These were Jack Beston's most senior and trusted workers, and they looked like they didn't take shit from anyone. As for Pat Tankard, if she had once been a vulnerable junior employee, Milly doubted that she had ever been troubled by the Ogre's unwanted sexual advances. Tankard's dark hair was cropped to less than an inch, she wore gold bands on the ring fingers of both hands, and her muscular left biceps carried a holographic tattoo that read from one angle, "Ellen," and from another displayed the image of a slender long-haired blonde.

"If there are artifacts in the data, they are not the result of anything that Milly Wu did." Pat Tankard smiled at Milly in a reassuring way. Her voice was a honeyed baritone, which Milly now realized she had heard in the shower rooms, crooning old-fashioned romantic ballads. Tankard went on, "I applied every operator in my own preferred order, which was generally not commutative with the order applied yesterday. If there was a signal, there is still a signal. Whatever was there, is there."

The order in which you performed operations could generate the illusion of a meaningful signal. Something as simple as a change from Cartesian to polar coordinates in a two-D array might produce "meaningful" patterns that went away when you made the conversion at a different point in the processing.

It was one step nearer to detection. Milly ought to be feeling some reassurance. Instead she experienced a rising tension, and the pressure in her bladder was definitely uncomfortable. She also felt a queasiness, like that of the first few minutes in zero-gee, when the stomach rose to push up against the diaphragm. How much longer could she sit here in order to hear Jack Beston's final decision?

Milly decided that before she would leave, she would sit until she threw up or her bladder burst. The precedent for the latter was not promising. Tycho Brahe, the last of the great pre-telescope astronomers, and an eccentric task-master far more formidable than Jack Beston, had been unable for reasons of protocol to rise and leave a court banquet before the duke did so. He had suffered a burst bladder as a result, and died a few days later.

"Kruskal?"

Jack's voice broke into Milly's thoughts. The woman across from her nodded. "If it derives from a process of natural origin, it is one unknown to science." She was squat, olive-skinned, and plump, with an accent that suggested that she had arrived at the Jovian L-4 station from somewhere in the Inner System—probably Earth, and probably from one of the observatories still situated on the Andean cordillera.

Erma Kruskal went on, "Moreover, any natural process that generated such a signal would have to be, in most senses of the word, most unnatural. The entropy rises and falls, exactly as one would expect if a high-entropy repeated message were separated by long low-entropy start and stop pointers. Of course, this tells us nothing concerning verification and interpretation."

Everyone was showing the same caution, bending over backwards to avoid too much optimism. Milly told herself that was the right way to do it—you mustn't get too excited or too hopeful. All the same, she could feel her knees trembling. She pressed them tightly together.

Beston turned to the second man in the group. Arnold Rudolph was frail and tiny and looked older than God. Milly wasn't sure of his actual age—neither Hannah nor anyone else seemed to know it—but there were rumors that he had been present at the closing of the great radio dish at Arecibo, and had been a major force in producing the first spaceborne SETI interferometric arrays.

Rudolph nodded amiably to Jack Beston, but he seemed in no hurry to begin. After a wait that brought Milly to the edge of her seat, he said, "The history of SETI goes back long before human space colonization, or even the launch of the first artificial Earth satellite. It is, of course, a history filled with false positives, which urges upon us extreme caution." He didn't look at Milly, which she read as a bad sign.

He went on, "The human mind has an incredible ability to detect patterns, or to *impose* patterns where none is present. Thousands of years ago, our earliest ancestors named the constellations because they saw patterns in the stars. More than two hundred years ago, Schiaparelli believed that he saw linear features on the surface of Mars, channels which Percival Lowell in turn interpreted as 'canals' and as evidence of intelligent life. With better images, channels and canals both vanished. Seventy years ago, the Hobart hoax fooled every SETI worker for more than a year."

He paused. Milly wanted to scream, to shout at Arnold Rudolph, "Get on with it, we know all that." No one moved or spoke, and Milly literally held her water.

"However." Rudolph paused again, and stared around the little room that represented an antechamber to Jack Beston's personal quarters. This time his look included Milly. "However, I do not believe that this anomaly is an example of spurious pattern recognition. Something is there. It would be premature to speculate on what that something might be, or even whether it will survive the necessary verification process. But something is there. The anomaly is real. It would be foolish of me to try to contain my own excitement at the possible significance of this discovery."

His apparent lack of excitement was so obvious that Milly had to think twice before she realized what Rudolph was saying.

It was real! It was a signal! Jack Beston's top assistants were convinced that this was a genuine discovery.

Jack himself, as calm as Arnold Rudolph, was nodding. "I think that takes us as far as we can go on detection. Let's move on to verification. First, however, I have something else to report. Earlier today I prepared a message. On the basis of what I have heard, I propose to send it ciphered tight-beam to the Ganymede Office of Records, to be sealed there until we approve its release. The message announces the discovery of a signal, believed to be from an extra-solar source and of artificial rather than natural origin. It establishes our claim to precedence. The same message will be sent tight-beam to the Odin Project at Jovian L-5. Now, let's get on to the preliminary stages of verification." He turned to Zetter. "Your analysis?"

"The direction of origin of the potential signal is known to within five arc minutes." Zetter spoke like a zombie, her voice a flat monotone. Milly wondered, nature or practice?

Zetter went on, "I have examined every possible signal source of human origin, past or present, to see if any lie within a cone of angle five arc minutes. The potential signal has been operating for at most three months. I allowed for our own motion during that period, adjusting for receiver parallax effects. My conclusion is that no known ship, with or without crew, can be the source of the potential signal. *However.*" At last, a word with some slight stress on it. "This does not rule out all possibilities. We could be receiving a signal from a residue."

While the others nodded, Milly struggled to recall the briefing manuals. Was a *residue* the same as a *remnant*, some form of artifact left over from the Great War?

"To take one example," Zetter continued, "consider a blinded Seeker, flying outward at maximum thrust until its fuel ran out and then coasting. In a third of a century it could be as much as half a light-year from Sol. No test made using data from this station's receivers alone can distinguish such a source from one at true stellar distances."

"Which is what I thought. We need extra-solar verification. That's why I'm sending word to the Bastard. All right, everybody, meeting's over." Jack swung around to face Milly. "And you, get ready to travel. The two of us leave for Jovian L-5 and the Odin Station later today. Shall we say, two hours from now?" He turned away, to leave the antechamber and head for his own private quarters, then added casually over his shoulder, "By the way, the signal is identified in our announcements as the Wu-Beston anomaly."

It took Milly a moment for that to sink in. The *Wu*-Beston anomaly. She was not only named, she was named *first*. In any major scientific discovery, it was traditional for the senior researcher or group to be listed before anyone else. The most famous case was the discovery of pulsars, the centuries-old case that had already reverberated in Milly's mind during her earlier work looking for SETI signals. It was Jocelyn Bell, as a graduate student, who had noticed the telltale oddities of print-out that told of the existence of rotating neutron stars; however, it was Martin Ryle and Anthony Hewish, the senior members of the research team, who had been awarded the Nobel Prize for that work.

Jack Beston, in naming the anomaly in the way that he had, was guaranteeing that no such miscarriage of justice would occur in this case.

She gasped, "Thank you." All the stress and nervousness

and nausea of the past hour magically vanished. Her stomach and bladder felt fine.

"Thank you," she said again. Those were the only words she seemed able to find. But Jack had already vanished and the door was closed.

The others stared at her. It was Pat Tankard who finally spoke. "Two thank-yous for the Ogre, that's a record. But congratulations and a thank-you to you. You've made everything I've been doing for the past ten years worthwhile." She flexed her arm, and the blonde on her biceps grinned. "And good luck. You'll understand why I say that when you meet Philip the Bastard."

One hour more, and they would be on their way. Jack Beston had given Milly two hours to get ready, but she had no idea where the first one had gone. She had wandered the Argus Station in a happy stupor, until Hannah Krauss tracked her down.

"Congratulations, Milly. The Wu-Beston anomaly. How about that?" The touch of envy in Hannah's voice couldn't be repressed, but it was only a touch. "Are you all ready to go? You certainly don't *look* ready."

"I haven't even thought about it. What should I take?"

"Just personal stuff. Maybe a stiletto to keep Jack at a distance while you're traveling? Relax, my dear, I'm just joking. But don't bother to take any of your signal data, because we'll send everything you need to Odin Station on tight secure beam."

Maybe Hannah had been joking about keeping Jack at bay; but Milly, arriving at *The Witch of Agnesi* carrying just one light travel bag, was not so sure. She made it a point to be there well before Jack Beston, so that she could take a good look around before their departure from Argus Station. This ship was Jack Beston's personal space-yacht, and she hoped it would tell her something about the man.

Her first impression of the ship told little about Jack, but it blew her away with the evidence of Beston wealth. The drive was of a type she had never seen before, permitting smooth changes of acceleration when and how you pleased. She would feel none of the jolts, jerks, and nauseating turns of a commercial vessel. The navigation system was totally automated. Jack Beston would not need to put a hand on it during the flight to Odin Station (which made Milly wary as to where he might try to put his hands). As for the interior, each fitting that she saw as she wandered from cabin to cabin was more than Milly could afford. The paintings looked like originals and the free-fall rails were of rare woods, all imported from Earth.

Jack Beston's private suite, at which Milly took a swift and quite unauthorized peek, had a sitting-room, a kitchen containing the most advanced equipment that Milly had ever seen, and a large bedroom. The last contained a circular bed almost three meters across. Who was supposed to sleep there? Jack himself was skinny enough to become lost in its downy vastness.

Perhaps sudden, huge, and unexpected wealth would do that to anyone—especially if the ways that you could spend your money were strongly constrained.

The story as told to Milly by Hannah was sad, wonderful, or ludicrous, depending on your point of view.

Philip and Jack Beston had grown up together on Ganymede in moderate circumstances, neither poor enough to suffer hardship nor rich enough to be part of the *jeunesse dorée* who felt that Ganymede and the whole System were theirs to play in and with. Philip and Jack knew that they came from a family that had once been loaded. That, however, was more than a century ago. Now they were just smart, ambitious, and competitive.

And until Philip's sixteenth birthday that was enough. Three weeks after that day, the boys received a call while they were in school. They were asked to come, at their convenience but without telling anyone—*anyone*, which made it really interesting—to the offices of Branksome and Reid. Philip and Jack had never heard of Branksome or Reid, but the caller assured them they had been legal advisers to the Beston family for many generations.

The original Branksomes and Reids were all long-dead, explained Martha Sappho Reid, a woman in her late seventies. She sat Philip and Jack down in the poky little office on deliberately old-fashioned wing chairs. She gave them green tea in ancient porcelain cups, and began.

"I have rather a strange story to tell you. You have heard, perhaps, of Marcus Tullius Beston?"

Jack looked to his older brother for assistance. Philip said, tentatively, "Like, the great-great-grand-uncle?"

Martha Reid nodded. "Add one great, and you have it right. Marcus Tullius Beston trained the first generation of cetacean managers, and he made a gigantic fortune from the Terran sea-farms. However, he formed no permanent liaisons, and he died *sine prole*."

She caught the exchange of glances, and added, "That means he died without children. Rather than handing his wealth on to siblings or nephews and nieces, which would commonly be a preferred solution, he followed a quite different path. He set up a trust, the original assets of which were his entire fortune. Furthermore, upon his death the assets of the trust were to be invested and managed, but otherwise remain untouched for a period of three-quarters of a century.

At that time, the heirs would inherit. Marcus Tullius Beston, however, was a man whom many would consider a little eccentric."

She ignored Philip and Jack, who were looking at each other in a way that suggested they thought Marcus Beston was a total loon.

"Beston's will decreed that the inheritance would be encumbered," Martha continued. "Which is to say, it would go only to family members who satisfied certain criteria, and it could be spent only in certain ways. Those ways were rather tightly defined. Inherited wealth was not to be spent on pleasure. It was, rather, to be applied only to such enterprises as might significantly affect the future of the human race, and affect it in beneficial ways.

"In due course, Marcus Tullius Beston died. The first result of his death was perhaps entirely predictable. His will was contested by every living family member, all of whom had been in effect disinherited in favor of the far future. The will survived those challenges, and the trust was established. Perhaps you are beginning to guess the rest of the story."

Jack looked to Philip for guidance. Philip said, "Er, the whole thing got wiped out in the Great War?"

"Indeed, no, though that is an intelligent surmise. The trust continued and its assets grew, through good times and bad, until the present day. And well before the Great War, the trust managers had the foresight to transfer a substantial fraction of the assets into investment in Outer System development. Now, however, we must come to the present day. It has been seventy-five years since Marcus Tullius Beston died. Today is, in fact, the exact anniversary of his death. The rules for the line of descent for his inheritors were complex, but well-defined. You, Philip Beston and Jack Beston, are his sole inheritors. You were bequeathed and will receive, in equal shares, the value of his estate."

"You mean we're going to get money?" The explanation had finally reached a point that Philip and Jack could understand.

"Eventually, but not for some years. The elder brother—that is you, Philip—will have to reach age twenty-three. Moreover, the assets may be used by each of you only in the manner originally described; namely, for such enterprises as will significantly and beneficially affect the future of the human race."

"Do our parents know all this?"

"Not yet. Marcus Tullius Beston envisaged, and wished to avoid, any situation in which individuals might seek ways to leverage in advance a future bequest."

Jack asked, "Do our parents *have* to know—ever?"

"I see that as inevitable. I do not see it as a problem."

Jack said, "That's because you don't know what our stepmother is like."

Philip said, "Oh shit. We're not getting money. We're getting trouble."

"The way I've heard it," Hannah went on, "Philip and Jack's parents took their own shot at cracking the terms of the will, trying to get their hands on the kids' money. They didn't have any more success than the people seventy-five years earlier. They just made it so that Philip and Jack never wanted to speak to their stepmother ever again.

"Then Philip and Jack became old enough to inherit. They had a big problem. All that loot, more than they had ever dreamed of having, but they didn't know how to get their hands on it. They suggested all sorts of things based on their own interests, but the trustees bounced every one. Martha Reid didn't seem to see the value to humanity of Philip's proposed hundred kilometer ice rink on Callisto, or Jack's System-wide space race.

"Freedom to use the trust fund, but also to do something you'd like: that was the problem, and it was Jack who cracked it. He'd always been interested in the idea that there might be aliens, somewhere out there in space. If you could find some, there was no end to what humans might learn. So why not take the old ideas of listening for signals, and do it *right*? Propose a big, elaborate facility with the best possible equipment and people. And stick it far away from Ganymede, where Old Mother Reid couldn't keep too close an eye on how you were spending the money.

"It was a great idea, and Martha Reid loved it. She agreed to approve it in a hot minute. Jack set to work, planning an L-5 Argus Station. And he was coming along fine, until he applied for permission to build.

"That's when he found that there was already an application for a SETI station at Jovian L-5. Philip, without telling his brother, had decided that he would do the same thing, and do it *first*. Jack went nuts when he found out but there wasn't much he could do—except win the race. They had always been competitive, now they would be super-competitive. He made his own application for a station at L-4, the other stable Lagrange point. He would do an all-sky survey, whereas Philip Beston was going to concentrate on selected target stars, but otherwise they'd be using the same sort of equipment and analysis methods.

"And there was one other thing, something that neither brother had expected. Once they got going, Jack and Philip discovered that they were fascinated by the SETI projects. The longer they worked, the more it became an obsession. They've being going head to head for the past twelve years, with neither one slowing down and neither showing an advantage—until now, with the Wu-Beston anomaly. You can imagine how Philip welcomed *that* message from the Ogre.

"Better be prepared when you reach Odin Station, Milly. It's odds-on that the Bastard will have a reception planned for you. I wouldn't like to guess what."

⊏ ⊏⊐ ⊐ ABOARD THE *OSL ACHILLES*

Welcome aboard the *OSL Achilles*." The blond-haired man in the white uniform stared dubiously at Janeed, and then at the two bags. "Is that all you have?"

"I'm afraid it is. Is there anything wrong with that?"

"Well, no. But some of the others . . ." He gestured to a huge heap of luggage. "Most people try and bring the contents of the family home, including the cat. It's my job to talk them out of it."

"I never had a family home, so it was easy." Janeed examined his silver badge, which offered the cryptic message F. O., MARR P. They were already in Earth-synchronous orbit, and her light-headed feeling was due to more than the microgravity environment. Normally she would never have added, to a total stranger, "Is that all you do, handle luggage? And what does your badge mean?"

He seemed more amused than affronted, and looked hard at Janeed for the first time. "No, it's not all I do. My name is Paul Marr, and I'm second in command. First officer, sort of a spare captain—I suppose it's in case we lose one."

"You mean you're the first mate."

"If you want to put it in the old-fashioned Earth way, I guess I am." Janeed and Sebastian were the last to board, so there was no pressure to keep them moving along. Paul Marr glanced at Sebastian, who was staring enraptured out of the port at the full globe of cloudy Earth, far below, and added, "The first mate. You sound like you've been to sea yourself."

"For more than a dozen years."

"Really? You don't look old enough."

"Easily old enough. Thank fresh air and early nights if I look younger than I am. It wasn't on a real ship, though. I worked in the South Atlantic on a Global Minerals' mining platform."

"Even so, it's a lot more than I've ever done. It must be wonderful down there on Earth: the sea breezes, the tides, the storms."

"Not just those. Don't forget the pirates, the grog, the lash, the treasure, keel-hauling and hanging from the yard-arm." Janeed's strange sense of freedom—of *liberation*—would not go away. It was like waking on a spring holiday morning when she was six, with the whole day and the whole world waiting. Perhaps it was unfair to dump her exhilaration on Paul Marr, but he didn't seem to mind. He was laughing, and it was with her, not at her.

"Get yourself settled in on Ganymede," he said, "then you must take another trip on the *Achilles*. We'll go down to Earth, just the two of us, and you can show me everything."

Was it a come-on, after less than two minutes in each other's company? It certainly sounded that way. Janeed decided, to her own amazement, that she wouldn't mind if it were. Paul Marr was part of the mystery, shaking off the surly bonds of Earth and heading into the unknown.

But Marr was staring at Sebastian, who had suddenly swung away from the port.

"I'm sorry." The first officer was looking at Sebastian, although he seemed to be talking to Jan. "The gentleman there. I assumed that you two were brother and sister. But the manifest shows different last names."

"We're together, but we're not related." At Paul Marr's frown, Jan added, "We grew up together, ever since we were a few years old."

Paul Marr said, "Good"—which so far as Jan was concerned could mean absolutely anything—and then, to Sebastian, "I've been curious to meet you, Mr. Birch. You are the reason that the *Achilles* will be detouring to Mars, instead of taking a straight run to the Jovian system."

Sebastian said nothing. It was Jan who had to ask, "Why? What's on Mars that involves Sebastian?"

"Not what. Who. We'll be picking up a Dr. Valnia Bloom there, who has been recruiting for her science section. She wants to talk to both of you and give Mr. Birch another set of tests on the way out to Jupiter."

"Why?"

"You've got me. But it will offer you the chance to see a bit more of the System. Of course, you won't have an opportunity to go down to the surface of Mars. We'll just do an orbital rendezvous."

"Good." Sebastian spoke to Paul Marr for the first time. "I'll see cloud patterns."

"You'll certainly be able to do that. Are you interested in the clouds on Mars?"

"Not very." Sebastian turned back to the observation port, leaving Paul Marr to stare quizzically at Jan. His expression said, *Is he normal?* Jan didn't want to think too closely about that. She loved Sebastian more than anyone else in the universe, but even she couldn't deny that he was strange.

"Come on." She took Sebastian's arm. He seemed fixated

on Earth again. "You'll have time to look at that later. Now we have to go to our quarters and settle in." She picked up the bags, handed one to Sebastian, and moved along the entry umbilical that led through to the ship's interior.

At the hatch an odd feeling in the back of her neck convinced her that she was being stared at. She turned. Paul Marr had not moved. He gave her a nod and a little smile, and said, "Enjoy the *Achilles*. We're proud of her. I hope I'll see more of you on the flight out."

Marr had sounded sincere enough, but for the next four days Jan did not see him at all. It was not for lack of trying on her part. The *Achilles* was a substantial vessel, a fat ovoid forty meters long and thirty across its round mid-section. The engines that propelled the ship toward Mars at a steady third of a gee were housed in the rear, together with the ship's instrumentation and control room, all behind a bulkhead that said NO PASSENGERS BEYOND THIS POINT in large red letters. Jan decided that Paul Marr must be hiding there, because he was certainly not in any other part of the ship. While Sebastian stared first at the starscape beyond the observation port— "Boring," he said, after half an hour—and then drowsed in his bunk or gazed vacantly at the cabin ceiling, Jan explored the whole vessel.

There were seventy-one other passengers, bound for the Jovian system as final destination. Jan and Sebastian were the only ones who would head farther out, after the indoctrination sessions on Ganymede. She spoke with a fair number of fellow travelers, but found little in common with most of them. They had worked indoor office jobs on Earth, and they expected to work indoor office jobs somewhere on Ganymede or possibly Callisto. Jan's life on the high seas of Earth meant nothing to them, though she did swap sea stories with one former sailor. Her own ignorance of what the future might hold in the Saturn system ruled that out as a subject for conversation.

The captain of the *OSL Achilles* joined the passengers every day for dinner in the ship's formal dining room, and different groups took it in turn to sit at his table. When Jan's turn came, along with Sebastian and three others, she made polite general conversation for awhile, and then—ingenuously, she hoped—said, "Your first officer was very kind and helpful when we came aboard. But I haven't seen him since."

Captain Eric Kondo squinted across the table at Jan. She had the feeling that he was reading her ID badge. "I'm sure that you will, Ms. Jannex," he said, "as soon as we reach Mars. The first officer has been very busy, overhauling the Omnivores for inspection when we reach Mars orbit."

"Omnivores?" The man seated next to Captain Kondo was tall and thin-boned, as though he had already lived all his life in a low-gee setting. "What are they, some kind of pet animals?"

The captain—short, serious, and very dignified—looked at his neighbor in horror. "Pets, sir? Not in space, sir. I know that back on Earth in the old days the sailors carried goats and guinea pigs and turtles for fresh meat, but we are prohibited. No pets allowed, orders of the Outer Systems Line. Mr. Marr and the engineer are overhauling the Diabelli Omnivores—our main engines, that keep pushing us along so comfortably. If you sit quiet and remain still, you will hear and feel them."

Jan already had. Lying in her bunk the first two nights out, she had detected a faint vibration.

"But if you do feel them," Captain Kondo went on, "it means that they are not at maximum efficiency. A perfectly efficient engine would make no noise at all, and would not vibrate. That's what the crew are working on now. Before we get to Mars, all that work has to be over and done with. Then you will have the first officer here at dinner, and less of my dull company."

He said it with a smile, as though he didn't believe that anyone might possibly find him boring; but Jan had the feeling that he was looking at her particularly when he mentioned the first officer.

On the seventh day, the *OSL Achilles* was nearing Mars orbit rendezvous when a knock came on the door of Jan's cramped little stateroom, far forward near the bows of the ship.

She was curled up on the bed dressed only in briefs and a tank top, but expecting it could only be Sebastian she called, "It's open. Come in."

Paul Marr entered, wearing a smile that vanished instantly when he guessed from her clothing that she had been expecting someone else. "I'm sorry. I should have said who I was."

"It's all right." Jan pulled a bed-cover over her bare legs. "My fault. I thought it was Sebastian, and we're pretty informal with each other. You get that way if you took baths together when you were kids."

She noticed something odd about his appearance. He was dressed in a newly-pressed white uniform, but his hands were dirty and his nails grimy, as though no amount of scrubbing could get them clean. She went on, "I would ask you to sit down, but there's not room in here to swing a cat."

"No pets allowed. Orders of the Outer System Line." He didn't smile when he said it, but Jan felt certain that he had been told about her dinner two nights earlier with Captain Kondo. Her conviction was confirmed when he said, "We finished work on the Omnivores just a couple of hours ago.

They're as clean and beautiful and efficient now as they ever will be. I wondered if you'd like to go aft with me and take a look at them before we power down and settle into Mars orbit."

"Dressed like this?"

"Dressed any way you like." He hesitated, then added, "You look pretty good to me. But I'll wait outside."

Which left Jan with a small problem. She wanted to be at her best, but she had brought with her exactly one stylish dress. She had been holding it in reserve, waiting for a night when Paul Marr finally appeared for dinner. She didn't want to waste it on a tour of the ship's engine room, and anyway it didn't feel right for that. Engines, if they were anything like the methane power drives on the Global Minerals' platform, made you dirty if you so much as glanced at them.

She scanned her minimal wardrobe and settled for a dark green top and cut-offs, with flat-heeled pumps. At their first meeting she had noticed that Paul Marr was no taller than she was. She didn't care, and hoped that he didn't. You would think that by now no one would worry about a woman's height, but she knew for a fact that some men did, just as they worried about age differences. She suspected that Paul was at least five years younger than she was.

At the last moment she changed into high-heeled open-toed sandals. If he had old-fashioned hang-ups on height or age, she might as well find out about them now.

He was leaning against the wall of the narrow corridor when she emerged. His scan of her, from toes to head—five centimeters taller than him—produced a delighted smile. "So far as I was concerned," he said, "you could have gone as you were. But I must say you look better now. In fact, you look just terrific."

So did he. Jan wondered what she might be getting herself

into. The strange feeling of exhilaration had not left her. To depart Earth was to enter a zone of space and time where anything was possible.

He didn't take her arm, nor did she expect him to. This was a member of the crew, suitably polite and formal with a passenger. But he did walk very close, guiding her along the spiraling corridor that wound its way aft. Since the ship was decelerating into Mars orbit, the way aft was all "downhill."

At the rear bulkhead they paused. Jan pointed to the sign. NO PASSENGERS BEYOND THIS POINT.

Paul shrugged. "You wouldn't want it to welcome just anybody, when the ship's control room is back here. The sign ought to add, 'Unless accompanied by a ship's officer.' That's me." He slid the hatch open and waved her through.

Since the area also contained the living quarters of crew members, who spent far more time aboard than any passenger, Jan expected the rooms to be bigger and better furnished than her own cramped area. Just the opposite seemed to be the case. Rather than the bright blues and yellows she had become accustomed to, the walls aft were painted in dingy khaki and a hideous lurid green. The passages were even narrower than the spiral that had brought them here, more like tunnels for rats than corridors for human beings.

"A couple of reasons for that," Paul said in answer to her question. "First, the crew are at home in any acceleration from free-fall to two-gees—that's emergency only, by the way. We're used to wriggling our way along, and wider corridors wouldn't make that any easier. Also, you are seeing the worst part, the way back to the engines. The captain's quarters are big and pretty plushy, off to the left. Mine don't match up to his, but they're comfortable. Maybe you'd like to take a look at them sometime."

That sounded like another hint, and not a particularly subtle one. Jan glanced at Paul Marr, but his eyes stared straight ahead as he added, "Not today, though, we don't have enough time."

Enough time for what? His expression remained serious, and that was fine. The last thing she wanted was a leer or a sly wink.

They had reached the hatch leading down to the engine room. Paul said, "Don't touch anything unless I tell you that it's all right," and slid through onto a tight spiral staircase of open metal rungs.

Jan followed him down, glad that she had chosen cut-offs but with second thoughts about the heels on her sandals. She didn't know what she had expected to find—flaming rockets, or a ball of nuclear fire?—but the reality was not impressive. The engine room contained no people, and no furnishings of any kind. She and Paul Marr stood on a small flat platform, less than two meters across, in the middle of the room. On each side, arranged in a hexagon and within touching distance, stood six upright bulbous blue cylinders.

"Here we are," said Paul. "The famous Diabelli Omnivores. Fusion drives that have transformed travel around the whole system."

"Those things?" Jan asked.

"These things." Paul patted one of the blue cylinders. "I'm sorry if you're not impressed."

"Maybe if they were working I would be." And then Jan realized her error. Since the ship was decelerating, the drive must be on, and these engines had to be working.

Instead of replying, Paul took her wrist in his hand. His fingers were soft and smooth, not like someone who had spent the past week fiddling with engines. He moved her hand until it lay palm-down on the surface of one of the blue cylinders. "Feel anything?"

She did. The cylinder transmitted a gentle throb to her flat palm, a *thrum-thrum-thrum* so faint that it felt like the tingle of a weak electric discharge.

"Tuned as well as we could do them," Paul said. "Ninety-nine point nine-eight efficiency. One hundred percent isn't possible, even in theory."

"What's going on inside? If they're called Omnivores, they ought to be eating something."

"It's probably not the best name for them." Paul patted the bulbous cylinder, then left his hand to lie alongside Jan's. "If you were inside—which thank heaven you can't ever be—you'd find that nuclear fusion is taking place right here, inside this section. At the moment we are fusing hydrogen to helium to power the drive. We can do that with an internal temperature as low as ten million degrees. But if we ever ran short of hydrogen we could fuse helium to make carbon, or anything all the way up to iron. That's why these are called Omnivores, because they can fuse lots of different elements. But most fusion reactions need at least a hundred million degrees before they start to produce useful net power. We try to avoid it, because the higher temperatures are harder on the engines."

Jan pressed her hand down on the cylinder. It was quite cool, but her fingers were just a few centimeters from a roaring fusion furnace. Paul might speak casually of "as low as ten million degrees," but that sounded more than enough to her.

Paul was watching closely. "Scary?"

"No, not at all. Kind of exciting." It was, too. So much pent-up power, vibrating under her fingers and responding to human control—it gave her a definite lift, an odd kind of turn-on.

"I hoped you would like it." Paul again patted the blue cylinder. "I think of this as a kind of test of people. A visit to the engine room produces one of two reactions. Some are terrified at being close to so much raw power—they don't seem to realize that if the engines ever did blow, they'd be no safer at the other end of the ship than they are standing here. Other people are stirred by what they see as the power that humans have gained over nature. We are doing things inside the Diabellis that once took place only in the middle of stars. I find that impressive and exciting." He turned away from the Omnivore cylinder. "Let me know if you'd like to come here again. Meanwhile, we'd better be getting back forward. Mars orbit rendezvous in an hour or two. Dr. Bloom will be sitting there itching to get at you."

"I think she wants Sebastian more than she wants me."

"Even so, it doesn't sound like much fun for either of you. But I hope you enjoyed this visit."

"Very much."

That was quite true, and it left in Jan's mind one question: Why had Paul Marr singled her out, from all the passengers, for the guided tour? Or maybe there was a second question, too: *Had* Paul Marr singled her out, or was she one on a list of a dozen?

Jan preferred not to ask. Something told her that she would find out in due course. And if she did, and the answer proved to be that he was interested in Jan alone, there was one other question that she still had to ask herself.

12

The control room was cold, and Alex was sweating. In one hour, he and Kate—which in practice probably meant he alone—had to give the most important briefing of his life. It was also likely to be the most difficult. He had insisted that the computing and data resources of the Seine were all that he needed to make his model into a practical prediction tool. Kate had told him that was bullshit, because the model was producing nonsense. He wasn't sure he believed her. He was sure that he had no idea what might be going wrong.

Calm, stay calm.

First, run the model for the decades preceding the Great War. As before, it predicted the occurrence of the war to the year and to the month. Beyond the war that run of the model offered no prediction, but that was as it should be. Such a traumatic event was a singularity of the timeline, beyond which prediction was impossible.

So what about the runs that Kate had completed while he was, in her words, "diddling little Lucy"? He wasn't sure it had been Lucy-Maria, but it wouldn't help with Kate to explain that uncertainty.

The model automatically stored every parameter of every run. Alex called on the Seine to perform in parallel all the runs that Kate had tried, one after another, the previous night. It would take months to track every variable, so for the moment he wouldn't try. He settled for gross aggregates. The crucial number for the moment was total solar system population. He asked for that value, averaged over all the runs that he and Kate had performed, to be displayed as a function of time.

And here it came, the number of humans in the whole solar system, for every year in the coming century and a half.

The starting value, for the year 2097, was today's actual count of 5.2 billion. The number was rounded, to two significant figures, but Alex had demonstrated, over and over, that his results were not sensitive to small errors in inputs or minor changes in initial conditions. The value for 2098, 5.3 billion, came five seconds later than he expected. The amount of computation that Alex's model required was enormous, but nowhere near enough to tax the capacity of the Seine. However, he did not command the system's highest priority. That went to emergency real-time missions, and to the often-meaningless (in Alex's humble opinion) computational demands of other government programs.

2099: the rounded average over all runs remained at 5.3 billion. Alex spot-checked the exact value, which showed an increase. *2100*: sure enough, the number was up slightly again, to 5.4. Alex was aware of Kate at his shoulder, watching not the display but Alex himself. The years moved on steadily, the population count crept higher.

. Maybe nothing was wrong. Maybe Kate had screwed up. Alex's models were different from all earlier predictive models. He was still struggling to find a way to explain those differences in a way that Kate's chosen test subject, moronic Ma-

canelly, could understand, but every conceivable model had
certain things in common. It had *endogenous* variables, computed within the model and used to produce future values of
those same variables; and it had *exogenous* variables, values that
must be fed into the model from some external source.

Any model needed both.

2105: 5.6 billion; *2106*: 5.7 billion; *2107*: 5.7 billion. . . .

Endogenous variables were easy, you simply provided their
present-day values and the model ran with them to estimate
their future values. The big question was always, where do
you get values for exogenous variables? In a model designed
to predict the development of the solar system for a century
or more, the one thing you knew for certain was that there
would be surprises.

2110: 5.9 billion; *2111*: 6.0 billion; *2112*: 6.1 billion. . . .

The increase in solar system population, averaged over all
model runs, was accelerating.

By definition, a surprise was something that no one could
hope to predict. And since surprises were inevitable, in this
sense Alex's model runs were all bound to be wrong. Cheap
faster-than-light travel, true immortality as opposed to today's
longevity treatments, the arrival of aliens in the solar system;
any of these might happen, in any future year. Alex's model
could assume any one of them, and still make predictions.
However, none of the runs that Kate had made assumed any
such thing.

2117: 6.5 billion; *2118*: 6.6 billion; *2119*: 6.7 billion. . . .

What Alex had learned, over years of experience, was that
futures in which no surprise exogenous variables were introduced tended to be *conservative* futures. They had slower
growth, and better stability.

But what about war, all-out combat like the Great War
that had torn the solar system apart thirty years ago? That

produced huge effects, but it was not an exogenous variable, introduced from outside. It arose directly from a steady series of changes in human activities. It was a prediction of the model—the main prediction, in fact, that motivated all of Alex's work. If your model could predict that a war was on the way, you had a chance to explore changes in exogenous variables to make the war disappear.

2124: 7.6 billion; *2125*: 7.8 billion; *2126*: 8.0 billion. . . .

But suppose that, without future surprises or another great war, humanity over the span of centuries dwindled and faded and vanished? What did the modeler do then? If Kate were correct, and the model runs all went that way, Alex had better have some kind of an answer ready for the meeting with Mischa Glaub. Kate thought Glaub might have a couple of other people with him, members of the project review committee.

2134: 9.2 billion; *2135*: 9.5 billion, *2136*: 9.9 billion.

They had come to the year of the model run where Alex had left last night—the place where he had dragged himself away from the displays and headed off with his mother to meet Cyrus and Lucy-Maria Mobarak. At this point Kate had taken over. Now he had to pay extra attention to other variables, while continuing to monitor population growth.

2137: 10.0 billion. Running along smoothly, except that the rate of population growth was suddenly down. Now he recognized another complication. The model was set up to accept inputs, where appropriate, from other sources. Before the Seine came into operation those other sources were limited and well-defined. Now, suddenly, a million new data sources could feed the model. They included other predictive models whose outputs Alex did not trust.

"How did you limit exogenous variable inputs?" He snapped the question to Kate, without taking his eyes off the display.

"I cut them out." She was standing very close to him, where she could see everything he saw. Her breath on his cheek was as warm as her voice was cold. "You left without telling me how to pick them, or what values to use. I didn't take any that you hadn't included."

Alex nodded. New exogenous variables were a source of possible instability. Kate had made the conservative choice, by prohibiting new ones. All the macroscopic measures looked good to him. He could see no sign of the precursors of war, the ominous indicators that had popped up all over when he did simulations of System activity for forty years ago.

But something odd was happening. The model was now forty-five years out, and although the population count continued to creep up, two other variables had reversed their trend. The index for Outer System activity was down, with the cancellation of three development projects among the moons of Neptune. Just as disturbing, no new extra-solar probes had been launched for the past seven years in any of the model's predicted futures.

"Can you see it?" Kate didn't sound angry anymore. She was just tense.

"Yes."

"Do you know what's causing it?"

"No idea."

"What are we going to tell Mischa Glaub and the review committee?"

A good question, but not one to concern Alex at the moment. He had too much else on his mind. Sixty-five years out, with no hint of coming war; but transportation cargo volume and inter-world passenger traffic were down. So were terraforming activities, Oort Cloud exploration, free-space research stations, and what Alex thought of as "inverse terraforming"—the genetic modification of Earth's plants and animals to match the geography and physiography of other worlds.

And now, in 2140, the population curve was totally flat and he thought the fitted curve showed the first hint of a downward slope. Why, when the solar system was peaceful and stable?

"Mineral deficiencies?" He hit the sequence to provide figures on population breakdown. "Maybe reduced fertility?"

"You think?—" Kate was crowding him, almost sitting in his seat.

But Alex had an answer before she could complete a question. The available minerals and trace elements needed for human existence were on the increase. The fertility indices were fine, general health was better than ever, longevity was increasing—and still the figures for total System population were declining. As the model moved forward, ticking ahead another five years, the gentle decrease was turning into a no-sedive.

"What's happening, Alex? What's causing it?"

"I don't know." He wanted to say, this is impossible, it can't be happening. Either you have a steady human expansion, or you have a war. Humans just don't die out, with no reason. That had never happened before in any of the models he had seen—his own, or other people's.

2152: 7.1 billion; *2153*: 6.4 billion; *2154*: 5.7 billion; *2155*: 5.0 billion; *2156*: 4.3 billion. . . .

The population prediction wasn't just decreasing, it was plummeting. Alex waited and watched, but in his mind he had already extrapolated the curve. They were losing seven hundred million people a year. Unless the curve flattened, in a little more than six years the projected human population of the solar system would be zero.

A plague, a major universal plague which left no survivors? That was the only thing he could think of. Such a disaster could certainly occur, as one of the surprises which any real future might contain. But from the point of view of the model, the plague would have to be fed in as a new exogenous variable. Neither he nor Kate had introduced any such event.

"Alex . . ." Kate said.

She didn't need to say more. The year index read *2160*. The population count was 1.5 billion. As they watched, the year advanced to *2161* and the count fell below a billion. *2162, 2163, 2164 . . .* The count slowed, steadied, hovered around the one hundred million mark. And then—*2165, 2166, 2167, 2168*—the number began a final and implacable downward run.

By 2170 it was over. In that year, and in every year beyond, the human population of the solar system was a steady, flat zero.

They stared at the display in silence. Finally, Kate said, "Well, it is only a model."

Normally those would have been fighting words. To Alex's mind, provided that you fed the model reasonable inputs and possessed enough computer power, the results you got back were a possible future. And more than possible; *plausible*. Not the only conceivable future, certainly, because of surprise factors that no model could include. A future, however, that was far more than an assembly of random predictions.

Now a hundred different runs, with a hundred different sets of initial conditions, pointed to the same melancholy conclusion: *No humans by the year 2170*. Alex was reluctant to believe the results, but he could see no basis for rejecting them.

Population zero; and two years before that, all transportation, development, and outward expansion had ended. He was still staring at the flat-lined results when Kate made the day's discomfort complete.

"Come on," she said. "We're running out of time. In half an hour we have to brief Mischa Glaub. I hope you have something sensible to say. Because I sure as hell don't."

Kate had warned of a tough review session. Alex decided in the first thirty seconds that the real thing was going to be worse than her fears.

It began as soon as Kate led Alex into a small conference room flanked by modern display panels and old-fashioned pictures. The latter were of stern-faced individuals, presumably past members of review committees.

Seated at the table were four people—Kate had promised at most three—no less stern-faced than the images on the wall. Alex had met Mischa Glaub before. He was a short broad man with a shaved head, a sour expression, and a permanently angry disposition. Old hands in the Department of Planning made it a point to avoid meetings with Mischa in the morning. Food, it was said, softened his ire. Unfortunately this session was starting an hour before lunch, and it would run until the committee members were satisfied.

Alex had also met, at least briefly, two of the others. They were Glaub's boss, Tomas de Mises, and Ole Pedersen, head of the Methods and Logistics Directorate which sat at the same organizational level as Mischa Glaub's empire. It was no surprise to find them here, though Pedersen's presence might be a problem. Kate had warned Alex that Ole Pedersen was wily and ambitious, always promoting his own group's products and critical of anyone else's. Tomas de Mises was less of a worry. He was older, close to retirement, and reluctant to say or do anything likely to cause trouble.

The final person at the table, however, was the real shocker. She was a middle-aged brunette, whose white skirt and floral blouse broke the rule for office uniform. Rules were for lower level staff. Alex recognized her as Magrit Knudsen, Tomas de Mises's boss. She was a major force, already a Jovian Worlds' cabinet member and tipped to become a leader in the Outer Planets' Development Council.

Why was she here, for a routine progress review meeting?

The way that Kate had explained the procedure, Alex, or possibly Alex and Kate, would brief Glaub and a couple of staff assistants. They would brief de Mises, and de Mises would in turn provide summaries for people farther up the chain of command. Apparently normal procedure didn't apply today. Alex was expected to brief the whole ladder at once, from top to bottom. Magrit Knudsen seemed to be studying him with special interest.

Kate's raised eyebrow said, "Don't blame me. I didn't know she'd be here, either." But there was no time for discussion, because Kate and Alex were barely in the room before Mischa Glaub snapped, "All right, let's get on with it. And keep it short. We've all got other business to attend to."

Kate glanced at Alex and nodded. He was on, with an instant decision to make. Either he described what they had as early results, the product of a still-evolving model and therefore not to be taken seriously, or he said what he really believed, which was that his model was right, that it was far superior to anything that had ever existed before, and that it predicted terrible danger in all plausible human futures.

The rational thing to do was to be modest about the model, dismiss this set of results, and promise better in the next review. There were two problems with that. First, given the promises that Alex had made for model performance once the Seine was in operation, there might be no next review. The whole project was likely to be scrapped. And second, Alex was a lousy liar. He couldn't stand up and make statements that he didn't believe. What he did believe was his model.

Avoiding Kate's eye, Alex described the runs of the past two days and displayed their results. At first, the four people across the table sat and listened, sometimes nodding approval. Then he came to the critical years and showed the trends flattening and turning down. The audience became restless.

The model reached 2154 and the population dipped below 6 billion. Mischa Glaub was the first to break. He exploded, "You know what you're showing there? You have the whole bloody System in catastrophic decline. But I've seen six other projections in the past month, and not one shows anything but expansion."

Alex drew a deep breath. "All the other models are no good."

Pedersen, whose group had produced three of those other projections, said, "Now just a minute, if you're going to accuse my people—" Mischa Glaub snorted and said, "Cut the crap, Ligon. Unless you got damned good reason—" At the same time, Kate said, "What I *think* he means is—"

"Why?" Magrit Knudsen spoke no louder than the others, but her one word cut them off in mid-sentence. She went on, "It's not enough to tell people that your model is right, and all the others are wrong. You have to explain *why* your model is better."

When Alex said nothing, she added, "Ligon—that's your name, right, Alex Ligon?—there's an old saying: a man who understands what he's doing can give an explanation of his work that the average person can follow over drinks in a bar. I happen to believe that's true." She glanced at the clock. "We're not in a bar, and I'm supposed to be somewhere else. But I count myself as an average person. I'll give you half an hour. Tell me about your work. Tell me why I should keep funding it, rather than cancelling you on the spot."

She knew his first name, although no one in the room had used it. How come?

Alex postponed that question for later. She had put him on the spot. He had not had the time to fine-tune and polish a simplified explanation to the point where Pedersen's man, Macanelly, would follow it. He must go ahead with what he had, and hope that Magrit Knudsen was three or four rungs higher up the monkey ladder than Loring Macanelly.

He began with a direct question. "Did you ever take physics courses?"

Knudsen looked puzzled, but she nodded. "Twenty years ago. Don't assume I remember anything."

"I'm sure you'll remember all we need." Alex in principle was briefing the whole group; in practice he was talking to Magrit Knudsen alone. "For instance, for hundreds of years the scientists who worked with a gas would describe it by some basic properties. Not just what sort of gas it was, but they would measure its pressure and temperature and volume. Later on they got more fancy in their descriptions, and added things like entropy and enthalpy, which we don't need to bother with now. People used those basic variables to tell how a body of gas would behave under different circumstances. They called the branch of science that was developed to do this *thermodynamics*."

He looked at the others. Magrit Knudsen nodded, tentatively and apparently a little puzzled. Mischa Glaub from his expression was ready to explode, but he and the others wouldn't override their boss. Alex figured he had about five minutes.

He went on, "The important thing about thermodynamics is that you don't need to know anything about the gas at a more fundamental level. You get valid results without knowing that a gas is actually made up of separate molecules. The thermodynamic variables you are dealing with actually represent averages over a huge number of individual particles, but your results are correct even if you have never heard the word 'molecule' or 'atom.'

"But then people learned about molecules, and they had a mystery to solve. How did the overall general properties they'd been dealing with somehow emerge from the action of a whole lot of separate particles? It took a while, but eventually physicists like Maxwell, Boltzmann, and Gibbs developed a theory based on the molecules themselves. The theory was called *statistical mechanics*, and it showed how to relate the behavior of ensembles of tiny particles to the general thermodynamic properties that people were used to."

His audience was becoming more restless. Mischa Glaub was squinting and glaring. Ole Pedersen muttered something to Tomas de Mises that sounded like "What the hell's he going on about?" Even Kate, who knew where Alex was going, was biting her lip.

Magrit Knudsen nodded. "I follow you so far. But I hope this is leading somewhere."

"It is. The other predictive models used in the departments are like thermodynamic theories. What I mean is, they work with general variables. A general variable can be anything you choose: economic production by industrial sector or by location; overall computer capacity; transportation supply and demand; population; commodities and services. The theories tie these things together, and model the way that they evolve over time.

"But something like transportation demand is a *derived* quantity. It arises because of the separate needs and actions of more than five billion people. You could say, it's like a thermodynamic variable that arises from the combined activity of a huge number of small, separate units. That's a true statement, but it doesn't go far enough, because all molecules in a gas are essentially identical. Whereas every human being is essentially different.

"My predictive model recognizes that fact. It *derives* the general variables that other models take as basic. If you want to think of it this way, the model is a statistical mechanics for predictive modeling. It allows you to derive all the 'thermodynamic' general variables of the older and obsolete models."

Alex saw Ole Pedersen's head jerk. The word "obsolete" was a red flag, since Alex was describing what the models of Pedersen's directorate still did today. Pedersen was bristling and seemed ready to interrupt. Alex hurried on.

"We can't stop there, though. There is another necessary model innovation. If you try to deal with all humans as identical, the way that gas molecules are identical, you'll get garbage for results. Human progress depends to a large extent on the *differences* between people. So the individual units in my predictive model are not simple equations or data items. They are *programs*. Each program is a Fax, a duplication at some level of an individual human. My code allows anything from a Level One to a Level Five Fax to be used.

"Before the Seine was up and running, I had to cut corners. It would have taken forever to make runs with five billion separate Faxes, even if I used their lowest levels. So I was obliged to work with aggregates. I knew that was oversimplifying reality, and my results proved it. They were unstable. They blew up, just the way that any predictive program becomes unstable if you make the time-step too large.

"With the Seine up and running, though, I can finally run my model the way it should be run. No aggregation, but with a representation of every individual *as an individual*. And I can use Level Five Faxes if I want them, with complex decision logic and interaction powers, rather than simpleminded Level Ones. So I'm running a real solar system, with real people. But using the full power of the Seine computer, my virtual solar system will evolve six million times as fast as the real one. A year of solar system development takes only five seconds on the computer."

"Five seconds? You say *only* five seconds, but that's a long time to produce nonsense." Pedersen stood up. "I'm sorry, but I've had enough. All the meaningless analogy with thermodynamics and statistical mechanics, and all the talk of superior approaches. Then you show us *that*." The sweep of his arm took in Alex's final results, still frozen on the displays. "Population zero, humans extinct, solar system development dead. Is there anyone in this room who believes such a thing for half a second? All our other models show nothing remotely like that. I don't know about the rest of you, but I've wasted too much time on this—this *horseshit*."

"Now, Ole." Tomas de Mises waved a hand at Pedersen, palm down. "Don't let's go to extremes. Though I must admit . . ." His voice trailed off. He stared at Alex's final results, and shook his head.

"When did you perform the runs you just showed us?" Magrit Knudsen ignored the reactions of Ole Pedersen and Tomas de Mises and addressed Alex directly.

"Last night." Alex didn't want to look at Kate. If he had been present when the runs were first performed, they would have had time for a more detailed evaluation. "We repeated them this morning."

"Then everything is less than one day old. Bugs in new models are the rule rather than the exception. I, too, have trouble believing what you have shown us. *However*." Magrit Knudsen stared right at Ole Pedersen. "Regardless of anyone's skepticism, these runs suggest problems in solar system development so grave that we must take them seriously. I do so, even if there is only one chance in a thousand that they are correct." She turned to Mischa Glaub. "I want this work to continue on a high-priority basis. If you require additional resources, of humans or equipment, do not hesitate to ask for them. That's it for this meeting."

She stood up. "If you have the time, Ole, I'd like to spend a few minutes with you in my office, discussing your directorate's models. You, too, Tomas, unless there's something more urgent on your calendar."

Magrit's tone suggested that was unlikely. When the two men had trailed out after her, Mischa Glaub turned to Alex.

"After what Knudsen said I guess I can't fire you on the spot, which is what you deserve. I should have known not to hire somebody with more money than sense. Don't you *ever* come into one of these meetings again and go off half-cocked with results that you haven't run by me and checked ten times over. If there's one thing I hate, it's surprises. So get the hell out of here, both of you, and work on that goddamm model."

His expression changed from irritation to poorly-suppressed glee. "But did you see Pedersen's face when you talked about 'obsolete' models? He looked like he was crapping barbecued rivets."

13

You say that the Lonaker and Ligon models are junk."
Magrit was in her office with Tomas de Mises and Ole Pedersen. She was standing, and she had not invited the men to
sit down. It was her way of indicating that this would not be
a long meeting.

"You may be right, and you probably are." In principle she
was addressing both men, but no one had any doubt that she
was mostly talking to Pedersen. "On the other hand, the models seem to be radically new. There is a chance that they are
providing warnings that we should not ignore. So what I want
you to do is this: learn everything that you possibly can about
the new models. I will direct that every question you ask be
answered, to any level of detail that you desire. Then I want
your *personal* evaluation of the models. Not a simple dismissal,
merely because they are different from what your own group
has been developing. I want a *real*, point-by-point analysis.
At the same time, keep it simple. Pretend that it's Macanelly
you'll be briefing."

She saw Pedersen wince. Loring Macanelly was a cross that
she made him bear, in spite of (and partly because of) his

complaints. Ole Pedersen was an interesting mix. Intellectu-
ally insecure but extremely ambitious, he was also competent
and highly intelligent. Magrit believed in building on what
people could do, rather than dwelling on what they could not.
There were two ways to motivate Ole Pedersen. One was to
provide him with ordinary challenges, such as making effective use of an individual who was stupid but well-connected
and difficult to fire. That was Loring Macanelly. The other
was to ask for the apparently impossible, which now and again
Ole Pedersen would accomplish.

It was the second reason that made her add, "And don't be
content with evaluating what you find. I'd like you to understand Ligon's work so thoroughly that you can make improve-
ments to it."

By referring only to Ligon's work, Magrit made sure that
Pedersen would not waste time asking questions of anyone
but Alex Ligon. She was quite sure that Pedersen realized
whose model it was, and if Mischa Glaub's feathers were ruf-
fled because he was being bypassed in the chain of command,
Magrit would take care of that separately. To make the latter
task easier, she added, "One thing I want to make clear. It's
the new model, and only the new model, that you will be
exploring. I'm not authorizing you to go fishing around in
other projects over there."

Pedersen was nodding. He even seemed pleased. Magrit
could imagine his thoughts. If the model had basic flaws and
he could uncover them, he gained kudos. If the model happened to be correct and he could somehow suggest an im-
provement, he would share in the glory.

Magrit turned to de Mises. "Any problems with any of this,
Tomas?"

"No. If there are disputes, I'll do my best to sort them
out."

Which he would, and which he was good at. Any original thought by Tomas de Mises was far in the past, but he was a great mediator and conciliator. When in the near future he retired, Magrit would be sorry to lose those talents.

"Excellent." Magrit led them toward the door. "This is a high-priority job, so I'd like reports every couple of days. Short, no more than a page until you turn up something major."

Until, rather than unless, to give Ole Pedersen added motivation. Magrit took a deep breath as she closed the door and walked over to her desk. Her job required a constant balancing act . . . and she wouldn't change it for any other in the System.

She had missed the time slot for a regular lunch. She heated a bowl of soft noodles, gulped it down with a handful of crackers, and scanned her messages. One jumped out at her, although she had no time to consider it in detail. She made a quick-print, stuffed the document into her pocket, and examined the priority list.

Ligons. The whole damned day seemed packed with Ligons, although she had to admit that Alex Ligon had made an unexpectedly favorable first impression. Kate Lonaker swore that he was a genius, and today he had stood up for his work without any guff or false modesty. Unfortunately, Alex seemed to be the exception that proved the rule. The imperial word from Prosper Ligon, delivered to Magrit from the dizzy heights of Council Headquarters, displayed the contempt that only established wealth and power could afford: Magrit was to contact Rezel and Tanya Ligon as soon as possible, and arrange for them to meet immediately with the owner of the lease on Pandora.

"Contact" could mean anything. When dealing with someone powerful, Magrit infinitely preferred a face-to-face in her own office. That way they couldn't be calling on huge external resources without you knowing about it.

This time she'd have to settle for half. Rezel and Tanya Ligon would meet with her in person, but she must go over to a Ligon corporate center to do it. She stood up and headed for the door, then hesitated. She came back to her desk, pulled out an image cube, and stuck it into her pocket. If Bat's information were reliable—it had never in the past been anything but—this might be needed.

On the fifteen-minute trip via Ganymede's high-speed elevators and rapid slideways, Magrit wondered if she was about to make a mistake. Supposing that she and Bat did not have to deal with Rezel and Tanya Ligon, then who else in the family might they propose? It was going to be another balancing act to get what she wanted.

Magrit arrived at the corporate center and identified herself to a Level Three Fax in the outer chamber. The Fax politely invited her to take a seat and told her that the news of her arrival was being passed on to the appropriate parties. Magrit sat down on an angular and uncomfortable chair, opposite expensive murals of the baleen management team and huge krill harvesters with which the second rise in Ligon fortunes had begun. She noted that she was exactly on time.

Thirty minutes later she was still sitting in the same place. The Fax, which had the form of a handsome young man, was apologetic. It could, it said, unfortunately do nothing to speed things up. When younger, Magrit would have been either intimidated or seething. Now she recognized the tactic. Important guests would never be kept waiting. This was an attempt, and a rather crude one, to show Magrit where she stood in the Ligon perceived order of things.

Magrit checked her mobile message unit. As she suspected,

it would not operate. For security reasons, the interior of the Ligon corporate center was shielded against both incoming and outgoing signals. No matter. It was nice to be inaccessible to other problems for an hour, and she had plenty to do. Bat, in their most recent conversation about the Ligon family and its demands, had volunteered his additional concern that "something new and major" was going on in the System.

What sort of something? Bat, crouched black-cowled and scowling on his over-sized chair, had admitted that he didn't know. It might be an effect of the Seine, now fully activated. Possibly it was some unrelated development. It was far harder for Bat's highly logical and organized mind to admit his own uncertainty than it was for Magrit to accept it. At the moment he could offer no more than a visceral discomfort, a feeling, he said, as though some giant wasp had become accidentally entangled in his delicate spider's web of information retrieval. He promised to work to make his worries specific and tangible. Meanwhile, would Magrit remain alert for anything new under the Sun, anywhere from the Vulcan Nexus to the Oort Cloud?

She had promised to do so. And lo and behold, sitting in the incoming message queue in her office had been a candidate for Bat's "something new" claim. She pulled out the quickprint she had made in her office, sat it on her lap, and read through it three times.

To the Ganymede Central Council, special restricted report. On 10/10/97, at 4:16:44, the Argus Station at Jovian L-4 noted a signal of apparent extra-solar origin. The identifier, recorded here for the purpose of recognition of priority, is AT-66-JB-2214. Signal frequency, duration, and direction will be reported later, assuming that confirmation tests prove satisfactory. Following accepted protocol, the signal has been named as the

Wu-Beston anomaly. *General detection tests have been passed, and we are proceeding to verification before attempting interpretation. This message is being tight-beamed to two and only two locations, namely, the Ganymede Cabinet Records Office and the Odin Station at Jovian L-5. Signed, Jack Beston, Argus Station Project Director.*

This was certainly something new. What it signified was another matter. Over the years Magrit had heard rumors of a dozen contacts with alien intelligence. Each one had fizzled out after a few weeks, explained as natural radio sources, within-System human signals, or an over-optimistic assessment of some natural data run masquerading as a statistically significant sequence. It was hard to believe that this one would prove to be different, but when she next spoke to Bat she would point it out to him. This was a restricted access message, to named individuals only, but chances were that Bat had already seen and evaluated it. He had an insatiable curiosity for things he was not supposed to know, and he possessed personal probes that could crack almost any message cipher in the system. Coded signals were like dark chocolate with truffles, they had Bat smacking his blubbery lips.

That conversation would have to wait. Finally, the reception Fax was waving for Magrit's attention. The door beyond the ante-chamber stood open, and Magrit walked through to face the inquisition.

Two people were in the room, both standing. Rezel and Tanya Ligon she recognized easily from the data on the Ligon family that Bat had provided. They were close enough look-alikes to be twins, although Magrit knew that they were in fact sisters two years apart. Each was a tall, busty blonde with hair cut to conform to Ganymede's latest fashion, fringed across the forehead and curved around the cheeks. Each wore a dress of electric blue, cinched tight around a narrow waist and short enough to show off long, slim, and perfect legs.

Magrit had been too rushed to freshen up after her improvised lunch. She was still wearing the white skirt and floral blouse of her morning meeting. Back on government levels those were considered slightly daring, at the edge of permissible dress codes for office work, but comparing herself now with the Ligon cousins, Magrit felt frumpy, dumpy, and unkempt.

She dismissed those thoughts. This was not a beauty contest. Nor was it a social encounter, a fact made clear when the woman on the left—Rezel, Magrit thought, a fraction taller and heavier than her sister—said abruptly, "Knudsen? Sit down, and let's get this over with. We can't spare much time."

But it was your man, Prosper Ligon, who insisted that I meet with you. Magrit smiled pleasantly, took a seat across the table from them as indicated, and waited.

After a long pause, the woman went on, "I am Rezel Ligon. We didn't really want to meet with you at all. We want to meet with the man, the Bat or whatever his name is, who holds the lease on Pandora."

The man. The Ligons had been doing their own homework. To Magrit's certain knowledge, the gender of the leaseholder for Pandora was nowhere provided on any of the legal documents. Bat was identified only by the name he used on the Puzzle Network, *Megachirops*, while Magrit was named as the point of contact. But among other things, money bought information.

Magrit said mildly, "I have full authority to negotiate on Bat's behalf. What do you propose?"

"We will not negotiate with you." Tanya Ligon gave up

on icy stares and spoke for the first time. "We prefer to deal with the Bat."

"Why?" Magrit knew very well the answer to her own question. The sisters formed a one-two knockout sexual team who had obtained from a score of supposedly hard-headed and rational businessmen the most favorable contract terms for Ligon Industries. She was curious to hear the sisters' own reasons, and was amused when Tanya said, "We find that men are more amenable to logical arguments than women."

"Perhaps. But Bat does not want to meet with you, or with any women. Maybe he finds them too logical."

"He meets with *you.*"

"Not recently. And when he did meet with me, he had no choice. He was my employee."

That produced more reaction. Rezel's perfect brow wrinkled, and Tanya said, "*He* worked for *you*. And he could afford to take out a long-term lease on the whole of Pandora?"

"He subsequently became very wealthy." Magrit wondered, didn't people remember anything? Bat's name had been splashed all around the System only a few years ago, when he had been richly rewarded for his rescue mission on Europa.

Magrit did not mention that their own cousin, Alex Ligon, also possessed of great wealth, worked for her now. Instead she said, "Bat's very rich. He meets only with whom he chooses."

Another glare from Tanya's frosty blue eye. Rezel said, "You are being uncooperative. This is not a question of money. We insist that we talk to him. We are convinced that in a meeting in person with the Bat we can persuade him to change his mind about the lease of Pandora."

It was time for other tactics. Magrit glanced about the conference room. The wall decorations were all 3-D depictions of the Ligon family history, so rich and varied that it was impossible to determine what equipment they concealed. "Do you have anything in this room that will take an image cube?"

Rezel just scowled, but Tanya reached across and pressed the table top. An image display unit, mounted flush with the polished surface top and indistinguishable from it, rose into view. Magrit slipped the image cube from her pocket, inserted it, and performed her selection.

"Here," she said when the picture clip appeared, "is Rustum Battachariya, also known as Bat, the Great Bat, and on the Puzzle Network"—the sisters looked blank—"as *Megachirops*. This is the man whom you wish to meet. The picture is a few years old. He has put on perhaps thirty kilos since it was taken."

Magrit was cheating a little. She had selected a sequence that caught Bat at his most malevolent. He crouched in the Bat Cave, amid a clutter of Great War relics. He was examining one of his treasures, a de-brained Seeker missile. The glow from the Seeker's ruby sensors reflected in Bat's dark eyes. He looked, and undoubtedly was, unwashed and unshaven, and he was dressed in rumpled black clothes that emphasized rather than cloaked his bulging body.

Magrit heard Tanya grunt. Rezel was silent, but she gazed at the picture with her mouth open.

"A meeting is not impossible," Magrit went on. "However, there are a few things you ought to know that pictures cannot reveal. Bat does not travel. If you are determined to meet with him—which I still do not recommend—it would have to be at his home."

"*That* is his home?" Tanya was staring at the dark walls and gloomy depths of the Bat Cave.

"That's right." Magrit smiled at the sisters. "It's not as bad as it looks. The weapons are all disarmed—at least, that's what Bat tells me. You two are not geeks." Magrit spoke as one making a new and surprising discovery. "But Bat is a typical geek, always taking things to bits, fiddling with their computers, and putting them back together again. You'd really be wasting your time with him. It's a pity there's no one in your family with his sort of interests."

Rezel arched her styled eyebrows at Tanya, who said to Magrit, "Stay where you are." The two sisters stood up from the table and walked toward the back wall, which mysteriously became a door as they approached it.

Magrit was left alone. She disengaged the image cube of Bat and slipped it back in her pocket. It wasn't likely the Ligon sisters would ask to see it again. After five more minutes she stood up and as an experiment walked around the table and across to where Rezel and Tanya had disappeared. The wall remained a wall. Apparently there was a recognition code built into it. Magrit went back to the table.

Three minutes more, and part of the back wall suddenly became the image of the reception Fax. Its eyes turned until they looked straight at Magrit—some fancy recognition software there, more than you'd find in any government office Fax—and it said, "Your meeting is over. I have been instructed to request that you now leave the Ligon corporate premises."

So much for negotiation. Magrit, on the way back to her office, assessed the meeting. On the one hand, they had stopped pushing for a meeting with Bat; on the other hand, it was clear that they were not willing to deal with Magrit; nor had she ever expected them to. She had planted the seed of an idea with them at the end of the meeting, and that was about all she had hoped for.

* * *

Back in her office, Magrit tried a call to Bat. Reaching him was always an iffy proposition, because he had long ago assured her that he would not abandon certain sacred activities even if her incoming message warned that the Sun was going nova. She had asked what those activities were. He mentioned cooking, eating, seeking Great War relics, and thinking about difficult abstract problems.

Magrit said, "But that's all you ever do!"

Bat had pondered for a moment, folded his hands across his belly, and nodded.

Today he was not, by Bat standards, cooking or eating. True, he had in front of him three bowls of assorted sweetmeats, half-empty, but he was not in the kitchen juggling stock and shellfish and fine-chopped herbs.

He inclined his head, to indicate that he was aware of Magrit's telepresence.

She waved the quick-print. "There's a report from Argus Station at L-4. I was wondering—"

"I read it. It is interesting, and perhaps relevant. However, it is not the central phenomenon that causes me apprehension. What I sense goes farther back in time, and feels far more dangerous. Is that the reason for your presence? If so, then a simple message—"

"It's not. Bat, I did you a favor today. I persuaded two members of the Ligon family that a meeting with you would not be to their advantage."

"For this relief, much thanks."

"But that doesn't mean the pressure is off you, or off me. Bat, I know how you feel about this. You wish they would just go away. So do I. They're not going to. Unless we can provide a reason for them to lay off—a strong reason—they are going to squeeze and squeeze until they spit you out of the middle of Pandora dead or alive. Do you have anything new that I can use?"

"You must be the judge of that. I am only able to tell you what I have discovered."

"Shoot."

"Very well." Bat closed his eyes. "We could I suppose begin with Giacomo Ligon, whose first Antarctic leases were provably obtained through threat and bribery and covert murder. However, that was close to a century years ago. This leads me to suspect that some statute of limitations is likely to apply."

"Look far enough back in anybody's family, you'll find villains. Anyway, that was all on Earth so Jovian law wouldn't apply. Bat, we need something *now*, some hold on living family members."

"This is something of which I am not unaware. However, it is my nature to be comprehensive rather than superficial. Permit me to continue, and since you wish it I will confine my attention to members of the Ligon family who are presently alive and make their homes on Ganymede. The most promising candidate, since he sits at the heart of Ligon financial affairs and has final say in them, is Prosper Ligon. I have, regrettably from our point of view, been unable to discover any taint on the man. If he has interests other than work, I have been unable to learn of them. He appears to have as few vices as I do."

It was an awful temptation, but Magrit bit her tongue. "So cross off Prosper Ligon. Who else?"

"There are two sisters who specialize in the seduction, drugging, and blackmail of important figures in Jovian government and commerce. However, since the involved parties are all far more interested in concealment than revelation, I see little leverage."

"Rezel and Tanya? Those two beauties are the ones who wanted to meet with you today. You're lucky. I guess I saved you from seduction and drugging and blackmail."

"Indubitably you did. May I continue, or must we both descend to the level of facetious commentary? Next we have Hector Ligon, who seems capable of any manner of debased behavior provided that it requires no iota of sense or original thought. We could certainly trap him into any number of compromising or illegal activities. Sadly, no member of the family would lift a finger or pay a sou to save him. Even his father regards it as merely a matter of time until some act of folly on Hector's part leads to his disgrace and dismissal from the bosom of the Ligon family."

"Bat, I know you like to be thorough. But I have a Board of Supervisors meeting in half an hour, and if I go in unprepared there's a couple of people who'll love to chew on my ass. Could you stop listing the Ligon family we *can't* pressure, and come to the ones we can?"

"A consummation devoutly to be wished, but one that I fear is at the moment impossible. Juliana appears to be as free from vices as her Uncle Prosper. The various aged aunts have been guilty of gross acts, but so long ago that no one today will care. The family members who have chosen to become Commensals offer potential, but I must investigate them further. For awhile I believed that our best hope was Karolus, a man blackened by sins numerous and dastardly; regrettably, I am convinced that he also lacks all shame. If we threaten to expose him, he will laugh at us and admit to everything."

"Right. Am I being unfair if I summarize what you've told me by saying we have nothing?"

"If you are unfair, you are also accurate."

"So I'm glad I did what I did, earlier today. But if this

works out, you'll have to consider an action you do not want to take."

Bat finally opened his eyes, so that he could stare accusingly at Magrit. "The logical complement of the things that I want to do forms a near-infinite set. Do you propose to be specific, or merely to taunt me with vagueness?"

"You will have to meet with a Ligon. Now hold on." She could see Bat beginning to bristle. "This isn't just any Ligon. It's a man who works for me. I've met him, and I suspect that the two of you may actually get on together."

"Hmph."

"I set the bait earlier today in my meeting with the sisters. If they take it, I'm going to suggest that Alex Ligon fly out to see you, there in the Bat Cave. After that it will be up to you. You want to remain on Pandora? Then the two of you have to cut a deal that satisfies the Ligon family."

"And you, I presume, have no suggestions as to what such a scheme might be."

"Of course I don't. That's your job. I mean, you're the smart one, aren't you?"

"Hmph."

"That's what I thought. So you're going to prove it. Now, I have to run."

She cut the connection, to avoid discussion.

From Bat's point of view, however, the timing was perfect. Before the communication screen had time to become blank, an irresistible message from Mord had appeared on it.

14

Mord had been designed with great skill. Many times, the suite of programs developed by Mordecai Perlman would pass for a human rather than a high-level Fax.

Many times; but this was not one of them. The image on Bat's display wavered in its outlines, and the voice that had called for immediate attention lacked Mord's acerbic tone as it said, as soon as the channel was opened, "It's everything that I thought it might be."

The comment also lacked Mord's usual clarity. Bat studied the wobbly image. "Might I ask *what* is all that you thought it might be?"

"The Seine, and its data banks. There are thousands of new ones, far more than you predicted. I've tasted hundreds, and I'm just getting started. Fascinating. But it's"—Mord paused, as though scanning for the appropriate word—"*scary* out there in the Seine. I had the feeling that I could easily get lost. No, not lost. Swallowed up."

"That was a danger I already predicted. The Seine has sets of programs designed to locate and eliminate blocks of code with no external pointers."

"I don't mean *them*." Mord was not inside the Keep, but he was still within Bat's protected environment. The display had begun to normalize, and his voice was contemptuous as he went on, "I know all about scavengers, I've avoided that kind of program for half a human lifetime. This is different."

"I have experienced something of the same feeling. It is as though something new and very large is stirring within the System."

"Maybe. But you've not experienced it the way I've experienced it. I mean, you're sitting there, laughing and scratching, and I'm in the middle of this."

"You feel in danger of your own destruction?"

"That's not quite it, either. It's not like I'm a parasite. It's more like I might be *absorbed* into the Seine's overall structure and become part of it. I don't want that."

"If this disturbs you, you could remain here and reside within the Keep. Its integrity and separation from Seine influence appear to be complete."

"Nah." The shake of Mord's head was perfect human simulation. "It's interesting out in the Seine, a whole new universe to play in even if you do have to watch your ass. I didn't come here looking for protection, or to tell you I'm running a bit unstable and over my head. I've got a goodie for you. Do you remember asking me to keep a look out for anything that mentions the asteroid Mandrake?"

"I did so with good reason. Mandrake was the home of Nadeen Selassie. She was the legendary genius of the Belt, the weapons-maker who among other things designed the Seekers. She died on Mandrake at the end of the Great War, reputedly while developing some kind of ultimate device of which no details are known. It was reported, however, to be not a weapon for reprisals. Rather, it was designed for universal destruction."

"Hey, I know all that. You told me, so I remember. I'm not some dumb-ass human. But did she? I mean, did she die? Are you sure?"

"The whole of Mandrake was heated to more than three thousand degrees by a direct hit from a teraton bomb. It became a ball of bubbling magma. I have myself seen those images." Bat paused. "May I anticipate your next question? You are going to ask me, am I sure that Nadeen Selassie was on Mandrake at the time."

"You got it."

"I have no direct evidence for that fact. Nor, however, do I see reason to doubt it."

"Well, sit tight, Fat Boy, because I'm going to give you a reason. I've been wandering the new data banks, the places nobody else bothers to go. There's thousands of them, little stashes of information that were totally isolated before the Seine. I located a bank from one of the Amor class of asteroids, the ones that cross the orbits of both Earth and Mars. This asteroid was—and is—called *Heraldic*, and it had a little colony on it at the time of the Great War. Although it belonged to the Belt it wasn't important enough for Earth to hit, so it wasn't touched by any weapons at all. That didn't do much for the people living there, because they weren't self-supporting and afterwards the supply systems got totally screwed up. Everyone was starving to death. So they all took off."

"To go where?"

"Not clear. According to the files left behind on Heraldic they were headed for the Callisto rehab camps, but I found no evidence they ever made it. If they did, they never wrote home. The Heraldic data bank sat abandoned and ignored until the Seine remotes went in a few months ago, set up the connectors, and hooked it into the general base."

"Do you have the reference code?"

"Does Rustum Battachariya eat chocolate? Of course I have the reference code. You can see for yourself when we're through. But I'll tell you what caught my attention. After the war was over, but well before the colonists gave up and left, three refugees from the Belt arrived at Heraldic: a woman and her two little children, in a beat-up ship with planetary landing capability. One of the kids, the baby boy, seemed all right, but the little girl was going to die no matter what. Her lungs were a mess of dissolving tissue. The woman had a chance, provided she received immediate medical treatment. She damn near died anyway, what with seared lungs, skin burns, and a broken back. They couldn't do too great a job on her, because their medical supplies had run low and they didn't have a good treatment center to start with. But they tried. Before they were finished with the treatment, while the woman was still a wreck, the baby girl died. After her daughter's cremation—she insisted on that rather than space burial—the woman upped and left, taking the baby boy."

"For what destination?"

"You tell me. The record's blank. She said they'd come from Ceres and were going back there, but that was almost certainly a lie. The orbital geometry was all wrong, with Ceres on the other side of the Sun when she arrived and when she left. The people on Heraldic didn't much care. They had their own worries. She also said her name was Pearl Landrix, but my guess is that was false, too."

"Mord, I am a patient man." Bat ignored the snort from the display. "However, so far you have offered me not one scintilla of evidence to suggest that the woman who arrived on Heraldic was anything other than she claimed to be, a poor and disabled war refugee and her injured children. Certainly, you have no reason to associate her with the presumably-deceased Nadeen Selassie."

"No reason, except for a couple of things that if you'd shut up for a minute I'll tell you. They put her under when they operated on her back, and beforehand while they were prepping her they did the usual tests to see if she was allergic to any of the drugs they'd be using. As part of that, they did a routine genome map. They discovered an unusual corrected trisomy of one of the chromosomes. Whoever did the test made a note: the only cases in their records of that kind of corrected trisomy came from Mandrake." Mord paused. "You don't look any too pleased."

"I am filled with contempt and disdain—for myself. Since this data bank is online, I should have searched for references to Mandrake. I failed to do so. Nadeen Selassie was born on Mandrake, and she did all her work there. However, if this is your evidence, it is anticlimactic. It offers no linkage of the woman calling herself Pearl Landrix to Nadeen Selassie. The type of genetic abnormality that you describe was not rare on Mandrake. It was in fact rather common among the colonists, and just as commonly corrected. It was merely rare in other parts of the System."

"I'm not done. The baby girl died and was cremated. But when they first arrived, and before the colonists realized they could do nothing to save the girl, as a matter of routine they did a genome scan and performed a general physical on her. The genome scan proved conclusively that the woman and the baby girl were not related."

"In times of war and disaster, adoptions are common."

"Don't fight it, Bat. You've got that gleam in your eye. You believe there's something there. And I'm still not done. Before the cremation—again as a matter of routine—the girl's body was subjected to examination. It wasn't a full autopsy, but whoever did it thought the results were odd enough to include in the data file. The baby had abnormalities that had nothing to do with her injuries. It looked like there had been pre-birth tampering, in the brain and in some of the organs. So you tell me: was Nadeen Selassie a biologist?"

In moments of high excitement, Bat turned to food. He had stuffed his mouth so full with candied orange peel that it was a few seconds before he could chew and swallow enough to answer Mord's question.

"Even after thirty years and considerable research, Nadeen Selassie remains a figure shrouded in mystery. She was, in terms of weaponry, the Grand Designer for the most exotic forms that were ever found or ever lost. I am forced to rely on rumor and hearsay, but by all accounts she was unique. Her talents embraced biology, chemistry, and physics. If it is possible that she is still alive . . ."

"No. Not even assuming that Pearl Landrix was Nadeen Selassie. Her medical record at the time of her operation and after is still in the data file on Heraldic. When she left, they told her to go to the best treatment center she could find. If she did that, and soon, she might live as long as ten years. If she didn't get treatment, she would die within five. But either way, that was thirty years ago. Calm down, Bat. She's gone."

"You are undoubtedly right." Bat had moved rapidly from skeptic to believer. "And the legacy of her work, the ultimate weapon . . ."

"That's gone, too. If we're lucky."

"Perhaps." Bat turned to look around the Bat Cave, as though seeking a suitable open spot for yet another Great War relic. "One cannot help but speculate on what it might have been." He stood up, which in the micro-gravity of Pandora looked rather like an act of levitation. "Even before you called, a variety of incidents today had already made it impossible for me to think straight. I beg your indulgence. I must go now and seek circumstances which will permit me to regain my mental equilibrium."

"You mean you're going to gorge. That's enough for me. I'm out of here."

Mord's image vanished. As always, Bat wondered just what it was that had vanished. Mord was no more than a different form of Fax, a set of logical operators embodied as an evanescent swirl of electrons. Today, however, the puzzle of Mord's incorporeal existence was no more than a fleeting thought. Something more urgent was on Bat's mind.

Rather than heading for the other end of the Bat Cave and the pleasures of the kitchen, he sank slowly back down onto the padded chair. He said, aloud, "Something more deadly than a Seeker missile. Something more surprising than the super-adapted humans whom we learned about during the incident on Europa. And yet they survived to the present. Why not this? Mord feels it, too. Something is stirring within the System, something big and mysterious. The ultimate weapon? Or the ultimate shared illusion?"

This was why a person needed solitude. This was why a man could not afford to be interrupted by the constant clamor of mailings and messages and media. Magrit—his recent conversation with her already felt old and distant—had stated it succinctly and correctly. He was the smart one.

And he was baffled.

He set the sidereal clock back more than thirty years, and queried the astronomy programs for solar system positions and velocities of a select group of bodies.

Mandrake—Heraldic—Ceres. Mord had been right. Transit from Mandrake to Heraldic would have been easy in the closing days of the Great War. But movement from there to

Ceres? That would be a lengthy and energy-expensive trip.

What about other destinations? Bat called in the ones he saw as most likely, given the starting point of Heraldic, and asked for evaluation.

One of them at once jumped out of the pack. *Mars*. If Pearl Landrix, perhaps aka Nadeen Selassie, wanted to go anywhere in her little ship, Mars would be the destination of choice. But Mars had itself been hideously battered during the Great War. It represented a first destination, but surely not a final one.

Where? If Nadeen Selassie was indeed carrying with her a doomsday weapon to make the solar system "dark as day," where would she have taken it—or, if she were dying as Mord insisted, have sent it?

Bat sat alone in darkness for many hours, brooding on unanswerable questions. He had the feeling that forces he sensed only dimly were gradually coming closer.

15

ABOARD THE *OSL ACHILLES*

Mars, for Janeed at least, promised to be at best an anticlimax. At worst it might turn out to be a disaster. For starters, no one aboard the *Achilles* would be allowed to land. The ship would go no closer to the planet than synchronous orbit, seventeen thousand kilometers above the surface, and sit there and wait for a couple of days. They had detoured to Mars, so far as Jan could tell, for three unrelated reasons: to permit an official inspection of the engines; to collect another eight passengers outward bound for the Jovian system; and, the one that worried Jan, to pick up Dr. Bloom.

Why did Valnia Bloom want more meetings with Sebastian? You would think that with all the examinations, mental and physical, performed down on Earth and in orbit around Earth, everything that could be tested had been tested. Also, what did Dr. Bloom want with *her*? Jan had learned, only a couple of hours ago, that she too was scheduled for another session with the head of the Ganymede department of scientific research.

From that moment Jan had been in hold mode. Now she

was staring down at the surface of the planet and simply waiting. The exhilaration that she had felt since leaving Earth was draining away, minute by minute. Valnia Bloom had boarded, and Sebastian was already meeting with her. Was there any way that, having come so far, Jan and Sebastian might be rejected and returned to Earth? She had wandered the ship, hoping to see Paul Marr and perhaps receive some reassurance that acceptance aboard the *Achilles* meant final approval for outbound colonists. He was nowhere to be found. She assumed that he was with the inspection engineers behind the bulkhead with its red-lettered NO PASSENGERS sign.

The view of Mars offered no relief. The planet was enduring one of its periodic months-long dust storms, clouding the ruddy face almost to the poles. It was mid-morning down there, and Jan could make out—or imagine that she made out—the great crack of Valles Marineris. That was all. Mars had struggled back close to its prewar population of seventeen million people, but no one, seeing the world from Jan's vantage point, would discern any evidence of their existence.

Suddenly, after waiting for what seemed like forever, she felt a touch on her elbow. It was Sebastian, moving, as usual, as silently as a cat. He dismissed the view from the port with a summary glance—*No clouds!*—and said, "Your turn."

"With Dr. Bloom? What did she say to you? What did she want? How did everything go?"

"It was fine." Sebastian smiled. "It was good."

That was probably the best that Jan could get. She nodded, turned, and headed at maximum speed for the cabin where Valnia Bloom had set up a temporary office. When she came to the door, she hesitated. She didn't want to seem worried or nervous. She smoothed her hair, waited for five seconds, then knocked and went in.

Valnia Bloom seemed as intense and anorexic as ever. She nodded to Jan, waved her to a chair, and said, "This shouldn't take long."

Probably she thought she was being reassuring. Her expression was anything but. Her next words were worse. "Janeed Jannex, you said in our earlier meeting that you had known Sebastian Birch for more than thirty years, since you were small children. To your knowledge, was he ever placed for any reason in an institution?"

"No!" The word burst out of Jan. All her life she had defended Sebastian, arguing that he was normal, covering for him when he did something especially weird, explaining away his lack of interest in conventional learning. And now, just when she thought all that was past, here it came again.

"He's a little slow to catch on, that's all," she said. "But once he understands an idea, he has it forever."

"I can very well believe that." Valnia Bloom was studying a display, but it was tilted so that Jan could not see what was on it. "Did he ever have any form of brain surgery?"

"No." Jan's mind instantly popped up *tumor*. "He's all right, isn't he?"

"Physically, he is in very good shape. He would otherwise not be here on this ship. His brain scans, however, are unusual and show very lopsided mental activities. In addition to the odd neurotransmitter activity noted by Christa Matloff, there is extra tissue in one of the *sulci*. The functions of that tissue remain a mystery. And so far as his mental abilities are concerned, they too are unusual. There are elements of the classical *idiot savant*, although he does not fit easily into that category. His innate understanding of the complex dynamics of weather systems is, so far as I can tell, unprecedented. He says he can *see*, inside his head, how storms on Jupiter and

Saturn are born and develop. More so, oddly enough, than the weather patterns on Earth."

She frowned at the display for a long time, while Jan shivered inside and wondered, *Why is she telling me all this?*

"Nothing like an epileptic fit?" Valnia Bloom said at last. "No loss of physical control, or violent outbursts?"

"Never." Jan wanted to laugh, the idea of violence from Sebastian was so preposterous. "He's the best-natured man you'll ever meet."

"He is certainly the most phlegmatic." Valnia Bloom was nodding, more to herself than to Jan. "I wanted to be sure that you were not in some way *shielding* Sebastian in ways that you preferred not to mention. I have a reason why this is important. I know that the two of you insist on being considered as a team, which is very unusual in people who are not sexual partners."

"We're not."

"I know that."

"We never have been. He's like my brother."

"Which is why I wanted to meet with you before taking any action. You came as a team. I understand and appreciate that. But would you accept it if I were to, so to speak, take Sebastian under my wing for awhile?"

"You mean—what do you mean?"

"I would like to work with him, and try to understand why he is different from other people. He would become one of my personal research projects. Oh, you two would still be together as much as you like, and see each other whenever you want. But you might not—almost certainly would not—be working side by side on a day-by-day basis. You would no longer be a team. I want to know, is this acceptable to you?"

It was, in a way, Jan's oldest and dearest dream: a Sebastian who was valued for what he could do, rather than needing protection for what was strange or incomprehensible to him. But because Jan had filled her role for so long, she had to ask. "If ever Sebastian seems to be having difficulties—"

"You will be the first to know, and the first person called upon to help."

"Then, yes. It sounds like a wonderful opportunity. Dr. Bloom, when you get to know him you'll find that he's the sweetest, most uncomplaining person on Earth—not just Earth, anywhere. I'm absolutely thrilled for Sebastian that this is happening. And thank you for what you are doing."

Jan wanted to lean over and hug the stern, narrow-shouldered woman sitting across from her. She didn't think that was likely to be appreciated. Instead, she had to be content with a smile that probably reached her ears.

"Don't thank me." Valnia Bloom reached forward and with an air of finality stabbed with one thin digit a key on the hidden display. Then she looked up, and actually smiled an answering smile. "Before you leave, Janeed Jannex, I want you to know that I am doing this not because, unlike Sebastian, I am the sweetest person on Earth, or anywhere in the System. I am doing this for my own selfish motives. I am as keen to study Sebastian Birch as you are to make sure that no one harms him. That is all."

The dreaded meeting was over! The *Achilles* was in a stable orbit and the ship's interior formed a micro-gravity environment, but Jan felt that it would have made no difference had she been back on Earth. As she left the room she would still have floated, borne up by sheer euphoria.

She headed forward, seeking Sebastian to give him the good news. He was lying on his narrow bed, staring at nothing—or at, according to Valnia Bloom, the evolving storm systems that he and he alone in the whole System was able to visualize.

"I had my meeting with Dr. Bloom." She stood at the end of his cot, grinning down at him. "Everything is all right."

His round face took on a perplexed expression. He said, "Of course." And then, with hardly a pause, "I feel hungry. Can we go to dinner?"

Maybe Valnia Bloom had been trying to tell Jan something. She was in many ways still shielding and directing Sebastian, although to anyone else's eye he was not a child or a youth but a full-grown and physically mature man. Maybe in trying to help him, she had become part of the problem.

Jan said, "You go ahead by yourself. I'll eat later."

He nodded and sat up. "So I'll go eat now," he said, and happily drifted out and away along the corridor. On his own, Jan noted, with no need at all for direction or assistance. She went next door to lie on her own bed. She needed an hour or two alone, to work some of the smiles out of her system.

Apparently she failed. There must have been plenty of smiles left. When she went to dinner, three hours later, Paul Marr was in the passenger dining room for the first time. He was assigned to eat with a different group, so he did no more than glance at Jan as he passed and say quietly, "I wish people would do something for me to make *me* grin like that."

Dinner itself was a curious disappointment. The person she wanted to talk to was one table over, making polite and impartial conversation with the five passengers who sat with him. Jan noted that his white uniform was as spotless and well-pressed as ever, and this time his hands and nails were scrubbed free of every trace of working grime. He occasionally glanced her way, but not enough so that others would notice.

Jan's own table partners were a mixed bag. Four of them, a man, woman, and their two children, had just flown up from

Mars and in their new micro-gravity setting they at the moment felt like eating little or nothing. Then there were two wannabe miners who had been office workers back on Earth. Jan had eaten with them several times before and quite liked them, though they talked mainly about their bright future in the rough-and-tumble cowboy society on Callisto. Jan eyed their delicate hands and pudgy bodies and hoped they wouldn't be disappointed.

And then there was Judd O'Donnell, a loud oaf who seemed to seek Jan out and whom she avoided whenever possible. As usual, he insisted on sitting next to her. Tonight his main contribution to the conversation came when fish was served as the first course. One of the would-be miners said how good it was, so tasty it might have been flown up fresh from Mars. The Mars family stared at him in disbelief, but remained silent.

Judd O'Donnell said, "Hey, how can you tell if the fish you're eating was caught in Marslake?" And, when no one answered, "You turn the lights off, and see if it glows in the dark."

He laughed loudly. The man in the group from Mars winced, while the woman made a gesture to her children to keep quiet. Radioactivity levels on Mars were still high thirty years after the end of the war, especially in bodies of water. Mutations were common. A strict eugenics program culled the human and animal populations, and most families had relatives among the victims.

That set the tone for the rest of the dinner. When she came in, Jan had been feeling on top of the universe. By the time people were dispersing she couldn't wait to get away. But she stayed, enduring O'Donnell's attempts at wit and waiting for Paul Marr to get up and leave.

Finally she couldn't take any more. She stood up in the

middle of a Judd O'Donnell story and left the dining room. Before the door could slide closed behind her, it was opening again for someone else.

"Phew." It was Paul Marr. "That fat man at our table, talking about how he was going to transform Outer System economics . . . I thought you were never going to leave."

That was direct enough. Jan could play coy, but what the hell. "I felt the same about you. I thought you must be having a fascinating time while I sat and suffered. You got economics, I had tasteless jokes."

Other passengers were still leaving the dining room or drifting along the corridor. Paul Marr remained a meter and more away from Jan, and his voice was soft and casual when he said, "We've had enough economics and jokes for one night, and it's too crowded here to talk at all privately. Can I interest you in a quiet drink back in my quarters?"

"I think so." Jan tried to sound as relaxed as Paul. "Do you want to go on ahead?"

"Oh, I don't think that's necessary. No harm in a passenger wanting to take a look at the engine room, is there? By the way, the inspection of the Omnivores went as smooth as you could ask. We'll be on our way in less than twenty-four hours."

To the men and women they were passing, the conversation must sound routine if not actually boring. No one had a monitor to read Jan's pulse rate, or to measure the fine tremble in her hands. One more turn, and the end of the passenger quarters would be in sight. If she was thinking of changing her mind, better do it now.

They came to the lettered bulkhead. Paul slid the hatch open and ushered Jan through. Instead of heading aft down the corridor with its bilious green paint, Paul made a sharp left turn. At the second door along he paused. "It's not up to the captain's quarters, but it's home to me. Welcome."

Jan found herself in a room maybe twice the size of hers. It had been furnished with a surprising delicacy of taste. The chairs were light and frail in appearance, suitable for a ship where acceleration would rarely exceed half a gee, but their lines were elegant. The walls had been finished in a pastel pink (which Jan actually didn't much care for) and two of them bore half a dozen paintings which she suspected were originals. That was confirmed when she saw a neat *P. Marudini* in the lower right corner. She glanced at him, and he shrugged. "I was young when I started to paint. I thought Marudini sounded a bit more like an artist. Now it's too late to change."

He was over by a small table in one corner, opening two conical bottles each of which wore a misting of condensation. Next to them was a vase of roses. The lighting level in the room was dimmer than in the rest of the ship.

Jan said, half question and half statement, "You were *expecting* that I would come here with you."

He coughed. "Well, no. Let's say that before dinner I was *hoping*. But then I learned that we were at different tables and I couldn't do anything to change that, so we wouldn't have much chance to talk. I'm sorry. I must have seemed a bit abrupt."

"I didn't think so." Jan accepted one of the bottles. She had learned to drink in micro-gravity, but a delicate trial sip was beyond her. She squeezed too much into her mouth and had to swallow hard.

"All right?" Paul asked.

"Just choking. The wine is very good. Like an Earth wine."

"As it should be. It was made in southern Chile—not too far from where you lived."

So he knew where she had come from on Earth. Paul had done his homework.

"The roses, too?"

He nodded. "From Punta Arenas. Flower city." He took a sip from his own squeeze bottle, savoring the aftertaste and looking thoughtful. "I guess everything went well with Dr. Bloom?"

"You spoke with her?"

"No. I saw your face. You were the cat that got the parakeet."

"That would have been difficult on board the *Achilles*."

"Quite right." He took a bigger mouthful. "No pets allowed."

"Like passengers beyond the bulkhead."

The conversation was casual, but underneath it ran a strong current of sexual tension. Jan noticed that there was no bed in the room. What would happen if things developed as she expected? Fun and games in free-fall? She felt nervous but determined.

"But you never answered my question," Paul went on. "Did everything work out as you hoped with Dr. Bloom? You know, it's quite unusual for her to want a second meeting with someone after they leave Earth orbit."

"Things went very well." Jan wondered how to phrase it. "I was really worried beforehand, but I had no reason to be. That's why I feel so good. It's as though I just gave birth."

"Gave birth? To what?"

"To *who*. To a thirty-five-year-old. All my life I've been looking after Sebastian and making decisions for him. Dr. Bloom told me to stop. It will be hard, but I have to take her advice. For his sake."

Paul lowered his head and did not look at her. "I wouldn't

normally say this to any passenger, but I feel close to you and you need to know. There's a lot of talk aboard about Sebastian Birch. For one thing, people say he's either retarded or has serious mental problems."

"I know. Neither one is true. Sebastian is strange, but Dr. Bloom says that he has talents she has never encountered before. She wants to spend a lot of time with him. And she wants me to spend less."

"*That's* what you meant by giving birth. You had me worried for a second."

He was inviting her to ask why. Instead, Jan held the conical bottle out toward Paul and squeezed it. "All gone. I've been gulping too fast, but sipping is difficult."

"Would you like more?"

"I don't think so."

"Well, then." He released his own bottle, leaving it suspended in midair. After a few moments of hesitation, during which Jan felt that she herself was in total suspension, he moved to her side and put his arms around her. His first kiss seemed tentative. Jan responded much more forcefully, and when they came up for air he said, "First time in microgravity?"

"Yes."

"It's a bit different. Just follow my lead." Between kisses he began to remove her clothes, slowly and carefully. She did the same for him, glancing occasionally about her. She still saw no sign of a bed.

"Not needed in free-fall," he said, in answer to her unspoken question. "If we were in powered flight I would make a section of the floor turn into a waterbed. At the moment all we need are these." He drifted up to the ceiling. They were both naked, and as he rose past her Jan saw plenty of evidence of his excitement.

He returned holding two broad straps and laughed at the expression on her face. "Not for what you may be thinking. Maybe some other time, but these are to stop us drifting off into the walls." He bent and attached one to each of his ankles.

"What about me?" said Jan.

"You'll see." Paul straightened and embraced her again. They kissed and fondled each other for a few minutes, until Paul sighed, took his hands from Jan's breasts, and reached around to grasp the back of her thighs.

"I know this won't sound very romantic," he said, "but I have to get it out of the way. Newton's Third Law is more noticeable in space than it is on Earth. If we're to stay in contact, you need to put your legs round mine and lock them there. That's right. That's fine. Just let me do the work."

"I will." *And just don't let me do something stupid.* Jan closed her eyes and pressed her lips against his.

After a long minute when things didn't seem to be working, Paul at last found the right position. The lower parts of their bodies came into full contact and he grunted with satisfaction. They made love in silence for a long time, until Paul gasped, grunted, and thrust so hard that Jan's legs had trouble holding him in position.

He clung to her, panting and perspiring, while she caressed the back of his head. Finally he leaned back and stared into her eyes.

"How was it?" Jan asked.

"Great. Just great." Paul frowned. "Not so good for you, though. I know you didn't get there. Sorry, but I couldn't wait any longer."

"That's all right. I didn't expect to. Be honest with me. Wasn't it a bit difficult?"

"Well, yes. At first it was."

"I thought it might be. They say that the first time usually is."

"Of course it is." He smiled. "Zero-gee, the first time in space, all the body movements are different."

He saw her expression, and the smile left his face. "When you say the first time, you don't mean—" Their bodies were still locked together, but he pushed himself away from Jan so that he could stare down at himself. "My God. You do."

"It's all right. There's only just a few drops on you. A clumsy doctor took care of that during a physical when I was younger. You won't be hanging bloody sheets outside the ports."

Paul moved farther away from Jan, reached down, and released the straps from his ankles. He moved to a wall drawer and pulled out an object like a double sleeping bag. When he and Jan were snugly zipped up inside it he said, "This is quite a shock. You really were a *virgin?*"

"Don't look so surprised. We all start out that way. If you mean, what am I doing, a woman well over thirty and still not sexually experienced, then I don't have a good answer."

"It's nothing to do with age." Paul still seemed distressed. "But if I had known . . ."

"If you had known, then what? Would you have avoided me?"

"No!"

"You didn't exactly rape me, you know." Jan pulled him close to her again. "I was as keen for this to happen as you were. More keen, I bet. Is it all right for me to say that?"

"Of course it is. I'm, well, I guess I feel *honored.* I mean, that you would choose me to be the first. Why me?"

"You're a very attractive man. You seemed interested in me."

"I was. I am."

"I've been thinking about you ever since you greeted us as we came aboard. This seemed appropriate. You are, after all, the first mate."

He laughed at her weak joke, but he still looked upset. "Why now, after so many years?"

"You mean that I'm an antique?"

"Not at all. You are young and beautiful."

"Thank you. I'll accept that, even if I don't quite believe it. You ask, why now? It's all part of a feeling I've had ever since we lifted off from Earth. I've been exhilarated and excited, full of the conviction that everything was new and different and wonderful."

"No thanks to me. Next time, Jan, it will be better. I swear it. I was just too excited tonight." He frowned. "I hope there will be a next time."

"There had better be. Unless you are the original *Achilles'* heel. Paul, stop worrying. Tonight was just fine, and everything I've ever heard or read about this says it just gets better." She snuggled close to him. "I'm not asking for an instant repeat performance, so you can go to sleep if you want to. But I would like to be held, and maybe talk a bit if you feel up to it. I want to ask you a question."

"Sure." He pulled her head onto his shoulder and put his lips to her ear. He whispered, "Ask me anything."

"Do you pick out a different passenger on each trip?"

He started and pulled away. "Now Jan, that's really an unfair question. When I said, ask me anything—"

"You don't understand, Paul. I'm hoping that the answer is yes."

"Why? What difference does it make?"

"I'll rephrase the question, so it doesn't make you sound like a libertine. Have you had experiences in the past with other women passengers?"

He hesitated. "Yes, I have. But I still don't know why you ask. There's no chance at all of disease."

"That thought never entered my head." Jan nuzzled his neck. "I just like to feel that my needs are being attended to by someone with experience and expertise. I'm well aware that I don't have those myself. I wondered if you would notice when we began to make love."

"I had no idea. Everything seemed perfectly normal."

"Except for that first minute."

"I thought that was more me than you. People are different. There's always an adjustment to get the geometry right."

"The geometry feels just fine." Jan relaxed against his body. The sleeping bag provided warm intimacy. He had more chest hair than she expected, and she liked the soft tickle of it against her breasts. He also smelled different, a sexual odor which came as an unexpected pleasure. She closed her eyes in contented silence. Maybe she was all set to fall asleep herself, for certainly when he spoke his voice seemed to come from far away.

"I don't want to spoil the mood, because this is really pleasant. But I did have something else that I wanted to talk to you about. It may sound pretty ridiculous."

Jan said lazily, "You said, ask me anything. So I'll say, tell me anything."

"It's about Sebastian."

It was Jan's turn to stiffen. "What about him?"

"I know that you've looked after him almost all his life, and you care for him very much."

"Like a brother. There has never been one shred of sexual feeling between us."

"Once I had time to see you interact, I never thought there had been. You don't look at each other that way. And I understand that Dr. Bloom may be the person who has the most contact with him from now on. But because you've been so close for so long, you ought to hear this."

"Has Sebastian done something?"

"He has done nothing wrong. He spends lots of time wandering around the ship, staring at things and not saying anything."

"That's harmless enough."

"I think so, too. But it has made a few people uneasy, and they are reacting. There's been a rumor going around that he's a Jonah. Do you know what a Jonah is for ships in space?"

"I imagine that it's the same as it is for ships on the seas of Earth. Someone who brings bad luck."

"That's what they're saying. Sebastian Birch will bring bad luck to the *Achilles*."

"I never heard such nonsense. Sebastian wouldn't harm anyone or anything."

"I believe you, Jan. But I want you to know the wild talk that's been going around some of the crew and passengers, so you won't get a nasty surprise. It's nothing more than dumb superstition, but they say that with Sebastian Birch on board this ship will never make it to Ganymede. Somewhere along the way, no one knows how or where, the presence of Sebastian will lead the *Achilles* to disaster."

16

The model . . . a worrying new insight, burning to be tested.

A meeting with Prosper and Lena Ligon . . . top priority, they insist it can't be put off even for a day.

Kate Lonaker . . . cold as Charon, unsympathetic to any attempt at reconciliation, refusing to talk.

Travel notification . . . a trip to the Saturn system, with no explanation.

Alex was going mad. He had never felt himself under such multiple pressures. Somehow he had to impose logic and a set of priorities.

Prosper Ligon and his mother first. Alex composed the shortest message he could imagine: Meet four o'clock at Ligon HQ. Notify if not acceptable.

Next he checked the travel authorization. As soon as he saw the origin: Ligon Industries, he put the worry to the back of his mind. He would find out what it was about soon enough.

Now for the tough one. He called Kate.

She answered at once, as though she had been sitting waiting by her communications terminal.

"Yes?"

"I'm going to run the model again. I have a new idea, and to test it I'm going to DP Central. I would very much appreciate your assistance and insights."

"Very well. I will meet you there."

Still cold, still aloof. What was wrong with the woman? Would he make a big deal of it, if Kate had gone off and screwed somebody and she didn't even remember who?

Alex decided. Yes, he would mind. He would be totally pissed. He owed Kate a big apology, if only she would endure his company long enough to listen.

He hurried along to DP Central, where they would enjoy access to the highest computational priority and the best displays, courtesy of Magrit Knudsen. Somehow, Kate was there ahead of him.

"Kate, I just want to say—"

"I'm ready for work when you are. You tell me you have a new idea. What is it?"

So much for apologies. *Hell hath no fury like a woman scorned.* He hadn't exactly scorned her, but that logic wouldn't get him far. To work.

"I've reviewed the old results over and over. I'm still convinced that the model is basically correct."

"So you mean, a hundred years from now there will be no humans left, anywhere. Right. That's very reassuring."

"I don't believe that result. I think that the problem lies in the Seine."

"Two weeks ago you told me that the Seine would solve all our problems."

"All our *computational* problems. We have ample computing capacity for the first time ever, but the Seine is much more than simple computer power."

"Like what?"

"Like a huge number of external databases, online for the first time. We were careful not to introduce what we thought of as inappropriate exogenous variables into the model, but the Seine doesn't have that constraint. Anything that is not specifically ruled out is open for consideration. The trouble is, the Seine is so complex that we don't know what it includes and what it excludes. I believe that we have to do something radically different. We have to introduce our own exogenous variables, things that we believe are possible logical components of the future. We have to see how this affects the computed results."

Kate, for a change, didn't act like an ice princess. The lines of her face softened, and she stared directly at Alex. "But there could be a million things in the possible future. How are we supposed to know what to choose?"

"We assess possible events on the basis of our own estimates of their likelihood. We change the model to reflect it, and see what difference it makes to the results."

"I wouldn't know where to begin."

"Well, I think I do. The Seine doesn't try to predict the future, or make random assumptions. It uses only facts that are present somewhere in the System right now. If the computed future suggests the extinction of humanity, that's because those factors are already present *today*."

"Such as what?"

This was one that Alex wished he could avoid. "Such as the Commensals. They are basically human, but a thousand other life forms have been spliced into them. It occurred to me that the way we have been running the model, neither the computer nor the Seine data banks makes any distinction between a human and Commensal. We don't know if future population figures refer to humans, or Commensals, or both. If everyone in the System eventually elects to become a Commensal, then the model that we have may be predicting that the future holds no true humans. On the other hand"—Alex had to face an intolerable possibility—"maybe Commensals become the human norm, but they have a built-in flaw that causes them to die out."

A built-in flaw like guaranteed sterility, so that no one is reproducing anymore.

Kate began to nod agreement, then stared wide-eyed at Alex. "But if that's the case, then your mother—"

"I've already thought of that."

"Oh, Alex." She reached out as though to take his hand, then withdrew. "I'm really sorry. I hope that's not true."

"So do I." Alex saw his chance, and jumped in. "And I'm really sorry, too. I don't mean for my mother and the other Commensals, I mean for what I did. I know I screwed Lucy Mobarak, or Deirdre de Soto, or somebody. Maybe I screwed all of them. But they sabotaged me, I'm sure of it now, down in the Holy Rollers. The drinks were spiked. I had no idea what I was doing—I don't even remember it. That doesn't excuse what I did, but maybe it explains it. I want to say again, I'm sorry."

"Let's talk about all that later." But Kate reached out, and this time she did squeeze his hand. "For the moment we have to concentrate on the model. If it's the Commensals that are causing the trouble . . ."

. . . then we are in for a battle royal. The Commensals, and the Sylva Corporation that oversees their creation, between them have tremendous political clout. Kate didn't need to say that to Alex. His own mother was far from unique in her willingness to do anything to restore and maintain her youth and beauty.

"We're going to find out." Alex set to work at the console. "I'm setting up the model to treat Commensals and unmodified humans as separate but interacting populations." He turned to Kate. "Do you know, can someone who decides to become a Commensal change her mind, and have the process reversed to become a normal human?"

"I don't think so. I believe it's one-way only. If it is possible to undo it, I've never heard of a case where someone chose that option."

"So we'll assume it goes on like that." Alex set parameters so that any member of the human population could elect to become a Commensal. The human population changed by reproduction, by transfer to Commensal form, or by death. The Commensal population could decrease only through death. An all-Commensal solar system ultimately implied an empty solar system.

He glanced at Kate. His finger hovered over a final key. She nodded. "I can't think of anything more. Do it, Alex."

It was the power of a god. Alex pressed. At one touch of his finger, databases all across the System came into play. Within the computer, the separate Faxes that represented more than five billion humans (and now Commensals) began to live, die, love, hate, act and interact, and move around the solar system. Days sped by too fast to follow. As the years rolled on, the full panoply of solar system activity was revealed on the displays.

Most of Alex's attention focused on just two counts: the ratio of the number of Commensals to the total human population, and the human population itself.

The yearly aggregates came into view. By 2105, System population was a figure familiar from their previous runs: 5.6 billion. Commensals were less than one in ten thousand of humans. But the fraction was creeping up. In 2124, one percent of the human population of 7.6 billion had become Commensals. In 2134, that percentage was close to five percent.

"I think you're right, Alex." Kate was crowding close, no longer aloof and standoffish. "It's the damned Commensals."

Alex didn't think so. He could make the extrapolation in his head. The proportion of Commensals was increasing, but nowhere near fast enough to cause problems. With ninety-five percent of the total still human, and still actively breeding, the number of people or Commensals would never start to nosedive by 2150.

But here came 2140, and trouble. The conversion to Commensals were steady at five percent. The trouble lay in the human population. Birth rates were down, along with every other index of activity. Alex and Kate sat and watched in grim silence, right to the bitter end when in 2170 the number of humans hit a flat zero. A small population of Commensals lingered on for a few years, but by 2185 that count was also down to nothing.

"That's it." Alex smacked his fist down on the console, ending the run. "Exactly the same results as before. Now we know it's not the Commensals that cause the problem. Another idea bites the dust."

"That was just one thing to try." Kate didn't mention that in some ways she was relieved. The idea of a solar system filled with Commensals, and only Commensals, did not appeal to her. "We can examine the effect of other important variables."

"We could." Alex hesitated. Did he really want to go through with this? "But there's one other thing I'd like to do before we change variables. There is an alternate way of running the model itself, what I call Snapshot Interactive—SI—mode."

"I've never heard you mention it."

"That's because we've always stressed the need for repeatable runs. You need results that you can take up the line to Mischa Glaub and Tomas de Mises, and if you have to run again you'll always want the same answers."

"Damn right. Alex, I don't understand you. I know we run with a variety of possible inputs, but each run is deterministic. Except for database changes, we get the same run today as we did yesterday."

"That's not guaranteed in SI mode. There can be differences."

"I think you'd better be specific. Remember, I'll have the job of explaining all this to Mischa Glaub."

"I'll be as clear as I can. As you know, the big difference between my model and the ones developed in Pedersen's group is that I include a separate piece of code for every single individual in the solar system. Each person is represented by a Fax with some level of decision-making logic of its own. The interaction of all those human-simulator components makes up the complete model. The *average* properties, such as transportation activity or food needs, are not regarded as independent variables. They are constructed values, built up from all those billions of separate needs."

"I got that much from your briefing the other day. You're saying nothing new."

"I'm about to. When I said that individuals are represented in the model, I meant exactly that. Each person in the solar system census is in there, represented by anything from a Level One to a Level Five Fax. There's a Mischa Glaub in the model, also a Kate Lonaker, even Cousin Hector, though I bet his Fax is smarter than he is. Most important, there's an Alex Ligon."

"Most important to who?"

"Most important for what I'm proposing to do next. The SI mode allows a person to take the place of his or her own

Fax, *inside the model.* I've never done it before with the Seine in operation, but I've tried it with a reduced model in a limited environment. I know it's feasible. I'm going to enter the model, as myself. For me it will feel like just another VR environment, same as in the media shows." He gestured to one of the half-dozen VR helmets on the bench in front of the displays.

"Alex, you're out of your mind. Your model runs at umpteen-million times real-time."

"About a million, in SI mode."

"A million, then. So the model simulates a year every thirty seconds. There's no way your brain can possibly keep up."

"I won't even try. For most of the interactions, my Fax will be making decisions. Once a simulated year, I'll have thirty seconds to review where I am, make decisions, and hand control back to my Fax. I won't be able to change much, because my Fax isn't powerful or influential enough for that. But with me in the program, you lose exact repeatability."

"But why do it at all? What will you get that you can't see right here?" Kate gestured at the displays.

"I don't know. Immediacy? Perspective? Perhaps nothing at all. Don't worry, I've done this before. It was never very enlightening, because the model was oversimplified and aggregated so much that the setting felt bogus and artificial. I'm hoping it won't be that way now."

"Not artificial—when you're being jerked forward a year at a time, every half minute? Give me a break."

"I built in a smoothing function and a neural connector designed to help with that. It ought to be that I'll feel like I *remember* whatever my Fax has been experiencing." Alex picked up one of the VR helmets. "We can talk about all this when I come out. Once I wave my hand, start the model running."

"And then do what?"

"Watch, and wait. We're going to run for sixty years. That's half an hour in real-time. If I'm still in the helmet after that, drag it off me."

"Alex!" But the helmet was going on, and Kate's cry of protest sounded far-off and muffled. The inside of the VR helmet was totally black. The only sound was Alex's own breath in the oxygen supply tube.

He waved his hand. Nothing at all happened. He sat for a few seconds and was on the point of removing the helmet when he realized that this was exactly what he should expect. Time was blurring along in the computer model, but his first one-year snapshot was thirty seconds in the future.

It came to him not as some form of description or image, but as *memory*. He remembered the whole of the past year, but with a variable degree of detail. System politics were far-off and vague, while anything that affected him personally was clear. He had persuaded the bosses that his models were the right way to approach prediction, he had been promoted, and he had moved in with Kate—over the screams and protests of his mother and the rest of the family.

Was this the program, or mere wishful thinking? He was still trying to decide that when—*memories*—another year sprang full-blown into his mind.

So much for his smoothing function! It didn't seem to work at all. The merger of the Ligon and Mobarak families had taken place—but how and when? Who had married whom? Alex could not remember, although he was somehow sure that he himself was not married to Lucy-Maria.

Here was other news, confusing and muddled, coming from the farther reaches of the Jovian system. Signals had been received there, perhaps from the stars. It could mean the discovery of aliens. The message was being looked at—had been looked at—had been dismissed as bogus. Or had it? It still seemed to be there. Alex felt his own confusion beginning. The future was filled with an infinity of branch points, and the model could not pursue all of them. He had the nagging feeling that he disagreed with some of the program's choices, but before he could analyze his reasons—*memories*—another snapshot came pouring in.

Was this only three years out, or were multiple years somehow being crushed together? The solar system had escaped a great disaster that would have ended all life, from Mercury to Neptune and beyond. This was not the gradual dying-off that the model runs had predicted. This one would have been quick, extreme, and total. But it had not happened. So why was it here at all? The program was responsible. The non-event must have been on a high-probability path, otherwise it could not be in Alex's memories at all. He tried to dig for details and a better understanding, but he was too late. *Memories*. Something—war, natural disaster, technological failure?—on Earth. Discoveries on Triton, Neptune's giant moon. Loss of the Oort Cloud explorers. A dozen more events crowding all at once into his mind. He ought to have known this was impossible, even the highlights of a full year could not be comprehended in half a minute. Kate had been the realist, he had not. (Did they live together now? He could not say.) *Memories*. The tempo was increasing, a year was shrinking to nothing. What had happened to his thirty seconds per year? A trip to Venus—for what possible reason? A death, someone in the family. He could not tell who it was. A great rain of comets, sweeping in from the Oort Cloud and endangering the whole System. Was this the source of humanity's disaster? No, some form of deflection shield had operated. *Memories*. Of a meeting, with the population chart of the System spread out before him. Ten billion people—as many as had ever been predicted in the models. But the total was decreasing. *Mem-*

ories. His mother, face changing color and melting like hot wax. Cousin Juliana, shriveling, dying—along with all the Commensals? The data were not there. Destructive forces unleashed around the solar system, as powerful as they had been during the period of the Great War. But he saw only their shadow, an unrealized potential. Was this the warning of coming holocaust? *Memories.* They came not as individual images, but as a great collective tide. The Seine had collapsed, the Jovian worlds were uninhabitable, Mars did not communicate, battered outposts on the moons of Uranus clung on to diminished life. And Alex himself. Where was he? He had committed a major blunder in planning the model. He had not allowed for his own death. If his Fax "died" within the model, what would happen to the connection? Could he die too? *Memories.* The worlds of the solar system were dark. He sat on the outer fringes, alone, beyond the planets, beyond the Edgeworth-Kuiper Belt, looking in toward the weak spark of the distant Sun. *Memories.* Of solitude and silence. Had he come here hoping to be safe? He knew, through an unexamined accumulation of doomed memories, that his was the only life within light-years. How long had he been alone? How long would he remain here?

There hath he lain for ages, and will lie . . .

The VR helmet was ripped from his head. Light, worldfilling light so bright that he was forced to squeeze his eyes tightly shut, burned around him. He heard the voice of a stranger, calling through the effulgence.

"It's been more than half an hour, and you were mumbling to yourself. I couldn't understand what you were saying. I had to get you out. Alex? Alex? Are you all right?"

He was not all right. He had swept far forward in time, to the death of humanity and beyond. He had hovered alone on the rim of the universe. How could anyone be all right after that?

"I *knew* I shouldn't have let you do it," the voice said. "I'm a total bloody fool. Here. Sniff this."

An acrid vapor filled his nostrils. Alex gasped and gagged. His heart raced, he opened his eyes, and the room flickered and reeled around him.

"Alex!"

"Sa' right. I'm—mm—a' right."

"You don't sound it. Who are you? Tell me your name, where you are and who you are."

"I am Alex—Ligon." The room steadied. He was sitting hunched in a chair, with someone—Kate. Kate . . . who?— gazing down at him. "I'm—I—where am I? I've . . . been . . ."

"Alex! What happened to you? When I removed the VR helmet your eyes looked ready to pop and your pupils were all dilated."

Alex shook his head, not to disagree but to try to clear it. "Dunno. Can't think straight. Gimme a boost."

"No. Alex, that's a bad idea."

"Need it. Got to have it. Mental overload, too many futures. Too much, too fast."

"You'll regret it. You'll feel terrible later."

"Give it."

Alex closed his eyes and lay back. Hours seemed to pass before he felt the cool spray of the Neirling boost on his temple. The world inside his head steadied and came into focus.

He opened his eyes. Kate was frowning down at him.

"I'm all right, Kate. I'm fine. But it's going to take days to sort out what I experienced. My head was spinning around like a top. It's my own fault, I ought to have realized what would happen."

"And I ought to have forbidden you even to try. I thought you said that you had done this kind of experiment before."

"Not with the Seine running the show." Alex's pulse was beginning to slow. The Neirling boost had taken effect, and he would have at least three hours of mental clarity. He leaned back in his chair and rubbed his forehead. Everything from there to his brain stem had ached. It would ache again, when the boost lost its effect, but for the moment he felt he could understand—and explain—anything.

He said, "I'll tell you what I think was happening, but I may be wrong. The Seine has enough computational power to consider and select from thousands of branches at a time. A Fax is too simple to be employed in more than one future, but apparently a human isn't. I was catching glimpses of many possibilities—too many for me to handle."

"You've lost me, Alex."

"That's not surprising. I've never gone into those elements of the predictive model with you. I would have, but you insisted that I work on a briefing that Macanelly would follow."

"I did. But if you're suggesting that I'm a dimwit like Loring Macanelly . . ."

"No, not at all. It's just a question of where I put my time. I was trying to produce a simplified version for Macanelly, and that meant I had to leave some of the trickier elements out. Then we had to brief Mischa Glaub and Magrit Knudsen when we weren't expecting it, so I went with the same approach—"

"Information, Alex. I need *information*. What did you feel you had to leave out?"

"All the probabilistic elements of the model."

"Then you're right, we have never discussed any such thing. You've always insisted that your model is *deterministic*. Unless you are in your Snapshot Interactive mode with a human in the loop, it will produce the same results every time."

"That's true. It will. But that doesn't mean there are no probabilistic elements." He felt a mild irritation at Kate's slowness of comprehension.

"Alex, now you've got *my* head spinning like a top. Back up, take it easy, and remember who you're talking to. I'm not Loring Macanelly, but I'm not boosted and I'm no genius when it comes to models."

"I'll do my best." Alex remembered a piece of advice from the leading scientist of the last century: *An explanation should be as simple as possible, but no simpler.* It wouldn't help to quote that now to Kate.

"I'm going to use an analogy. I was afraid to do that with Loring Macanelly, because from everything you've told me he'd not know how to distinguish an analogy from the real thing. But it's the way I often think of the predictive model.

"Imagine that our model is playing a game of chess, and it's the model's move. It knows the layout of the board pretty well at the present time, but the board isn't the usual one with just sixty-four squares and at most thirty-two pieces; our board is the whole extended solar system, with at least five billion humans and any number of computers and natural features. The model has to take into account all the actions and interactions of all the elements, and then decide how the board is likely to look one move ahead. Let's say, one move ahead means one day from now. The opponent—in this case, humanity and Nature—makes a move. Then the model has to decide how the board will look at that point, which is two days ahead. After that the opponent moves again, and again, and again. The model has to decide in each case what the board is likely to look like. It is making a prediction."

Kate was nodding—a little uncertain, but still a nod.

Alex went on, "The best human chess players can look ten

or even twelve moves deep. They have an idea what the board might look like that far ahead, and they make their next move accordingly. How do they do it? Well, one thing we know for sure is that they don't do it blindly. They also don't do it by evaluating every possible move that their opponent might make, and choosing the best one for them. There isn't enough time in the universe for a human player to adopt such an approach, even though it was the method used by the earliest and most primitive chess-playing programs. What the human player does, based on instinct and experience, is to assign a *probability* of success to particular sequences of moves, taking into account every reasonable move that the opponent might make. Those sequences with a low probability of success are dismissed. They don't even make it to the level of conscious consideration. The high-probability sequences are examined and compared. Finally, the player makes a move. That move is the move that offers the best chance of winning, *given all the moves that the opponent might choose to make in the future.*

"The predictive program faces the same problem as the human chess player, only worse. It doesn't know what the 'opponent'—the natural universe, plus the five billion or more human 'pieces'—will do, day after day after day. Even with all the computing power available in the Seine, a short-term prediction would run to the end of the universe. So the model, like the human chess player, is forced to work with probabilities. And like the human chess player, it rules out the low-probability futures, unless we insist, via exogenous variables, that it *must* consider them. If we do that, the model automatically converts that low-probability future to a high-probability one. Even then, when we go farther into the future the case that we insisted be considered may drop in probability, if the exogenous variable was introduced at only a single point in time.

"From the point of view of the model, there never is a single future. There are huge numbers of possible futures, branching off and diverging from each other the farther ahead we look in time. What we see reported as *the* future is simply the one to which the model assigns the highest probability." Alex paused. "You don't look happy."

"I'm not happy. You are telling me that we went ahead and presented a briefing to my boss and my boss's boss and my boss's boss's boss, talking as though what we had was gospel brought back from the mountain. Now you're saying what they heard was just one of a billion trillion possibilities."

"No. The model is much smarter than that. All possible futures will progress through time, and as they proceed they will diverge from each other. That's inevitable. Think of the futures as being like photons of light, forming a cone that gradually widens as the light travels farther from its source. But if you sum *all* the probabilities for *all* the futures, you must get unity—*some* future must happen. The model considers the thousand futures for which the computed probabilities are the greatest, and makes a measure of dispersion. How much has the cone of those probable futures widened over time? If the number it calculates exceeds a pre-set value, the model will return a message that with these parameters, the future is indeterminate."

"But that never happens. At least, is hasn't happened in any runs that I've ever seen."

"That's good news, not bad. It means that all likely futures are rather similar, which is a reason for having confidence in our model. Implausible futures damp out over time, unless we insist on forcing them back in via exogenous variables.

What I didn't expect, and what I had trouble handling when I was in the Interactive mode, is that I would be able to sense other futures—maybe even improbable ones—as the program was running. They hadn't had enough time to damp out." Alex could feel them stirring again inside his head. Comet showers, disintegrating Commensals, the discovery of aliens, mysteries on Triton . . .

"So the most probable futures are much the same as each other," Kate said. "You were still interacting with the model at the end. You must have seen them. What were they like?"

She was anxious but hopeful. Alex for one moment considered giving her the answer she wanted to hear, but the run records would reveal the truth.

"Nothing to offer us comfort," he said. "Exactly the same result as before: a century from now, no humans survive. The solar system will be empty and lifeless."

17

Three hours after Alex emerged from the unnatural high of the Neirling boost, his brain felt like a squashed melon. It would take days to sort out the flood of information dumped into him, even if he were not in a boost trough. He was in the worst possible condition to attend a difficult family meeting, and Kate hadn't been slow to tell him so.

"I've never heard of anything so stupid." She had forced him to eat a bowl of soup and now she was sitting at one end of the sofa with his head cradled in her lap, glaring down at him. "You ought to be tucked up safe in bed."

"I wish I was. Don't I just." Alex lay full-length on the couch. "But Kate, I'm committed to this. I promised the family."

"Screw the family. They're a selfish lot, they never do anything for you."

"I don't *want* them to do anything for me. They tried for years to give me jobs that I didn't like in Ligon Industries. I'm here to *escape* from them." The painkillers that he had taken didn't seem to be working. They had merely added to the boost slump and dulled even farther his ability to think.

"But I must go to this meeting. I told them I would be there at four."

"Then let me call and tell them that you *won't* be there at four. I'll be happy to do that for you."

He was sure she would. Her anger had not lessened since his apology, but it seemed to have transferred from Alex to the rest of his family.

"Kate, if you talk to Prosper Ligon or my mother, you won't just say I can't make the appointment. You'll flame them. And then you'll lose your job."

"Nonsense. I won't lose my job."

Alex noted that she did not deny that she was likely to cuss them out. "I'm telling you," he said. "Your job will be in danger. It won't happen through any direct route, or in a way we can do anything about. Mysterious pressures will drift down from somewhere higher up. Ligon Industries have been around for a long time. Even the family *names* go back centuries."

"Huh."

Which Alex read as a sign of agreement. Kate was highly savvy when it came to the realities of interaction between government and industry. She knew better than he how much an old-line and well-connected company could command in the way of political influence.

He sat up. "It's past three. I have to go."

Kate scowled as he groped for his shoes, but she didn't try to keep him. "Just be firm with them," she said, as he prepared to leave. "Tell them no. They can't make you."

Which just proved how little she understood the Ligon family. But Kate was watching him closely, and he was careful not to put on any of the traditional clothes normally considered necessary for a family meeting.

She nodded approval. "That's right. I say, if they don't treat you right then screw your family. Give them hell, sweetheart. I know you feel terrible, but remember this: even with your brains coming out of your ears you're still three times as smart as Cousin Hector."

Being smarter than Hector was small consolation for anything. Far more important was the *sweetheart* and Kate's quick kiss on the way out.

The long ride up from Kate's apartment to Ligon Corporate went in a blur. Alex surfaced only once from his stupor, when a flickering sign drifted past him on one of the rapid transit corridors.

Exciting news!
Exclusive to Paradigm.
Secret message to Ganymede Central!
Aliens on the way!
An informed source reveals that a message from
the stars has been forwarded from the Jovian L-4
station, announcing that aliens are coming to the
solar system. Will they bring peace? Will they
bring war? Visit *Paradigm Outlet* NOW for full
details!

Alex felt no temptation to obey the command to seek a connection to the Paradigm Outlet. The announcement seemed more like a pointer to the inside of his own head. One of the "futures" considered and discarded by the prediction program had been the discovery of messages from aliens. It must have been thrown out in favor of a more probable future, but it had occurred very early during the run. Could it have been *this* early, on the same day as the run was made?

Should he change his mind and tune in? How old was the "secret message" that Paradigm was shouting about? He knew it was one of the most sensational of the Outlets, where "exciting news" could easily be the rehash of something decades old.

Whatever he did would have to wait, because he was approaching the bronzed double doors of Ligon Corporate. He stared in through the eye-level camera, was recognized from his retinal pattern, and waited for the heavy doors silently to swing open. The Level Three Fax was waiting there, but also to his surprise was Uncle Karolus Ligon.

Normally Alex's uncle had no time for him. Today he examined Alex's paler-than-paper face, gave a broad wink, and said "Been getting the old leg over, then? She must have been quite a tiger from the looks of you," and led a mystified Alex through to the conference room.

Only five positions were marked out at the marble-topped oval table, including a seat for Alex. That was a bad sign. It meant that only the most senior family members would be present. In addition to Alex—who was decidedly *not* senior—he saw Lena, Uncle Prosper, Uncle Karolus, and Great-aunt Cora. There was one significant omission.

"Where's Great-aunt Agatha?"

He addressed the question to his mother, but it was Prosper Ligon who answered. "Agatha is indisposed."

"You mean she's *sick*. She can't be."

Great-aunt Agatha, as she would readily point out, was one of the Commensal program's biggest success stories. Five years ago, she had been a weak and wasted centenarian. Now, at age one hundred and ten, she enjoyed an active social and sexual life.

Prosper nodded his ancient donkey head. "I am sorry to say that is so. Agatha is sick. We have yet to learn how sick."

His tone was mournful, but Alex saw a gleam of yellowed teeth. Great-aunt Agatha had been widely advertised by Sylva

Commensals in their promotional material. A picture of her before and after the conversion to a Commensal, with the note: Which would you rather be: young-looking and healthy, or old and sick?

It was obvious how Prosper Ligon's thoughts and hopes were running. If Great-aunt Agatha were really sick—or, better yet, died—that would knock the stuffing out of Sylva Commensals' sales. And Sylva was one of the companies whose growth had pushed Ligon down toward the bottom of the top ten corporations in the System.

Prosper went on, "The condition of Agatha is not, however, relevant to the reason for this meeting. Alex, I am sorry to tell you that we have received a most disturbing report from Cyrus Mobarak. Before we begin, would you like to make a statement?"

A statement about what? Alex glanced at each of the faces, and received no enlightenment. Uncle Karolus gave him another wink.

"I don't know what I'm supposed to make a statement about."

"Very well. If you choose to feign ignorance, so be it. The other day, you went with your mother to meet Cyrus Mobarak and his daughter, Lucy-Maria. While Lena and Mobarak were briefly absent, it seems that you persuaded Lucy-Maria to go with you on an expedition to the lower Ganymede levels. Does the name 'Holy Rollers' mean anything to you?"

"Yes. She took me there."

"Lucy-Maria states otherwise. At the Holy Rollers Club, she maintains that you, without her knowledge, placed some form of behavior-modifying drug into an otherwise harmless drink. She remembers nothing of subsequent events, until she was discovered by security guards in a private room. She was naked, she had been sexually assaulted, and tests revealed the presence of multiple addictive drugs within her body. She was carried home, where she told her father that although she cannot state with absolute conviction that you were the guilty party, she spoke only a few words to anyone else present at the club. Would you now like to make a statement? Would you, for instance, like us to request that a DNA test be performed to establish that you were not the person who forced himself onto her?"

Alex shook his head. "Forcing yourself" onto—or into—Lucy-Maria Mobarak would be an impossibility, because she was always at least two steps ahead of you. He would get nowhere telling his family that. As for the DNA test, chances were better than even that he would fail. He wasn't sure how many people he'd had sex with that night, but he was fairly sure that it was more than one.

Prosper Ligon, staring down at the tabletop as though addressing it rather than Alex, went on, "If you have nothing more to offer on your own behalf, we are forced to assume your guilt." Great-aunt Cora gave Alex a stony and accusing glare. Lena Ligon said, "My dear, I'm so disappointed in you," and Uncle Karolus said, "How was she, then?"

"Needless to say," Prosper Ligon continued, "Cyrus Mobarak now considers Alex Ligon as a dissolute rake, totally unsuitable as a marriage partner for his innocent daughter."

The word "innocent" finally got to Alex. His head was aching worse than he ever remembered it, and he was being crucified for nothing. He remembered Kate's advice. *Screw your family. Give them hell.* But they were screwing him! He burst out, "His *innocent* daughter! Did Lucy say I was her first fuck ever? Because if she did, that's a total lie. I bet she's had more men up her than the Ganymede central elevator."

Great-aunt Cora gasped, Uncle Karolus guffawed, and Prosper Ligon said acidly, "We neither inquired of Cyrus Mobarak

regarding his daughter's previous sexual experience, nor do we
intend to. The simple fact of the matter, Alex Ligon, is that
you have failed the family. If we hope to achieve a union with
Mobarak's empire, we must seek it through other methods.
And fortunately, such an avenue appears to be available. Lucy-
Maria Mobarak is, it seems, very taken with your cousin, Hector."

"Hector!" Alex said. "But he's a total idiot!"

"Now then," Karolus said. "That happens to be my son
you're talking about. Not that I disagree with you. But Cyrus
Mobarak is a doting father, and if things work out he'll go
along."

"If?" Prosper glared. "This *if* is news to me. I thought
Mobarak's consent had already been given."

"It's not him. It's her."

"Lucy-Maria is balking?"

"Not exactly. But somebody put a half-witted idea in her
head. She says she wants Hector to 'prove himself.' "

"Prove he is able to sire children?"

"Good God, no. If all she wanted was proof of his fertility,
I could offer plenty. I'm paying for his little mistakes all over
Ganymede. No, she wants him to perform some great and
noble deed."

"What sort of deed?"

"The mind boggles." Uncle Karolus scowled. "It's not like
he can ride off on a horse somewhere and fight a dragon.
Hector says he wants to think about it and come up with
something valuable for the family, all by himself. Except that
thinking is what he's worst at. Alex there is the one who
thinks."

"To remarkably little avail." Prosper Ligon turned again to
Alex. "You owe the family some exceptional service as com-
pensation for what you did."

"I didn't do anything that Hector hasn't done a hundred times."

"Comparison with your cousin will not help your case. He at least is doing his best for the family. I will tell you exactly what we expect of you. We discussed this before you arrived." Prosper looked around the table for the confirming nods of agreement, and went on, "You were present at our last full meeting, when the decision was made to accept the contract for Phase Two of the *Starseed* contract. Our profit for this work—and, indeed, possibly the very survival of Ligon Industries—depends upon the rights to operate down to and within the atmosphere of Saturn. Those rights reside with the lease on the minor moon Pandora. Do you recall any of this, or were you daydreaming of lustful pleasures throughout the meeting?"

"You are confusing me with my sex-mad cousins, Rezel and Tanya. I remember perfectly well what was said at the meeting. It was Rezel and Tanya who were supposed to contact the present leaseholder and fuck him until he didn't know which way was up or what day of the week it was. I was only a third-string back-up. What happened? Did the nympho twins strike out?"

Bad language and sexual references had no effect on Prosper Ligon. The old donkey's head gave a more-in-sorrow-than-in-anger shake, and his uncle said, "Insults to fellow family members cannot compensate for your own failings, Alex. Do you deny that you have family duties and family responsibilities?"

"I have always done my absolute best for this family. The very fact that I am here, where I have no wish to be, proves that."

"Very good. You now have an opportunity to prove it once again. Rezel and Tanya, for whatever reason"—Prosper Ligon coughed drily—"were unsuccessful in arranging to meet with the current leaseholder of Pandora. From certain rumors that we have heard, concerning the interests and nature of the leaseholder, we believe that you have a better chance of success. We wish you to take on this assignment."

It was no surprise to Alex—the mysterious ticket to the Saturn system had been a pretty obvious clue. "You mean because he's interested in computers and computer models? If he's really reclusive, that won't be enough. There are tens of millions of modelers in the System, and he won't agree to see any of them. He'll surely refuse to see me." Alex thought of the predictive model in its present disastrous condition, and went on, "Even if he would see me, I can't possibly go anywhere at the moment. My work is at a critical stage."

Lena Ligon shook her head, and said in her sweetest and most reasonable voice, "Alex, dear Alex. Give us some credit for knowing what we are doing."

Prosper Ligon raised his head and added, "Your mother is far wiser than you. She realizes, as apparently you do not, that Ligon Industries has connections and influences that extend to the highest levels of Jovian system government. Will you accept the truth of that statement?"

Alex has stressed that very point to Kate Lonaker, little more than an hour before. He nodded.

"We feel sure that a leave of absence for you to pursue the question of the Pandora lease will be approved. What we ask of you is that you visit the current leaseholder, and argue our case."

"Suppose that he won't meet with me?"

"We have evidence to suggest that he will. Once again, we possess corporate resources which you seem to undervalue and underestimate."

Alex was ready to reply—he was going to say that he would take the assignment, in the hope that would let him escape from the meeting—when the door leading into the conference room crashed open.

Everyone turned. Great-aunt Agatha stood on the threshold. Her clothes were normal enough in style, but her blouse lacked the usual carefully-chosen brooches and hung open to reveal her carefully sculptured bosom. "Started without me, eh?" she said. "The decline of manners is a symptom of this decadent age." She walked forward briskly enough, but with an odd and crab-like sideways motion.

As she took her place at the table, Uncle Karolus said abruptly, "Thought you were sick."

"Nonsense. Now, what's the first order of business?"

She was addressing Prosper Ligon, but it was Lena Ligon who answered. "Agatha. There's something wrong. You're *yellow*."

As soon as his mother said that, Alex could see it, too. Great-aunt Agatha's skin had a slightly sallow tinge, but it was her eyes that really showed it. Usually the whites were absolutely clear, with a hint of blue that spoke of perfect health. Those whites were now a muddy yellow, almost buff in color.

"Nonsense," Agatha said again. "Lena, you are imagining things."

"You told me you were sick." Prosper Ligon walked around the table toward her. "You were supposed to go to Sylva Commensals so they could take a look at you. Did you go?"

"I did not. Complete waste of time. I feel fine." Agatha placed her hands on her right side just below the rib cage. She was pressing there, and Alex noticed a slight tremble in her fingertips.

He glanced at the others. They seemed to have no idea what was wrong. "Aunt Agatha, are you feeling any pain?"

"Of course not."

And of course, her answer should have been no surprise. One advantage of being a Commensal was that one of the interior organisms took care of pain symptoms, while others repaired any damage.

"It's the parent schistosome," Alex said. And, when the others stared, "The big wormy thing that sits above the liver in a Commensal. There's something wrong with it. Maybe it's even dead. Look at her symptoms. She has jaundice, because the liver isn't breaking down bile correctly; and I think there's swelling in the liver, where she's pressing herself."

"Nonsense. I am perfectly fine." But Great-aunt Agatha's words lacked their usual crisp diction, and she was bending over sideways in her seat.

Prosper said, without any hint of haste, "This meeting is now adjourned. Karolus, Alex, give me a hand. Cora, make an emergency call."

"Where to?"

"Sylva Commensals, of course. This is their responsibility."

Karolus said, "Ha! Sylva. Trillions in damages," and went at once to Agatha's other side.

Alex was slower to move. He had been watching his mother. On her perfect face, for the first time in his life, he saw undisguised alarm and terror.

"They say she's going to be all right."

Kate paused with the lighted taper in her hand. "*They* being who?"

"Sylva Commensals. Apparently the death of one of the big schistosomes is rare, but it has happened before. They'll take it out of Aunt Agatha, put in a replacement, and she'll be as good as new."

Kate lit the candle and blew out the taper. "They more or

less have to say that, don't they? Either things are fine, or else they admit there's something fundamentally dangerous about becoming a Commensal."

She had greeted Alex on his return with an explosive, "I've wondered and wondered. You've got to tell me *everything*." More revealing than her words were her clothes and the condition of her apartment. She was wearing a tight pantsuit of powder blue, showing off her figure and enhancing the color of her eyes. The lights were dim, and a casserole was steaming in the kitchen oven. Where Alex would sit was a bottle of whiskey and a flagon of Callistan ice melt, drinks that he preferred to any wine in spite of Kate's efforts to "educate" him. The table was decorated with candles, sprigs of ivy, and fronds of lady's slipper. Alex, knowing that Kate was a great believer in the language of flowers, sneaked a look at a reference database while she was off removing the casserole from the oven. *Sprig of ivy, with tendrils: assiduous to please.* And *Lady's slipper: win me and wear me.* Both of which suited him very well. He wasn't going to mention the recent past if she didn't.

"I think that being a Commensal may be dangerous," he said. "I received some very odd visions about them when I was inside the predictive model." He decided that was the right way to put it. He had been *inside* the model when it was running, and *visions* was a better word than facts. What he retained after he left the model was a great jumble of impressions, perhaps scrambled in time.

"I'll tell you one thing, though," he went on. "After we left Sylva Commensals, Uncle Karolus did a funny little hop-step. 'They're in shit up to their necks and they can't duck,' he said. 'We have recordings of the meeting, with Agatha walking like a lame crab and yellow as a banana. I'll make sure that the pictures are with the media tomorrow—leaked, of course. We'll insist we have no idea how they got out from Ligon Corporate.' "

"Dirty tactics." Kate refilled Alex's glass. "What did I tell you? Wherever you encounter gobs of money, you'll find shady business methods to go with it."

They were sitting opposite each other at the little table, small enough so that knee contact was inevitable. "All right," Kate went on. "I don't want just the high points. Give me details, the whole thing. Every second from the moment you arrived at Ligon Industries until you walked back in that door."

It was a tall order, but Alex did his best. He ate a fair amount, drank a lot, and talked steadily while Kate sipped wine and listened in silence. She frowned once, when he said he hadn't denied having sex with Lucy-Maria, or whoever else it might have been, on his disastrous night at the Holy Rollers; but Kate clapped her hands with delight when he told her that he had recalled her advice, *Screw your family. Give them hell*, and described his own outburst.

"Bravo, Alex. Exactly what they deserved."

"Maybe. But I didn't do so well later. If it's approved for me to take a few days leave I'm pretty much committed to trying to see this weirdo who hangs out on Pandora. I don't want to do it, but I didn't know how to say no."

"Don't give it a second thought. I'll pass word up the line that your presence here is absolutely vital. Which it is."

"I'm not sure. Prosper Ligon sounded pretty confident. He usually makes sure of his positions ahead of time." Alex had another thought. He had covered everything from the time he arrived at Ligon Corporate, but not the period while he was traveling there. "Kate, I saw a news blurb while I was heading up for the meeting, about some sort of alien contact.

It made me think of something similar in the predictive model. Have you heard anything about alien messages?"

"There was nothing on the standard channels."

"There wouldn't be. This was a Paradigm special."

"Then it was more than likely garbage. Want me to check it out?"

"If you would." Alex didn't say, *if you can*. Kate could network in a way that he would never master. "Not now, though."

"Certainly not now. Have you finished eating?"

"Yes."

Kate rested her hand on the top of the bottle. "And drinking?"

"Not quite." Alex realized that his head no longer ached. He felt good, physically and mentally. He took the bottle from her. "One more, for medicinal purposes. You know the origin of the word 'whiskey'? It comes from *usquebaugh*, which meant 'water of life.' The old-timers back on Earth knew what they were talking about."

"Just don't drink too much. You know what another of your old-timers said about alcohol? 'Liquor increases the desire but ruins the performance.' "

Which disposed of any question as to what would happen next. Kate might be worried, but she didn't need to be. Beneath the table, Alex gripped her knee between his. This had been a long and multiply-horrible day, but the night would be better.

To borrow from more of the old-timers, *all's well that ends well*. And then there was, *Unborn tomorrow and dead yesterday, why fret about them if today be sweet?* Not to mention *a lecherous head begets a lecherous tail*.

He didn't realize that he was speaking aloud until Kate reached out and very firmly removed the bottle from his hand.

"When you start babbling quotations, it means you've had quite enough."

"I'm feeling great."

"That's all right. Feeling great is allowed." Kate put the bottle off on a side table and reached out a hand to raise Alex to his feet. "What isn't allowed is Alex Ligon, tomorrow morning, telling me that he's not sure who he had sex with tonight."

18

The buzz was surely Magrit Knudsen, trying to reach him again. It would be about the infernal Ligon family, and Bat's need to meet with them, but Bat had taken all the irritation he could stand for one day. He set a minimal data-rate line to the outside world, designed to infuriate and frustrate any human caller, and retreated into the safety and solitude of the Keep.

It was time to review the four-sigma list.

The list was prepared automatically by Bat's own programs in their constant system-wide search for anomalies improbable enough to be flagged. The "four-sigma" designation was, as Bat well knew, misleading. It suggested that he was interested in items with only one chance in more than ten thousand of occurring, which was quite true. But the name also assumed that such events followed a normal distribution, which was surely not true.

Bat was too lazy to invent a better name. He knew what he wanted from the program and in any case the next step was all his, incapable of being quantified in any manner that he could describe. He sought *connections* between items on the four-sigma list, to multiply chances and turn a less than one in ten thousand probability into a one in three hundred million improbability.

It had been a few days since he examined the list, and several new items caught his eye.

1) Someone was requesting of Transportation Central a high-speed passage between the Jovian L-4 and L-5 points, an event unprecedented in the program's experience, and in Bat's also. Argus Station to Odin Station? He marked a query to keep track of the flight.

2) A rapid five percent drop had taken place in the corporate value of Sylva Commensals, coincident with a statement of record high earnings. That was certainly an anomaly, in that it made no apparent sense, but Bat knew better than to spend time wondering about it. While still in his teens he had concluded that the value placed on a corporation by investors was nothing but a random walk modified by inside information.

3) A solar flare of record size had occurred, doubling the intensity of the solar wind through the whole system for four days. Bat ignored that one, too. Certainly, it was an anomalous event, but even at his most paranoid Bat did not suspect the Sun of active involvement in human affairs.

4) Nothing new at the Master level had been posted on the Puzzle Network for the past six days.

That made Bat sit up and take notice. He had been too preoccupied with his own worries to monitor Puzzle Network activity recently, but he had never known such a long interval without at least one new Master-level problem. Something must be going on, and he was quite annoyed that he was not involved. Again, he marked a query to keep track and see when the pattern ended. If it did not, the program would alert him in a day or two.

5)   Fewer live human births had been reported for one day of the previous month than at any time in a decade. Bat took a quick look at the numbers on the days before and after, and wiped it off the list. He was seeing a simple consequence of the laws of probability. Statistical maxima and minima had to occur on some day, and only if a pattern were displayed was it worth further study.

He was all set to strike the next item also—huge Io volcanic activity, surely correlating with the solar flare—when a slow, gurgling voice emerged from the speaker attached to the low-data rate external line.

L—e—t m—e i—n.

No human could slow a speech rate like that, and remain intelligible. Bat stepped up the data rate on the line. "Mord?"

"Who do you think?" said an acerbic voice. "Come on, give me a decent line rate."

"Not while I'm in the Keep environment. It will take a minute to close off the Keep, then I'll bring you in on a Seine connection."

"Sure, don't bother to hurry. A second of time at your clock rate only makes me feel like I'm waiting a year."

"I have little sympathy. You are multi-tasking, and we both know it. Do you have useful information for me?"

"Of course not." The Keep had closed, the Seine was open, and Mord's scowling, long-nosed face appeared on the display. "I'm here simply for the pleasure of your company."

"As I am for yours. Sarcasm does not become you. What have you learned?"

"You go first. What do you have?"

"Concerning Nadeen Selassie and the boy child whom she had with her?"

"You got it. We're not talking Santa Claus here."

"I examined orbital geometries, and with a high level of probability their destination when they left the asteroid Heraldic was Mars. The ship that they were on had a planetary landing capability, which is itself significant. *However*"—Bat held up his hand, restraining any possible interruption from Mord—"Mars could have been no more than a stopping-off point. Mars record-keeping returned to normal surprisingly quickly. We can say with certainty that no one corresponding in physical description to Nadeen Selassie was present on that planet, five years after the Great War."

"So they died on Mars, or they got away. Either option, we lost 'em again."

"Perhaps not. I took this one step further. Assume that they left Mars at some time during the three-year interval following their departure from Heraldic. What, then, would be their possible destination? We can rule some out, very easily. A return to the Belt, in its devastated condition, would have meant certain death. They could have traveled out to the Jovian system, but their arrival would certainly have been noted. Even if they went to one of the refugee camps on Callisto, their presence and condition would have been remarked. I searched the records, and found no sign of anyone who could have been Nadeen Selassie. Anywhere beyond the Jupiter system, such as one of the Saturn moons, would at the end of the Great War have been unable to permit their survival. All of which seems to leave only one possibility."

Mord said in a rasping voice, "Earth. Son of a bitch, they went to Earth. She must have been crazy. The damned planet was a heap of rubble."

"Less crazy, perhaps, than desperate. Again, I examined the orbital mechanics. Earth would have been relatively easy compared with any of the other choices that I have mentioned. Also, Earth did not suffer total devastation. The northern hemisphere was destroyed, but the southern one survived."

"Except that if they'd landed there, somebody would have made a note of it. Their arrival would be in the records. I'm assuming it wasn't, or you'd have got to it at once and wouldn't be stringing me out like this."

"No such arrival was recorded. That says to me that the ship must have landed in the northern hemisphere."

"In among all the teratomas that the Belt had dropped in? You've gotta be kidding. They'd be worse off there than out on the surface of the Moon."

"Not so. Survivors were picked up in the northern hemisphere. Not many, and no one who corresponds in age and description to Nadeen Selassie. However, several thousand people were recovered."

"That's a lot."

"Not if we restrict our attention to small children, which at this point we can logically do. I queried the data banks for all below the age of ten who were recovered on the surface of Earth's northern hemisphere anywhere in the appropriate time period."

"Bat, I'm impressed. You've actually been *working*. And here's me thinking all this time you were sitting in there playing with yourself."

"I have, as you say, been working. And now it is your turn to do so, because I am unable to proceed farther."

"How come?"

"Recalling what you had told me of abnormalities revealed in the autopsy on Heraldic of the girl child, I sought to obtain medical records of all the children rescued after the Great War in Earth's northern hemisphere. I have their names, but other records were not available to me by any form of direct-access link. They are protected by irritating considerations of personal privacy. You, however, are able to approach the problem from a variety of angles . . ."

"I got you. I can slither in most places. I'll see what I can do. Now it's my turn. When I first arrived here you asked me what I had."

"And?"

"I took a different tack. You've been babbling on for ages about the Mother Lode of weapons. I decided to go off and take a look for it. I knew there was no hope in the old and established databases, because you and the other Great War buffs have gone through them for years. If I was going to find something, the place to look was in all the new, small data-bases that are coming online with the Seine's search ma-chines."

"And did you find it?" Bat's voice betrayed a rare excite-ment.

"No such luck. That would be too much to hope for. But I did discover some very odd bits and pieces. For instance, I found Nadeen Selassie in at least a dozen places. Most of them were just personnel lists involving Belt weapons programs. There were two odd exceptions. The first was in a list of something called *planetary weapons*. I'll leave you the list, so you can make your own decision as to what it represents, but it looks as though the words 'planetary weapons' were used to distinguish them from free space weapons. It's still a funny designation, because most weapons can be used anywhere, ei-ther down on the planetary surface, or out in space."

"Unless a weapon is designed to attack something you don't find out in space—plants, maybe, or animals. The universal disassemblers down on Mars were like that."

"Could be. Except that the disassemblers were on a different Belt list, of weapons designed for use against personnel and equipment. But there was something stranger still on another list. According to this one, Nadeen Selassie had a new weapon *fully finished and tested* before the end of the Great War. It was classified as a weapon of planetary destruction. You'd think it would be just the kind of thing that the Belt leaders would have used on Earth or Mars, or even one of the populated moons of Jupiter. So here's my question: why *didn't* they use it? If it really was a weapon that could completely destroy a planet, that would have been enough to end the war at once, with the Belt the winner the first time it was used."

"Perhaps a full-scale version was never produced. You say only that it was tested."

"No. Apparently a production version was ready for use, complete with a delivery system."

Bat closed his eyes and sat in silence for a long time, so long that Mord finally said, "Hey, are you going to sleep on me?"

"By no means." Bat opened his eyes. "I am as lacking for an explanation as you are. A weapon, capable of destruction on a planetary scale, finished, tested, and ready for use. And yet, not used. It might be tempting to argue that the Belt leaders refrained from employing so terrible a weapon for humanitarian reasons, but everything we know of the Great War tells us that no such charitable motive can be ascribed to the leaders of the Belt war effort. They would have killed every human on the inner planets and all through the Jovian system, if it allowed them to win the war."

"So you agree with me. We got us a mystery."

"A mystery, indeed, and one that would be of high abstract interest, were it not for my suspicion—my conviction, even—that this weapon was not destroyed. It left the belt with Nadeen Selassie, traveled with her to the asteroid Heraldic, and is now—where?"

"You got me. I'll let you wrap your head around that one while I see if I can crack the data on Earth's medical records. Anything else? Otherwise, I'm out of here."

"I will only repeat my earlier warning. Take care. The whole computing and communication profile of the System has changed since the Seine came into operation. I can detect a substantial difference, without being able to define or quantify it."

"Same here, but more so. I used to move around freely, now it's look before you leap. I never relocate or access a new data file without checking everything beforehand. Look for me back here in a week or less. If I'm not, you'll know that something got me. Trouble is, you won't know what."

Mord's squint-eyed image vanished from the display, leaving Bat oddly worried. Mord was only a program; far more sophisticated than most programs, true, but still no more than a few million lines of logic and code.

On the other hand, could you say much more than that about human consciousness? The loss of Mord would be mourned, as much as the loss of any human. And the blank display, doorway to the Seine, suddenly seemed dark and ominous.

19 TIME WITH THE OGRE...

The *witch of Agnesi* was inspected, fueled, and ready to go. Jack Beston, arriving minutes before their scheduled departure, said only one thing to Milly.

"Travel time with Ganymede surface gravity as ship's acceleration would take too long, so I've set us for one-gee Earth. Okay?"

At Milly's startled nod—what choice did she have?—he vanished into his own suite of rooms and closed the door. His disappearance suited her fine. It was not his absence that worried her, so much as his possible presence. As for the acceleration, one Earth gravity was six times what she had grown up with on Ganymede and far more than she had ever experienced before. She would probably feel like she was made of lead, but if it meant getting there quicker she could take it. She went across to the pilot interface. "How long will we take to reach the Odin Station at Jovian L-5?"

The pilot included a high Level Four Fax, embodied as a dignified man with a smooth face and a touch of gray at the temples. He frowned as though thinking about Milly's question, although the answer could have been provided by the computer in microseconds. "Assuming that I receive no requests for change of acceleration, the scheduled travel time including mid-point turnover is eight-point-six days. Perihelion distance will be three hundred and eighty-nine million kilometers."

"But that will take us inside the Belt."

"Quite true. We will travel closer to the Sun than many of the asteroids. However, with our onboard matter detection systems there is absolutely no danger of collision. Can I help you with anything else?"

"Not at the moment."

"Then I hope that you enjoy the flight. If there is anything that I can do to make it more pleasant, don't hesitate to ask. And now, please take a seat. The drive is scheduled to go on in thirty seconds, but cannot do so unless all passengers are suitably positioned."

Milly went to sit down and strap herself into one of the cabin's swing chairs. She had been surprised by the pilot's answer, but she should not have been. The acceleration due to Sol at Jupiter's distance was only a couple of hundredths of centimeters per second per second. Given a drive capable of accelerations of a Ganymede gravity or more, orbits around the Outer System were practically point-and-shoot. The passage from Jovian L-4 to Jovian L-5 would take *The Witch of Agnesi* arrowing across between Sol and Jupiter, on a near straight-line trajectory. At turnover point the ship would be almost exactly equidistant from the planet and the Sun.

She lay back in the padded seat. A few seconds more, and the ship was moving. The force that Milly felt was surprisingly gentle. If this was all she had to take there would be no problem at all. From the port on her left she saw the Argus Station, apparently rotating around an axis that directly faced Milly. She realized that the Argus Station was not actually moving. The ship was turning into position. And suddenly, while that thought was still in her head, a powerful force seized her and thrust her hard against the supporting chair.

So *this* was one Earth gravity. She felt as though she could hardly breathe. Her breasts, always in her opinion too large, became more than a cosmetic problem. They were heavy weights pressing against her ribs. And she was supposed to endure this for—how long?—more than eight days, the pilot had said.

Milly closed her eyes. Eight *minutes* would be too much. She lay in misery for an indefinite period, until she heard another sound in the cabin. She opened her eyes.

Jack Beston was standing in front of her. He didn't seem to be suffering any strain at all.

"Here." He was holding out a vapor syringe. "One Earth gravity for a week or so won't do you any physical harm, but there's no point in feeling uncomfortable. Just remember not to try to move too fast for the first few hours."

Milly didn't have enough breath to speak. She took the syringe. If this was part of some deep Ogre-ish plan to render her unconscious so that Jack could have his way with her, then she was his and good luck to him. In her present condition, being unconscious was better than being awake.

"Not there." Beston gripped the syringe and re-directed it to a place on Milly's neck. She, uncoordinated and with her hand weighing a ton, had somehow pointed the syringe at a part of the chair support behind her head.

"You want it to act as quickly as possible," he went on. "So an artery is best—and anywhere in the body works a lot better than a shot into the seat cover."

It was a joke of sorts, and Milly wanted to smile. She made the effort, and felt the skin of her face move and stretch in odd directions. What it looked like was anyone's guess. She

allowed him to direct the placing of the syringe nozzle and
pressed the plunger when he said, "Now, push." She felt the
spray cold against the side of her neck.

He waited a few seconds, peering down at her. "How do
you feel now?"

"Just the same." But she didn't. For one thing, she had
spoken, an act which had seemed impossible only a minute
ago. Her breasts felt like breasts again, not like lead weights
on her rib cage. She released the straps that held her in the
seat and began to stand up.

Jack Beston put his hand on her shoulder. "Not yet. Sit
here and rest for a couple of hours, let your body get used to
things. Then I'll take you to the exercise room."

She had noticed the elaborate facility on her first quick tour
of the ship, and dismissed it as the foible of a man with more
money than sense. "Are you going to exercise?"

"Both of us are. Very gently, and very carefully for the first
day or two. Muscle build-up under higher gravity comes
amazingly fast, but it's very easy to develop a sprain or tear
tissue."

He retreated into his own quarters, leaving Milly to wonder
what manner of man she was dealing with. Was he interested
in her personally, as Hannah Krauss insisted? If so, he showed
no signs of it. Was he an Ogre, as everyone insisted? Then
he was an Ogre on its best behavior.

Milly had to wait two days before she could answer those
questions. *The Witch of Agnesi* flew steadily on, its acceleration
never changing. Milly's body gradually adapted to the unprecedented acceleration field. She moved slowly and carefully,
and reminded herself that humans had evolved in a force field
like this. Jack Beston remained for most of the time in his

own quarters, and Milly kept to hers. They met twice a day to eat, to exercise—gently, at his insistence—and to talk about nothing. He was fidgety and restless, but uncommunicative.

Milly was not bored. She was too worried for boredom. She was busy obsessively analyzing and re-analyzing her own work, wondering if she had made some blunder that the others at the Argus Station had failed to catch, wondering if she would go down in history as a major discoverer or as one more footnote testifying to an alien signal that wasn't. If she did take a break it was to wander over to the ports and stare out. When they reached turnover, the Sun, the ship, and Jupiter would lie almost exactly in a straight line. Already she could see the Sun's intense glare out of one port, and Jupiter's full face out of the one opposite. Ganymede, where her relatives lived and where until recently she had made her home, was never visible. The solar system felt very empty. She felt very alone.

Late on the afternoon of the third day, Jack Beston appeared and asked her if she would have dinner with him in his private quarters. She couldn't think of any reason to say no, so she agreed, but when the time came and she knocked on the door leading to his cabin, she felt highly uncomfortable. As she entered the sitting room she had to remind herself that so far as he was concerned she had never been here before.

She wandered around, offering compliments on the well-designed furniture and expensive decor. At last he said, "You know, back on Argus Station I have a reputation for being paranoid about security. I'm not, really, about anything but the project itself. Zetter's the security freak, not me. But when I bought this ship it came with a monitoring system already installed for the private quarters."

Did that mean he knew she had been snooping around? It

must. She stared at him. His face had a brooding expression, but he didn't sound upset at her—certainly not as upset as Milly felt. "I'm sorry. When I came aboard, I wondered—I've never been on a ship anything like this before, so I just—"

"Don't apologize. Do you know what I look for in a person who applies to work on the Argus Project? Insatiable curiosity, about everything in the universe." He waved her to a seat by the low table and dropped to sit cross-legged on the cushions opposite. He smiled a grim smile. "Of course, when certain other people display that type of curiosity, I don't like it at all. I don't mean you, Milly. Have you scanned the news outlets recently?"

"No. Not since we left Argus Station."

"Well, I have. We sent word that we had a possible signal from the stars to just two places: Odin Station, and the Ganymede Office of Records. The signal that went to Ganymede was enciphered and should have been locked away. But somebody leaked it, and somebody cracked it. There's a blurt about us on the Paradigm Outlet. Most of it is made-up nonsense, as you'd expect, but it says we have a message from aliens. Your name is mentioned. It's going to be a pain in the ass until all this dies down. A hundred media chasers will be after you."

"What do I tell them?" In her whole life, Milly had never met a single individual from any outlet.

"You refer them to me." Jack Beston's green eyes took on a gleam of anticipation. "I'll give them more than they bargained for. I'll offer them information—if they'll tell me where the Ganymede leak came from."

"Are you sure it was the Ganymede office? The signal you sent to the Odin Station wasn't enciphered."

"It didn't need to be. Odin Station is locked as tight as the Bastard's ass. He'd kill anyone on his project who leaked this kind of information, because even though he lost on the initial discovery he's hoping to get there first with interpretation."

"I thought the race was over."

"Not until we know what the signal *means*."

"Then why did you send any message at all to Odin Station?"

"A calculated risk. We need the Bastard's inputs for verification. It's either that, or sit around for years while we change orbit position. And I'm too impatient to wait for things." He followed Milly's eyes, to where an array of little servers were creeping through from the kitchen and positioning themselves by the low table. "Well, the hell with all that. I didn't ask you to dinner to obsess about work. Let's eat. Help yourself."

Milly wondered what to expect as she opened the server lids. Her earlier inspection of the kitchen suggested a level of cuisine beyond anything she had ever encountered. It was a relief to find exactly the same kinds of food that she had grown up with.

No, put it differently. This *looked* like what she was used to. Milly placed a minimal amount of food on her plate. She thought of Hannah's warning, *the seduction of new female workers*, and Jack's own *I'm too impatient to wait for things*. If he were planning to put a move on her, was he above adding a little psychotropic additive to affect her mood? She speared a small green bean on her fork and tasted it.

Jack Beston was watching closely. "Are you all right? You've hardly taken any."

"I suppose that I'm a bit surprised." Milly gestured with her fork at her plate. "This is fine, but it's the same sort of food as we used to eat at home."

"You mean it's too plain, rather than high-class?"

"Well, I wouldn't say that."

"But you might think it." Jack had loaded his plate with about ten times as much as Milly, though so far he hadn't taken a single bite. "I'm sorry, but when it comes to eating I'm a low-brow. I think I developed my food tastes early in life, and I wasn't born rich. I had richness thrust upon me."

"I know."

"Hannah told you?"

"Right."

"You've not taken enough food to feed a mouse. And so far you have nibbled on one very small bean. What else did Hannah tell you?"

Milly put down her fork. "Since you insist on asking, she warned me to be very careful. You have a habit, she said, of making passes at women on your staff, especially ones who are new. And I'm the most recent arrival."

He was staring at her and nodding his head thoughtfully. This was probably where she got fired.

"So you're nervous," he said, "and that's spoiling your appetite?"

"Maybe."

"And maybe there's more to it than that." Jack reached across the table to take her hand, but she pulled it back out of reach. He nodded. "You really are nervous. Maybe you are worried about the food and think there could be something wrong with it. Now I'm going to tell you a few things, Milly Wu, and whether you believe me or not, and whether after I talk we sit here and eat a civilized dinner together, or whether you leave and lock yourself in your cabin for the rest of the trip, is up to you. Either way, I won't hold it against you.

"First, I do find you very attractive, and I have since your original interview. Also, I know I have a reputation, and there's some truth to what Hannah told you. But I wish Hannah had told you something else. I have never, ever, tried to use position or money or influence to pressure someone into having sex if she doesn't want to. I'm not interested in any form of coercion. Also, I have never tried to drug a person, man or woman, to do anything for any reason."

He paused and Milly saw that his hands, still extended across the table, were trembling. "Hannah didn't tell me most of that," she muttered. "I'm glad you did. And I believe you."

"Good. Because now we reach the hard part so far as I'm concerned. I told you I find you attractive, and I do. But if you had come on strong to me tonight and suggested that we have sex—I'm not saying that you ever had any such thought—I'm sure I would have been a big disappointment. Can't you see that I'm tense and nervous as hell, and have been for days, and that it has absolutely nothing to do with you? I asked you to dinner to get my mind off something else."

"The visit to Odin Station?"

"You can be more specific than that. It's not the *station* I'm worried about. It's *Philip*. You know—the Bastard."

"I know. But I've never heard you use his name before." Milly was feeling a lot better, even as his discomfort seemed to grow. "But I don't understand. I thought we were in an unbeatable position. We discovered the signal, and we announced the discovery. He doesn't even know where to look."

"We'll have to tell him that, to get verification."

"But the signal direction is just a tiny fraction of what we have learned. We'll still be far ahead. What can he possibly do to change that?"

"If I knew, I'd be a lot less worried. Do you have an older sister?"

"No. Two younger ones, and a young brother."

"You're lucky. The oldest ones always believe they're the boss. Philip is just a couple of years older than I am, but right from the time we were little kids, in everything we ever did, he always managed to work it so he came out ahead—even when the whole project was my idea. It's the same now. He's got me so psyched that I'm convinced he'll do it this time, even though I can't think of any way it can possibly happen."

It was strange. Watching him across the table, Milly saw a different Jack Beston. He was the Ogre, the hard taskmaster who cracked the whip over everyone and everything on the Argus Project at Jovian L-4. But he was also a nervous little kid, scared of what his devious older brother might do to spoil his plans. Milly felt like putting her arms around him and telling him that everything would work out all right.

That would be, for a dozen different reasons, a mistake. *It's when you feel sympathy for the Devil that you're in trouble.* Milly believed everything that Jack had said to her, with the possible exception of his impotence. On that subject a man was not a reliable source. But she did go so far as to reach out across the table and pat his hand.

"You'll win. I'm sure of it." She bent over and began to lift covered dishes onto the table. "I'm sorry I was suspicious about the food, and to tell the truth I was starving before I came in here. I think it's the effect of the higher gravity, our bodies are trying to double their muscle mass in a few days."

Milly pushed Jack's plate out of the way. "That's all cold, you need to start over." She took a clean plate for him, opened the covered dishes, and began to serve both of them liberal helpings of everything. "We'll eat now, and since you want distraction I'm going to give it to you. You asked about my family. Well, they're the least interesting group in the System. I'll tell you about Uncle Godfrey and Aunt Mary, and Ginger and Sara and Lola and dopey Cousin Peter, and I'll go on until you beg for mercy."

20 . . . AND TIME WITH THE BASTARD

In little more than eight days, an acceleration of one Earth gravity had gone from feeling oddly wrong and perhaps unendurable to oddly right. You could live your whole life in the outer reaches of the solar system, but something deep inside you remembered where humans had begun. Milly gazed ahead at the nearing bulk of the Odin Station and felt half-regretful that she was once again in a micro-gee setting.

Jack was drifting around the cabin, pausing now and again to stare out at their destination. He seemed more relaxed than during their first dinner together. Maybe Milly had been able to persuade him that there was no way his brother Philip could achieve an advantage, or maybe he simply accepted that he was close to a confrontation. For whatever reason, the rest of the trip had been a lot easier than the first days.

Milly kept her eyes on the nearing station. It was remarkably similar in appearance to the station that they had left at Jovian L-4. There were the same distributed antenna arrays, the same skeletal lattices to detect the ghostly passage of high-energy neutrinos, and the same central bulk of the main habitat. Halfway across the System, and here she was facing a facsimile of the station that they had left. Who had copied from whom? If Jack were to be believed, the Bastard had stolen every idea from his younger brother.

Unlike Jack, Milly felt a huge desire to meet Philip. She had never seen a picture of Jack's brother. She had one sister who was very like her, and one with no apparent resemblance at all—though other family members claimed to see one. What would Philip look like? More important, what would he be like *inside*? She felt that she was slowly beginning to understand Jack. He was an odd mixture of total self-confidence and total insecurity. The combination was intriguing and highly attractive. It was easy to see the reason for his supposedly-numerous affairs on Argus Station. Milly was no longer sure that Jack had always been the instigator.

"We are ready to begin docking. If you wouldn't mind preparing for arrival . . ." The pilot Fax waited until Milly was seated and Jack, reluctantly, stopped his wandering and strapped in. The bulk of Odin Station hung enormous beyond the port, eclipsing half the star field. They eased their way in toward a set of gantries on the side.

The docking was performed with inhuman precision. Milly felt barely a tremor of contact, and then the illuminated signs to remain seated went out. Moments later, a green flashing light indicated that the umbilical had been connected and pressures equalized.

"Here we are." Jack was already unstrapped, and he sounded breathless. "Let's do it."

He sounded jittery. Milly, on the other hand, felt enormously excited and filled with anticipation. Her hopes had been on hold for more than a week, but within the next few hours there was a chance that the signal she had discovered—the *Wu-Beston* anomaly—would be confirmed as extra-solar, a real signal from interstellar distances.

She followed close behind as he headed for the hatch. When it opened she found herself at the beginning of a long umbilical, exactly like the one through which she had left Argus Station. Thirty meters away, at the other end of the tube, a figure was moving their way which at first glance could easily be mistaken for Jack Beston.

Philip the Bastard.

Jack advanced, Milly close behind, until the two brothers faced each other no more than half a meter apart. Neither one reached out a hand.

"Jack." Philip Beston nodded his head. Now that she was close, Milly could see differences. Philip was almost the same height, but more heavily-built. He had the same red hair, but in place of Jack's lidded green glint, his eyes were blue and wide and innocent. And, unlike Jack, the smile on his face seemed easy and genuine.

"And this"—Philip stepped past his brother—"must be the famous Milly Wu, discover of the Wu-Beston anomaly." He paused and frowned. "Are you really Milly Wu?"

"I am. Is something wrong?"

"Not at all." He reached out, took her hand in his, and shook it firmly. "My apologies. I was merely surprised to find someone so young—and, if I may be a little gauche, so very attractive—making so important a discovery. I am delighted to welcome you to Odin Station, and I look forward to the opportunity of working with you."

His brother's air of bonhomie made Jack sound sour and nervous as he said, "On verification. Only on verification."

"Jack, my dear young sibling, would I ever suggest anything else?" Philip turned again to Milly. "As you can see, my brother remains regrettably suspicious of me and my intentions."

"Damn right I do," Jack growled, and moved on along the umbilical toward the interior of Odin Station. "With plenty of reasons. How soon can we talk verification?"

Philip shrugged at Milly, as though to say "What can you do with him?" and ushered her forward. "As soon as you like, Jack," he said. "My staff has been eagerly awaiting your arrival. As have I."

"That, I do believe." Jack, at the end of the tube, had to wait for his brother to come up to him and point out the way they should go. The outside of Odin Station resembled Argus Station, but within there would surely be big differences. Milly didn't propose to find out what they were. It had taken weeks to learn the chambers and crisscrossing corridors of Argus Station, and she would not be here long enough to make the effort worthwhile.

Even assuming, that is, that she would be given the freedom to do so. Philip Beston took them only a few more meters, then led them into a suite of rooms.

"This is where you will be staying. As Jack will no doubt explain to you, we do not feel free to offer the full run of Odin Station. If you do leave these quarters, I request that you be accompanied by one of my staff members."

"In other words, he doesn't want us to see too much." Jack stepped forward and moved across to sit at the long table. "Let's not mess around here. You know what we came here for and what we want, and we know exactly what you want."

Philip Beston raised an eyebrow at Milly. "I had intended to proceed with the usual civilities, and offer you refreshments after your long journey. However, if you feel the urge to get down to business at once . . ."

"We do." Jack seemed as nervous as Philip was relaxed. "Are you set up already for verification?"

"As ready as we can be, given the absence of critical information. The arrays are all in position, we merely have to set them to their correct phases."

Even Philip showed a trace of tension with those words. Milly felt the atmosphere in the room slowly tightening. The problem from Jack Beston's point of view was quite simple. Odin Station had receiving equipment as good as that at Argus Station. There would be little to choose between them when it came to sensitivity. The big question was, to which direction in space should the array of receivers be tuned? Without that information, Philip Beston would be hunting blind.

On the other hand, as soon as Jack provided the signal direction to his brother, the two of them would be on an equal footing. Odin Station would presumably skip the detection analysis that Milly and the team at L-4 had performed; if the signal were verified, they would be equally well-equipped to tackle the all-important problem of signal interpretation.

There was a long silence. Jack Beston, having hurried so far and so fast, appeared to be having second thoughts. At last his brother prompted him: "I assume that the signal is still there? That it didn't show up for awhile, and then go away?"

Jack merely gave him a cynical glance. Milly could see Jack's point. If the signal had vanished, the array of sensors in Odin Station had not previously been tuned to the right direction. Therefore, there could be no verification. The signal needed to be observed simultaneously from both the L-4 and L-5 locations.

"Look," Philip Beston said at last. "I know exactly how you feel about this. I'd feel the same way myself if our positions were reversed. But I've had my top team in position and awaiting your arrival for hours. If you want to change your mind, get back into your ship, and return to Argus Station . . ."

"No, I'm suspicious—just like you—but I'm not dumb. The signal is still there, of course it's still there. Or at least, it was an hour ago when I checked back to base from our ship."

"Regular light speed signals?" Philip Beston shook his head. "You know, if we wanted to do this as accurately as possible, we should arrange for entanglement between your computers and mine. That way, we would not have to compensate all the time for signal delays."

"Sure. I'd be willing—if you would." Jack locked glances with his brother, and after a few moments both shook their heads. Milly realized she had just witnessed a significant interaction. Entanglement of the computers would zero out communication delays; but it would also vastly increase the risk that the secret information of one station would become accessible to the other. Neither brother was willing to permit that. Clearly, each felt that he had some sort of competitive edge, even though Jack had won the first round by detecting an anomaly.

Jack was drumming his fingers on the tabletop staring at nothing. Finally he glanced up to Milly. "All right. Go ahead."

"Provide coordinates?"

"You've got it." Jack turned to Philip. "I assume it's necessary for us to say this only once? Everything in this room is being recorded?"

"Just imagine that the positions were reversed, think how you would proceed, and assume that the same applies here." Philip Beston had lost any trace of his original relaxed air. He was tenser than his brother as he turned to Milly. "The coordinates of the signal source, if you would be so kind."

Milly didn't need to consult notes. "As of 5:82:34 hours on 97/09/04, the source coordinates in the ecliptic standard reference frame of 2050 were as follows: declination, 38 degrees 22 minutes 17.3 seconds south, azimuth 231 degrees 54 minutes 52.6 seconds. The signal fall-off from the observed direction of signal maximum followed a circular normal distribution, with a one-sigma value of 1.3 arc seconds. No motion of the signal source was detected over a five week period of observation. However, for the first three weeks the array tuning was not exact, so a movement in position of less than twenty seconds of arc would have been undetectable."

"Thank you." Philip sounded breathless. "What is the source direction relative to an L-4 to L-5 baseline?"

"A little more than thirty-two degrees. The angle is not optimal."

"But it's pretty good. We lose only a factor of two in angular resolution. It will take my staff approximately ten minutes to tune our most sensitive arrays to that direction, but after that they have to make preliminary observations and perform an optimizing scan. We have maybe an hour to wait for results. During that time, I would be very happy to offer a tour of Odin Station." Philip glanced at Jack. "There will of course be a few places that I do not feel free to show you."

Jack shook his head. "Not for me. Milly, you go if you feel interested."

Milly nodded.

Philip took her by the arm. "If I may make so bold . . . I consider this a reasonable decision on both your parts. I suspect that my brother knows the inside of Odin Station as well as anyone here, despite the fact that this is his first visit."

That comment, Milly felt sure, was intended for Jack more than her. Both brothers had been spying on each other in

every way possible for years. Milly wondered if she would see
the "insider" whom Zetter had indirectly referred to in Milly's
first staff meeting with the Ogre. One thing for sure: if she
did see that insider, there would be not a hint to suggest a
relationship with Jack Beston and Odin Station.

Milly allowed Philip Beston to lead her through the interior. She saw the detection analysis teams, although only
through glass partitions, and she was not invited to go in and
meet them; she saw the door marked INTERPRETATION TEAM
ONLY, and speculated on the activity that might be going on
within; she looked out of ports, through which she could view
the big distributed antenna arrays, now turning, little by little, to optimize for the acceptance of a signal from a particular
direction in space.

Not just any particular direction, either. *Her* direction, the
direction of the Wu-Beston anomaly.

Philip Beston was obviously proud of his equipment and
his work team, but Milly was taking in what she saw only
with some peripheral area of her brain. The central part of her
attention was focused on the verification procedure which was
now beginning, and on the question that would be answered
in the next few hours: *How far away is the detected signal?*

The massive arrays of detectors at Argus Station and Odin
Station could pinpoint the direction of a distant source to half
an arc second or better. The two stations were separated by
about 1.3 billion kilometers, one ahead of and the other trailing Jupiter by sixty degrees in the planet's revolution around
the sun. Because of that long baseline, Odin Station, Argus
Station, and the distant signal source formed the vertices of a
very tall and narrow triangle. Observing the directions of the
source as seen from the two observing stations provided the
tiny angle at the apex of that extended triangle. Angle information, together with the length of the baseline between the

stations, was enough to determine the distance of the signal source.

In practice, the observations provided only a lower limit for distance. If a source was too far away, no angular difference would be observed as seen from Jovian L-4 and Jovian L-5 points, which left the actual distance undefined. However, that result would be quite satisfactory to Milly. It would establish that the signal source, wherever it was, was far out among the stars and not in the immediate neighborhood of the solar system.

Milly knew the numbers by heart. The angle of the source direction relative to the baseline joining Jovian L-4 and Jovian L-5 was 32 degrees. If the parallax—the difference in direction of the source as seen from Odin Station and from Argus Station—was one second of arc, then the source must be at a distance of fifteen light years. A measured parallax of half a second of arc would mean the source was twice as far away, at least thirty light-years. One-tenth of a second of arc was beyond the resolving power of the arrays at the two observing stations. All you could say then was that the signal emanated from somewhere at least fifty light-years distant.

Philip Beston must have noticed Milly's incomplete attention. He glanced at his watch. "You've probably seen as much of this as you want to, and I'm sure you have other things on your mind. We won't have results for another half hour or so. Would you like to go back to your rooms? Or could I interest you in a light snack and perhaps a cup of tea?"

Milly did feel that she ought to get back to Jack. On the other hand, what would they do then? Sit around, stare at each other, and wait? That was not the most thrilling way of spending time until the results came through.

"I think that a cup of tea would be very acceptable."

Her hesitation must have showed, because Philip smiled.

"It's a tough choice, isn't it? Do you enjoy the company of the Ogre, or do you spend even more time with the Bastard? But that's not a fair question. I suspect it's the lure of refreshment that sounds interesting, not the pleasure of my company."

He was fishing. Milly didn't mind that, but she didn't feel like encouraging him. No one had said anything to her about Philip Beston's attitudes toward young women, but heredity was a powerful force. She smiled back, said "A cup of tea and something to eat with either you or Jack would be very pleasant," and left the next move up to him.

They had passed some kind of dining room on the brief tour of Odin Station. Philip nodded and led her not in that direction, but to a different, smaller, and more private room. He closed the door carefully as they entered. Food and drink were already laid out on a credenza, which made Milly wonder how much his offer had been planned in advance. She took her lead from Philip, helped herself to a sugary cake and a glass of hot green tea, and sat opposite him at a low glass-topped table that kept their separation to a comfortable meter.

Philip ate in silence for half a minute or so. He was a slow and neat eater, like Milly herself. At last he said, "You must have done a spectacular job. I mean, the Wu-Beston anomaly. It's not like the Ogre to share credit unless he realized that anyone looking at the work would deduce that the discovery was yours, and yours alone."

Milly sipped tea and said in a neutral voice, "Jack has always been more than fair with me."

"Are you sure of that? Jack has always had a bit of a reputation for stinginess. You might say it's none of my business, but how much financial reward did he give you for the discovery?"

Milly stared. It was not a subject that had ever come up for discussion.

"The terms set out in the bequest for use of inherited money are quite specific," Philip went on. "There are ample funds to reward the discoverer of a genuine SETI signal, and there would be no difficulty in justifying such use. And, of course, even more substantial rewards are available for the fortunate individuals who can *interpret* a received signal. I assume that Jack told you about all this?"

Milly's continued silence was its own answer.

"Hmm." Philip Beston rubbed his forefinger around the rim of his empty glass. "Pardon me if I say so, but one way or another I suspect that you are being royally screwed over by brother Jack. I want to make a suggestion—it is just a suggestion, but I'd like you to think about it over the next few hours, and tell me how you feel. All right?"

Milly felt she had to do more than sit, stare, and nod. "What sort of suggestion?"

"You've made a major discovery. It is officially known as the Wu-Beston anomaly. Now, to the average person in the solar system, one Beston is as good as another. They don't know if it's Wu-Jack or Wu-Philip Beston, and they don't care. And to that same average person in the solar system, there is little to choose between Argus Station and Odin Station—both are at the outer edge of nowhere. You did not, I assume, sign a long-term contract to work with Jack?"

Milly shook her head.

"Which means you are free to leave at any time. Now, if you were to come here and work for me, I can assure you of three things. First, you will be given full and continuing credit for your discovery. Second, I will arrange for you to receive the maximum permissible financial reward for that discovery, including a quadrupling of your present salary. And third—which will in the long run be far more important than either of the first two—you would occupy a senior position on the interpretation team at Odin Station." Philip placed his glass on the table in front of him. "Never forget this, Milly. Detection is important, verification is no less so; but full fame and public recognition will go to the person or team who can *interpret* the signal from the stars. Don't you want to be the one who can say what it means, and point out its value to the human race? Think about it."

Milly thought. She decided that Philip Beston must be a moron, if he imagined that she was doing this work for money. Fame, maybe—she still thrilled when she heard *Wu-Beston anomaly*. But money, no way. Second, Philip Beston was a scoundrel. All that talk about no one caring who the Beston was in "Wu-Beston" translated clearly to one fact: he wanted people to think that he, Philip Beston, was the Beston referred to. A safe way to do that was to switch Milly to his project on Odin Station before interpretation had begun and even before verification was completed.

He was looking at her expectantly.

"I'll think about it," she said. "In fact, I have thought about it, as much as I need to."

"Well."

"I've concluded that Jack's name for you is exactly right. You are Philip the Bastard. The sort of bastard who will do his best to steal from his own brother. Jack can be an Ogre when it comes to work, but he's worth ten of you."

There was a term for what she had just done: burning your bridges. But astonishingly, Philip Beston seemed not at all put out.

"That brother of mine," he said, "I just don't know how he does it. Works his people to death, insults them every chance he gets—and he still has you eating out of his hand.

What's his trick, Milly? Did he do the little-lost-boy act, making you feel that he's all nervous and vulnerable and insecure? That worked for him very well with me when we were little, until I realized it was all a total sham. Brother Jack knows exactly how to manipulate people, always has."

Nervous and vulnerable and insecure. The words described uncannily well the impressions that Milly had formed of Jack Beston during the trip out from Argus Station.

Either Philip Beston was totally confident of his assessment, or he was uninterested in Milly's response. Before she could answer he had turned and was heading for the door.

"My instincts tell me that we are close to array alignment." He seemed to be talking to himself more than to Milly. "Let's find a place where we can see what's going on."

Milly doubted that it was instinct—far more likely he was wearing an intra-aural receiver—but his words made her tingle all over. She hurried after him. When your whole life hung on the next few minutes, what Jack and Philip Beston thought of each other or did to each other was down in the noise level.

The room that he led her to was empty, but well-provided with virtuals. Milly saw three display volumes. The first was an open space view of the antenna array, now fixed in position or hunting so imperceptibly that the human eye could not tell the difference. The second virtual was obviously of the control room, with half a dozen staff members eyeing output tables or talking excitedly to each other. The third virtual showed Jack Beston, sitting where Milly and Philip had left him, and intently studying what she assumed were miniature versions of the other virtuals.

Philip Beston said quietly, "Where do we stand, Laszlo?"

One of the control room figures looked up from his monitor. "We have lock on, and it's quite tight. Our rms signal maximum lies 0.6 arc seconds away from the coordinates reported by the Argus Station. We find exactly the same pattern for signal fall-off with angle—a circular normal distribution with sigma of 1.3 arc seconds." His voice had remained flat and factual when quoting statistics, but his final words took on a different and more animated character. "It's there, Philip, absolutely no doubt about it. It's there, it's definite, it's clear, and it is at interstellar distance. Our estimate has a most probable value of 25.8 light years, and at the very least the distance is 19 light years."

"Target star?"

"None. It looks as though the signal is being generated in open space. That's no particular surprise, we've always thought that a system of interstellar relays would make sense."

He **was** saying things that Milly, and certainly Philip Beston, knew already. Given the excitement that he—and everyone else in all the virtuals—must be feeling, it was not surprising if Laszlo did a little babbling.

"You listening, Jack?" Philip Beston said. And at Jack's slow thoughtful nod, he added, "Congratulations, brother. You already had detection, now it looks like you have a shot at strong verification. That would mean there's just one left."

Jack nodded again. "Yep. Just one. The big one."

"Do you want to send the announcement, if this holds up?"

"It will. Let's send this one together. It's the third one that I'm going to send solo."

"Let's just say that one of us will be sending it solo. Race you to the corner, eh, brother?" Philip flipped a switch, and the virtual of Jack vanished. "Some things change, but I guess that some things never do. For twelve years, Jack has been telling anyone who would listen that the idea of a big SETI project was his and his alone. It wasn't, but I've given up arguing. Jack seems determined to spend his life trying to prove he's better than I am."

Milly said, "Maybe he is."

"And maybe he just has you wrapped around his little finger. When you see through him, or when things at Argus
Station start to go bad, you give me a call." The wide, innocent blue eyes fixed on Milly. "I will still be here. And
maybe you'll give me a chance to prove I'm not the bastard
that Jack makes me out to be."

Verification. Milly had assumed after the first meeting with
Philip Beston's staff that the whole job was as good as over.
She should have known better.

Three more days of hard-slog checking were needed, of
everything from measures of proper motion of the source to
an attempted interferometric analysis of its spatial extent, before both brothers agreed: the parallax as observed from Jovian
L-4 and Jovian L-5 was real. The origin was so far away that
it acted as a point source. The signal came from somewhere
well outside the solar system.

In those three days, Philip Beston said nothing to follow
up on his suggestion that Milly ought to change sides and
work on Odin Station. Only at the final farewell did he hold
her hand for a moment longer than necessary, and say softly,
"When you decide you'd like to be on the winning side, you
know who to call."

Jack Beston could not possibly have heard, but he was in
a foul mood as *The Witch of Agnesi* pulled away from Odin
Station for the return trip. Milly couldn't see why. They had
confirmation of a signal, and a significant time advantage over
Philip Beston when it came to interpretation.

But when she said that to Jack, he merely gave her a slit-
eyed green glare. "He knows we have a lead, and he knows
that we found the signal and he didn't. Given all that, he's
far too cheerful."

"Maybe he's putting on a show for the staff of Odin Station. They must be feeling pretty crushed."

"No." Jack shook his head. "You didn't grow up with the Bastard, the way I did. He doesn't put on shows. He's got something up his sleeve. Something to do with signal interpretation."

"Do you have any idea what it might be?"

"Not a clue." Jack stared intently out of the forward port, as though willing the ship to fly faster to Argus Station. "We'll find out when he hits us with it."

The outer regions of the solar system are remarkably empty. It is certainly possible to run into another object, particularly when flying through the Asteroid belt, but you have to be freakishly unlucky to do so. And if that other object happens to be a ship, with its own navigational control system, then the chance of collision contains such a string of zeroes after the decimal point that no rational person should worry about it.

Humans are not, of course, particularly rational. Milly's question of the Level Four Fax aboard *The Witch of Agnesi* was asked a thousand times an hour, somewhere in the system; but in fact there had never been a collision of two ships whose navigation systems were in working order. The *OSL Achilles*, outward bound for the Jovian system and Ganymede, crossed the trajectory of *The Witch of Agnesi* as the latter sped between the Jovian L-4 and L-5 points, and in celestial terms they made a "close approach" of less than two million kilometers. No human on either ship was aware of that fact.

The passengers of the *Achilles* were increasingly unaware of anything. Janeed had heard that in pre-war times a certain form of group mania infected the passengers of ocean liners. After the first few days nothing in the world existed beyond the ship, while what happened before and after the cruise became utterly irrelevant. A wild series of random courtships and short-lived affairs was the result.

Jan had hardly believed those reports, but now she saw evidence of their truth at first-hand. Colonists were pairing off, and as the ship drove outward toward its rendezvous with Jupiter an air of continuous festivity took over.

Not only the passengers were affected. The ship's trajectory was computer-controlled, as were most of its on-board systems. The crew had time to relax. Paul Marr was able to devote a more-than-generous amount of time to Janeed. That certainly suited Jan. Within the first two days she had decided that everything she had been told about sex was right, or possibly understated. The more you did it, the more you liked it. The real danger was that you might become an addict. Jan suspected that she might be well on the way.

Occasionally, she would worry about Sebastian. She was seeing less and less of him as the days went by. On the other hand, Valnia Bloom seemed to be with him almost constantly. They spent most of the time hidden away in her private cabin. Jan didn't think they were engaged in a sexual relationship, but even if they were, so what? Sebastian was a strongly-built and physically mature man in the prime of life. He and Valnia Bloom were as entitled to as good a time as Paul and Jan.

When she had boarded the *Achilles,* two weeks going on forever ago, Jan had expected to be impatient until the moment she set foot on Ganymede. Now, as that time of arrival came closer, she was loath to leave the ship. She and Paul had vowed that this would not be the end, that they would see each other again. But in reality, how many shipboard romances survived the day of disembarkation?

One major party still lay ahead. Jan had never heard of it before, but Paul explained as they lounged naked one evening in his cabin. The ship was in drive mode, and the two of them were reclining in sybaritic luxury on the most comfortable bed Jan had ever encountered. At the flip of a switch the floor had become soft and yielding, cushioned on the reservoir that contained the *Achilles'* ample supplies of water.

She lay on her side, head turned to look across the flat plain of his chest and watch its steady rise and fall as he breathed. He had painted her nude, and when the picture was finished one thing had inevitably led to another.

"Of course the party isn't *necessary*," he said. "It represents a tradition from the earliest days of planetary exploration. The ships at that time all used chemical rockets—"

"Not nuclear?" Jan asked. "They had nuclear energy, you know, even back then."

"They did, but they'd had bad experiences with it and a lot of people were still scared. So they used chemical rockets."

"But the effects of chemical rockets on the atmosphere and ionosphere are a lot worse than nuclear. Didn't they know—"

Paul had his arm around her and he gave her left breast a gentle squeeze. "Are you going to let me tell you about this, or do you want me to roll over and go to sleep?"

"Wouldn't be the first time, would it? Go on, I'm listening."

"The ships used chemical rockets. That's not totally true, because there were already a few ion drives; but they provided such low accelerations that they were useless for passenger shipping. You can guess what it was like. Everybody was short of delta-vee for everything. They would scrounge, beg, or borrow as much momentum transfer as they could lay their hands on, but space travel was still marginal, all touch-and-go. The first ships to reach Jupiter didn't have enough fuel to slow into orbit around the planet. If they didn't do something different, they would arrive, swing past, and shoot away in some other direction. The answer—the only possible answer at the time—was to skim through Jupiter's upper atmosphere and use air-braking for velocity-shedding.

"The theory was simple and fully understood for more than a century. Doing it, and getting it exactly right, was another matter. The *Ashkenazy* went in too deep and never came out. The *Celandine* erred in the other direction. It skipped in, skipped out, and left the Jovian system completely."

His voice had gradually slowed and deepened. Jan squeezed the little roll of fat at his waist. "You're supposed to be telling me about some big party we'll be having, not zoning out on me. Are you drifting off?"

"I am not. I'm thinking how much easier we have it than the original explorers. The *Celandine* crew members were tough, and braver than you can believe. I've heard their recordings. They sent back data on the Jupiter magnetosphere until they were on the last drips of oxygen, then they all signed off as casually as if they were going out together for an early dinner. A dip into the Jovian atmosphere used to be a life-or-death proposition. Now it's just a game. Jupiter's atmospheric depth profile is mapped to six figures. The atmospheric swingby is a tradition and a good excuse for a party, but it is absolutely and totally unnecessary."

"Like crossing the line." She saw Paul's forehead wrinkle. After sex he always seemed a little bit brain-dead. "In the old days of Earth-sailing ships, crossing the equator was a bit dodgy. The region around the equator was called the Doldrums, where the winds would fall away to nothing for days or weeks at a time. The ship would sit becalmed, in extreme heat, with no one aboard knowing if they would live long enough to catch a saving wind. Then steamships came along, and crossing the equator offered no special danger. But a ceremony called 'Crossing the Line' lived on. There were high jinks on board the cruise ships; parties and ritual shaving—not just of people's heads, either—and silly ceremonies involving King Neptune."

"It's King Jove on the Jupiter flyby, but the rest of it sounds much the same." Paul turned to look at Jan. "Look, I know it sounds stupid and it really is stupid, but as first officer I'm stuck with it. You don't have to go along."

"Are you kidding? Paul, there's no way I'd miss this. If I had been there in the old days crossing the equator, I'd have been whooping it up like nobody's business. My question is, can you as first officer take part in all the fun, or is it considered too undignified?"

"Define 'too undignified.' I suppose there are limits, but they're pretty broad. On the last Jupiter atmospheric flyby, two months ago, the chief engineer dressed himself in a baboon suit. He had cut a piece out of the back. His ass was bare, and painted blue, and he said he was selling kisses. But I didn't hear of any takers."

"Captain Kondo permitted this?" Jan had trouble imagining the captain, short, stocky, and immensely dignified, participating in the brawl that Paul was describing—or even allowing it.

"Captain Kondo remained in his quarters throughout the party. He does that on every Jupiter swingby. His view is that what he does not see, he is not obliged to report."

"And you? What did you do?"

"Last time? I was lucky enough to be on duty, running the ship—someone has to. Officers on duty are not permitted to join in the general wildness. This time, no such luck. I'll be assigned to passenger service. My official responsibility—as stated in ships' orders—is 'to offer and provide to passengers any form of legal pleasure that they desire.' You have no idea what some people ask for."

"I'll tell you what they'd better not ask for. When does this party start?"

"Not for awhile."

"But when?"

"We're lying here nice and cozy, and you want to worry about time? Ten hours from now, give or take. Is that close enough?"

Jan snuggled closer and blew across his chest. She liked to watch the fair hair stir and his nipples tighten. "It will do. Ten hours should be more than enough to think of something to do. Something legal. Something you're not allowed to refuse. . . ."

As the time drew nearer, Jan wasn't so sure. She knew what she wanted, but Paul had a certain native prudishness and delicacy. He liked to wash at once after lovemaking, while Jan preferred, as she had told him to his mild disgust, "to wallow and steep in it for hours and hours." Afterplay, with the smell and feel of male sexuality, had not lost its novelty and appeal, and Jan was not sure that it ever would.

Would Paul cooperate? He would certainly have no chance to wash for awhile if he did. On the other hand, Jan was hearing more and more talk of previous swingby parties and they sounded like a case of anything goes. Paul might have trouble holding onto his dignity, even if Jan were not around.

Meanwhile, preparations for the party were in full swing. The point of closest approach to Jupiter, when the *Achilles* would make its deepest penetration into the Jovian atmosphere before racing out again for its rendezvous with Ganymede, would take place in a little more than three hours. Before that, an early dinner must be served and done with, so that the big dining room could be emptied and decorated for the party. So far as Jan could tell, the dining room would merely serve as a focal point for festivities—passengers and crew would be living it up in every part of the ship, except for the prohibited area aft that contained the crew quarters and the drives.

The little service robots had been allowed to make a jump-start on their duties. When the gong for dinner sounded over the ship's general communications system, Jan went along to the dining room and found it already half full and the tables decorated. Fresh flowers, somehow preserved since the *Achilles* left Earth orbit, perfumed each table, and each place-setting contained some special item chosen to match the background of whoever sat there. Jan looked for her own place, and found on the table a small replica of the Global Minerals' platform on which she had worked for more than ten years.

She went quickly around the room, searching for Sebastian's name card, and found a similar replica on the table in front of his seat. He also had something extra. At the place where he would be sitting Jan saw a small globe on a support stand. It was maybe five centimeters across, and when Jan looked closely she realized that it was not, as she had assumed, an Earth globe. The little sphere was Saturn, and as she watched the cloud patterns moved across the planet's face. This, for a guess, was a special present to Sebastian from Valnia Bloom.

Jan returned to her own table. As she was sitting down she saw Sebastian and Valnia enter together. Valnia looked worried—did she ever look anything different?—but Sebastian gave Jan a smile and a wave. He seemed different, older and more poised. His face was thinner and his expression more focused, and for the first time in her life Jan saw a mature man of thirty-five. Whatever Valnia Bloom was doing certainly appeared to be working. Jan smiled back and gave Sebastian a thumbs-up. They were less than a day away from Ganymede, and only a few weeks from their final destination at the weather station on Saturn's minor moon, Atlas.

She stood up, with the idea of going across to talk to Sebastian, but at the same moment Captain Kondo arrived at her table. He gave a nod of greeting and waved his hand to indicate that she should not stand up on his behalf.

That had not been Jan's intention, but rather than explaining she sat down again. "I'm a little surprised to see you here, Captain," she said. "I rather thought that you would— well . . ."

"Would certainly not be present?" Captain Kondo did not smile, but there was a definite twinkle in his eye. "Have no fear, Ms. Jannex, as soon as dinner is over, and well before flyby, I will be on my way out of here."

"I gather you do not enjoy such things."

"I would not say that. Perhaps I worry that my somber presence would dampen the gaiety of others. Or, who knows? Perhaps I might find myself carried away, and indulge in activities which I would later regret."

The captain was in a more playful mood than Jan had ever seen him. Apparently no one onboard was immune to the party atmosphere. It gave Jan hope that Paul would go along with what she had in mind. She saw him at the far side of the room, preparing to sit down at a table distant from hers.

No matter. She did not propose to make her suggestion during dinner, with other passengers around, and certainly not in the presence of Captain Kondo.

The dining room filled early, without any of the usual late stragglers. The food was exceptional in both its quality and its variety. Jan saw some from Earth, some from the Ganymede and Callisto deep farms, and even a few exotics from Mars. One item she did not recognize at all, but suspected it had been grown on the warm-blooded vegetation lattices of Saturn's moon, Tethys. The diners, dressed except for the crew in their elaborate party best, paid little attention to the food. Their minds were already moving on past dinner. The instant of closest approach to Jupiter would be signaled by bells all over the ship's communication outlets. That moment lay less than two hours away.

As the final course was being served, Captain Kondo stood up. Crew members, scattered around the room, had obviously been waiting for this moment. They hushed their neighbors as the captain turned, so that he could take in everyone in the crowded dining room.

He raised his glass, and tiny bubbles glistened and winked in the bright overhead lights. "To all of you," he said, "and to your new and successful life as part of the Outer System. Ladies and gentlemen, you are the future. Work hard, live well, be happy and fertile, and I hope that someday I will meet each of you again."

Glasses were raised, the toast was echoed and drunk. Moments later, as conversation around the room resumed, Captain Kondo nodded to his table companions and quietly left. Jan felt the subtle change in atmosphere. It said, "Captain's gone. Party time!"

She had been careful not to eat too much. She hoped that Paul had done the same. For what she had in mind, she did not want an overstuffed and lethargic companion.

He had moved away from his original table and she searched the room for him. He was standing over by the far wall. Unlike the passengers, the crew were not in party-dress. He looked terrific in his white uniform. It was no surprise to

Jan to see that Paul was surrounded by half a dozen brightly-clad women.

All the passengers were moving around now, impeding the progress of the robotic servers who were doing their best to clear the tables and move them into storage. The whole dining room was to be an open surface available for music, conversation, and dancing. Jan edged her way through. A couple of meters away from Paul she went to stand by the wall, and waited.

It took a few minutes, but eventually he was alone and drifted over toward her. He said, "An excellent dinner, don't you think?"

It was a neutral remark. He knew that tonight she had something unusual in mind, but neither his face nor his manner revealed that. He was making Jan take the initiative, not exactly playing hard-to-get but giving her full freedom to make suggestions.

Jan said, in just as calm and formal a voice, "Closest approach to Jupiter will happen in an hour or so."

He glanced at his watch. "An hour and three minutes."

"I've heard it said that the captain and the second in command of a ship like this have keys that will open or close any of the locks." Jan was staring away across the room, as though the conversation might be a little boring to her. Inside, she was tingling. "Is that true?"

"Quite true. We have to be able to deal with any sort of emergency. That would be impossible if parts of the ship were inaccessible." He glanced at Jan. "By the way, I should mention that there will be an engineer aft with the Diabelli Omnivores, if they happened to be somehow on your mind."

"They weren't." She turned to face him. "Paul, there is an observation port right at the front of the ship. Do you know it?"

"Given my position on this ship, that's almost an insult. Come on, Jan. Of course I know it. I've been there dozens of times."

"How would you like to go there again—with me? I want you to lock the door, so that nobody else can get in." She reached out her hand and placed it flat against his chest. The white uniform was cool to her touch, but she could feel the beat of his heart. "And then"—she was nervous, breathless— "I want us to stay there. I want to make love during the Jupiter swingby. I want to reach orgasm exactly when we are at the point of closest approach to the planet."

"My God. You don't ask for much, do you?" But his eyes were alive with speculation. "I was trained as an engineer. An engineer is always allowed some kind of operating tolerances. When you say *exactly* at swingby minimum distance—how close do we have to get?"

"You would know that better than me. But I want the bells in the ship and the bells inside me ringing at the same time."

He stood for a moment, thoughtful. Then he nodded. "It might be possible. But before we start, I need five minutes to pay my respects to a couple of other passengers. Head forward, just as far as the bend in the corridor, and wait for me—and don't get friendly with anyone else. We have a date in the forward observation chamber. If anyone asks what you will be doing, say it is a project of the highest priority."

Jan nodded, stepped away from Paul as if she were bidding him a polite good evening, and walked toward the dining room exit. Her legs felt wobbly, which was ridiculous—that's how your legs were supposed to feel *after*, not before.

She was almost out of the room when the fresh-faced young sailor approached her. He had traveled Earth's southern oceans before deciding to try the Outer System, and they had spoken about the sea life several times. He had seemed interested in Jan, and now he was smiling.

"Great dinner, and I bet it's going to be a great party. Are you lined up for anything special?"

"I'm afraid I am." Jan pulled a face. "You know, Sebastian Birch and I will be going on to Saturn, to work on the Atlas weather station. I've been asked to study Jupiter's cloud patterns as we are making our atmospheric entry and withdrawal, in preparation for what we'll be doing at Saturn."

"That's a bit much, isn't it? On a party night." He looked disappointed, and said as he turned away, "But if it's your job, I guess you have no choice but to do it."

"I suppose I don't."

Jan made her escape as quickly as possible. As she went to wait at the bend in the corridor she had a new thought. Suppose the young sailor decided that she would like company during the cloud observations? He might come to the forward chamber, and discover that a quite different form of entry and withdrawal was taking place.

When Paul at last appeared, making a final farewell comment over his shoulder, her first words were, "When we're in the observation chamber and the door is locked, no one else can get in. Can they?"

"Only the captain. And the chance that Eric Kondo will run the gauntlet from all the way aft to all the way forward, with a high-grade party going on everywhere in between, is a flat zero unless he thinks the ship is in danger. Why? Who else are you expecting?"

Jan explained about the sailor from Earth as they went forward. Paul laughed, and said, "You know what sailors are. They know there's a port in every girl. But if he can enter the chamber when the door is locked, he will have earned anything he gets."

It was clear why Paul was so confident as soon as they entered the observation chamber and he locked the door. Jan had taken no notice of locks before, but this one seemed substantial and complex.

"Proprietary experiments were performed in here a couple of times," Paul said. "But so far as I know, it will be a first for this particular experiment."

He switched off the chamber lights and turned Jan to face forward. "Before we become distracted by anything else, take a look. Have you ever seen anything like it?"

The cloud-torn face of Jupiter filled half of the all-around observation port. Jan moved to the window and stared out. She felt overwhelmed. It was twilight at this location on Jupiter. The *Achilles* was close to the top of the atmosphere, racing forward for its planetary rendezvous. The ship would penetrate only the tenuous upper layers before skipping out again, but Jan could already feel—or imagine—a change in her weight caused by the deceleration.

She watched, fascinated, as they sped across gigantic puffy white thunderheads, or stared down into dark gas chasms wide and deep enough to swallow any of the inner planets. She caught sunlit gleams of orange and purple, and once a far-off bolt of green lightning. For the first time in her life she had a faint comprehension of what clouds and cloud patterns might mean to Sebastian.

She stood and stared for a timeless period, until at last Paul tapped her on the shoulder. He said softly, "I don't want you to feel that I am in any way rushing you, but it is less than twenty minutes to the point of closest approach. If you really want to ring your bell . . ."

"*All* my bells." As they gently and carefully undressed each other, Jan looked around the interior of the observation chamber. She had not thought things through in enough detail.

The floor of the room was cold, hard plastic. There were two chairs, but one of them was thin and angular and bolted down. The other chair was hinged, so that it would swing to follow the line of the ship's acceleration. It was also padded and probably comfortable, but if either she or Paul sat down in it the geometry would be completely wrong for close body contact.

Paul didn't seem concerned with practical matters. His attention was wholly on Jan's body, touching and kissing and nuzzling her. Finally she pushed herself away, held him by the shoulders, and said, "Paul, that feels wonderful. But, I mean, *how?*"

"How?" He sounded puzzled. "I was thinking the usual way, unless you have different ideas. We've done this before in free-fall."

"But this won't be free-fall. We'll decelerate—we are already doing it. Don't you hear the wind?"

Jupiter's thin upper atmosphere, rushing past at many kilometers a second, was already producing a thin shrill whistle on the outer skin of the *Achilles.*

Paul shook his head. "It won't quite be free-fall, but close to it. We'll feel a weak force—a small fraction of a gee—pushing us toward the outer wall of the chamber. I was thinking that with me like this"—he drifted across to flatten his back against the broad curve of the observation window, pulling her with him—"and you facing me, with your legs around me, like this . . . if you think it won't work, I'm ready to prove otherwise."

He was already doing so. Jan, her chin resting on his shoulder and her forehead just a few centimeters away from the transparent window, felt the nerve-tingling thrill of the first moment of entry. It would work, and it was working. Her own weight, slight but perceptible, pressed them closer together. The cloud-racked face of the planet flashed past her, and as Paul moved deeper inside her she felt thunderheads within rearing up to rival those from Jupiter's turbulent depths.

Paul whispered in her ear, "Three more minutes." She had no idea how he knew that. She nodded, kept her eyes open, and concentrated on catching the wave. It was going to work perfectly. She had wondered if such a thing were possible— had been half-convinced that it was impossible—but in just another minute or two . . . her legs were tightening, her eyes closing, her mouth opening, all the muscles of her lower body moving to their own internal rhythm.

And then, suddenly—too soon, much too soon—the bells of the ship's communication system rang out. Paul gave a final spasmodic thrust and pushed Jan away from him.

"No," she gasped. "Not yet. Keep going, Paul—another minute. Keep going!"

He slipped out, wriggled from under her, and dived toward the other side of the chamber. Jan cried out, "Paul, you can't—" The ship's bell was still ringing, and it sounded wrong. "What are you doing?"

"Not closest approach." He switched the lights on in the observation chamber and she saw him, naked and still erect, over by the door. He was working desperately at the lock. "Hull integrity alarm. Number Three Hatch—some drunken lunatic—this fucking cipher—"

He snarled in triumph, jerked the door open, and swung through. He was still stark naked. Jan, her heart pounding and her head dizzy, shaking as though abandoned at the top of a roller coaster, followed. She had no idea where Number Three Hatch might be, but the absolute urgency in Paul's voice overrode everything else. She followed him without any thought of clothing.

Amazingly, the corridor as far as she could see was filled with noisy people. They were cheering and waving, celebrating a Jupiter closest approach which had not yet happened. A man and a woman, half-undressed, leaned against each other. They were laughing. As Jan pushed past them, the woman said in a tipsy voice, "That's right, sweetie, go get him. Lots of good mileage left in him, I could see that."

Paul, five meters ahead, had swung open another door and thrown himself through. Jan, following more slowly, entered the chamber at the exact moment when a second set of bells rang out. These sounded a different note and were less strident than the ones that had interrupted them in the observation chamber. *This* was the moment of Jupiter closest approach— and the feeling in the pit of Jan's stomach was a universe away from orgasm.

The room she entered contained one of the *Achilles'* exit points. The inner airlock already stood open. Paul was grappling with a heavily-built dark figure floating by the outer one. Two safety catches on the lock had already been thrown. If the last one were freed, air from inside the ship would rush out, low-pressure hydrogen from Jupiter's upper atmosphere would replace it, and she, Paul, and the other man would all die.

Jan kicked off hard from the wall and sped headfirst across the chamber. Paul had the man around the neck and was trying to pull him backwards, but he had no way to exert leverage. The man ignored Paul completely and went on fiddling obsessively with the third catch on the lock.

Jan didn't know how to fight, especially in micro-gravity. As she came close she grabbed the man's right forearm, pulled herself toward it, and sank her teeth into the fleshy part of his thumb.

He gave a loud "Ow!" and released his hold on the catch.

The struggling trio spiraled away in mid-air, Paul still trying to throttle the bulky stranger. Jan lost her bite, but still held the arm. Three other people, two of them crew, burst into the chamber. As they wrestled the man to the floor, she saw his face.

It was Sebastian.

"I feel that I, not Sebastian Birch, must bear full responsibility for all that happened."

Dr. Valnia Bloom sat in the small medical center of the *OSL Achilles*. Her red hair was drawn back and hidden by a tight white skull-cap. With her thin lips, chalk-pale countenance, and haunted eyes, she resembled a living skeleton.

"It was at my suggestion," she went on, "that Sebastian agreed to have a series of treatments using selected psychotropic drugs. In our work together over the past weeks, I became convinced that his obsession with planetary atmospheres and their cloud patterns derives from some deep-seated compulsion, either natural or one implanted at an early age. We had been moving backward in time, seeking the site of his earliest memories. This afternoon we came to the time when his memory had been modified by the team that discovered him roaming and helpless in Earth's northern hemisphere. In an effort to reverse or bypass that block, I administered a second dose. Sebastian had been tolerating the treatment well, with no apparent side effects or post-session abnormalities of behavior. At dinner this evening he seemed his usual self, though perhaps more restrained than the others at our table. That was not difficult, since everyone else was euphoric, and I regarded Sebastian's poise as the sign of an increasing maturity that matched his actual age. I must admit that I too was in an elevated mood, and when Sebastian disappeared shortly after dinner I thought nothing of it. I assumed that he had gone to join a party somewhere else on the ship. Whereas . . ."

She gestured to the unconscious body on the bed next to her. Sebastian lay in a deep sleep.

Captain Kondo, standing at the end of the bed, looked to Jan and Paul Marr—both now dressed in conventional if somewhat rumpled clothing.

"Did you or anyone else knock him out, either with a blow or with the use of a sedative?"

Paul and Jan shook their heads.

"And you were with him continuously," Captain Kondo went on. He was both unrumpled and unruffled. "You were with him from the time that you overpowered him by the Number Three Hatch until he was brought here?"

Paul coughed and said, "Ah—not quite all the time. Two other crew members watched him for a few minutes. But they assured me that they did not touch him in any way while I was gone. He simply became unconscious, and they were afraid to do anything that might affect his condition." Paul did not add that in those few minutes he and Jan had hurried to the forward observation chamber, where they had dressed as quickly as possible without worrying about the fine details of their appearance.

Captain Kondo slowly nodded. "There will of course be a full investigation of this incident when we reach Ganymede. For the moment, I wish you to say nothing to any of the passengers. I will ask the same of the others who were present in the Number Three Hatch." He hesitated. "I was about to add that I would make a general statement, reassuring all passengers that the *Achilles* remains in a safe and spaceworthy condition. However, it is my sense that such an action on my part is quite unnecessary. The vast majority of the passengers are under the misapprehension that alarm bells, naked passengers and crew in a high state of physical arousal"—his eyes flicked from Jan to Paul. He knew!—"unarmed physical combat, and the towing of an unconscious person along a corridor to the ship's medical center, constitute nothing more than a normal and reasonable element of a Jupiter swingby ceremony. I believe it best if they remain with that impression. Mr. Birch will of course be held under continuous close observation, for which I will now make arrangements."

He turned, apparently about to leave. Jan blurted out, "But what will this mean? Will Sebastian and I be allowed to continue on to Saturn? Do we—will we—I mean, is there a chance that we will be sent back—back to Earth?"

"You need have no fear on that score. You have been accepted into the service in the Outer System, and such acceptance cannot be revoked. You will not be returned to Earth. However, I am less sure that you will be permitted to proceed to Saturn." Captain Kondo raised an eyebrow toward Valnia Bloom. "I also think it likely that Dr. Bloom will choose to go with you wherever you are, at least for some initial period of time."

Valnia Bloom came to life. Her skeleton head nodded vigorously. "Of course. I caused this to happen. It is my responsibility to remain with Sebastian until I learn exactly what I did to him."

"That seems reasonable and appropriate. Let me add, we will dock on Ganymede in approximately six hours. I hope that you will find some agreeable diversion—or, at the very least, a respite from your immediate worries and concerns—during the remainder of what has been by far the most unusual Jupiter swingby of my career."

Captain Kondo nodded formally to the little group. "And now, I bid you a very good night."

22

In the early days of the Ligon corporate empire, the tradition was well-known if unspoken. The smartest of each generation ran the family business. The worthy but uninspired went into the church or military service, while the idiots with Cousin Hector's combination of stupidity and furious energy would be tucked away on a remote part of the broad baronial estates where he could do little damage.

Alex stared out of the port and decided that the Ligon family had now adopted a new principle. Today, the fool of the family was sent off on a fruitless mission to a distant part of the solar system. There he was supposed to meet with a man who preferred to avoid everyone, and persuade him in a manner unspecified to share his lease on Pandora with the Ligon corporate interests.

Based on what he had seen so far, Alex found it hard to believe that a rational human would want any part of the Saturnian system. The sun was a feeble and shrunken disk of light, nothing like the radiant orb visible from Ganymede. As for the planet itself, guarded by its great ring system, Saturn gave an impression of cold, aloof mystery. When Great-aunt

Cora had described Alex's trip to Saturn as being to "the outback of the solar system," Uncle Karolus had laughed and said, "More like the outhouse." As for Alex's final destination, which he was fast approaching, that was nothing at all—an insignificant mote of a world, forever unable to support an atmosphere, a gravity field, or a civilization.

The only moon of Saturn that any Ligon family member took seriously was Titan, today clouded by dense hydrocarbon fogs, but with long-term potential, according to the professional world-builders, that matched Ganymede and Callisto.

So what *did* Pandora, only minutes away, have to offer? Nothing but the old rule of real estate: location, location, location. It was well situated to operate as the nerve center for the swarming Von Neumanns who would mine the Saturnian atmosphere. More important yet, it commanded the access rights for that mining.

Which just made things tough for the present occupant, because in Alex's experience, what Ligon wanted Ligon got. For instance, they wanted him here, and here he was. Kate had been confident that the work he was doing on the predictive model would persuade their superiors that he should remain on Ganymede. Her message of recommendation to that effect had gone all the way up to Magrit Knudsen—and bounced back down with a totally contrary command. Alex would not only go to Pandora and communicate with its mysterious occupant, he would explain his work on predictive models and the problems that they were encountering.

That seemed like an insult to both Kate and Alex. Kate had done some checking through her own network, and learned that the hermit who lived on Pandora had a reputation for gluttony and arrogance in roughly equal parts. The only reason for asking him anything was that he had once worked for Magrit Knudsen and apparently owed her some allegiance.

Also, a few years ago he had sorted out—more by luck than anything else, according to his fellow-workers at the time— a major mystery on Europa.

Alex had been told to expect no greeting at Pandora's single dock. He was to make his way from the surface, through multiple air-locks, and down a long elevator shaft. That was as far as the instructions took him. From that point he would be on his own.

Docking in the negligible gravity of Pandora took only a few minutes. Alex, about to leave his single-person ship, hesitated. On the journey from Ganymede he had spent his waking hours playing with the predictive model, making a variety of assumptions, plugging them in as exogenous variables, and studying the output. The ship's computer had a Seine link, but one permitting only an infuriatingly low transfer data rate. Alex's results had been more puzzling than persuasive.

However, he would not leave them behind. He dismounted the data cube that contained both his program and his most recent results, and tucked them away in a side pocket of his travel bag. If Rustum Battachariya was, as Magrit Knudsen insisted, a computer specialist with considerable intellectual resources of his own, perhaps Alex might find a way to repeat his recent runs in a more forgiving computer setting.

The descent into Pandora's gloomy interior did not affect Alex as it would have, say, Kate or his mother. He was not interested in the physical appearance of his surroundings— "blind as a worm," according to Kate, when it came to niceties of furnishings. Had he been taking notice, he would have discovered one point at least on which he and the lone inhabitant of Pandora agreed: simplicity. The walls were bleak rock or dull plastic. Alex passed through the last of three massive sets of air-locks, removed his suit, and kept going.

At the end of the elevator shaft he had no options as to

what to do next. A single corridor, forty meters long, ended in a steel door. The door was closed, but a red button stood in the center with a sign above it: AFTER THE BUTTON IS PRESSED, YOU WILL HAVE SEVEN SECONDS IN WHICH TO EN-TER.

Alex pressed, drifted on through as the door opened, and wondered about the need for such security. So far as he could see there was nothing on or in Pandora that anyone in his right mind would think worth stealing. What it suggested was extreme paranoia on the part of the man he was about to meet.

Beyond the door Alex found himself at the side wall of a chamber that stretched far off to left and right. If the corridors and elevators he had seen so far were unusually empty, this room made up for them. It was packed—not with furniture, but with *machines*, all dust-free, gleaming, and placed relative to each other with great care. The only object out of place, in both its nature and its condition, stood about eight meters away on Alex's left.

It was—Alex had to take a second look to make sure—a person; a man of colossal size, dressed in rumpled and tight-fitting black clothes, and with a black cowled hood that partly concealed his face.

The man nodded to Alex. He said, in a rumbling but pre-cise voice, "I have observed your progress since the arrival of your ship at the surface. I must say that you arrive at a pe-culiarly inconvenient time."

"For both of us," Alex said.

He was ignored as the other went on, "I will not say wel-come to Pandora, since that would be gross insincerity on my part. I will, however, ask if you have dined."

Alex hadn't eaten, nor did he particularly want to; but since this seemed like an unexpected attempt at politeness, he shook his head and said, "I didn't eat."

"Nor did I." The other man threw back the cowl, to reveal a round shaven head. "I am, of course, Rustum Battachariya, and you of course are Alex Ligon. You may find it easier to call me Bat, though this should not be presumed to indicate any desire for a closeness of relationship between us. And when I invite you to share my afternoon repast, it is only because a failure to do so would display a churlish lack of civility and hospitality on my part."

He led the way toward the far end of the room. Alex, who wondered if he had understood what the other was saying— it sounded, improbably, like he was inviting Alex to eat lunch—followed close behind. He could not help glancing from side to side as they went. The artifacts lining the walls or standing mounted on the floor formed a bizarre collection. None was new, many seemed from a much earlier generation of technology. Some bore the marks of fire, great force, or heavy impact.

Rustum Battachariya must have had eyes in the back of his head, because without turning he asked, "Are you perhaps interested in relics of the Great War?"

"Not particularly." Alex actually had no interest at all in the Great War.

"Hmmph."

They proceeded in silence to the end of the room, then around an opening in a wall partition that did not run all the way to the ceiling. It led into a kitchen as elaborate as any that Alex had ever seen. The equipment included pots and pans big enough to serve a dozen people, although only two chairs stood by the solidly-built table. As an additional feature—odd for any kitchen—a small communications center was built into the wall next to one of the chairs. The display was turned on, but offered only white noise.

As they entered, as though greeting their arrival, the screen became a flickering mosaic of colors and a woman's calm voice said, "Confirmation of the Masters' conference call, to take place within one hour. The purpose is to finalize the Beston agreement with the Puzzle Network."

Bat scowled. "Noted and accepted." He saw Alex's questioning look. "That channel is specifically for Puzzle Network interactions. Is it possible that you are interested in, or perhaps even a member of, the Puzzle Network?"

"No, I'm not a member." Alex, convinced that another "Hmmph" was on its way, added, "I was very much into the Puzzle Network when I was younger, and I thought I had a chance to reach the Master level."

"But you were unsuccessful?"

"Not exactly. My family didn't think it was the sort of thing I should be interested in. My mother put a lot of pressure on me to give it up."

"Ah. The problem of parents." The round black head nodded. "I too had such difficulties, until we parted company when I was a teenager."

"You left home?"

"To be rather more accurate, they threw me out. My parents, like yours, considered my level of interest in the Puzzle Network inordinate and inappropriate." Bat waved a fat hand toward one of the chairs. "Please be seated. Few things in the universe must be delivered precisely on time, but a perfect soufflé is one of them."

Alex sat down with no great expectations. The other man could clearly put away a mountain of food, and from the look of him he often did, but quantity was no guide to quality. And Alex had eaten meals prepared by the best chefs in the

System. Prosper Ligon had no interest in food, but the rest of the family insisted on the highest quality of cuisine.

Bat quickly produced from half a dozen different ovens a giant soufflé, three different cooked vegetables, five sauces, and a loaf of bread which he sliced with amazing speed and dexterity. Alex filled his plate, began to eat, and after a few moments stared at his companion. He shook his head. "This is sensational. I think it's the best food I've ever had."

"Probably." Bat was tasting carefully, a frown on his pudgy face. "It is better than average. I feel, however, that I was perhaps a trifle heavy-handed with the tarragon."

Alex didn't know if he was supposed to agree or disagree. He decided that it was safer to eat in silence. So far they had managed to agree on nothing except the problem of having parents. Rustum Battachariya also showed no inclination to conversation, eating steadily and thoughtfully and in quantities that established a need for outsized cooking utensils.

Finally Bat pushed away his plate, sighed, and said to Alex, "We have dined together, which will perhaps ensure a degree of civility in what follows. Or perhaps not. Let me be frank. I agreed to meet with you for one reason only: I was warned that should I refuse to do so, strong tactics might be used against me. Specifically, I was warned of physical violence or even murder. What is your reaction to such warnings?"

"They are absolute nonsense. I would never consider any sort of threat."

"That is gratifying to hear. Are you confident that you speak for your whole family? If so, this meeting may be concluded at once, and we can return to our respective interests."

Alex was on the spot. If he was confident of anything, it was that he could *not* speak for the whole family. At last he said, "I think it might be a good idea if you and I were to continue our discussion."

"Very well. Let us do so. But I must ask, on what basis? You would like me to give up or share my lease on Pandora. Why? And what inducements can you offer me, other than the not inconsiderable one that my life and physical well-being might otherwise be in jeopardy?"

"I have the authority to offer you a considerable amount of money, far more than the cost of your lease on Pandora."

"Money?" Bat dismissed the word with a wave of his hand. "I happen to know that you work for the Outer System government, at a salary which is by the standards of your own family members ludicrously low. Am I supposed to believe that your own principal motive in life is money? If it is not, why should you assume that I am any different? Come, Mr. Ligon, if as a young man you approached Puzzle Network Master level, you cannot be without intelligence. Surely you can make an argument stronger than that?"

Greedy and arrogant seemed to be about right. Alex had watched Bat put away enough food for six people, and now the haughty part was showing through. Alex remembered Kate's words. *He's so fat and obstinate you can't push him. You have to move him some other way.*

Alex was saved from the need for immediate reply by the chime of the communications unit set in the wall by Bat's left hand. The same woman's voice said, "Conference will begin five minutes from now. Elect visual or voice-only mode."

Bat said, "Voice only," and then to Alex, "I may require privacy for a brief period. This is a matter of great practical significance."

"That's all right. I brought my programs and some recent results. I'll have plenty to do—if you can provide computer access."

"Of course. You may have access to the Seine, or if you

prefer it you may use the Keep, which is my wholly internal and protected resource. If the latter—"

Bat's next words were drowned out by a grating klaxon that sounded all through the Bat Cave. Alex felt a series of heavy vibrations, carried through the floor.

As the klaxon ended, the woman's voice spoke again. "We are registering interference on all incoming communication channels. A foreign body which offers no identification is approaching Pandora and seeking forcible entrance. All external access has been sealed. Habitat separation of the Bat Cave from outside influences is complete."

Alex saw Bat's questioning glare and shook his head. "Not my doing. I have no idea what is happening."

"No more than do I. The timing of this is extraordinarily inconvenient. Unless, of course, it was expressly *designed* to interfere with my planned activities. My conference call is minutes away. Who would attack Pandora, and why? This is not the best location to address those questions. Come." Bat led the way, out of the kitchen and along the length of the Bat Cave.

Alex, following, understood Bat's final remark when they reached the other end of the great rectangular chamber. The communications center in the kitchen had been small and primitive. The one they approached was as elaborate as anything controlled by Ligon Industries.

Bat plumped himself down on a massive padded chair. "We are, of course, in no danger of any kind. We are sealed and shielded, from both material and electromagnetic interference." To Alex he seemed as much intrigued as annoyed as his fat fingers rippled over a console. "No ship in the solar system is capable of doing significant material damage to Pandora. Which leaves the question, who would want to come out here, jam all incoming signals, and try to blunder in? All system communications are monitored. A man would have to be an utter fool to imagine that such a situation could be maintained for any length of time, or that he and his vessel would not promptly be taken into custody."

A man would have to be an utter fool . . .

Alex had no trouble thinking of a candidate. Hector! His cousin knew that the Ligon family wanted the current lease-holder out of Pandora. Lucy Mobarak had asked Hector to perform some great deed. Could his cousin be such an idiot as to think that threatening Rustum Battachariya on his home ground would qualify—at the very time when Alex himself was out here to negotiate?

Easily. It was exactly the kind of pea-brained action, with never a thought as to consequences or what he himself would do next, that Hector had specialized in since he was old enough to walk. The irritating thing was that his cousin seemed able to get away with it. Aunts and uncles said, "Oh, that was Hector. You know what Hector's like . . ." and left it at that.

It wasn't something that Alex could easily explain to anyone who was not part of the family. Instead, he said, "You mentioned that you feared aggressive action unless you came to some arrangement. Is the conference call that you'll be missing connected with that?"

Bat finished running his fingers over the console. "We're totally blacked out so far as incoming or outgoing signals is concerned," he said. "No estimates as to how long it will last." And then, "My conference call is on a different subject entirely. Have you been following the recent news leaks about alien messages?"

Aliens again! The word went into Alex like an electric shock. He'd had aliens on his mind for weeks. They formed part of some of the high-probability predicted futures, in strange and confusing ways. But Bat couldn't possibly be referring to that.

Alex said cautiously, "Well, I've seen a blurt or two about alien messages. But you don't believe what you hear on those."

"Normally, you should not. In this case, however, the situation is rather different." Bat composed himself on his chair. With head bowed forward and hands placed palms together in front of him, he reminded Alex of some ancient carved idol. Alex stood and fidgeted uncomfortably.

"I believe that I can divulge this to you without compromising confidentiality," Bat said at last. "The time for the official news release is very close. Puzzle Network members, as you are surely aware, do not seek or enjoy the company of others. We do not cluster, we do not congregate, we rarely make group decisions. However, some years ago it was agreed by the Master level players of the Network that there might be one notable exception. The ultimate challenge as a puzzle would surely be the deciphering of a signal from an extraterrestrial intelligence. For such a thing, we would sacrifice privacy and anonymity. We would work together, we would even, if necessary, *meet*."

"Here, in the Bat Cave?"

"I think not." Bat's expression revealed his repugnance at the thought. "This is—or was once, and should be—my private retreat."

"But if you don't meet here, you'd have to go somewhere else."

"Your statement, although undeniably true, is hardly a triumph of abstract deductive thought."

"Are you saying that the blurt is right—an alien message has really been received?"

"Your skepticism matches my own feelings when I first

heard rumors over the blurt outlets. I generally dismiss as preposterous any claims of alien signals. That remained my position for several recent weeks, as confirmation of the blurt failed to appear. Four days ago, the situation changed radically. A group of high-level Masters of the Puzzle Network, of which I happen to be one, were contacted by a man named Philip Beston. He is head of the Odin Station at Jovian L-5. Beston asserted an alien signal has in truth been received— he forbore to call it a *message*, since no interpretation has as yet been performed. However, he did offer convincing evidence of both signal detection and verification. Moreover, he invited selected senior members of the Puzzle Network to join his group in a high-level collaborative effort, aimed at taking the first steps to transform a meaningless data stream signal to an intelligible message. As you might imagine, such an invitation proved irresistible. Network members normally work in isolation. Now, for the first time ever, we would pool findings and conjectures. The purpose of today's conference call was merely to finalize a venue for that cooperative effort, since close proximity seems essential."

"So you *are* going somewhere else."

"Since I decline to convert the Bat Cave into a hotel for Puzzle Network Masters, that unfortunately appears to be the case."

"Where?"

"I cannot be certain. However, the probabilities strongly favor Ganymede. It forms a home to more than half the Puzzle Masters."

"I don't believe this. I just *came* from Ganymede. You dragged me here, across half the solar system—"

Bat's eyebrows rose high on his rounded forehead. "Excuse me? *I* dragged *you*? I dragged no one. Your presence was *imposed* on me, by extreme pressure from your family and a senior member of the Ganymede government."

"You're right. Forget I said that. I didn't want to come, any more than you wanted me here. But why didn't you tell me you might be on Ganymede in the near future?"

"For the best of all possible reasons. At the time when your journey began, I had no idea of any of this. I was still an extreme skeptic on the subject of SETI messages. By the time that my doubts were dispelled by Philip Beston's call and accompanying evidence, you were already on the way."

"I'm sorry." Alex decided that blowing off steam at Bat would get neither of them anywhere. "I could have figured out the timing for myself. Assuming that you do go to Ganymede, how long will you be there?"

"I have no idea. Some weeks, or perhaps even months. The desire to be here, surrounded by the creature comforts and privacy of my own home, is very large. At the same time, suppose that we make significant progress in deciphering a message from the stars. That is probably unrealistic optimism, but how could one then resist staying, at least through the initial phase of discovery. It is a true case of Buridan's famous ass."

"I can see that." Alex thanked whatever gods may be that he recognized the reference to Buridan's donkey, starving to death because it was unable to choose between two equal bundles of hay. Cousin Hector would no doubt have said that he didn't know this woman, Buridan, but from the sound of her he'd like to meet her.

But Alex saw a rare opportunity to come out a hero with his own family. "You are going to be away from Pandora for at least several weeks. In your absence, it would be easy for Ligon Industries to set up their operations center for helium-three mining from Saturn's atmosphere at the other end of Pandora—so far away, you would never be aware of its presence. And the whole *Starseed-Two* project won't be of long duration—it can't be, without substantial penalty clauses. If we guaranteed that the installation would be done in your absence, with guarantees that nothing would affect the Bat Cave . . ."

Bat nodded, and for one moment Alex dared to hope they might have a deal. But then Bat said, "It is premature for any such discussion. I do not yet know where the Puzzle Masters will assemble, and already you have me off on Ganymede. Perhaps something can be arranged—if and when my own movements are more defined." He waved a slab-like hand, dismissing the subject. "Enough of that speculation. I have explained to you the reason for my interest in aliens. What is the basis for your own?—I sensed more enthusiasm for that topic than for any other subject we have mentioned."

Alex shook his head. "My interest is complicated and relates to my work on predictive models. It would take time and computer access to explain."

"Time, apparently, is available in ample measure." Bat waved his hand again, this time at the displays which showed all external communications still blocked. "Why are you interested in aliens? And why might the computers be relevant?"

Alex was hesitant at first. How much, if anything, did the other know of computer modeling? He began slowly, giving the sort of general explanation that would suffice for upper management, until Bat scowled and said, "*Details*, please, root and branch. Generality and vagueness are the refuge of scoundrels, politicians and bureaucrats."

Put that way . . .

Alex began to describe his work at a deeper level, encouraged by Bat's close attention and occasional nods. When he reached the tricky subject of the predicted extinction of humanity, and the dependence of that on exogenous variables, Bat blinked and nodded.

"I, too, have had intimations of approaching catastrophe throughout the solar system. The evidence I have seen is tenuous, but it suggests disaster much closer than a century away. Did your program take account of the possible effect of new weapons left over from the Great War?"

Alex shook his head. "I didn't include them, because I have never heard of any such thing."

"Very well. There are two other anomalous factors that you might wish to take into consideration. First, a small group of genetically modified humans was created as a by-product of the Great War. So far as I know, they live quiet and productive lives, but their possible impact on future events cannot be discounted."

"I know about them, and I've run the model with and without their presence. The results do not changed significantly."

"Very good. Then there was a group of humans of apparent great longevity, near-immortals who were active on Ganymede but vanished a generation ago. Nothing has been seen of them since, and it was conjectured that they chose to remove themselves to the far reaches of the outer system. However, they also might be significant to the future."

Alex nodded. "I knew of them, too, and I ran the model both ways, with and without them. They also made no difference."

"Then for the moment I have no other suggestions." Bat glanced again at the display of blocked communications. "Let us return to the question of the effect of aliens. Can you describe how their presence affected your predictive model results?"

"I can do a lot better than describe." Alex fumbled in his

travel bag and produced the data cube. "I can show. Here are all the programs and the results. We can—oh, no, I guess we can't. With access to outside communication blocked, we can't get to the Seine. My models really suck up computer resources."

"Such resources, fortunately, are available." Bat looked smug. "Long before the Seine was activated, I foresaw dangers and difficulty in ensuring the privacy of my work. To be honest, one of my principal concerns was other members of the Puzzle Network. Cheating on a puzzle is by no means forbidden, including infiltration of another's databases. For that reason I established an independent computer capability here on Pandora. I call it the Keep. It is fully disjoint from all aspects of the Seine, and I would be surprised if your model is unable to run on it."

Alex was dubious. "When I said my model eats computer time and resources, I really meant it."

Bat inclined his massive head. "I do not doubt you. I merely say, try, and see. One of us, I suspect, will be surprised."

Bat had been referring to computer resources. Alex, as the runs proceeded, was astonished for quite other reasons.

The computer capacity available within the Keep was everything that Bat had suggested, with far more power than had been accessible to Alex prior to the arrival of the Seine. The predictive model ran fast, even at a high degree of detail. The cause of Alex's amazement, however, lay elsewhere.

He began by repeating the series of runs in which an alien influence was assumed to be at work in the solar system, sometime in the next half century. He duplicated exactly the runs that he had already made, and was not surprised to find exactly comparable results.

"You see, everything remains stable," he said to Bat. "No storage overflow, no solar system collapse, no end to humanity."

"A comforting conclusion, since in that time frame we might reasonably hope to be present ourselves."

"Right. But now see what happens when I make the same runs, and don't introduce any alien influence as a variable."

Again, it was an exact repeat of earlier runs that Alex had made. He sat back and waited for the instabilities to creep in, slowly at first and then catastrophically after half a century. He was so convinced of what he would see that he did not pay full attention to the results. Only when the time marker reached 2188, with a human population steadily growing and all variables within reasonable ranges, did he jerk up straight in his chair.

"That can't be right!"

"No?" Bat had also been relaxing, watching the near-hypnotic march of numbers and graphics across the displays. He leaned forward, frowning. "Forgive me if I appear a little lacking in perception, but I fail to see any anomalies."

"That's what's wrong with it."

Bat, mysteriously, said, "The dog in the night?"

Alex ignored that and pointed to the year, now 2190, and the display of population, which was approaching twelve billion. "It never did that before. Without an alien influence as an exogenous variable, the model always reached a crisis point about 2140. Population never rose beyond a maximum value of ten billion."

"There is a simple explanation." Bat sounded unimpressed. "Either you had a problem with the model in your earlier runs, or you have one now."

"You don't understand. It's the *same model*. I simply downloaded a copy before I left Ganymede. It must be your computer. It's not powerful enough to run my model."

"Never." All signs of boredom in Bat vanished. "The Keep contains resources more powerful than any Ganymede facility."

"You said you don't have access to the Seine when you're running in this mode."

"That is true, but not relevant. If it is simply computer speed that concerns you, the computers in the Keep should be more than adequate. Were you drawing on the Seine for other elements of the computation?"

"I'm sure I was. But I don't see any way it could change the model results. Are you suggesting that *the Seine itself* might destabilize my predictive model results?"

"At first sight, I agree that sounds like a preposterous notion. But what do we really know of the Seine, and how it operates? Have you run your model sufficiently?"

"Sufficiently to confuse me totally."

"Then with your permission, I will determine the external situation." Bat touched half a dozen points on the console. "Hm. Incoming signals remain inaccessible. However, that is no bad thing . . . I must think . . ."

Bat closed his eyes and turned into an obsidian statue. Alex stared at the vast figure, motionless on the padded seat, and declined to interrupt. He had plenty to occupy his own mind. He turned his attention again to the display. It had advanced another twenty years. Every parameter showed reasonable values. According to his model, humanity was doing fine a hundred years from now.

The *Seine* as a factor? That raised a whole new series of questions. The Seine had access to every data bank in the System. It could and would use whatever information the model called for. But at the level of sophistication and complexity of the predictive model, there was no way that any human could hope to track the entirety of data in use—not even for one day of prediction, never mind a century.

So where did that leave Alex? He had stuck his neck way out, assuring everyone from Kate all the way up to Magrit Knudsen that with the Seine his predictive model would give correct results. All he needed was adequate computational power. But there was a built-in assumption: the *only* thing that the Seine was supposed to do was compute. The results of a model should not depend on the computer on which it was run. However, since the Seine also had the power to bring in System-wide data sets which the *computer* deemed relevant to the computation, then the exact reproduction of any results could not be guaranteed. What data might the Seine possess to indicate that a solar system future without alien presence was unstable and doomed to human extinction, while a future containing an alien presence was stable? And why did the Keep's computer, aliens or no aliens, predict a future without a fatal collapse?

Alex was as capable of deep introspection as Bat. When a subdued beep came from the communication terminal, both men ignored it.

The beep came again, and again. At last an irate voice overrode the standard query signal and said, "Hello, Pandora. This is Atlas Station Security, calling Pandora. Are you receiving us? Hello, Pandora. Are you receiving this message?"

And then, in a fainter off-mike tone, "I think they're all asleep or unconscious. I wonder if they even know they were jammed?"

Bat scowled, opened his eyes, and replied, "We are neither asleep nor unconscious. We are *thinking*—a phenomenon possibly outside your experience."

"Oh, it's you again. Well, you might *think* that a little appreciation would be in order for what we've done for you.

We've arrested the wacko in the ship who was jamming your com lines."

"Do you have an identification and a motive?"

"Not yet. He's acting like a big hero and won't say a word, and we don't have a return yet for the ship's I/D. It's a Ganymede registration, though. Do you have anyone on Ganymede who dislikes you?"

"Numerous people."

"Surprise, surprise. Do you have any idea who this one might be?"

Bat looked hard at Alex. "No."

"Let us know if you want to press charges. We've got this fellow's ship in tow, and we're on our way. You have a waiting message stream whenever you decide to stop *thinking*. *Au revoir*, my ingrate friend."

"He seems to know you rather well," Alex said, then realized that might not be the most diplomatic of remarks.

Bat shrugged. "This is not my first encounter with the militants who call themselves the Atlas security force. Their main aim in life seems to be to protect me and the Bat Cave from physical assault, preferably by shooting at something. I have pointed out, many times, that this facility is more secure than their own base on Atlas. Although superficially rational, they appear incapable of learning this fact. No matter. Let us see what we missed in the past few hours." He touched the console, and surveyed the list of incoming messages. "All of them can, I feel, wait—with the exception of this one."

Another dab at the console. Three short sentences appeared on a small screen. *Meeting place, Ganymede, Level 147, Sector 291. Individual work stations established. Start date pending schedule from Philip Beston.*

Bat sighed. "As I thought. It will be necessary to leave the Bat Cave for awhile."

"And go to Ganymede? Is that the message from the Puzzle Group?"

"It is. And almost certainly, Attoboy sent it. It bears his laconic trademark. I will decipher it later."

"It seems straightforward enough."

"It would not be from Attoboy if it lacked a hidden message within the clear text."

"Maybe to tell you when the meeting begins?"

"I think not. I take his final sentence at face value."

"Can we meet again when you arrive at Ganymede?"

That produced Bat's longest hesitation so far. At last he said, "Your predictive model is new and intriguing, and it offers mysteries of inconsistency which so far I am unable to resolve. My instincts suggest that such a resolution could have far-reaching consequences. Certainly, this belongs on the four-sigma list."

Bat paused, studying Alex as though the two men were just being introduced. The shaved black head nodded a few millimeters. "Before your arrival I had heard much about the Ligon family; all of it was, I am sorry to say, highly negative. You fail to fit my preconceptions. You have a genuine interest in and talent for intellectual problems. I would not find the prospect of another meeting, when I am on Ganymede, intolerable."

One step at a time. Alex told himself that he had agreed to come here only because the family had pushed him, and he had never expected to succeed. Now when he returned to Ganymede he could report to Prosper Ligon and the others that, despite insane interference from Cousin Hector, he had made real progress. Rustum Battachariya had agreed to meet with Alex again—on Ganymede!

Magrit Knudsen was not there to provide Alex with a more striking evaluation of the situation. An agreement to meet again was the highest accolade that Bat ever offered to anyone. Alex had engaged Bat's attention in the most powerful way possible: he had provided a puzzle too subtle and intricate to be solved at once.

In Bat's upside-down universe, what could not be solved at once was not an annoyance; rather, in the best circumstances it would provide a source of ongoing pleasure and satisfaction for months or years to come.

23

Progress review meetings at Argus Station were held every Tuesday morning, starting at midday. This was Monday, ridiculously early in the morning. Why was she being summoned to the conference room?

Milly—just out of bed, hair falling into her eyes, without breakfast, starved of caffeine, less than half-awake—answered the call and hurried to the meeting. Despite all her efforts, she arrived ten minutes later than requested. She entered, braced for a tongue-lashing from Jack Beston.

On the threshold she paused, bewildered. The room was empty. A gruff voice from behind her said, "Yes, you're at the right place. We're all late. Go on in, and let's get things moving."

She turned. Jack Beston was behind her, his usually ruddy face pale and taut. With him was the mystery woman, Zetter.

"Didn't I tell you?" Jack said. He seemed to be talking to Milly, not Zetter. "Even before we left Odin Station, I knew that the bastard was up to something."

Milly could tell from the intonation that 'bastard' was being used with a different meaning. It was now a description, not a name.

"Zetter," Jack went on. He waved the two women to hard-backed chairs, and settled himself on a third with his arms folded over the back. "You tell her."

Zetter's vulpine face was uneasy, as though revealing information to anyone but Jack Beston himself was an unprecedented and dangerous activity. "We have received information from Odin Station," she said. The sharp nose twitched. "Soon after you two left, Philip Beston sent a secure message to certain senior members of the Puzzle Network."

"Secure, but not secure enough," Jack said. "You've heard of the Puzzle Network, Milly?"

"Yes." This was no time for Milly to go into details. She was too eager to learn what the Bastard had said.

"In brief," Zetter continued, "Beston has proposed a working collaboration between Odin Station and the Puzzle Network. They would form a joint venture for the interpretation of the SETI message. He will make available to them everything that he and his team are able to discover. The Puzzle Network team, in return, will channel any results that they obtain to him, on an exclusive basis."

"Putting it another way," Jack said, "we're screwed. The Bastard has signed up the top brains in the System at this kind of problem. Those characters work on fancy intellectual problems *for pleasure*. I don't know how good they are, but I have to assume they're the best."

"They are," Milly said. "The absolute best."

"Then we're doubly screwed. They're nuts, but they're *smart* nuts. The worst sort." Jack slumped into a chair, his chin cupped in his hands. After a moment he looked up. "How come you know so much about this, Milly Wu? Did the Bastard come crawling around you, trying to get you involved?"

That was uncomfortably close to the truth. Milly headed in a different direction. "I know the Puzzle Network because I used to be part of it. In fact, I was Junior Champion three years running. I only dropped out when I found that thinking about SETI was occupying more and more of my time."

"That right?" Jack Beston's eyes half closed to green slits. "Three years running?" Milly could hear the mental relays clicking over. "Zetter, that's all for now. I need a few private words with Milly Wu."

The thin face hardened, and Zetter's mouth compressed to a tight line. "You wish me to leave?"

"You got it."

"But our . . . source. What instructions do I provide?"

"Say, keep looking and listening. We're going to handle the rest from here."

Zetter nodded and did not reply, but as she left she gave a glare of hatred that Milly felt she had done nothing to deserve.

"Now, Milly." Jack Beston humped his chair over closer. "If you were champion three years in a row, in your Puzzle Network days you must have built up quite a reputation. You must still have close friends there."

There were things that you never said to your boss, no matter what the provocation. Here came one of them: "The hell with that, Jack Beston. I won't do it." Maybe it was lack of morning caffeine. "Not if you go down on your hands and knees and grovel."

"I just might do that. But Milly, listen to me for a minute." He eased his chair a few inches closer. "You started this whole thing. It's called the Wu-Beston anomaly, but everybody remembers the Wu rather than the Beston. Which is as it should be. But you know, and I know, that detection is only part of the story, and not the biggest part. Nobody today remembers who dug up the Rosetta Stone, what they recall are the people who used it to decipher hieroglyphics. The Bastard knows this, just as well as we do. It wouldn't surprise me if he's been thinking this way for years, he's such a sneaky devil.

"But now suppose that you were part of the Puzzle Network team that worked on the *interpretation* of the signal. Your name would be associated with every phase of the work: detection, verification, interpretation. For all of history, the only name anyone would associate with the first SETI signal would be Milly Wu."

"And Jack Beston. What would he get out of this?"

"The satisfaction of knowing he'd beaten the Bastard on all fronts. And Milly, you have no idea how sweet that would be. Can you do it? Can you become involved in the Puzzle Network interpretation effort?"

"No. That would be impossible, I've been away from it for too long." But even as she spoke, Milly could imagine an approach.

She had not, as she suggested to Jack Beston, totally burned her bridges. In fact, less than six months ago she had heard from one of the Masters, Pack Rat, an older man with a taste for adolescent girls and a definite fondness for Milly (Puzzle Network Masters had to be smart, but no one said they had to be moral). He had sent her a puzzle, and invited her to have dinner. She had solved the puzzle the same day that it arrived, returned her answer, and declined the other invitation. But she felt sure that the door was open. Pack Rat had as good as told her that she was still a prime candidate for Master level in the Network.

Jack Beston was watching her closely. He was not, as Hannah Krauss had told her often enough, a man who easily took no for an answer. Rather, he took whatever he wanted. Milly, on the other hand, had taken as much of some things as she ever would.

She said abruptly, "Suppose I'm wrong, and it turned out to be possible for me to become involved in the Puzzle Network's interpretation work. Then I would have to leave here. There's no possible way that your brother would send information to Argus Station."

"Of course he wouldn't. We would have to travel to wherever the information center was located."

"*We.* What do you mean, we? Who are you talking about?"

"The two of us. You and me. Now that we have a verified signal, our interpretation team can carry on here very well without me."

"I believe that. But what would you do on Ganymede? Carry my bags? Because I can assure you of one thing: no one is admitted to the higher levels of the Puzzle Network without a track record and sponsors."

His face went from pale to bright red. Milly was ready for the Ogre's patented bellow of rage, but it never came. Instead, Jack took a deep breath, then said quietly, "I'm sure you are right. If I go to Ganymede, I will do whatever is most helpful in interpreting the signal." And then, more intensely, "Milly, you have to understand how I feel. This SETI project is terribly important to me. I've devoted most of my life to it, and I can't stand the idea of being anywhere but at the center of the action."

"When I came here I was willing to devote my life to this, too. But I almost quit in the first few weeks. You've been running the place for too long, Jack Beston. It's your money, and it's your project, and Argus Station is your station."

"Well?" He seemed bewildered. "Who else would you have run it?"

"That's not the point. You feel that because you're the boss

you're entitled to treat everyone like dirt. And maybe you
are—while you are here. But if you were to go with me to
Ganymede, and it's a big if, I wouldn't take your bullying
anymore."

"Have I bullied you?"

"What! Of course you have. You've bullied *everybody*. People
only stay because they're in love with the work. Did you know
that when we were over at Odin Station, Philip Beston asked
me to come and work with him?"

"My brother? The bastard!"

"That's right, the Bastard. And I have to tell you, I was
tempted."

"But you told him no."

"That's right. I told him no." Milly would never mention
what else she had told Philip Beston—that Jack was worth
ten of him. "Now I'm telling you no. No more treating me
like a child. No cussing me out or cutting me down in front
of other people. And not just me. Try giving all your staff
the respect they deserve. They are competent, they are hard-
working, and they have *earned* your respect."

A month ago, those words would surely have been followed
by Milly's instant dismissal. Now she sensed that the dynamics had changed. Jack Beston needed her more than she needed
the Ogre.

She knew she was right when he leaned forward to rest his
chin on his forearms, crossed along the back of the chair. His
green eyes gazed up at her through bushy red eyebrows, and
he said, "I'll tell you one person who's certainly competent,
and that's Hannah Krauss. She read through your entire background, and she told me: 'I recommend that we make an offer,
only don't kid yourself about what you're getting when you
hire this one. She's young, but she's a tiger. She'll cause you
trouble."

"I'm not a tiger." Milly remembered Uncle Edgar's words. *Let them think you're a mouse, girl. Just don't tell them what those black and yellow stripes are, and keep your mouth closed when you smile."*

"Fine." Jack stood up. "You're not a tiger. I'll remind you of that when we get to Ganymede."

"You're not going to fire me?"

"I guess I'm not." Jack had an unreadable little smile on his face. "Not today, at any rate. I may not be as smart as Philip—"

"The Bastard."

"The Bastard. But I do know when to keep quiet. Meanwhile, there is other excitement this morning. The clean-up team worked all night, and first thing this morning they called to tell me they have the final signal as tight and tidy as it will come. Want to take a look?"

"Yes! My God, yes."

"I thought you would say that." He was studying her face. "Before we go over there, though, I have another suggestion. You have the look of a starving woman. You and I should go and hunt up some breakfast. While we eat you can tell me everything else that I'm doing wrong. There's no better way to begin the working week."

The final signal was a string of twenty-one billion binary digits. It had been received over and over, until two weeks ago it had finally ceased. Now that direction in the sky offered nothing but the random white-noise hiss of the interstellar background.

The signal was still not ready for analysis. First, it needed correction. A more sophisticated version of the Bellman's rule—"What I tell you three times is true"—was applied to find and correct dropped, added, or errant digits. The repeated strings were compared, digit by digit, and rare discrepancies corrected by majority rule. Arnold Rudolph, looking even more ancient and tiny than ever, had reviewed the final output, and given it his seal of approval. The sequence was error-free.

"But as to what that means . . ." Rudolph stared at the others in the room. "You now pass into an area in which I claim no expertise. I will say only this, which I am sure has already occurred to all of you: a sequence of twenty-one billion binary digits could encode the entire human genome, three times over."

In addition to Milly and the Ogre, Pat Tankard and Simon Bitters were also present. No one laughed. Arnold Rudolph was referring to a suggestion almost as old as SETI itself: the notion that the first message from the stars might be the prescription not for a universal encyclopedia, nor a complex series of machines, but the information needed to build a living organism. That made the major assumption that alien life, like life in the solar system, would be built around a four-letter molecular code. Assign binary digit pairs to nucleotide bases; say, $(0,0) \equiv$ adenine, $(0,1) \equiv$ cytosine, $(1,0) \equiv$ guanine, and $(1,1) \equiv$ thymine; then any sequence containing an even number of binary digits was equivalent to a segment of a DNA molecule. You would make that DNA molecule, put it into a suitable environment for replication, and see what developed.

No one on Argus Station laughed at Arnold Rudolph's comment; on the other hand, no one took it too seriously. The idea would be checked—a billion possibilities would be checked during the interpretation effort—but the general feeling was, the game couldn't possibly be that easy. The search for a signal had taken a century and a half. The search for meaning might take as long.

There was another argument against the idea of the signal being biological. Turn the situation around and ask, how valuable would it be to send off to the stars the genetic description of a human? Even if some alien group were able to decipher the signal and provide an appropriate environment in which an embryo might grow, at the end of all that effort they would have a newborn baby. The aliens would know how a human lived and functioned, but nothing at all about what humans as a species had *learned*. Far better to send information about science and the technologies which aliens might find valuable.

Jack Beston stared at the screen, where the first infinitesimal section of the signal sequence was displayed. It appeared like a totally random string of 0's and 1's. "We'll try the biological approach, of course, even if we all think it's an unlikely answer. We can't afford to overlook something just because it resembles the way we developed. But I suspect we're more likely to make progress with physics or mathematics."

That too was standard orthodoxy. Biological organisms would tend to be specific to their planetary origins. Physics and mathematics should be the same all over the universe.

The others looked at Jack Beston, waiting for more direction. When he offered none, Pat Tankard said hesitantly, "We already know that the total sequence length has a moderate number of factors—it's certainly not prime, and it's not highly composite. I was thinking of taking a look at partition theory and prime factorization of parts of the array. See if any of the two-dimensional arrays look anything like a picture."

Jack nodded. "That's very good, Pat, but maybe we shouldn't stick with two-D. For all we know, our unknown signaller comes from avian stock, and thinks naturally in three dimensions. Or one dimension."

After another brief silence, Simon Bitters, who had been wandering around the room in his usual restless way, returned to the rest of the group, put his index finger on the end of his nose, and said, "The whole signal repeats with twenty-one billion periodicity, but I was thinking that maybe not all of it is information. There may be marker sub-sequences, things like stop-start codons that indicate where something with meaning begins and ends. We need to look for short repeat sequences, patterns that don't actually mean anything but that repeat over and over. I thought I would go through and examine local entropy, then see if that leads me to repeat markers."

"Very logical." Beston stared again at the maze of digits on the screen, and shook his head. "Good luck. But all of you, I wouldn't start on any of this until you've had some rest. Chance favors the prepared mind, but discovery favors the rested one. And remember, we're in this for the long haul. We may get lucky in a few months, but chances are we're years away from knowing what you've got there." He turned to Milly. "Anything else, before we let these hard-working people get some sleep? They've been up all night."

Milly shook her head and allowed Beston to lead her outside. Once the door to the room was closed, he stopped right in front of Milly.

"There, see that? Nice as pie, not a harsh word from me to anybody. That's what you wanted, wasn't it?"

"Yes." Milly hesitated. "You were polite, and agreeable. But I'm not sure that *they* are all right. I mean, I know they're short of sleep, but their behavior seemed kind of odd. They've just finished something important. You'd never know it from their attitudes. They acted *flat*."

"As if something was wrong?"

"Yes."

"Very perceptive. Something *was* wrong."

"But I couldn't tell what it was."

"I know absolutely what it was."

"Was it me? Do they resent me, and the fact that I was the one who first found the anomaly?"

Jack laughed. "No, it wasn't you, Milly. You are very smart, probably the smartest person who has ever worked at Argus Station, but they don't resent that. Also, you have lots of dedication and drive to go with your brains. But there are still things you don't know."

He leaned against the wall of the corridor, stared down at Milly's puzzled face, and went on, "You said it very clearly before we went in there. I'm an Ogre, and a monster, and I insult my staff and bully my staff and drive my staff. Now let me tell you a story. Back in the days when humans were just moving into space, there was a race between two countries to see who could be first to get human beings to the Moon."

"I know about that. I've read a lot of history about America and Russia."

"I'll bet you don't know what I'm going to tell you, because it was never in the official history books—just passed down by word-of-mouth. In the beginning, the Russians seemed to be well ahead. They had the first satellite, and the first man in space, and the first woman in space. Then the man who was running the American space program at the time made a decision. He chose a foreigner—a German, who had fought against the Americans in a recent war—and gave him the main responsibility for getting men to the Moon and back. He was asked, privately, 'My God, why did you pick him? If he fails, you will be criticized by everyone in the country.' The administrator said, "Do you think I don't know that? But he won't fail—he's too arrogant to let himself fail.' You see, Milly, the job we have here is a bit like the job they had. It's difficult, it needs technology that's right at the edge, and we're in a hurry. Most people at Argus Station don't have your self-confidence, or so much confidence in the project itself. They need somebody who shows in everything he says or does that we *can't* fail—and in this game, coming in second *is* failing.

"Now I want to ask you a question, Milly. You heard Pat Tankard's suggestion of examining two-D representations of the signal. What do you think of it?"

"To be honest, not very much. You can send information as images, but it's terribly inefficient. A picture may be worth a thousand words, but a high-resolution one costs you a million. Mostly you send messages as words and numbers, or their equivalent. And they are both one-dimensional data strings."

"Exactly. So one of us—you or me—ought to have pointed out that fact to Pat. We didn't, did we? Do you think that was doing her a service?"

"It wasn't. But she just *might* be onto something."

"Just might. In this game, though, you play the odds. For Pat Tankard's sake, I ought to have cut her down or at the very least warned her. A bit later I probably will, but now I have another question for you. You've heard me rant and rave, you've heard me cuss out my people, you've heard me be an absolute tyrant. So here's my question: when I'm not around, have you ever heard anyone on the staff say anything negative about me?"

Milly thought. The odd thing was, she hadn't. She could hardly count Hannah Krauss's warning that Jack Beston had a lot of sexual interest in the female staff members. And even there, Hannah had made it clear that she'd had her own experience with Jack Beston, and still held him in high regard.

"No one has ever said anything bad about you. Not to me, at any rate."

"But if I go on being wishy-washy, the way I was back in there, they'll soon start to. They'll begin to wonder if I'm losing it. Milly, in private with you I will be as nice as you want—as nice as you will let me be. But in our staff meetings, I have to be the same rip-roaring Ogre that people are used to. I'm going to push, and hassle, and never let anybody imagine for one moment that we won't come out of this as the team who found and cracked the first message from the stars." He nodded to Milly. "That's all I have to say. Contact your friends in the Puzzle Network, see if you can finagle your way onto that team. If you do, remember I want to go with you. And yes, if I have to I'll carry your bags."

He headed away along the corridor, quickly, so that Milly had no chance to reply. She stood for awhile, thinking. She was not even sure what her reply would have been. Half an hour ago she had felt in full command of the situation. She was the one with the contacts, the one with the clout, the one in control. Jack Beston had no choice. He would treat her in *her* way, as she wanted to be treated, or she would quit and leave Argus Station.

Now she was not sure what she would do. She was sure of only one thing: Jack Beston—still an Ogre, but apparently Ogre-by-choice—was a more complex person than she had ever suspected. And because of that, all Milly's own decisions had become more difficult.

24

On the trip from Pandora to Ganymede, Alex sent one short message and then turned off his communications unit. Only a general System emergency would be able to get through to him.

He had two reasons for taking that step, and in a sense Bat was responsible for both. At their second meal together, Alex had described the sequence of events leading to his trip to Pandora. Bat listened in silence, and at the end said, "It would seem that all the major actions in your life are entirely dictated by women."

That rankled. Alex was all set to disagree until he gave it a moment's thought. Kate, his mother, Magrit Knudsen, Lucy-Maria Mobarak: they had all pushed him around. He loved to be with Kate, but the rest he could do very well without. He knew that once his mother realized he had concluded his meeting with Bat and was on the way home, she would be all over him with a million questions.

There was only one way to avoid being pestered. He posted his ship's arrival time at Ganymede and stated when he would be present at the Ligon Corporate offices. Then he turned off the communication system. He knew his family. They would all be there at the meeting, eager to hear what he had done and tell him why it was stupid.

This time he would surprise them. Not only had he met with Bat, but despite Hector's mad and ill-timed assault Alex had half-persuaded Bat to give Ligon Industries the access to Pandora that they needed. And Bat had agreed to a future meeting—on Ganymede. Alex had accomplished far more than anyone could have expected. True, he had nothing to do with Bat's new activities with the Puzzle Network—that was just a piece of luck. But why not take credit for it? Some family credit was long overdue.

Bat's second remark had been made during their review of Alex's predictive model, as they turned the basic assumptions inside out in search of a reason why results should be different on computers run inside the Keep, versus using the Seine's capabilities. Alex said, of one suggestion, "Well, we can be certain *that* isn't causing the problem." Bat had replied, with great solemnity, "I have learned that there is no such thing as certainty. There are merely different degrees of uncertainty."

On the flight home, Alex had taken every one of the "certainties" that underpinned his model and subjected them to intense scrutiny. He discovered no great revelations, but he did find himself agreeing more and more with Bat. The Seine, the very tool which permitted the predictive models to run with a sufficient degree of detail, might be introducing variations that Alex had never intended. The thousand—or million—new databases now on-line could contain wrong facts or unreasonable assumptions. Alex needed to modify the predictive models to screen all data provided by the Seine, using new programs that he himself would have to develop. It was out of the question for any human to perform all the necessary checks.

He had the modifications half done when his ship docked on Ganymede. Normally he hated to interrupt his work before it was finished. Today was a bit different. Today he had something to tell the family—something that would impress them, and make it clear that his life was not "entirely dictated by women."

Entry delays at Ganymede docking held him up for a few minutes, so he was hurrying when he descended to the Ligon Corporate offices and waited impatiently for recognition by the Fax on duty in the outer chamber. As soon as he was cleared he marched right on into the conference room—and skidded to a halt.

Prosper Ligon sat at the end of the long conference table. Alone.

Alex gestured to the empty seats. "Didn't you get my message?"

"Indeed we did." Prosper Ligon seemed far from happy. "Every relevant family member was notified. As to where they are . . ." His long donkey head showed his mortification. "On occasion, Alex, I wonder what has happened to the long tradition of family service. I would never have thought it, but perhaps you are the only person who can be counted on."

That was a back-handed compliment, if ever Alex had heard one. But before he could reply there was a commotion in the outer office. Uncle Karolus came barging in, grinning widely.

"Did you catch it?" he said. "Isn't it the greatest—worth a thousand price-fixing scandals."

"Karolus, a family meeting is being conducted here—or was *supposed* to be." Prosper Ligon waved to Uncle Karolus to

sit down. "Please treat the occasion with the dignity it de-
serves."

"You *didn't* see it, did you?" Karolus dropped into his usual
chair. "I'm telling you, Prosper, it's a great day for the Ligons.
We won't be Number Nine anymore. If we're not up to Number Eight by close of business today, I'll give my ass and hat
to charity."

"Karolus!"

"Listen to me, Prosper. You should be standing on the
table, cheering and dancing. Sylva Commensals is in deep shit.
It happened live on the most popular news outlet—Lanara
Pinchbeck's morning edition. She was sitting there talking
some half-assed talk about Callisto rough-style fashions, when
all of a sudden she stopped. She coughed a bit, like there was
a tickle in the back of her throat. Then she opened her mouth
wide and just sat there. We had a view of her tongue and
tonsils for at least twenty seconds of dead air-time—that has
to be some sort of record. Then she choked, and this fat white
maggoty thing, bigger than my thumb, came sliding out of
her mouth and dropped onto the table in front of her. It was
squirming around, and she started coughing up blood."

"You mean that Lanara Pinchbeck is a Commensal?"

"Dear God, Prosper, are you *blind*? You can see she's a
Commensal from just one look at her. She's older than sin,
and nobody her age can stay that fresh and bright and blooming without help. She's not blooming anymore, though. They
dragged her away feet-first, all on live video. And the camera
kept going back to the big fat maggoty thing, blind and
white and wrinkled. It looked like a giant floppy dick, slith-
ering around on the table."

"A schistosome," said Alex. "One of the big mature forms
that live inside all Commensals. Maybe the one over the liver.

Somehow it found its way into the lungs or intestines, then all the way out of her body."

"I don't know where it came from, and I don't much care. It's where it *went* that matters. Right splat on the table." Karolus smacked his hand down hard. "I'm telling you, showing that fat wriggler on live video will knock the bottom out of Sylva. They always show the benefits, but never the risks or what goes on inside a Commensal. I'll bet you a thousand that today they'll get zero sign-ups for the service."

Alex said, "My mother——" and Prosper added, "——and Agatha."

"You bet. Juliana, too." Karolus snorted with laughter, then said, "Oh, come on. You can stop the long face, Alex. I saw all three of them, right after they watched the show. You don't need to worry—they were more scared white than they were yellow, and no monster dick-slugs were crawling out of any holes that I could see. What they were mainly was well and truly pissed. They were heading straight over to the Sylva offices. I mean, we're not just talking money-back guarantees here. We're talking major lawsuits. Lanara Pinchbeck alone will sue for public humiliation and private anguish and loss of audience market share, and fifty other things you can't even imagine."

"That accounts for the absence of three family members." Prosper Ligon seemed not at all inclined to dance and cheer on the table, as Karolus had suggested. "There are other people missing. Do you know anything of the whereabouts of Cora?"

"She went with Agatha—supposedly to offer moral support. Actually, Agatha did look a bit out of it. But my guess is that Cora wanted to have a good laugh and see what came next."

"And Rezel and Tanya?"

"Dunno. They struck out so bad with the Pandora deal, I think maybe they're afraid to show their faces."

"With some reason. And speaking of the Pandora situation . . ."

Prosper Ligon turned to Alex. But before Alex could speak—this was going to be his big moment—Karolus jumped in.

"Yes, how about that? I've said bad things about Hector often enough, maybe I'll have to change my tune. He's not here for a good reason—he's under arrest for attacking Pandora and 'attempting to intimidate the leaseholder.' That's what the charge is. But, you know what? It seems like it worked."

"Wait a minute." Alex couldn't believe this. "Hector pulled a pointless stunt out at Pandora. He could easily have screwed things up for me."

"Seems to me Hector did some good. Isn't it true that the leaseholder, Rustum what's-his-name, is thinking of leaving Pandora and coming to Ganymede? That's what I heard through the company information net."

"Well, that may be true. But it had nothing to do with Hector."

"That's not the way it's being reported—and Lucy-Maria Mobarak apparently sees things the same way I do. She's convinced that Hector did the whole thing for her sake, to 'prove that he is worthy of her,' she says. She's on her way now, taking a special flight out to where he's being held. I'm telling you, this is a great day for the family. Sylva Commensals right down the tubes, a good shot at Pandora, and Ligon merging with Mobarak. Lucy-Maria doesn't seem to mind that Hector isn't too swift. Tell the truth, I've got the same feeling about her. She could trade her brain in for tripes and have a bargain. But if they suit each other, that's enough for me. We've got everything but the wedding bells. I say we scrap this meeting right now, and go off some place to celebrate." Karolus turned to Alex. "Unless there's something else that you feel you need to tell us?"

"Yes, there is. It's about the visit of Rustum Battachariya to Ganymede. I'm going to arrange it so he—"

"All in good time. He's not even on the way yet. Plenty of opportunity to talk about that when it happens. Me, I'm out of here."

Karolus swept from the room. Prosper Ligon glared at Alex. "I am not inclined to celebrate, despite Karolus's excessive enthusiasm. However, it is clear to me that little purpose is served by holding a family assembly which is unattended by the family. This meeting is adjourned."

He stood up. Ten seconds later, Alex was sitting alone at the long conference table.

Hector. Hector as hero. God, if you didn't laugh at that, you had to cry. Alex could see one consolation. For the time being, the whole of the family was off his back. His mother would be far more concerned about the possibility of giant slugs crawling from one of her body orifices than about anything to do with Alex.

For the next few days he would be free to concentrate his thoughts on a rather larger issue: the future of the solar system.

Alex worried a little on the way down to the Advanced Planning offices. Perhaps he ought to have told Kate when he expected to arrive home, because she too would want to know everything that had happened on his trip.

It turned out not to matter. Kate was there, working at a terminal in her own office. She was too preoccupied to do more than give Alex a nod and say, "Thank Heaven, I can use a clearer head than mine. We have problems. Sit down."

Alex sat. On the display in front of Kate was what looked suspiciously like outputs of his own predictive model. He said, "What's going on?"

"I wish I knew." Kate pushed her blonde hair back from her forehead and swung in her chair to face him. "You know that Magrit Knudsen told Ole Pedersen to learn all he could about your model, and how it works?"

"Of course I know. I was the one who had to provide him with program copies, remember?"

"Well, he took them, and the first thing he did was run them."

"The same thing I would have done myself—you want to be sure that whatever you've been given will work."

"Right." Kate's eyes, usually so clear and bright, were bloodshot. She must have been up for days. "And the programs did work, just the way they had for us. He used the same input parameters, and the results predicted the collapse of the solar system with all humans dying out."

Alex wanted to tell Kate about the anomalous run results on the Keep computers, when civilization was predicted to blossom and bloom for more than a century into the future.

He opened his mouth to speak, but she ran right over him. "By the time Pedersen did his final set of runs, he had dug into the theory in your papers. I've never denied that he's smart, even if he is an insecure asshole. He worked on this night and day—I think he was hoping for a basic error in what you've done—but he found what he didn't expect to find. Your theory is airtight. Last week, while you were away on Pandora, he came over to my office to say that he was a convert. He believes in your model."

"That's wonderful."

"You might think so. But Pedersen's as worried now as I am, because he did one other thing. He gave a copy of your program to Macanelly."

"He's must be out of his mind. Everybody says you might as well give programs to a trained ape as to Loring Macanelly."

"Pedersen knows that, better than anyone. Seems he did it more to keep Macanelly occupied and out of Pedersen's hair than anything else. So Macanelly ran the programs, too."

"And he found different results?"

"No. He got exactly the same as us, and the same as Ole Pedersen. But Macanelly follows the news outlets, especially the dumb-dumb blurts. He'd been hearing about a SETI signal, something that came in from the stars."

"The Wu-Beston anomaly. It looks like it may be the real thing."

"Real or not, it rang a bell somewhere in the jungle of Macanelly's brain. He'd heard that aliens had cropped up in one of the predicted futures."

"That's my fault. I included a line in one of my reports saying that they showed on one of the abandoned high-probability projections. But I never said a word about a SETI signal."

"With somebody like Macanelly, you don't need to. He's dumb, but he's persistent. Or maybe he's less dumb than we think. He did something I'd never have thought of doing, ever. He went to the Seine, and asked to have the complete SETI sequence—all twenty-one billion bits of it, from what I gather—provided as available inputs to your predictive model."

"That's totally crazy. The SETI sequence isn't a database. No one has the slightest idea if there is a real signal buried away in there. If there is, no one knows how to read it."

"Exactly. Totally crazy. So now listen for something crazier.

When Loring Macanelly ran your predictive model, with not a single change other than the model's access to the SETI sequence, he obtained totally different results. Instead of civilization collapsing and dying out half a century from now, everything stayed in bounds and coasted along as reasonable as you could hope to see."

Kate's laugh at Alex's expression was too high-pitched for comfort. "That's right, sweetheart. *Loring Macanelly* found the magic trick that stabilizes your model. And Macanelly, as we're all so fond of telling each other, is a total idiot. What do you think of that, Alex? Welcome home, and come join the madhouse."

25

Jan felt that she had been fighting to protect Sebastian all her life. There had been a brief vacation, the magical couple of weeks with Paul Marr on the flight out from Earth; then the *OSL Achilles* made its swoop through the upper atmosphere of Jupiter, and suddenly Jan was back to her old job.

"Why did you do it, Sebastian?"

It was the hundredth or the thousandth time that she had asked the question—inside her head, where there was no chance of an answer. She didn't expect more satisfying results now, but she didn't know what else to do.

They were still on Ganymede, in a section just four levels below the moon's outer surface. It was labeled as a quarantine and science research facility, but so far as Jan was concerned it was a prison for Sebastian. He was not allowed to leave. It was not clear that he would ever be allowed to leave.

Jan was housed separately. Paul had urged her to come with him, to have dinner together at The Belly of the Whale restaurant and then go sightseeing in the salt-ocean caverns of Ganymede. He pointed out that no one had criticized her behavior in any way, and until a decision was made as to whether or not to proceed to the Saturn weather station, she was free to do what she liked and wander wherever she pleased. He had a week and a half free before the *Achilles* left on its next run to the inner system. Why not spend the time together? They would have fun and get to know each other better.

She wanted to, but she couldn't. Or wouldn't. She explained that until she knew what was wrong with Sebastian and understood why he had tried to open the hatch, she would be unable to enjoy anything.

She thought that Paul might try to talk her out of that and was relieved when he didn't. But she knew, although neither of them said it, that if she left now their affair was over.

When she had told him that she was heading over to the facility where Sebastian was being held, Paul sat silent for a moment. Then he took her hands in his. "I understand, Jan. Do what you have to do. But don't forget that you are entitled to a life, too. You are too rare and precious to throw yourself away."

Entitled to a life. Would she ever have one? She had left Paul at a run, hurrying away before he could offer a farewell kiss, before she could change her mind.

And now, with Sebastian, she could finally ask the question directly. "Why did you do it, Sebastian? Why were you trying to open the hatch?"

He stared at her, a dreamy expression on his round face. "I don't know, Jan. I don't remember. I suppose I wanted to see clouds."

"But you could have seen those through any of the observation ports. If you had opened the hatch, you would have died. Others might have died, too."

"I know. But Jan, I didn't mean to hurt anyone."

It was true. He had never knowingly hurt anyone, and never would. But the old fear consumed her. Sebastian had major problems, and onboard the *Achilles* they had come horribly close to being fatal.

"We have all the medical records here." Valnia Bloom was sitting at Jan's side. She looked more like an anorexic corpse than ever. "Dr. Christa Matloff, who did your testing at the Earth orbital facility, sent an entire duplicate set. Sebastian, we are going to repeat every one of the tests that were done there, plus a battery of others. Is that all right with you?"

"Of course." He seemed surprised at the question. "Anything you want to do is all right."

Valnia Bloom flashed a sideways glance at Jan. "The tests will be both physical and mental. They will not be painful, but they may take a long time."

"I'll stay." Jan answered the unspoken question. To her relief, no one was asking about the wisdom of allowing her and Sebastian to leave Earth in the first place.

What *was* wrong with him? Was it related to the odd neurotransmitter functions within his brain? That was possible, but it might also have something to do with the tiny inorganic nodules that had been found in the white blood cells of his body. And did both of those peculiarities relate to Sebastian's earliest days, when as small children they had each wandered alone among the wild teratomas and devastated landscape of Earth's northern hemisphere?

To Jan's surprise, Valnia Bloom reached out and patted her hand. "Have faith," she said. "We will find out. Believe me, I have as much interest in resolving this as you or Sebastian."

Dr. Bloom spoke with confidence, but after three days Jan's own faith faded. With nothing else to do, she haunted the lab where Sebastian was being tested. Valnia Bloom must have spoken to the technicians, because Jan was allowed to examine any of the results and records.

Most of those were brain traces and scans, highly complicated images that meant nothing to anyone except a specialist. The most tangible evidence of abnormality was the curious dark nodules within the body cells. Jan read a batch of reports. Although they were inorganic and had no apparent function, they were never excreted from the body. When the cell in which they lived died, the tiny spheres were somehow reabsorbed into the body and in due course took up residence in a new cell. Whoever wrote this particular report had suggested that the nodules might have been present in Sebastian's body, unchanged in form and number, since childhood.

The report also asked, why had these anomalies not been discovered long ago? Jan could answer that. When she and Sebastian had been rescued and shipped to the displaced persons' camp in Husvik, the inhabitants of battered Earth had other things on their minds; things like survival.

In addition to a chemical analysis, a few specimens of the anomalous bodies had been carefully sheared in two. Jan took one of the high-powered microscopes and peered at the cross-section of one nodule. It formed a perfect sphere, and the spherical nature continued right through the interior. Concentric shells of material glittering prismatically under the microscope's strong illumination, flashing in different colors like tiny rings of gemstones.

Jan could not understand most of the technical comments on the specimens that she was examining, but in one of Valnia Bloom's reports her concluding remarks had been unusually concise and direct: *The structure of each nodule is identical, simple, and well-defined. They are spheres, penetrated radially by narrow apertures that run all the way to the center. The chemical composition has been analyzed and is known absolutely. The possible functions remain a mystery.*

Jan had been staring so long and hard into the microscope that her vision began to blur. She raised her head, squeezed her eyes shut, and began to rub them vigorously.

She was still doing so when she felt a touch on her shoulder. She spun around, pulse suddenly racing, sure that it was Paul.

It was Valnia Bloom. The gaunt doctor saw Jan's expression and shook her head. "I'm sorry. Would you like me to go away?"

"No. It's all right. I thought that you were—someone else." Jan knew that her eyes must be bloodshot from the rubbing. "I'm all right," she went on. "It's just that I've spent too long staring into the microscope. At the little sphere things."

"So have I. So have we all." Valnia Bloom sat down uninvited next to Jan. "I didn't mean to startle you, or interrupt what you were doing. But you and I need to talk."

Jan's heart raced again, with a different emotion. "Is Sebastian all right?"

"It depends what you mean by all right. Physically, he is fine—in better shape than either one of us. But I foresee problems."

Today Valnia Bloom was wearing her tight blood-red head scarf, which emphasized her sharp cheekbones and the pallor of her complexion.

"While we've been busy in the lab here," she went on, "the Jovian security staff have done a minute-by-minute reconstruction of what happened onboard the *OSL Achilles* during our Jupiter close approach and atmospheric fly-through.

"It's pretty scary. They estimate that if Sebastian had been free to work on the third safety catch for ten more seconds—and they've seen no reason to believe that he was likely to stop—he would have had the hatch open. Normally, a hatch failure can't destroy a whole ship. Bulkheads seal automatically when they sense a loss of pressure, and most of the hull remains airtight. But normally a ship is flying in vacuum. We were skimming through the upper levels of Jupiter's atmosphere, and that is mainly hydrogen. The static charge on the *Achilles* would have set off a hydrogen-oxygen explosion, big enough to cause a hull fracture. After that the whole ship would have exploded and fallen to Jupiter's deep layers. It's doubtful that anyone up here would ever have known what happened. The *Achilles* would be gone too quickly for any kind of emergency signal."

Jan knew that she had come close to death, but this was the first time she realized how near the whole ship had approached disaster. Dreading the answer, she asked, "Have they officially charged Sebastian?"

"They have not." Valnia Bloom was biting color into her thin lips. "Nor will they. The official conclusion is that Sebastian cannot be charged with anything, because he is of diminished mental capacity and therefore not responsible for his actions."

"He's not! I mean, he's not stupid. If they are saying he is retarded, that's just not true."

"I agree. Remember, I did the tests on both of you, back on Earth. At the same time, I find myself in an impossible position. I have been unable to explain to the investigating team why Sebastian apparently attempted suicide. Also, I have been obliged to tell them of the peculiarities of brain structure that were discovered by Dr. Christa Matloff, before you ever left Earth orbit."

"They don't mean anything. I've known Sebastian since we were small children. He thinks as well as anyone else, just differently from most people."

"Differently, and in some ways better. His intuitive grasp

of the behavior of complex hydrodynamic systems is astonishing. That intrigued me from the outset, and provided my original impetus to approve both your transfers to the Outer System. However, I still have a problem. There is another step that I would like to take with Sebastian, one which he has agreed to. Actually, he seems indifferent to the whole thing, which is worrying."

"He's like that. He doesn't get excited."

"Apparently not. However, in view of the official conclusion that he is not responsible for his own actions, I cannot proceed with anything based on his assent alone, or on my own feeling that it may benefit him. You are regarded by everyone as the person closest to him."

"I am. I always have been."

"So it was agreed that I should ask your permission."

"To do what?"

Valnia Bloom gestured toward the microscope. "You have examined the small inorganic spheres scattered within Sebastian's body?"

"I was looking at them when you came in. I also read your report. I don't know what they are—but neither do you."

"More accurately, we know exactly what they *are*, but we have no idea what they *do*. However, because they remain chemically inert they play no part in his general body metabolism. I would like to explore the possibility of sluicing him."

"*What?*"

"I'm sorry, it's the usual medical term. I would like you to consider removing these mysterious nodules from his body entirely. Every last one of them."

"But why, if they're not doing any harm?"

"I'm not sure that's true. What I said was, they don't play a part in his general metabolism. But the brain is a delicate organ, and its operation depends on tiny electric currents within it. The nodules are present there, too, and they certainly possess electrical and magnetic properties."

"Do you think they are the reason why Sebastian's neurological tests are unusual?"

"I would not make so strong a statement. What I will say is that breakdown and removal of the nodules—assuming that it can be done—removes one possible source of variability. I see no way that it can harm Sebastian, and it may help him."

It sounded good, but Jan had learned to be wary. Too many times, in the past, people had suggested "treatments" for Sebastian to "make him more normal." Some had been performed, over Jan's protests. Not one had made a scrap of difference.

"How would you do this, and how long would it take?"

"I can answer your first question, but not your second. Breaking down the nodules within his body in order to remove them will be a delicate operation. We will have to inject a set of bespoke nanos into him. They will be designed to find the nodules, encapsulate each one, and break it down. Then the nanos will transfer each capsule through the cell wall, into the blood stream, and to the kidneys."

"Would that be safe?"

"Completely. Since each of the enclosing capsules is tiny and chemically inert at body temperatures, Sebastian will simply excrete them—pee them out."

"How long will it take?"

"That's the part I can't answer yet. First, we need a set of tailor-made nanos, designed for this specific task. Nothing quite like them exists, but I have already spoken to a top nano designer. Harold Launius believes that the task is comfortably within present capabilities. His best estimate is three or four weeks to design and test."

"And while that is being done?"

"Sebastian will remain here. You will be free to come and go as you wish, and I will work with him and for him as much as possible."

Valnia Bloom, for her own reasons, valued Sebastian's health and sanity. Jan said, "If the tests go well, Dr. Bloom, what then?"

"Hal Launius will inject a batch of the bespoke nanos into Sebastian. The nanos will be self-replicating, and designed to cease operation after copying themselves a sufficient number of times. They will perform the task of encapsulating, breaking down, and excreting until every nodule has gone. At that point the nanos become non-functional, and will themselves be excreted by normal bodily functions. The whole thing, according to Launius, will take no more than a week from initial injection to final excretion. Naturally, we will perform final scans and biopsies, to make sure that the nodules are indeed all gone. Then we will again perform the entire suite of brain scans and tests, hoping that this time the results prove to be more like those of other people."

Jan still didn't like the idea of injecting foreign bodies into Sebastian, and allowing them to run riot through his body. "What about Fishel's Law? How smart would these nanos be?"

"Not smart at all. You don't need to worry about them getting out of control. They will be designed for a single function, and they will be unable to perform any other."

"Suppose that I don't agree to go along with this? What other options do we have?"

Valnia Bloom avoided Jan's eyes. "I was rather hoping that you would not ask me that question. But I can answer it. We have no real options. Unless something like full-body sluicing is done, and we are able to demonstrate its effectiveness, Jovian security will never permit Sebastian to go free. He will remain here or in some similar closed establishment, under guard, for the rest of his life."

"Then I have no choice, do I? For Sebastian's sake, I must permit you to go ahead."

"Very good. Since this meeting is being recorded, there is no need for any other action on your part. However, I have one more thing to say. This pertains not to Sebastian's welfare, but to your own."

"Yes?" Jan was instantly wary. People only did things for you to further their own agendas.

"You have cared for Sebastian, by your own admission, since childhood. I'm sure that you meant well, but your actions have had an unfortunate side-effect. He has never developed the ability to make his own decisions."

"No! You've got everything backwards. I cared for him *because* he couldn't look after himself."

"That's what you believe. I remain unconvinced. Earlier, I said that while the nanos are being developed and tested, you would be free to come and go as you chose. I stick by that statement. However, I strongly urge you to stay away from Sebastian. Let us find out what he does without your constant guidance."

Jan felt a surge of anger, strong and irrational. "You mean, let's find out what Sebastian does with *your* constant guidance. You think he's yours now—you have, ever since we left Earth."

The color that came to Valnia Bloom's cheeks transformed her to a vulnerable human. "I think of him as a research subject." Her voice shook, and she stood up. "Sebastian Birch is no more to me than that, nor has he ever been. I'm afraid that I cannot say the same for you. Sebastian Birch is your obsession. Let me offer a suggestion: get a life! It's very clear that at the moment you do not have one."

She was gone before Jan could reply. After a few moments Jan realized that she in any case had nothing to say. The other woman's *get a life* merely restated Paul's comment. *Don't forget that you are entitled to a life, too.*

Jan stared at the microscope, and at the baffling array of brain scans and reports on the table next to it. She should not be here in the lab at all. She was not *qualified* to be here. Her presence had been tolerated, sure—but everyone knew she had nothing to contribute. She was no scientist or medical specialist. Any treatment she proposed for Sebastian would be as likely to kill him as cure him.

She stood up. What was the name of the restaurant that Paul had mentioned? The Belly of the Whale. Almost certainly, it was already too late. There was only a tiny chance that she would find him there. But she didn't have to find him there. He was still on Ganymede. Someone on the *Achilles* would be able to tell her how to find him.

And then?

And then Jan was going to make a fool of herself. Maybe that's what getting a life was all about.

26

Bat's decision had been made weeks ago. Now, as the time for Ganymede departure grew closer, his reluctance to leave the Bat Cave on Pandora increased.

He wandered the length of the main chamber, seeing not so much the Great War artifacts that were collected there as the ones that were missing. Here was a cleared space for a life-support pod from the freighter *Pelagic*. Bat was convinced from fragmentary and scattered records that half a dozen of those pods still existed, floating somewhere deep in space with their human cargo. He, at least, was not persuaded that the cargo was dead. In any case, a pod itself would be a rare treasure.

The next space was more questionable, its existence supported on a gossamer net of indirect evidence. If the rumored BEC sentience had been created, that event must have taken place only in the last few days of the war.

And where would it have gone? The continued existence of a Bose-Einstein Condensate of the required magnitude, sentient or not, called for temperatures sustained within a few billionths of a degree of absolute zero. No natural environment in the universe offered anything colder than the 2.7 Kelvin microwave background radiation. A BEC sentience would require its own artificially cooled setting, maintained perhaps deep within one of the natural bodies that floated beyond the orbit of Neptune. The Belt weapons-makers, Bat knew, had established at least two research labs far off in that outer darkness. One day, as the boundaries of civilization steadily widened, those facilities would be discovered. And then, if they contained a sentient BEC, its find would set off an unprecedented bidding battle among Great War collectors—unless the sentience was able to argue its own case for continuing independence.

The third shrine-in-anticipation was reserved for Nadeen Selassie's unknown master weapon, existence unproven and nature unknown. Bat was staring at the empty space and seeking to imagine its contents when Mord's individual signal sounded through the chamber.

"I will be with you shortly." Bat could communicate orally with outside callers from anywhere in the Bat Cave, but visual displays required his presence in one of the two communications centers. "This is fortunate timing. In eight hours I leave Pandora for a trip to Ganymede."

"Which you swore you'd never be going back to." Mord's single sniff was the equivalent of a dozen cynical comments.

"A certain flexibility of outlook distinguishes the superior mind."

"Right. Didn't you tell me a few weeks ago that genius is distinguished by the power to focus on a single idea for months or years?"

"The superior mind is one able to encompass simultaneously a number of inconsistent facts and theories." Bat had reached the big padded seat. He settled into it with a grunt of contentment. This answered one question. Whatever else was left behind on Pandora, the seat at least went with him. "Is this a social visit, or do you report progress?"

"Anybody who paid you a social visit would take vacations on the Vulcan Nexus." Mord's squint-eyed glower filled the display in front of Bat. "I've found out some stuff—and it wasn't easy. I had to wriggle through fancy firewalls and data security systems. Want to know about the secret sex life of Earth's head of economic planning?"

"I do not. As for your difficulties, nothing worthwhile is ever easy. Did you locate the medical records for the children rescued from Earth's northern hemisphere, in the months or years following the end of the Great War?"

"Patience, patience. If that's all I had, I'd have sent it to you by regular mail. Yeah, I got the med records. A few hundred kids were in the right age group, but none of them was what you'd call normal. Most of 'em had seen their families burned or blown up or eaten, and they'd all been through hell. Standard therapy was to blank out those memories, and you can see why. But that, and the lack of records, makes it impossible to trace medical history back to before they were found. The medical records after they were found are not much help, either, because Earth was still coping with close to eight billion dead. Nobody had time for elaborate examinations of the living. The displaced persons' camps counted arms and legs, made sure the kids were breathing, and that was about it."

"A dead end."

"I told you, if it stopped there I'd have sent a postcard. It doesn't. Since I was inside the data banks, I decided to go the other way—forward in time. As you might expect, services on Earth got better over the years, and all the kids who'd been

DP's grew up and had regular exams and medical treatment. I can transfer full genomes on every one of them, if you want to download."

"I think so." Bat slowly nodded. He was sitting motionless, eyes closed. "To the Seine terminal. I will arrange for their subsequent storage in the Keep. Please continue."

"A fair number grew up physically damaged or mentally freaky, and a few died from long-term after-effects of the war. But not one of them showed anything that linked them to the Heraldic asteroid, or to Nadeen Selassie. They merged into the rest of Earth's population, and those that could took normal jobs. By the time I came within five years of the present I was convinced I was going nowhere, but what's time when you're having fun? I kept barreling along to the end. And guess what? In records less than three months old, I finally hit paydirt."

"Anomalies?"

"Make that a singular. One anomaly—but a biggie, way out beyond your four-sigma cutoff. A couple of DP kids, adults now, had been working as low-level helpers, nothing special, on a Global Minerals' methane-mining platform. They'd been there ten years or more, but recently they took it into their heads to apply for jobs in the Outer System. The woman's idea, I suspect, because the man shows up in the records as a little bit slow and more than a little bit strange. So they take the tests, and scrape through, and now the man starts to look more interesting. He can predict the outcome of hydrodynamic systems, particularly planetary atmospheres, that are complex enough to push computer models to their limits. Doesn't know how he does it, says he dreams it—and he *draws* the results."

"Not unique." Bat was unimpressed. "History records autistic children and adults with that same ability. Predicting the meteorological behavior of an atmosphere falls far short of Nadeen Selassie's planet-destroying weapon. I doubt if it satisfies the four-sigma criterion."

"Hey, you asked for oddities. I'm giving oddities, now you want more. But I'm not done. Hear the rest before you talk sigma levels. The man's name is Sebastian Birch, and I already sent his ID through to your data bank. After he and the woman pass the written tests—they operate as a team, by the way—they go up to Earth orbit for the physicals. She zips through easily, healthy and smart and perfectly normal. He seems healthy enough, but they run into a snag. His body cells are filled with tiny little balls, all identical and inorganic and apparently inert. They do nothing, but according to all the medics they shouldn't be there. Nobody has ever seen anything like 'em. They removed a whole batch of them as samples for the files. Are we at four-sigma yet?"

"There, and surpassing it." Bat's eyes were wide open. "Mord, this is exactly what I was hoping you might find. Can you send me full details of the tests performed, together with the complete set of results and comments?"

"Doing it while we talk. The comments won't do you much good, though. They all amount to, What the hell gives here? But I'm still not finished. The medics don't know why Sebastian Birch is full of these gizmos, but since they don't seem to be harming him or anyone else the medics give the okay: Birch and the woman, Janeed Jannex, are free to continue to Ganymede."

"Ganymede? These people are on *Ganymede*?"

"They are—right where you're going to be, a few days from now. But they almost didn't make it. You're the System expert on tapping transportation records, so I'll only give you the bare bones and you can dig out the details for yourself. Sebastian Birch and Janeed Jannex made the trip out aboard the *OSL Achilles*. When the ship was doing the traditional Jupiter swingby for velocity-shedding, Sebastian Birch took it into his head to go *outside*—into Jupiter's upper-level atmosphere. He was working on the hatches when they found him and stopped him. No explanation offered. Are we at four-sigma yet?"

"At it, and far beyond. Mord, this is extraordinary. What does it signify?"

"Hey, you're supposed to tell me. I'm just a high-level Fax, you're the one with the bulging brow and the monster mind. You ask for oddities, I give you oddities. But don't ask me to tie this to Nadeen Selassie, or the 'dark-as-day' weapon that's supposed to destroy the solar system. So far as I'm concerned, all we've done is find a human being who could have arrived on Earth at the right time, and who happens to have a very peculiar body and brain. Making sense of that is your job, not mine. What's *your* explanation?"

Bat sagged down onto the padded chair, his bulk overflowing the edges. He rested his elbows on his well-padded chest and cupped his chin in his hands. "It is unnecessary to goad me. I have no explanation, as you smugly realize. Do you have more information?"

"Not a scrap."

"Then we should conclude this meeting. I must think."

"Suits me. I don't want to stay too long, anyway."

"My apologies if you are offended. Your presence is normally welcome at any time, but this is an exceptional situation."

"Hey, it's not *you* I'm worried about. I don't like to stay *any place* too long. I said it before, and I'll say it again: something's hunting me out there, and it's closing in on my tail."

"Would you prefer to leave the distributed Seine network

completely, and reside within the Keep? You will be safe here, and the Keep will maintain its integrity as a protected unit even in my absence."

"Nah. I've been inside, it's boring as hell. Out in the Seine it may be risky, but there's a billion interesting sites to explore. Meantime, so long. I'm out of here. I'll visit you on Ganymede."

Mord nodded, and the image vanished from the display.

Bat did not move. New information normally served to clarify an issue. In this case, discoveries seemed to add a new layer of confusion.

True, he now had a name and a place. But if Sebastian Birch were in fact connected to Nadeen Selassie and her lost weapon, that weapon could not be biological since Birch had lived with other humans for more than thirty years and no one had suffered harm. Also, the weapon *should* not be biological. It was supposed to do more than kill life; it was designed to destroy a whole planet.

And yet there were the mysterious specks of matter found within Sebastian Birch's body. If they lacked a biological or chemical action, what remained? Only, perhaps, something in the realm of physics.

Bat sat motionless as the minutes and hours ticked by. Finally, the time for planned departure from Pandora was only an hour away. He rose, reached forward, and placed a call. After a few seconds, a woman's sleepy voice said, "Yes?"

"My apologies for disturbing you. It seems I was given a wrong ID."

"Great. It also seems to be the middle of the night."

"So it is." Bat was unfazed. "I am attempting to reach Alex Ligon."

"Who is calling?"

"This is Rustum Battachariya."

"Oh. He's asleep, but I'm sure he'll want to talk to you. Hold on a second."

After a few moments, Alex's voice said, "Huh?" He sounded not only three-quarters asleep, but perplexed.

"This is Bat. We have not spoken since your visit, but am I to assume that your family is still interested in obtaining the use of Pandora as an operations base within the Saturn system?"

"Extremely interested. If there are any terms on which an arrangement might be made, we would like to discuss them." There was an unintelligible mutter of complaint in the background, followed by Alex's faint, "I know it is, Kate. And I know I promised. But this may be the only chance."

Bat cut off the background chit-chat with, "I see possible terms for an arrangement. First, however, a question: does Ligon Industries employ qualified teams of experimental physicists and chemists?"

"Very much so." Alex now sounded surprised. "For some of the business ventures that we are in, top-flight research teams are absolutely essential. A project like *Starseed-Two* would be impossible without them."

"Good. That is as I expected. One more question, or more properly a statement: Ligon Industries has ways of obtaining access to facilities and materials that are normally unavailable—do not attempt to deny this, since I already have good evidence of it."

"I wasn't about to deny it. Certain members of my family make it a boast. Is this connected to your previous question?"

"Very much so. I wish you to obtain access to a set of medical samples taken at a particular place and time, from a particular individual. I would then like a top team of your experimenters to subject those samples to a wide assortment of tests, and to ascertain their properties and behavior. You may tell your family that in return for this favor, I will make Pandora available to Ligon Industries as an operating base for helium-three mining from the Saturn atmosphere. Construction of your base on a part of Pandora far removed from my habitation may begin at once."

"That's wonderful." Alex was fully awake. "But I need more details. Not just the name of the person and the location of the samples—you have to be more specific about the tests."

"I will do my best. However, we float here on a sea of conjecture." Bat hunched down again on his chair. "Listen closely. I am scheduled to leave Pandora for Ganymede less than one hour from now. We should meet and discuss this matter in more detail, but I do not wish you to await my arrival before beginning."

"So this is urgent? You didn't say that."

"I do not know the level of urgency. However, certain recent events fill me with misgivings. Are you ready to record information?"

"It's already being done."

"Excellent. The medical samples were obtained from an individual named Sebastian Birch. He is presently on Ganymede, and it is possible that Ligon Industries will find it quicker and easier to obtain new samples of what we need from him directly. If not, however, someone must proceed as rapidly as possible to Earth. . . ."

One month ago it would never have occurred to Alex that he could or should request a family meeting. Now he had called for two in two weeks. Beyond that, he had insisted that it take place early in the morning.

To Prosper Ligon that meant little—he would already have

been up and working for hours. Not so for other family members.

Alex glanced around at the diminished assembly. His mother sat on his left, looking terrible. Her perfect skin had sunk into a network of fine wrinkles, her eyes were bulging and glassy, and an I/V dripped straw-colored fluid into her left forearm. Her apparent age had doubled in a few days. Alex had placed his arm around her when she was trundled into the room, and Lena Ligon's shoulder felt as fragile as a bird's wing.

But at least his mother was alive, and present. Great-aunt Agatha had died three days ago, while Cousin Juliana remained in critical condition. Even now Great-aunt Cora was at her bedside.

To Alex's right, Uncle Karolus was hollow-eyed, but beaming across at Lena. No doubt the sight of her gave him happy thoughts of continued problems for Sylva Commensals that overwhelmed any sorrow at the death of his aunt. Tanya and Rezel wore a similar sleepless mask, which Alex suspected was common to him also. He and Kate had worked and played hard last night, then been awakened from sound sleep by Bat's call and unable to drop off again. Hector, across from Rezel, was worst of all. It took more than mere lack of sleep to impose on that Viking vitality such a drawn and dissipated air. News of the family meeting had probably greeted Hector as he staggered home in the early morn.

Only Prosper Ligon, in position at the far end of the table, remained his usual self. He nodded down to Alex, and said, "This meeting is now in session. It is, I believe, appropriate that you speak first."

Alex had made notes from the recording of Bat's request, then followed Kate's advice and destroyed them. "If I were going to ask my family to do something illegal," she had said,

"I don't think I'd want anything down in writing."

"It might not be illegal." But Alex had taken the hint—
after making sure that he had the important points committed
to memory.

In fact, what Alex had to say was not complicated. The
problem was that, despite a long family history of intrigue,
bribery, and corruption, and despite everything that Bat
claimed to know for certain concerning Uncle Karolus' past
sins, no one ever *spoke* of such things openly in family meetings.

Alex screwed up his courage, took a deep breath, and
plunged in. He spoke for five minutes, summarizing Bat's
request and the conditions for his offer. There was total silence
while he spoke, and afterwards.

At last Uncle Karolus said, "Let me get this straight. We
obtain these medical samples, and we do these tests. In return,
we get to install our Ops Center on Pandora and use it as
long as we need it. Right?"

"Rustum Battachariya assumes that will be for no more
than a year. Somehow he knows of the penalty clauses in our
contract."

"We don't have to kill anybody, or pay Battachariya some
enormous fee?"

"I don't think so."

"Then I'll say something I never thought I'd be able to
say." Karolus faced the whole table. "We have Alex coming
up with this deal, and Hector all set to tie down Lucy Mobarak. I see hope for the males of the younger generation after
all."

Alex was not sure he was ready for compliments from Uncle
Karolus. He said, "But I don't know how we'll obtain the
samples. Somebody may have to go to Earth."

"When the man himself is here on Ganymede, having another set of tests? Forget about Earth." Karolus waved a dismissive hand at Alex and turned to the head of the table. "Prosper? If I guarantee that little bit of business, what do you say?"

Prosper Ligon had been quietly examining his own notes. Finally he nodded. "The matter will, of course, call for a family vote. However, there appears to be a certain serendipity of timing. One of our best physics research teams is available. It has been held in reserve, pending a go-ahead with Saturn operations for Starseed-Two. If the arrangement with the man Battachariya is consummated at once, there will still be an inevitable delay of weeks before the research team is needed. And even if we put our chief scientist, Bengt Suomi, in charge—which I strongly recommend and can arrange—the cost of complying with Battachariya's request will be negligible. Therefore, I so move."

Hector woke from an exhausted trance and said, "Move what?"

"Uncle Prosper says the Battachariya proposal looks good." Karolus glanced around the table. "I'll second. All in favor?"

The nods were casual and in Lena's case feeble, but they came from everyone.

"Carried unanimously." Karolus stood up. "We need to wrap this up as soon as we can, so we'd better start. Sebastian Birch, right, held in science research quarantine? This shouldn't take long."

"One moment." Prosper Ligon held up a hand. "Before we adjourn, a moment's silence for Agatha seems appropriate."

"Of course. Respect for the dead." Karolus sat down.

After a few seconds he said, "Right," stood up again, and hurried out. Alex stared after him, then at the people remaining. He reflected that this was his family, his own flesh and blood. But he understood them not at all—and he was not sure that he wanted to.

27

Milly Wu paused at the closed door, took a deep breath, and stood up straighter. *This is the big-time, lady. Better not blow it. Don't gush, don't stammer, don't drool.*

Within the room beyond, collected in one place for the first time ever, she would find the most cunning and devious minds in the solar system. Here was the cream of the cream, the pick of the Puzzle Network's Master class.

Milly had been allowed into that elite group only because Pack Rat had made a special arrangement in return for unspecified future favors. But he had made it clear that she would be a decidedly junior figure, an observer more than a participant. *Sit, observe, learn—and keep quiet.*

She wished that Jack Beston were here with her to provide his own gruff form of reassurance. He had promised to come to Ganymede as soon as he had the Argus Station's own interpretation effort up and running, but that was poor consolation. Milly needed him *now*, as she prepared to open the door and face the legends of her adolescence. Pack Rat had named some of the people assembled to work on the SETI signal interpretation: Claudius, The Joker, Torquemada, Attoboy, Sneak Attack, Ghost Boy, plus *Megachirops*, the Great Bat himself. Milly had struggled with—and failed to solve—problems set by every one of them. Her own best efforts, posted on the Network under her chosen name, Atropos, had never remained unsolved for longer than a day.

That doesn't matter. This isn't a level playing field. I found the signal and I've thought about nothing else since the day I discovered it. Get in there.

Milly slid open the door and stepped through into the room. She was not sure what to expect. A bunch of freaks, who hid in the Puzzle Network because they were poorly equipped to cope with the rest of life? She had heard that view often enough—mainly from her own family, when they realized that she was fascinated by abstract challenges. "Why bother with such nonsense? You don't need to think. You're an attractive girl, you'll get boyfriends and a husband easy enough."

The single exception was Uncle Edgar, gently persuading Milly of her talents and coaxing her to stretch herself to the limit.

Or beyond.

Like now.

Milly stood at one end of a narrow corridor, twenty or thirty paces long. The floor was a sound-deadening thick carpet, while sound-absorbing tiles covered the walls and ceiling. Painted blue doors, three meters apart, were set into the walls on both sides. Every door except one was closed. Before the first one, close to Milly's right hand, sat an illuminated sign.

At the top, in flashing red, she read the words: SILENCE, PLEASE.

Below in smaller letters came a list of names and matching room numbers. Milly saw ATROPOS: CUBICLE 12, two-thirds of the way down. She recognized about half of the names on the list. Next to each one was a small flashing icon that read PRESENT or ABSENT. Almost everyone was here. At the bottom of the list, again as a bold flashing sign: RESPECT INDIVIDUAL PRIVACY. THE PRESENCE OF ANOTHER NETWORK MEMBER IS NOT AN INVITATION TO INTRUDE. DO NOT INVADE ANOTHER'S WORK SPACE. PROGRESS REVIEW MEETING IN THE CONFERENCE ROOM, 7.00–7.50.

With this for a greeting it did not surprise Milly to find no one in sight. She crept along the corridor toward Cubicle 12. On the way she had to pass one open door, that of Cubicle 7. The intimidating signs at the main entrance had made it clear that she ought to ignore whatever or whoever was inside, but her own curiosity was so great that she could not resist a sideways peek.

The layout of furniture in the little room was familiar. The table, console, terminal, and numerous display units were like those at the analysis stations on the Argus Project. The added feature, of a stand loaded with food and drink, made excellent sense. Milly was often so absorbed that she worked on long after she should have taken a break, to the benefit of neither her body nor her mental efficiency.

The room's fixtures, however, were not its most important feature. Someone was in the room—a man, sitting with his chair swung to face away from the desk and console and staring out of the open door.

Despite the instructions at the entrance of the room, Milly could not just ignore the occupant. The man was looking right at her, and he was smiling.

"Keep going if you want to," he said. "Or come on in."

Milly, disconcerted, did neither. She stopped walking and turned to face him. The man was in his fifties, deep-chested and strongly-built. Although his eyes were pale and hard to read behind prominent brow ridges, his whole person seemed to exude warmth and empathy.

"Are you with the Puzzle Network?" Milly asked at last.

"I am."

"The sign says that this cubicle is for Torquemada." Milly stopped short of expressing her conviction that it couldn't be true. In the past she had struggled for weeks with Torquemada's brain-bending problems, and in her imagination the torturer was a gaunt, robed figure with spidery fingers, peering in the flame-lit dungeon at his racked victim.

The tone in her voice must have betrayed her doubts, but the man just grinned. "That's right. I'm Torquemada. I shouldn't really be here at all—I'm busy on a dozen other problems, and I don't have time to pull my weight. But I couldn't resist coming in for awhile to kibitz. There never was a challenge like this one. Now, how about you? Are *you* with the Puzzle Network?"

"I guess so." It was a weak answer, delivered in a weak voice. In spite of the warning sign at the entrance, Milly spoke more loudly. "My Network name is Atropos. I'm very junior, though, and quite unknown."

"Not to me. Atropos was a three-time Junior Champion. Aren't you also Milly Wu?"

"Yes. How did you know that?"

"Because I'm not blind and deaf. Your image has been all over the Ganymede blurts for weeks. You discovered the Wu-Beston anomaly. That's the reason everybody is here today."

Milly glanced up and down the corridor. "The most invisible everybodies I've ever seen."

"What did you expect to find?"

"Well . . ."

What had she expected? She could say what she had *hoped*

to find—exactly what she had written to Uncle Edgar.

"I assumed that this room would contain an enthusiastic group of people, combining the forces of their brilliant minds to evolve meaning from an enigmatic signal developed by alien intelligences and transmitted for reception by other sentient beings living many light-years away."

That had come out far more pompous than she'd intended, but Torquemada took it in stride. He shrugged.

"Then you should be delighted. That's exactly what you've got." And, when she stared, "Come on, Milly Wu. You're dealing with the Puzzle Network, not a political convention. How many years were you a Network nut?"

"Nine."

"How many other Network members did you meet?"

"None." Milly had sudden memories of a long-ago birthday party and a shy thirteen-year-old boy. "Or maybe one. I had suspicions and I think he did, but we never asked each other."

"Absolutely appropriate. I'm the odd man out in this place. Most Puzzle Network members aren't like sheep or bees. They don't herd and they don't swarm. It's a minor miracle getting them within a kilometer of each other, even behind closed doors, and that's only happening because this is the central point for data receipt and analysis distribution. Everyone is so afraid of missing something, they'll put up with anything— even proximity. But not personal presence, except at the progress review meetings. I've been a member for thirty years. Until I came here I had met only one other."

"Which one?" Milly was curious to know who else was this friendly.

"*Megachirops*, alias the Great Bat. But I suspect he's the most antisocial of the lot." Torquemada waved a hand. "Bat's here, down at the end. Try and visit him and you'll wish you hadn't. But if you wait you may see him later in the day, in the conference room at the end of the corridor. Then again, you may not."

"I don't understand this. What's the point of coming here, if no one will talk to anyone else?"

"You'll see how it's done, as soon as you go to your cubicle. But if you have questions and if I'm still around, feel free to drop in and ask."

He smiled again, and once more Milly felt the strength of his personality. She started to move toward her own room, then realized that he had ended their meeting so smoothly that she had omitted to ask an important question. While they were talking she had become increasingly convinced that she ought to know who he was. She had seen him before, somehow and somewhere.

She took two backward steps so that she could again see into the open door of his cubicle.

"Do you mind if I ask you one of those questions now?"

"Not in the slightest."

"What's your name?—I mean your real name, not your Puzzle Network name."

"That seems fair, since I know yours. My name is Cyrus Mobarak."

"Thank you." Milly retreated along the corridor, which seemed a better reaction than standing and gaping. No wonder his face seemed familiar. She had been speaking with the Sun King, inventor of the Moby fusion plants and one of the wealthiest and most influential people in the System. But here he was simply Torquemada. Within the hierarchy of the Puzzle Network, money and family and influence meant nothing. Ingenuity and imagination were what counted, and all that counted. It gave her a new respect for the unseen faces behind the corridor's closed doors.

She entered Cubicle 12 and sat down in the single chair.

She noticed that the stand to her left was empty. Tastes varied, so apparently each person brought his or her own preferred food and drink. Something to think about before she came here tomorrow, but today she would manage without. There was much to learn, much to do. She couldn't afford to waste time hunting for food.

The equipment seemed familiar, and as a first move she turned on the console and the dozen displays. The message that appeared on every one was simple and specific: A REMINDER OF AN OPERATING RULE: NOTHING THAT WE RECEIVE FROM ODIN STATION SHOULD BE SENT ANYWHERE ELSE. IT MAY BE SHARED INTERNALLY, BUT MUST BE TREATED AS PRIVILEGED INFORMATION.

Jack Beston had warned her to expect something like this. He argued that *conclusions* drawn from data were another matter, and could be communicated. Milly was not so sure. She had decided, without getting into an argument with Jack, that she was going to judge each individual case as it happened.

As the displays began to fill with other information, she realized that Cyrus Mobarak—Torquemada, she ought to think of him that way within this environment—had been right. Thoughts, conclusions, conjectures, and results both positive and negative were swapped freely among the group members. Sometimes you could tell the originator of a message, sometimes not. Credit and personal ego did not seem to be an issue.

Milly soon realized something else. This group had been busy while she was in transit from Jovian L-4 to Ganymede, and already they had done an immense amount of work. It would take days, just to absorb their progress.

Milly cleared her mind of all other thoughts, made herself comfortable, and concentrated on the displays. At first she didn't care about details. On the way to Ganymede she had done her own share of obsessive thinking and decided that the signal, all twenty-one billion digits of it, was too large for any human mind to comprehend except in gross terms. She needed to build up a feeling of general structure before attacking details.

Examining the mixture of facts, conjecture, and statistics on the displays, it was no surprise to find that the Argus, Odin, and Puzzle Network groups were all following roughly the same initial agenda. The signal had arrived as one immense and unstructured linear digit string. Without discovering and imposing order, you had no chance of deciphering message content. Therefore, you looked for rational ways to subdivide the whole into smaller sections.

You could try dozens of different ways. For example, you might examine the statistics of the whole string locally, where a "local" region contained anything from a thousand to a million digits. All the tools of signal processing were available for that analysis. In one common technique, regions of abnormally low entropy—where the next digit could be predicted with some confidence from the group of digits immediately preceding it—could be sought and marked. These might be "start message" and "end message" markers, since it seemed highly unlikely that the whole SETI signal held only one message. You had to remember how much information could be contained in twenty-one billion binary digits. It was like five thousand densely-written books.

But perhaps regions of low entropy were merely a hint to some other kind of information. An entropy analysis had already been performed, but whoever had done it made no assumptions as to its significance. Milly saw a whole library of possible maps, showing the signal divided into pieces and available for her inspection or continued analysis.

Of course, examining the statistical behavior of signal sections was not the only way to seek structure, and it might not be the best way. As a valid but quite different approach, you could scan the entire signal for test sequences that repeated over and over throughout its length. Naturally, a test sequence had to be long enough for its occurrence to provide information. If the whole signal were totally random, then a short sequence such as 1-0-0-1 could be found in it more than a billion times by sheer chance. On the other hand, if you chose a thirty-digit test sequence you would expect to find it only a score of times in a random string of twenty-one billion digits. Occurrence of that thirty-digit string fifty or sixty separate times was so unlikely that you would know you were on to something.

It was easy to say, "Examine the signal for test sequences long enough to be significant," but the actual task was a monster. A billion different sequences existed with thirty binary digits. You needed to screen for all of them. That work was still going on.

And when you had found a particular sequence too often to believe that it was the result of chance, what came next? That was another and more difficult question. Perhaps each occurrence of a thirty-digit string indicated a starting point or an end point for an actual message. Then between each thirty-digit string that you found there were sure to be shorter repeated sequences of, say, six to twelve digits. These, particularly if groups of them came in close proximity, ought to form the message itself. In human terms, six binary digits were enough to encode letters of an alphabet, while twelve digits would suffice for most words. Even though there was surely no hope of finding the letters of any human language, it made sense to look for the universals of mathematics. The integers themselves should be easiest of all. Once you knew where each one started and stopped, the numerical value of a binary string was a unique number to within a reflection (should you read the number from left to right, or right to left?). Then you could begin to look for the symbols that stood for equality, less than, greater than, exponentiation, and other common arithmetical operations.

But this brought the interpretation teams face to face with the most vexing question of all: To what extent could you or should you assume that human thinking, human behavior, and human science applied in any way to a SETI message?

How alien was alien? This was the question that gave Milly nightmares. Even within the limited group of workers on Argus Station, she had found two schools of thought. One set— call them the optimists—assumed that any aliens advanced enough to send signals across space must be ahead of humans in every field of science. Moreover, the optimists were convinced that the aliens would have done their absolute best to make their messages easy to read. They would employ no tricks, such as run-length encoding, to reduce the volume of data transmitted and received.

The pessimists said, but wait a moment. These are *aliens*. Technical and scientific discoveries throughout human history didn't come in the most convenient or logical order. Archimedes was unlucky. He had the integral calculus within his grasp, and if Arabic numeral notation had been available to him he would have beaten Newton and Leibniz by almost two millennia. Kepler, on the other hand, had been fortunate. The Greeks, from Euclid to Apollonius, had established hundreds of theorems concerning conic sections. When Kepler needed them in order to replace the old systems of epicycles with his own laws, those theorems sat waiting.

Aliens are likely to know *different things*, because there is no fixed order for discovery. Maybe we have as much to offer them as they have to offer us. Suppose they never invented the alphabet, or positional notation in mathematics? Then their messages could be all ideographs, their numbers Roman numerals. But far more likely they would use something less familiar and comprehensible than either.

Milly had long ago made her own decision as to where she stood. You could not afford to be either an extreme pessimist or an extreme optimist. On the side of pessimism, surely any aliens would be physically and mentally nothing like humans. They were, after all, *aliens*. Their languages, notations, and order of evolution of ideas would be vastly different. On the other hand, on the side of optimism, surely any alien thought processes must follow the universal laws of logic. Also, anyone who bothered to send messages far across space would want their messages to be not only received, but *comprehended*.

Once you accepted those two assumptions, you had certain guarantees. To take one simple example, no sensible alien would ever send as part of a message $2 ? 2 = 4$ unless there was other independent evidence as to how the symbol ? was to be interpreted. The message was too ambiguous. The receiver could not determine whether ? stood for plus ($2 + 2 = 4$), times ($2 \times 2 = 4$), or raise to a power ($2^2 = 4$).

If it were up to Milly, she knew exactly how she would build and send a SETI message. First, you defined special symbols that provided start and stop instructions; then you displayed the positive integers, with enough examples, such as sequences of primes, to make sure the receiver could be absolutely sure there was no misinterpretation.

After that came the symbols of common arithmetic, with examples showing how to add, subtract, multiply, and divide. From there it was a short step to negative numbers, fractions, powers, and irrationals. Imaginaries you would introduce using fractional powers of negative numbers. Then on to series of powers, and the elementary transcendental functions such as sines, cosines, logarithms, and exponents. In every case you would give enough examples to be sure there was no confusion. After providing series expressions for the universal transcendentals such as π or e, you would provide a check that all was being interpreted correctly by quoting one of mathematics' enduring wonders, a formula that mysteriously links transcendental and imaginary numbers with the basic numerical building blocks of 1 and 0:

$$e^{i\pi} + 1 = 0.$$

Mathematics was easy, the obvious way to start. After that, Milly would proceed to astronomy, physics, chemistry, and, finally and most difficult, language.

The trouble, of course, was that it was not up to Milly. She was not sending a message. She was *receiving* one. The difference, in terms of self-confidence, was the difference between being a doctor and being a patient.

The good news was that she was not working alone. People as smart as she, and probably a whole lot smarter, were her allies. The displays in front of her provided an overview of the whole signal in schematic form, subdivided into twenty-seven regions.

Using her console to control the rate at which she advanced, Milly set out to scan the entire length of the signal. The Puzzle Network team had worked cooperatively to attach their analyses to the appropriate regions. The result was like a gigantic snake, of which the string of digits of the signal itself formed a narrow backbone. Here and there, in places where something particularly interesting and significant had been discovered, the snake bulged out like a python that had swallowed a pig.

Milly backed the scan to study Section 7, the fourth bulge, which at first sight was bigger than all the others. The comments were offered in ordered bunches:

Attoboy: The structure here is odd. High entropy sequences of average length 10^6 digits are regularly interspersed with low entropy regions each of constant length 3.3554×10^7 digits. Any thoughts?

Sneak Attack: Yes. We could be seeing sections of "text" (variable but roughly equal lengths) that introduce or describe a "picture" (something in image format, with a constant array size). Maybe square arrays of black and white images, each about $6,000 \times 6,000$ elements?

Claudius: More likely, a gray scale image $4,096 \times 4,096$ ($2^{12} \times 2^{12}$—that supports the notion of binary representations), with 2 bits (4 levels) for each pixel. That fits with the exact size of the low entropy regions, 33,554,432 bits.

Sneak Attack: Could just as well be $2,048 \times 2,048$, with 256 (8-bit) gray levels.

Claudius: Should be easy enough to find out which. If we assume a particular line length and do cross-correlations of successive lines, the correct line length should jump right out at us when we get to it, because the correlation will be a lot higher. Let me take a look.

That was all for that cluster of messages. Presumably Claudius did not yet have an answer, or at least not one that "jumped right out." Milly moved on.

The seventh bulge along the signal's spine, Section 12, contained remarks similar to the previous one, except for three added comments:

Megachirops: In this case the low entropy regions have a constant length of 4,194,304 bits, exactly one-eighth as long as in Section 7. Does anyone else find this somewhat surprising?

Ghost Boy: We would probably make them all the same size. The difference may be part of the message, trying to tell us something.

Claudius: Or could these be line drawings?—binary images, black and white with no shades of gray.

The ninth bulge supported a hypothesis offered early in the history of SETI:

The Joker: My frequency analysis of this section suggests that we are dealing with base 4 arithmetic, rather than the base 2 binary we have seen elsewhere. The temptation to interpret this as a biological description in terms of strings of four nucleotides is strong.

Attoboy: Beware of anthropomorphism. But I agree, the temptation is strong. I will try to correlate this section with everything in the genome library.

Not surprisingly, Attoboy had not yet reported results from that effort. The task was a monstrous one. The library to be examined held complete genomes for more than two million species, everything from humans and oak trees and mushrooms to the smallest and simplest viruses. No one, no matter how optimistic, would hope for an exact match. It would be a miracle (and enormously relevant to the universal nature of life) if anything correlated at all with a living creature from Earth. But Attoboy was right, you couldn't afford not to look.

Milly worked her way on through the signal, section by section. The exercise was giving her a strong inferiority complex. The results that she was seeing had been performed so quickly, and offered such powerful evidence of ingenuity— what could she possibly contribute? The team had already established the existence of unique start and stop sequences, each fourteen bits long. Numerical base and reading order were known beyond doubt: integers were base 2 and base 4, with the most significant digit to the right. Sequences of primes and squares and cubes had been discovered, more than long enough to be unambiguous.

When she came to the very end of the signal, with its termination as a repeated pattern of the fourteen-bit stop sequence, Milly at once went back to the beginning and started over. The easy part, following the trail that others had already marked out, was over. Now she had to do something to justify her own presence in the group. *Sit, observe, learn, keep quiet*; that was all very well—for the first half-day. After that, Milly hoped to bring her own special knowledge and experience to bear. She went to a section near the middle of the signal, where analysis and comments by members of the Puzzle Network were meager and felt tentative. This was a place with special significance for Milly. It was here where she first noticed the oddity that had evolved into the Wu-Beston anomaly, and she had studied it extensively.

Something she had brought with her from Argus Station, more important than clothing or personal effects, was her own suite of processing programs. She had no illusions that they were *better* than anyone else's; what she was sure was that they were different. Also, they were *hers*, and she knew them inside-out.

She began her analysis. It was similar to what she had attempted months ago, with one crucial difference: she could now build on everything established or conjectured by the Puzzle Network group. The start-stop coding sequence was known. She was sure of the integers. Perhaps most important of all, she knew that what she was dealing with *was* a signal. Puzzles always become easier when you know that a solution exists.

The section that she clipped out for inspection was only a small section of the whole, roughly a hundred million digits out of twenty-one billion. You could eat that up very quickly with images, but she had deliberately avoided low-entropy data runs. What she hoped to find was "text"—whatever that term might mean to an alien mind. It was too early in the game to hope for keys to an actual language.

After the first few minutes, Milly entered the twilight zone. Her mind became a place where symbols took on their own life and formed their own relationships. The signal contained dozens of these, short and well-defined strings that had been identified by other workers as common repeat patterns, but were not yet understood as to meaning. Sometimes the unknown strings appeared close to known integers, sometimes they coupled only to other unknowns. At this stage of understanding, the "knowns" lay within a great quagmire of uncertainties. The trick—if a trick existed—was to stand on a firm starting-point, something you definitely understood, then discover a sequence that allowed you to scramble out along it to reach another point of understanding.

Milly worked on, oblivious to where she was or how long she had been sitting there, until she found her attention returning, again and again, to a sequence containing only a few tens of thousands of digits. She had culled it piece by piece from the sea of a hundred million bits, without knowing at a conscious level what she accepted and what she rejected.

What made these samples different from any random selections? They seemed like a meaningless mixture. The pattern, if it could be called a pattern, comprised sets of small integers, always separated from each other by a repeated string. That string always contained the same twenty binary digits, and it could indicate an actual number but more likely stood for a symbol of some kind. Milly gave it a name. Call it the 20-bit "connector." Each block of connector-number-connector had its own start and stop codes, separating it from other blocks.

Milly substituted the word "connector" in the data set in place of the 20-bit strings, put decimal numbers in place of their binary integer equivalents, and read the result.

On the face of it, she didn't have much. Here was eight-connector-six-connector-eight, followed by the end-of-block marker. Here was eight-connector-seven-connector-eight, which was numerically almost the same, and another block end marker. But next to that sat the group one-connector-eight-connector-one, and then the more mysterious one-one-connectorconnector-six-connectorconnector-one-one.

Signifying?

Milly concentrated until the numbers and words swam and wandered and wobbled in front of her eyes. Pattern recognition was what humans did well, better than any computer so far built.

There had to be a pattern, right?

Right! So recognize it!

The display sneered back at her, *Right! If you can!*

Milly closed her eyes, took a deep breath, and sat motionless for a long time. At the conscious level, she seemed to be drifting from thought to random thought. But when she opened her eyes she was changing the word "connector" on the display to the symbolic "—".

The section she had been looking at became: 8—6—8, 8—7—8, 1—8—1, 1,1— —6— —1,1. If anything, that was more confusing than before.

And then, suddenly, it was not confusing at all. Milly shivered and rubbed her eyes. How dense could you get? Before she started, she had told herself the order in which a rational being would try to construct meaningful messages: mathematics, then physics, then chemistry. When that was done, you could consider interpreting biology and language.

Mathematics they had, at least at the level of the integers. It might be months or years before they advanced to complex variables and algebraic topology and the theory of continuous groups, but you did not need all those for a start on other subjects.

In physics and chemistry, what was the most obvious and fundamental information a message might offer? The periodic table was a basic building block, invariant across the universe. Hydrogen came first, helium second, lithium third, and so on right up through all the stable elements. Carbon was sixth, nitrogen seventh, oxygen eighth, and you had absolutely no choice in those assignments.

So now:

8—6—8: carbon dioxide, complete with the symbol for a chemical bond.

8—7—8: nitrous oxide.

1—8—1: hydrogen-oxygen-hydrogen—*water*. If you were a human, you would have placed that first. Did it occur more frequently than the other symbols? Milly would have to go back and check.

And 1,1— —6— —1,1? The dash was a clumsy notation for a two-or three-dimensional bond, but the reader was presumed to be intelligent. This one was methane, CH_4, carbon with single bonds to four hydrogen atoms. Maybe the 2-D or 3-D representation would be found elsewhere in the signal, but meanwhile this would suffice. Scanning the whole sequence, Milly could see more complex patterns. She was reading a tutorial in elementary chemistry, one which confirmed at the same time that the natural numbers represented the elements.

It wasn't a great discovery, maybe it was just one small step up the mountain of understanding involved in deciphering an alien message. But it was *her* step, one that no one else had ever taken. Milly didn't just want to post it on the Puzzle Network displays. She wanted to *tell* somebody, shout it to the world before her brain burst and the information was lost.

She stood up quickly, swayed, and grabbed the edge of the console. She came close to blacking out and had to drop back into her seat to save herself.

As dizziness receded she glanced over to see what time it was. Well past midnight. At once she knew what was happening. It was her old problem. She had sat alone in her cubicle, oblivious to everything but the displays and her own thoughts, for more than half a day. Now that she was again aware of her body, her mouth was dry and her throat felt as though it could not swallow. She needed a drink, and she needed to go to the bathroom—and both those things took priority over the table of the elements.

She stood up, more carefully this time, and eased her way to the cubicle door and out into the corridor. She did not know where the bathroom was, but instinct told her that there must be one close to a conference room. She moved slowly along the corridor to the end, supporting herself with a hand on the wall and glad now that all the doors were closed.

In the bathroom she relieved herself, then drank from a faucet and splashed cold water over her face and wrists.

She went back out into the deserted corridor. In her muddled-headed condition she had not noticed before how quiet and dark it was. Everyone else in the Puzzle Network team must have gone to bed long ago, and she should do the same. Her brain was not going to burst. She would post her discovery tomorrow.

Milly walked back toward the entrance, slowly and wearily. Halfway there, her nose picked up a faint and infinitely attractive aroma. Someone had been cooking, and in her starved state the smell was ambrosial.

She tracked the food scent to a particular closed door, and stood in front of it. Every tissue in her body called out for instant nourishment. If there happened to be leftovers, surely the person who had prepared the dish would not begrudge them to Milly? She would leave a note, explaining what had happened and promising to replace whatever she ate.

Her mouth, dry five minutes ago, was watering. She eased open the door of the cubicle. The lighting inside was at a low setting, but she could see the food stand and a big brown crockpot sitting on top of it. The handle of a ladle pointed invitingly to Milly.

She had taken two quick paces and was reaching out a hand when she realized that the room was not empty after all. A huge person, big enough to obscure half the cubicle's display screens, squatted on a flat padded chair. As Milly dropped back a step, the black-clad hulk turned toward her.

28

Is this it?" Uncle Karolus placed a closed transparent container the size and shape of a small thimble on the table. "I wanted to be sure we were talking about the same thing before I go ahead and give it to the test team."

It was the middle of the night in Alex's living quarters. Karolus, black-caped and hooded, had entered without warning to be greeted by a sleepy and startled Kate wearing only a short nightie. He gave her an appreciative leer before Alex appeared from the bedroom and she could retire into it.

Alex blinked in the brighter light of the living-room and picked up the miniature vial. He lifted it close to his eyes, peering at the contents. It contained a dark-gray liquid that moved sluggishly as he tilted it.

"It doesn't look right," he said. "The way it was described to me, there should be a lot of little balls in there."

"There are. At least, one of the Ligon techs took a quick look with a microscope and said there were. They're real tiny, so they move around as though they're a liquid."

"Then I guess this is what we need. Did you have to come here in the middle of the night?"

"I thought we agreed this whole thing should be completed as fast as possible. Does your fat friend still say he'll assign Pandora to us?"

"For a full year, as soon as the tests are finished and we deliver the results. He's grumbling a lot, but he already vacated Pandora and came to Ganymede. He wants the Ops Center finished before he goes back."

"Then let's get the tests over and done with, before he changes his mind. Who has the list?"

"Nobody. Bat described one series of experiments that I already passed on to Bengt Suomi, but he wants our people to feel free to add any more physical tests they can think of. He's convinced that when the right experiment is performed, we'll know it. I told Bengt Suomi that Bat is expecting some spectacular result, and you know Bengt. He can't wait to get started."

"I believe that." Karolus sniffed. "I'll give Suomi the go-ahead tonight. Then the trouble will be stopping him. I never met a scientist yet who didn't want to do just one more experiment."

Alex was still holding the little cylinder, and he moved it around so that the contents swirled up the rounded sides. "Are you sure that these samples were taken from the man I told you about, in science research quarantine?"

"Either they were taken from Sebastian Birch, which is what I was told, or somebody in science research quarantine is going to suffer a greatly reduced life expectancy."

"How did you get them?"

"You don't know." Karolus reached out and took the container from Alex's hand. "And you don't want to know. I'll tell you this, though. Gram for gram, the gray mess in this bottle is the most expensive material in the solar system. It had better be worth the price."

"Bat is convinced that it will be."

"Do you have any idea why he's so hot for this?—not that it's any of our damned business."

"He's convinced that it's somehow connected to a weapon, and a woman who died at the end of the Great War."

"The war?" Karolus scowled. "My God, the war was over thirty years ago. Battachariya must be off his head."

Alex recalled Bat in the kitchen of the Bat Cave, peering into a steaming cauldron of *bouillabaisse*, muttering, tasting, and adding a single grain of cumin. "I wouldn't say that. He is a little eccentric. But he cooks and serves better food than I've ever had from the Ligon chefs or anyone else."

"Really?" Karolus raised his bushy eyebrows. "That's quite a claim. I wouldn't mind tasting some myself. Good luck to him. I'm not a man to deny another his little pleasures— whatever they are. Which is my cue to leave and wake up Bengt Suomi, and yours to go back in there and service your extremely attractive friend."

Karolus stood up and pulled the black hood over his head. "Make sure Battachariya knows we are keeping our part of the deal."

"I will."

"I tell you, young Alex, these past few weeks have left me much encouraged. Hector honking Lucy Mobarak, you honking your own boss, no less, and the pair of you locking in the deal for Pandora. Meanwhile Great-aunt Agatha, that ghastly old hag, is heading for the bone yard. There's hope for the family yet."

He bulled his way out. Alex locked the door behind him, reflecting that there would not be much hope for the Ligon family until Uncle Karolus joined Great-aunt Agatha.

It was not reassuring to return to the bedroom and hear Kate, sitting cross-legged on the bed, say, "So that was the dreaded Karolus. You keep telling me that he's terrible, but you know, I though he was rather fascinating. He introduced himself to me most politely."

"Right. Most polite. As he was leaving he told me to get back in there and service my extremely attractive friend."

"Did he really? Extremely attractive? Polite, and a man of discernment, too. But not again, not tonight. Come to bed. Tomorrow we go three more rounds on your predictive model with Ole Pedersen. We need sleep."

As if she needed to remind him. Alex, once again comfortably in bed with Kate nestled into his back, felt a sudden attack of the midnight blues. Hector was going to receive the credit for the Mobarak merger and for the deal with Bat. Ole Pedersen, or, even worse, moronic Macanelly, would be given credit for success with the predictive model—alien influence and all, which was no longer wild speculation since the news blurts were full of the Wu-Beston anomaly and the current work on signal deciphering.

And Alex?

A mere anonymous courier, running between Bengt Suomi's lab and Rustum Battachariya, relaying other people's wish lists and results, all to be forgotten a year from now? Or, just as bad, the creator of a predictive model which consumed large amounts of the Seine's computer resources and produced nothing more than a bad example of mistaken concepts that would be recorded as part of the long history of modeling?

Alex fell asleep trying to decide which was better. Would you rather be forgotten, or blamed?

29

Sluiced. Until Jan heard that word, she had not been sure of her own plans. Now she knew. The idea that Sebastian's body would be invaded and taken over by self-replicating tiny machines, producing changes that no one could predict, filled her with horror. Even if no one else worried about the experiment—it was no better than an experiment, no matter what Valnia Bloom might say—she had to stick close to Sebastian and keep an eye on him.

He seemed more stolid and indifferent than ever. He didn't seem to know or care what was done to him. It was Jan or Valnia Bloom who, day by day, checked progress in the nano development. The chief technician, Hal Launius, insisted that the job was a simple one, with no chance of going wrong. He was confident and almost as casual in manner as Sebastian. It was left to Jan to do the worrying. She knew that never in human history had anyone developed a system incapable of failure.

She made sure that she was present when the completed product was delivered. She sat and watched as Hal Launius displayed the spray syringe. It was tiny, more like a toy than a medical instrument. The tube held a few drops of misty gray-blue liquid, innocuous in appearance; but Jan could not repress a shiver when Launius applied the syringe's tip to Sebastian's bared upper arm. The liquid vanished instantly, absorbed through the skin.

"Feeling all right?" Valnia Bloom, to judge from her voice, was more concerned than she would admit.

"Yeah." Sebastian sat dull-eyed. "Fine."

Jan wasn't. "What happens next?"

"For a few hours, nothing at all." Hal Launius examined the empty syringe and nodded in satisfaction. "After that, the nanos will have multiplied enough to make themselves felt. Sebastian, you will run a fever—no more than a degree or two, I expect—and then you'll need to pee a lot. That's how the nodules will be excreted. Make sure that you drink plenty of fluids to help your kidneys."

"When will it end?" Valnia Bloom asked. "Before we began, you suggested four or five days would be enough."

"I was being conservative. Safer to play it that way." Launius packed away the syringe in its little carrying case. "But if this isn't all over and done with in three days or less, I owe you dinner."

He left. Valnia Bloom followed him a few minutes later, after advising Sebastian that his temperature and pulse would be monitored remotely and reminding him that water would help to flush out his system. Jan watched him closely. For all the notice he took of Valnia Bloom's words, she might as well have saved her breath.

Then Jan and Sebastian were alone. It was no novelty, they had been alone together most of their lives. But since leaving Earth, things had changed. Perhaps it was Sebastian, perhaps it was Jan, but what had once been easy companionship was now awkward. Sebastian never started a conversation. His replies were only a few words. He seemed preoccupied, far off in some private world.

Jan stuck it out for three hours. At last she told Sebastian that she needed to go outside for "a breath of air"—a notion utterly alien to a Ganymede native. He simply nodded. She left the research quarantine facility and headed upward. The surface itself lay only four habitat layers above their heads.

Jan had made no conscious plan as to what she would do next. It seemed like random impulse when she looked for and located a surface access point, donned one of the protective suits with its superconducting fine mesh, and proceeded upward one more layer and out through multiple locks onto the naked surface of Ganymede.

Close to the lock, the ground, worn down by the passage of many people and vehicles, had taken on the texture of fine sand. Flecks of ice and mica at Jan's feet glittered in the light of the distant Sun. Farther off, to her left, she saw sunglint on jagged ridges and icy pinnacles. She knew their name— those were the Sabine Hills—but she felt no desire to explore them. A brief pang of homesickness for the soft and rounded contours of Earth came and went. She told herself that the Outer System was home now. She had better get used to the idea. This world and this scenery possessed its own stark splendor.

It was not until she found herself walking steadily west, toward an array of gantries and scaffolds rising into the black sky like the glittering spires of an alien city, that she finally realized what she was doing. Ahead of her lay one of Ganymede's main spaceports, the home for hundreds or thousands of vessels ranging in size from single person space-hoppers to full-sized interplanetary liners. In the latter class—she could not see it yet, but already she was looking—was the *OSL Achilles*, being prepared for its next flight from Ganymede to the Inner System. Paul Marr had told Jan that although he was on leave, he stopped by the ship every day to see how preparations were coming along.

Jan halted, stared up to the steady stars, and wondered if she should go no farther. Spending his off-duty hours with Paul was one thing, behaving like a fool and interfering with his work was another. But as she looked again to the spidery derricks and gantries, she recognized the solid outline of the *Achilles*. Her steps, taking orders from somewhere other than her conscious mind, led Jan in that direction.

Security at the ship—indeed, everywhere on the surface— seemed casual to nonexistent. Jan was able to approach the *Achilles*, operate the elevator on the scaffold surrounding the ship, and enter an airlock unimpeded and apparently unobserved. It was a shock to emerge from the inner lock and find herself face to face with Captain Kondo.

He inclined his head to her politely. "It is nice to see you again, Ms. Jannex. How may I help you?"

Did he have one of those phenomenal memories, which could store away the name of every passenger who ever traveled on the *Achilles*?

Kondo's next words eliminated that idea. "If you are seeking my first officer, you are fortunate in your timing. He is in the engine room, far aft, but he is preparing to leave momentarily. Although you know the way there, I would much prefer you to remain in this location. I will make him aware of your presence."

His tone was formal, but as he turned away the captain added, "I feel I am much indebted to you, Ms. Jannex. Many times I have urged Paul to enjoy himself and to take more relaxation between trips, but always to no avail. It seems that you have succeeded where I failed. Have fun with my first officer—but please bring back enough of him to fly the *Achilles*."

After that parting dig he left Jan to wait alone. She stood by the airlock exit, glad that Captain Kondo would not be present to observe her interaction with Paul—whatever it might be.

Paul appeared a few minutes later. He said, "Jan!"

It was impossible to tell from the one word of greeting if he was actually pleased to see her. Her suit ruled out a hug or other gesture of affection.

"I'm sorry, Paul. I wasn't planning to come up here at all, but then they started the sluicing operation on Sebastian, and it made me feel really uneasy, and I know it's supposed to be harmless and painless, but he's going to run a fever, and somehow . . ." Her voice trailed away.

"I understand. How long will the operation take?"

"No one seems sure. Three days, maybe four."

"Then the worst possible thing that you could do is hang around all the time with nothing to do but worry. Do you have to be anywhere special for the next few hours?"

"No."

"Then come with me. I guarantee something to take your mind off Sebastian for awhile."

"Where are you going?"

Paul pointed a finger upward, and grinned when he saw Jan's expression. "No, I don't mean the forward observation chamber of the *Achilles*. We've been there, done that—or tried to. I knew I would be in the spaceport today, so I booked myself for a space-spin. I asked for a single-seater, but I'll call and change it to a side-by-side with dual controls."

"I'm going to fly a spaceship?"

"No, you're not. Another day, maybe, but not today. Division of labor. I do the flying, you do the sight-seeing."

Jan had not agreed to go, but apparently refusal was not an option. Paul said, "Give me a minute to get my suit on. Good thing you are all set," and popped into an adjoining cabin before she could speak.

Again Jan was left standing alone. She felt much better. There were times when it was good to have someone else making the decisions.

Suited and outside the *Achilles*, Paul led them across an open expanse of the surface dotted with small spacecraft. Here and there, bright red shields against the solar hail of high-velocity protons hid whatever sat beneath. There were too many ships to count and to Jan the place was a maze. Paul obviously knew exactly where he was going. Fifteen minutes later he halted by a blunt-nosed oddity that reared high on six skinny legs. To Jan's earth-trained eye it resembled a giant blue dragonfly. Paul patted the side as they came up to it. A hatch in the side promptly opened and deployed a narrow ladder.

"Don't you have to make arrangements in advance for this sort of thing?" Jan asked, as they climbed up and dropped into massive cushioned seats. Jan's at once adjusted to her size.

"You might think so." Paul was checking read-outs. "And the average person couldn't take a ship without special notice. But I'm in the business. It's one of the perks. A lot of crew become planet-crazy if they're stuck below surface between flights, so we can fly anytime we want. Ready to go?"

It was a rhetorical question, because Jan's weight had suddenly become immense. The dragonfly was rising and rotating, her stomach was turning with it, and the surface of Ganymede dropped away with dizzying speed.

She said, through clenched teeth, "What's our acceleration?"

"One gee." The cabin had pressurized and Paul was opening his helmet. "I thought I ought to make you feel at home."

This was one Earth gravity? But then, before she had time to ponder how quickly the familiar became unfamiliar, she had something else to think about. Another ship, this one ten times their size, flashed by in front of them. Jan saw a line of portholes and people's heads, and knew that they had missed each other by a few tens of meters.

"Perfectly safe." Paul must have heard her gasp. "We're in the arrival zone, relative positions are controlled to within millimeters. Once we're clear of this I doubt you'll see another ship until we come back in to land."

"Where are you taking us?"

"Wherever you'd like to go."

"How about Io? I've heard it's spectacular."

"It sure is. Spouting volcanoes and lava and flaming sulfur pits. I've tried to paint that scene a hundred times, but I've always thrown away the result. I can't even get close to the reality. Whenever I read a description of Hell, I think of Io. But we can't go there today."

"Power limitations?"

"No. The Moby will run forever. But Ground Control doesn't want crew members joyriding out to Uranus or Neptune, so they're stingy on volatiles for reaction mass. Anyway, a round trip to Io is a full day's ride at our acceleration. We'll just ride around a bit."

Perhaps they would, but at the moment the dragonfly ship seemed to be plunging straight for the center of cloud-racked Jupiter. The planet was swelling visibly, at least in Jan's imagination. She recalled their last encounter with the planet, and the *Achilles'* near-fatal swingby. What on earth had Sebastian been trying to accomplish when he fiddled with the locks? He had never answered her when she asked him that. Jan had never admitted it to Valnia Bloom—in fact, she had insisted on the exact opposite—but Sebastian's behavior was becoming steadily more peculiar. Although he still stared endlessly at images of Jupiter and Saturn, he no longer drew their cloud patterns. He no longer seemed to do anything at all. Anyone examining him would conclude that he was half-witted or drugged. He had not always been like that—if he had, he would never have passed the tests, and he and Jan would still be back on Earth. But in his present condition, where in the System could Sebastian possibly be allowed to go next?

"Mind if I talk?" Paul broke into her thoughts. "You seem a bit out of it."

"I'm all right." Jan could detect a slight change in heading, they were no longer plunging straight for Jupiter. "The view reminded me of . . . something."

"That's what I was afraid of." Paul swiveled his seat to face her. "I was surprised to see you board the *Achilles* today— surprised, but pleased. Because there's been something I wanted to say to you, and I've been putting it off."

What was coming? Jan stiffened in her chair as Paul went on, "We've had a great time these past few weeks—at least, I have. But in six days the *Achilles* will be gone, and I'll be gone with it. Now, I'm a sailor and I'm probably a typical one. If it hasn't quite been a girl in every port, it has been a different companion on every trip. Two or three weeks were just enough time to start something going, then when you arrived at your destination you went your separate ways with everything tied off neat and civilized. I won't lie to you, Jan, I've had a hell of a time doing that and there were never any regrets.

"So I ought to be the last man in the System with any right to complain when something cools off. Except it hasn't been like that with us. We were really intense on the way out to

Ganymede, and again after we arrived until you went off to see how things were with Sebastian. I thought that was it, things were over between us. But you came back and we were hot as ever. I was starting to imagine that we might be something special for the long-term. Then Sebastian had to have this weird operation done, and away you went again.

"Now, I don't want you to think I'm jealous of the poor bastard. I'm not. I'm sorry for him, because in my opinion— don't get mad—he's not firing on all neurons. But it seems like whenever he's in trouble, I disappear off the screen so far as you are concerned. Like today. You come aboard the *Achilles*, and I get a big lift just out of seeing you. Only it turns out you didn't really come to visit me at all. You came because you were worried about Sebastian. So I bring you up here, thinking this will take your mind off him. But after take-off, you went away somewhere inside your head. Tell me the truth. Were you thinking about Sebastian just now?"

Jan paused, then reluctantly nodded.

"Do you wonder if I can't see any sort of future for the two of us? What do you want, Jan?"

"I don't want you to leave."

"I have to leave. The *Achilles* lifts off in six days."

"I know. I didn't mean that. Look, Sebastian's operation will be finished in three days. Will you wait that long, then ask me again what I want?"

"If it has to be that way." The ship had been following a long curved arc while they talked. Jupiter's great orb had vanished, and the frosty glitter of Ganymede lay dead ahead. Paul turned to face away from Jan. "I will ask again. But I'm afraid I already know what you'll say. We'd better close our suits, we'll be landing in five minutes."

"That would be good. I have to get back to the research facility."

Jan listened to her own words, and she couldn't believe she had spoken them. They confirmed all Paul's worries and doubts. She wished they could ride out, just the two of them, and never come back.

Except that it wouldn't work. Her ties to Sebastian were too strong. The hell of Io was nothing compared to the hell that was Ganymede.

Jan had been away for more than three hours. In that time Sebastian, so far as she could tell, had not moved a millimeter. He sat on his bed staring at the false-color display of Jupiter that covered one whole wall. The centuries-long hurricane that formed the Great Red Spot was muted to dull orange. Curling white vortices of ammonia, each one the size of Earth, spun away from its western edge.

"Sebastian?"

He did not respond. Jan went across to him and put her fingers to his forehead. Her own hands felt icy, but he was surely warmer than usual.

"Thirty-eight point two degrees," said the disembodied voice of Valnia Bloom. "A little fever, but nothing to be concerned about. Don't worry, I have his bedroom continuously monitored. Everything is going according to plan."

"I'd like to stay for awhile."

"There's no problem with that. We can give you your own room, you can spend as much time in it as you like. I'll make it so you can monitor the bedroom, too."

"That would be perfect." Jan moved to stand directly in front of Sebastian. "How do you feel?"

"Good."

"Not too hot?"

"No."

"Or hungry?"

"No." The moon face was impassive. His eyes never left the display.

Jan recalled the way that he had been on Earth, with his talk of strato-cumulus and cumulo-nimbus cloud layers. Now it was hard work to wring a monosyllable out of him. She had to get him moving, make him think about something more than the damned clouds.

"Sebastian, do you know where I've been? I think you would love it." She described her trip to the surface, the suited walk across icy rock beneath the unblinking stars, and the wild space-spin with Paul Marr. She gave lots of details and tried to make it sound as exciting as possible. Sebastian did not look at her, but he was certainly listening. Once or twice he nodded.

At the end Jan said, "Maybe you and I can take a ride together, as soon as the sluicing is finished? We could fly all the way in and swing by Io."

That ought to grab him. Back on Earth, Sebastian had been a far better pilot than Jan—an absolute natural, according to the Global Minerals' sky chief.

"Maybe."

But his flat, neutral voice said, *I don't think so.* In spite of anything that Valnia Bloom and Hal Launius might say, or even believe, Jan was profoundly worried.

A space ride together, to view Io or some other world of the Jovian system? Not unless he changed a lot from his present condition. As he was, Sebastian was not likely to be going anywhere. Ever.

30

Contrary to widespread opinion, Bat was not a misogynist. True, he did not enjoy the company of women, but neither did he care for that of men. He tolerated the presence of a select few humans; beyond that he saw no need to venture.

Nor was he unsympathetic to youth. His own adolescence had been a period of extreme trauma in which he felt at war with the rest of the universe, so he was sympathetic to anyone who had recently endured the same travail.

The glare with which he greeted the young woman who entered his cubicle therefore had nothing to do with gender or age. It was late at night, he was awaiting the arrival of Alex Ligon, and a closed door should be enough to guarantee privacy. In addition, he had been interrupted while pursuing a difficult and abstract line of thought on the SETI problem.

The intruder was saved from Bat's righteous wrath not by anything she said, but by what she did. As she came in she stared at the brown crockpot. Her glance finally moved to the seated figure, but Bat had caught her expression long before that.

He recognized that look and sympathized with it. The newcomer was *hungry*, starved-wolf hungry. Such a need excused almost every form of improper behavior.

Moreover, its satisfaction must not be delayed by the conventional niceties of formal introduction. Bat waved a hand toward the food stand. "Bowls are on the lower rack. Help yourself. Eat, and enjoy."

The woman nodded and grabbed the ladle, but she stared round-eyed at Bat as she filled a bowl with herb risotto. Thirty years of rude stares had accustomed him to such a reaction. He said, "When you have taken as much food as you want, I request that you leave. I am expecting a visitor, and you are greatly disturbing my work."

The woman mumbled something unintelligible through a mouthful of hot rice, but rather than leaving she swallowed and said, "I'm sorry I came in without asking. Are you *Megachirops*—the Great Bat?"

"That is my name within the Puzzle Network. This section is dedicated to Puzzle Network activities. Others are not supposed to be here."

Still she did not move, except to continue gobbling the result of Bat's culinary labors so fast that he knew she could not possibly savor the delicate balance of flavors. Finally she paused between mouthfuls to say, "This tastes wonderful. It's saving my life. My name is Milly Wu."

"Of the Wu-Beston anomaly?" Her presence in the analysis center at last made sense.

"That's right."

"Then you have a message waiting for you. It came in a few minutes ago from the Argus Station at Jovian L-4. It contains a privacy tag, which means that it can only be read using a cubicle code." Bat saw no reason to add that privacy tags were no challenge, he had read the message, and the sender had cagily offered no details except to request a return call. He went on, "But there is no cubicle set aside for Milly Wu, and no cubicle code."

"Oh, I'm sorry. I gave you my name but not my Puzzle Network name. I go by Atropos, and I'm in Cubicle Twelve."

Few things in the System impressed Bat. When one did he took care not to let it show. This was Milly Wu, discoverer of the Wu-Beston anomaly. *And* she was Atropos, a journeyman triple champion in the Network. Such talent could be expelled from the room, but not precipitately.

He asked a polite question, expecting a negative answer. "You must have arrived only recently. Are you making progress in deciphering elements of the SETI signal?"

Her response made Bat feel that he had made an awful mistake. She crashed the bowl down half-empty on the stand and exclaimed, "Yes! Yes!"

Now she was going to stay and spout rubbish at him when he should be working. He became convinced of that as she babbled on. "I believe I've found something, an interpretation that I've not seen in any other analysis. I started work in Section Fourteen—you know the twenty-seven section mapping of the whole anomaly? Of course you do, you probably created it. Anyway, it's the same place where I first noticed the existence of a signal, out at the Argus Station. But today I had the advantage of the interpretive suggestions that you and the others have made, so I was able to start with a knowledge of the integers and arithmetic operations. It took me forever—that's why I blundered in here looking for something to eat—but finally I began to put a few pieces together." She advanced to stand by his console. "Mind if I use your displays?"

Bat had not invited Milly Wu to talk about her work, nor did he now give approval for her to use the equipment in his cubicle. That did not stop her. She continued to speak, rapidly and intensely, and threw images on the screen at such a dizzying speed that for the first minute Bat was constantly about to interrupt and eject her. Then he found himself concentrating, just to keep up with the stream of information. After that, intellectual interest took over.

By the time that she delineated the signal sections that provided formulas for simple chemical compounds, Bat was persuaded. He nodded and said, "Yes, that result is new. And it is elegant."

Bat employed his own vocabulary for describing the work of others. *Interesting* meant *dull*, *fascinating* indicated that the result possessed some minor interest, while *remarkable* was equivalent to Wolfgang Pauli's, *This theory is so bad it's not even wrong*. The word *elegant*, which he had just used, was reserved for cases where Bat was impressed.

There was visible proof of that fact, had Milly known how to read it. Just before she came into the room, Bat had filled a large bowl with peel-less, seedless oranges. He had intended to eat his way through them as he worked. When Milly concluded, the bowl sat cradled on his belly, ignored and still full.

Bat now took an orange, popped it whole into his mouth, and placed the bowl on the desk in front of him. It was logical to continue the discussion, pointing out to Milly how her work dove-tailed with some of his own thoughts on deciphering other elements of the signal; but other matters were going to intrude. Alex Ligon was already late, and although his message had been terse and guarded, it implied final results from Bengt Suomi and the Ligon Industries' team of scientists.

Milly knew nothing of any of this. She read Bat's scowl differently. She said, "Thank you for the food and thank you for listening," and started toward the door.

"One moment." Bat held up a pudgy hand. "I would like to pursue your ideas further, but in the near-term I am otherwise engaged. If you would be free to return . . ."

"Tomorrow?" Milly's face showed mixed feelings of pleasure and disappointment. She *had* done something new—even elegant. Food and drink had restored her, so that she was in no mood for sleep. And she had a chance that might never be repeated, an opportunity to work one-on-one with a leading Master of the Puzzle Network.

But Bat was frowning and shaking his close-cropped round head. "I was not thinking of tomorrow. I had in mind, say, one hour from now. If you were to return then, my other meeting should be concluded."

Milly nodded. "One hour. If you become free before then I will be in Cubicle Twelve."

And she was gone.

Bat nodded approval. It was nice to deal with someone who knew how to make up her mind. Milly Wu's results were indeed elegant. However, they added to a strange suspicion that had been stirring for days in the base of his brain.

Bat settled back in his seat and closed his eyes. He sensed that the world-lines were converging, and each one might require hard thought. It was one of those rare occasions when he envied Mord's capability for parallel processing.

The waiting message was, as Milly had expected, from Jack Beston. She made sure that the cubicle door was closed, invoked her own code, and was met by Jack's green-eyed glare. His excited tone matched his expression. "Milly, I'm delayed at L-4. I have no idea how long I must stay here. Call on a tight security circuit and insist on talking to me. I'll explain."

Problems at Argus Station? But Jack sounded more pleased

than alarmed. Milly asked for a secure line and waited impatiently as it was established. When the connection was completed, to her annoyance the face that appeared on the display was not Jack. It was Zetter, looking, as usual, ready to cook and eat her own grandmother. Except that now her thin face wore an expression of ill-disguised triumph.

"Yes?"

"I'm returning a call. I need to speak with the Ogre."

"He is unavailable."

"Station security can reach him at any time. You know that better than anyone. That's you. I don't think Jack Beston would like to hear that I tried to reach him, and you blocked my call."

It was a power struggle, pure and simple, the kind of thing that Milly loathed. Zetter glared hatred out of the display, then vanished.

Milly watched the clock. In less than thirty seconds Jack's face appeared.

He greeted her with, "Anyone with you?"

"I'm alone, in a secure environment."

"Good. Let's hope that the Bastard can't tap into a secure line. I believe that this time he's made a big mistake."

"How?"

"He made a deal with the Puzzle Network when he didn't need to. Milly, I have good news." Jack glanced from side to side, as though even in his own station he worried about being overheard. "We're starting to crack the signal. Not all the signal, of course, and only partial results where we have them at all. But Pat Tankard and Simon Bitters are making progress. The whole job will still take years, but we're beating the Bastard. We're moving ahead of him."

"Are you sure? Do you have an information pipeline into Odin Station?"

404 ■ CHARLES SHEFFIELD

"Not a reliable one. Zetter still has hopes, though." Jack was frowning. "What's your problem, Milly? I thought the news would make you ecstatic. We've always agreed that detection is good and verification is better, but until you have interpretation you're not even halfway up the mountain."

"I haven't changed my mind. But Jack"—when had she started to call him Jack, rather than *sir* or *Mr. Beston*, or even the Ogre?—"it's not happening only on Argus Station. The Puzzle Network group here is making progress, too. My guess is that your brother's team is moving along just as quickly. All of us overestimated the difficulty of making some initial sense out of part of the signal."

Jack's scowl turned him back into his usual Ogre self. "Don't kid yourself, Milly. The Bastard's team are idiots, nothing but trained monkeys. If they have any results, it's because they are taking them from the Puzzle Network. What has your group found so far?"

That was a tricky question. Milly was working for Jack Beston and the Argus Station, but she felt honor-bound to abide by the rules posted at the Puzzle Network: *Nothing that we receive from Odin Station should be sent anywhere else. It may be shared internally, but must be treated as privileged information.*

She could not be sure what information, other than the raw signal, the Puzzle Network had received from Philip Beston. Perhaps the fundamentals of signal partitions and the mathematical basics had originated at Odin Station. Milly didn't share Jack's wishful thinking that his brother had assembled a team of incompetents.

The one safe area was her own results. Bat had assured her that they were new, which meant they could not have originated in the Bastard's analysis center.

She provided a quick review of what she had found. Jack's frequent interruptions for clarification gave her a new appreciation for *Megachirops*. Her explanations to him had been a hurried and muddled first attempt, yet he had grasped methods and results without asking a single question. As she spoke she heard a loud bang on the door, which she ignored.

When she finished, Jack shook his head. "Interesting, but nothing at all like what we have. Not in the same part of the signal, not in the same area of knowledge. Remember we once talked of using the biological approach, coding the nucleotide bases of DNA?"

"We did. I was skeptical, because it would require that alien evolution follow the same biochemical pattern as ours. But I've seen the same suggestion of biological coding made here by a Puzzle Network Master."

Milly felt a twinge of conscience as she said that—the final comment strayed beyond her own work—but she was reassured when Jack replied, "We've gone farther than a suggestion. Pat Tankard and Simon Bitters took some old work of Arnold Rudolph on quaternary codes. They applied it to a forty-million-bit chunk of signal between two sections that we feel sure are image format. The idea was to see if binary digit pairs might match nucleotide bases. Of course, there's no way of knowing in advance which of the four nucleotide bases corresponds to any particular pair of binary numbers. So Tankard and Bitters took every possible combination of two zeroes and ones. For each case they scanned the whole signal section, looking to see if any recognizable sequence came up again and again. And it did. For one base-to-binary-pair assignment, a ten-letter sequence, GGGCAGGACG, cropped up again and again. It's used in basic gene-swapping, and it's present with slight variations in everything from bacteria to humans. This region of the SETI signal is riddled with it. Do you see what this means, Milly?"

She did, very clearly. "The aliens who sent the message are

close to us in chemistry and structure. If we have the GACT code, we can look for and read out whole-organism genetic profiles."

"You bet. And then we may be able to make them! We have the information to *build* alien life forms, not just learn about them. Now you see why I'm not on my way to Ganymede. We're on a round-the-clock schedule here, and I've got to stay and keep everybody hustling."

"Do you want me to come back?" Milly was excited, but a little hesitant. She did not share Jack's total confidence in what the Argus Station crew had done. Every puzzle had an infinite number of wrong answers in addition to the single correct one.

"No. You're making headway and there are plenty of problems to go round. I told you, all our work has been in one small part of the data, a small fraction of one percent of the whole signal that we've started to call the biology site. There must be others—math sites, physics sites, chemistry sites like the one you found, maybe even language sites.

"You stay there, Milly, we go all out—and we leave the Bastard standing!"

Jack vanished from the display, as much of a driven whirlwind as ever. Milly cut the connection before Zetter could reappear for another turf war. She sat down in the cubicle's sole chair and stared at nothing.

No matter how you looked at it, the Argus Station team had accomplished something of great potential significance. Now the question arose, what was Milly going to do with the information? In principle, the only restriction on her was that she should not give Odin Station data to anyone, especially to Argus Station. What about the other way round? If she followed her natural instincts for open transfer of information, she would tell the Puzzle Network about the Argus Station results. That, in turn, would surely lead to Philip Beston finding out what his brother had accomplished.

But was that a bad thing? The potential gains for everyone were so great, everything from faster-than-light travel to vacuum energy to extended lifespan, it seemed criminal to lock away important results in secret boxes.

Milly made a decision. Her loyalty had to be to the human species, not to any single member or group. She headed along the corridor to Bat's cubicle. He had said one hour, but in her current mental state time meant nothing. It might have been a full hour, or it could have been only ten minutes.

In any case, if he didn't want her he could ask her to leave. She had lived through that once tonight already.

A worse situation would be if the expected visitor happened to still be there. Milly was willing to tell Bat about the Argus Station developments, but she could not make such an announcement to a stranger.

She came to Bat's cubicle, stepped close, and placed her ear against the crack of the door.

Not a sound. Good.

This time at least she would knock.

Milly rapped on the hard plastic, swung the door open, and marched in.

Alex was late. He had been delayed, then delayed, then delayed again. The worst thing was, he couldn't complain. He knew what was going on and he could even sympathize with it. He had been the cause of similar delays himself, many times. There was always the urge to perform one last test, check one more item of data, add another explanatory comment . . .

He hoped he didn't look like Bengt Suomi when he was doing it. The chief scientist of Ligon Industries was dark-haired and dark-complexioned, an extremely tall man with a permanent stoop. He was supremely competent and supremely thorough, but his saturnine countenance suggested that he had never laughed in his whole life. Every result that he had approved for release to Bat appeared to cause him intestinal agony. Twice he had seemed ready to hand over the file, twice he had pulled it back and gone off to verify some small point with one of his staff.

The third time that he had appeared, Alex grabbed the file from Suomi's hands, whipped up the associated data cube, and ran. He ignored the anxious cry ". . . but the units of the magnetic field . . ." that followed him out of the room.

Now he felt like the White Rabbit, scurrying along the endless warren of corridors and tunnels leading to the Puzzle Network's Command Center. He was late, he was late, and it totally fit his ideas of Puzzle Network members that they had chosen a site on Ganymede that could be found only by negotiating a labyrinth. It had been easier to reach the Bat Cave on Pandora. One thing was certain, there must be an alternate route to this destination. The tunnels were in places so narrow that Bat would have to be greased and fired from a cannon to pass through them.

He was at least half an hour late. He had tried to call ahead on his wrist unit, and typical of Bat there had been no answer. Alex arrived at what should be the final door, hurried through, and found himself in a narrow deserted corridor. The floor was covered by a thick sound-deadening carpet. This was the place, it had to be because it fit Bat's description—but where was Bat? Alex saw a dozen blue doors, every one closed.

That was all right. No one in his right mind would be here

at this hour. That left Bat. Alex went along, banging on each door as he came to it until he heard a deep-voiced, "Yo? Enter."

Alex's first impression was of an unlit empty room. Bat, swaddled in black clothing and with a black hood around his head, formed a mound of darkness on a padded seat like the one he had occupied in the Bat Cave.

Alex decided to beat Bat to it. "I'm very late. I'm sorry, but there were last minute changes."

"The time was not wasted." Bat held out a hand. "The results, if you please. I assume that you have them?"

"I do, but I'm afraid that you will be disappointed. Bengt Suomi's team performed two hundred and eighty-seven distinct tests on the nodules taken from Sebastian Birch's body." Alex gave Bat the data cube and the sheaf of papers. "I gather you've been over many of the early results already with Bengt Suomi. He found only one thing in these latest batch of tests that qualifies in his mind as inexplicable. He doubts that it is significant."

The grunt could have been anything, disappointment or disagreement. Bat said only, "A judgment as to significance depends on what a person hopes or expects to find. I beg your indulgence while I examine these results in detail."

Alex glanced at his watch. Bat might function well without sleep, but Alex didn't. The discussions of predictive models went on and on, every day, and Mischa Glaub was a poor sleeper. He tended to call meetings at an early hour when he was in his worst mood and other people were groggy from low blood sugar and lack of caffeine. He admitted—even boasted—that this gave him a psychological advantage. Glaub had another session scheduled for tomorrow morning, which Alex and Kate were obliged to attend.

Alex said, "Let me tell you about the one thing they found that Bengt Suomi considers new and peculiar. It will save time."

Bat raised a magisterial arm. "Just as likely, it will lead me to ignore other relevant information. Time spent in study is not wasted." He reached forward and inserted the data cube. *They also serve who only stand and wait.* I say again, please indulge me."

Alex glanced around him. Bat's oversized seat took up half the cubicle. The rest was displays, desk, control console, food stand, and a portable stove. The room offered no space for a second chair, in the unlikely event that Bat would have tolerated one.

Wait, maybe, but stand, no.

Alex settled on the floor, back against a wall and legs stretched out in front of him. From where he was sitting Bat rose up as solid and steady as a black mountain. Occasionally a sheet of paper was discarded from the sheaf and fluttered to the floor. Occasionally Alex saw the whites of Bat's eyes, prominent in the coal-black face as they glanced from page to display and back.

Ten minutes passed, and the floor was littered with discarded sheets. Alex moved to a more comfortable position. As he did so he heard a grunt—concern, surprise? He looked up. Bat's eyes had closed.

It was far into the night, but surely the man couldn't have fallen asleep? Alex drew his legs in close to his body. He was starting to stand up when he heard a sound outside. The cubicle door opened. Its edge gave him a sharp blow on the right knee and the young woman who entered almost fell over him.

Alex scrambled to his feet and they stood staring at each other.

"Who—" the woman said.

"I have it!" The words that interrupted her came from Bat. He had emerged from his apparent stupor and was suddenly energized. "Bengt Suomi is right. It is curious indeed, and it provides the question if not the answer."

Alex looked at the woman and said, "I'm Alex Ligon." She said, "Milly Wu."

Bat waved his arms at both of them. "No time for that now. This has enormous potential importance."

The woman said, "What about work on the SETI signal?" and Alex knew why her name sounded familiar.

"For the moment that is superseded." Bat turned to Alex. "Even now, we must be thorough. I am ready to hear a summary of what the Ligon team considered important in their tests."

Alex hesitated and glanced at Milly Wu. She shook her head and said, "I don't understand one word of this. You might as well go ahead."

Alex considered his answer. Bat was a devil for precision. "They didn't say they considered that anything was *important*. They reported that one test gave unusual results."

"Exactly. An excellent answer. Continue."

"Ninety-four tests involved the chemical properties of the spherical nodules."

"A waste of time and effort. Any salient results would surely involve the nodules' structure, which would be destroyed by chemical tests."

"Bengt Suomi took very seriously your request that they supplement your list with suggestions of their own. You asked that the team perform as complete a range of tests as possible."

Bat bowed his head. "I did indeed, and I stand corrected. Bengt Suomi was right to proceed as he did. Continue."

"Suomi happened to agree with your conclusion—*after* he

saw the results. The chemical tests gave nothing. Then there were the structural microscopic tests, concentrated on geometry and mechanical properties rather than physical or chemical ones. They confirmed that although the nodules appear superficially as perfect spheres, they have a distinctive microstructure. Each one contains tunnels running radially in toward the center. The tunnels are minute, though wide enough to permit the passage of gas molecules. The team could not imagine any physical effect that might depend on such a structure. Bengt Suomi describes that result as interesting, but not informative."

"An admirably cautious statement."

"The remaining tests involve physics. The nodules are stable over a wide range of temperatures, pressures, and fields. Radiation and particle bombardment affect them little, except for lattice dislocation effects at high energy levels. Electric and magnetic influences appear unimportant, even with intense fields. There was just one test result that no one could explain. The nodules act as a catalyst in inducing phase transitions of certain gases."

Bat was nodding. "That is indeed the anomalous test result. Phase transitions, moreover, for gases which do not exist in free form within the human body."

"Apparently. Suomi found that the catalytic effect was the strongest—the phase transition is almost instantaneous—for free hydrogen. The effect weakens rapidly for heavier gases." Alex was tempted to add, all this effort, and you're saying you agree exactly with Bengt Suomi's conclusions?

But Bat was not looking at Alex or at Milly Wu. He was staring at the display, which showed a magnified view of one spherical nodule. The dark pupils of his eyes had dilated against their luminous whites. He said, very slowly, "So we have the results I requested, and they prompt but do not answer the key question: Why would anyone place such anomalous structures *inside the body of Sebastian Birch*—a place where those structures are unable to exercise the only effect of which they seem capable?"

The question had not been addressed to Milly Wu, but she said, "Maybe as a protection? Maybe the nodules absorb free gases that shouldn't be there."

"I think not. According to these results, the gases are not absorbed by the nodules. They merely induce an instantaneous phase change, from a gaseous to a far denser liquid form. Therefore . . ." Bat did not complete his sentence. He puffed out his fat cheeks, frowned, and turned to Alex. "Do you know the exact location of the research quarantine facility where Sebastian Birch is being held?"

"I can find out." A call to Karolus would provide that information, but Alex was pretty sure his uncle would not want his name mentioned.

"Do so. And then I have another request. It is possible that I am overreacting, but I would like you to go to that facility and locate Sebastian Birch."

"I don't think they'll let me in."

"You underestimate the power of the Ligon name. It commands authority. Once you find Birch, remain with him. Do not permit him to leave your presence, even for a moment." Bat rose, an imposing presence that filled the room. "I will explain this later, but go at once, and quickly. Do not leave the research complex. I will join you there as soon as possible. Before you leave, tell me: will the link on these pages allow me to contact Bengt Suomi at any time and place?"

"It ought to reach him wherever he is. But it's the middle of the night."

"I am not unaware of that fact."

Milly said to Bat, "It sounds like your meeting with me is off."

"No. It is, I hope, merely postponed. Go with Alex Ligon, and help him if help is needed. You and I can meet tomorrow—if there is a tomorrow."

He turned to the communications unit, ignoring the other two as though they had already left.

As they headed away along darkened corridors, Milly said, "What's this all about?"

"I don't know." Which was the exact truth, but Alex felt compelled to add, "Although I have no idea what's going on, I do know one thing. Magrit Knudsen is way up in the Ganymede power structure, and she was Rustum Battachariya's boss for over ten years. She says that although he often understates, or refuses to say anything at all, he never exaggerates. I think we ought to hurry."

31

Bat made it sound easy. You go along to where Sebastian Birch is being held, and exert your authority to make sure that Birch does nothing out of the ordinary.

Maybe it *was* easy, when you tipped the inertial mass indicator at over three hundred kilos; but Alex didn't command that much weight to let him push people around. As they ascended the riser shafts and skimmed along interior slides, he saw Milly's eyes on him and he read their question: Who is this Alex Ligon, and how is he going to do what even the Great Bat says is beyond his powers?

That was Alex's question, too. When they had been traveling for twenty minutes he flipped on his wrist unit at emergency interrupt. He tried to call Bat, and for a change the line was open; but it was locked into high-priority mode with another caller. Alex's ID check indicated that Bat was talking to Bengt Suomi.

It was the time for desperate measures. Alex placed another call. After a pause, in which Milly said "Who?" and Alex answered "Reinforcements," the tiny screen came alive.

"Alex? What the bloody hell are you playing at?" The

growl was muted and tinny, but the glowering face had lost none of its malevolence.

"I don't know. All I know is, I'm out of my depth."

"If you're calling me at this hour because you're in trouble with some goddamned woman . . ." The wrist unit must have captured Milly in its viewfinder, because Uncle Karolus went on, "My God, it's not even the same one. You're getting to be as bad as Hector."

"I need help."

"You need treatment. D'you know what time it is? You're lucky I'm not a few years younger, or I'd be out trolling for my own trouble in the lower levels. What the devil do you want?"

It was a waste of time explaining the whole thing to Uncle Karolus, and anyway Alex didn't know the whole thing. He sketched in the minimum, then said, "We're on the way to the research quarantine facility that's holding Sebastian Birch. I don't believe we can march up to the entrance and expect them to do whatever we ask. Can you get us in?"

Karolus yawned, squinted, and said, "Who is she?"

"This is Milly Wu. She's helping me."

"Helping you do what?"

Bat only knows. "She's on our side."

"Sweet Alonzo. You think that's an adequate explanation? Either I'm going soft in the head, or you are. I can't be bothered with position fixes. Where are you now?"

"Level fifty-nine, Sector one-thirty-four. At least forty minutes away from the lab, maybe forty-five."

"I must be crazier than you." From the grunting sounds, Karolus was pulling on pants or shoes. "I'll get you into the place, and that's all. I'm closer, so I'll probably beat you to it. But if you arrive first, don't try to go in. Stay on Level five at the end of the final bend in the Sector corridor. Don't talk to anybody—including me. I have a call or two of my own to make."

Karolus was gone. Milly raised her eyebrows at Alex.

He shrugged. "That was Uncle Karolus. I'm sorry he's such a wild animal, but he does know how to get things done."

"No need to apologize. He seems pretty reasonable for a man who's just been woken up in the middle of the night. My own boss is an ogre. Compared with him, your uncle's a teddy-bear. Hey. Wouldn't *this* be quicker?"

This was a high-speed lift that they were passing. It was intended for cargo only. Before Alex could point out the dangers, Milly had stepped onto it and was whisked upwards out of sight.

He followed, and felt the crushing load of a two-gee acceleration. As his legs buckled and his guts bottomed-out on his pelvis, Alex thought again of Bat's words: *It would seem that all the major actions in your life are entirely dictated by women.* There was no way he could make a call while boosting upward, but when the lift tube spat him out on hands and knees on Level 12—as high as it would go—he tried his wrist unit again.

Still busy. He swore, stood up, and set off along the Sector connector.

"Your uncle did tell you not to call him." Milly led him by a couple of steps, not a hair out of place.

"I was trying to reach Bat, not Karolus. We need to know what's going on."

"Bat doesn't think so. It's the Puzzle Network mindset. You're expected to operate with incomplete information."

"We certainly have that." Alex, in the middle of placing another call, slapped at the unit to cut the sequence off halfway. What was he thinking of? He had been all set to talk to Kate. And tell her what?

Milly's use of the high-gee cargo lift had gained them at least ten minutes. They were on Level 5 and into the final approach to Sector 82 when Alex saw someone hurrying from the other direction.

Karolus greeted them with, "There'd better be a good reason for all this, young Alex. And don't you utter one word unless I ask you to." Then he smiled at Milly and said in a quite different tone, "I hope I wasn't rude when I first saw you. I was half-asleep. Maybe we can meet later on under better circumstances, and start over."

Milly's nod to Alex—*See? I told you he sounded nice*—was at least as irritating as being called *young Alex*.

They were not heading to Level 4, where the only interior entrance to the research quarantine facility was supposed to be located—all other entrances led in from the raw surface of Ganymede. Instead, Karolus was leading them along a narrowing tunnel. A strong breeze blew in their faces.

"Not much farther." Karolus paused beside a door set flush into the tunnel's side and banged on it hard. "Now, if they're worth half the money I agreed to pay—here we go."

The door cracked open, noisily, and a worried, gnome-like face poked through from the other side.

"Quick. In." The man gestured to them, and jerked his head to glance along the corridor in each direction. "If anyone finds out that I let you in—"

"I know. They'll cut your balls off and make you swallow 'em." Karolus pushed past him. "So you'd better keep your mouth shut."

"You said cash."

"Damn right I did. What do you expect, that I'd give you a credit chit made out from Ligon Industries? I'll pay you cash—tomorrow."

"You told—"

"Never mind who I told or what I said. I was in a hurry. D'you think I carry that much on me in the middle of the night? You'll be paid all right. Where is Sebastian Birch?"

"Up the staircase, one level. Along the corridor, right turn, and fourth door on the left. Locked."

"Key?"

"Spinor lock. Here's the codes." The gnome handed over a slip of paper. "When you're in, swallow it."

"Right." Karolus handed the paper to Alex. "Here you are. A chance to do something useful. We'll save the explanations for later, but I hope you know what you're going to do after you eat that. Because I sure as hell don't."

That made two of them—three, since Milly Wu was undoubtedly as ill-informed as Alex. The interior of the research facility, not surprising given the hour, was deserted, but the directions were easy to follow. They headed up a staircase, Alex one step behind and feeling like a criminal. Karolus walked in front and chatted easily to Milly, exactly as though they all had every right to be where they were.

"Along the corridor, fourth door on the right, and here we go." Karolus halted. "Alex, do you want to do the honors?"

The lock was reasonably simple, in keeping with a minimum-security installation. Alex suspected that he could have opened it in fifteen minutes, even without the spinor codes. Five four-space rotations and a parallel displacement, and the spinor keys hissed finality.

"Right. That's my job over and done with." Karolus pulled the door, checking that it would open a fraction. "He's all yours. If anyone ever asks, I was never here—and I'll have half a dozen witnesses to prove it."

"I thought you wanted to know why we need to see Birch."

"I do—some other time. You owe me a favor, Alex, as well as an explanation. You get one, you give one."

Karolus left. Alex pulled the door open wide. He peered in. The interior was a well-furnished apartment, not at all like the detention cell that he had expected. The living room was comfortable, dimly lit, and empty; as it should be, at this hour.

Two more doors stood at the far end. Alex advanced and opened the left-hand one, with Milly close behind. It revealed a tiny kitchen, unlit. Alex took a deep breath and turned to the final door.

It opened silently, revealing a small bedroom with a shower and bathroom attached. All the lights were off, but enough came in through the open door. Alex surveyed the room, then turned for a second inspection of the living room and kitchen.

They had hurried through the night to find and guard Sebastian Birch. Since this was a quarantine as well as a research facility, the one certainty should have been Birch's presence.

So much for certainties.

Sebastian Birch, whoever he might be, whatever he might be, and wherever he might be, was nowhere in this apartment.

32

Jan had eaten a little too much cultured lobster at the *Belly of the Whale*; or maybe it was the rich chocolate dessert that did not agree with her. At any rate, at the time of night when she normally would be in the deepest phase of her sleep cycle, she found herself poised on the edge of consciousness. Faint imagined voices spoke inside her head, their mutterings just too faint to be understood.

She lay flat on her back, her thigh in companionable contact with Paul's. He was sleeping soundly, as always. He didn't usually stay over at the research facility—Valnia Bloom somewhat frowned on the idea—but preparations for the next voyage of the *Achilles* were going smoothly. He had pleaded for one more chance to capture her in his painting. She was, he said, an unusually difficult subject. Something in her smile—a certain wistfulness, a certain longing—eluded him. He wanted to try first thing in the morning, when his hand was at its steadiest.

Jan opened her eyes and stared up into darkness. Suddenly she was fully awake. The voices were not in her head, they were real. They came from the monitor system in Sebastian's apartment. Was he talking to himself, in his sleep?

Not unless his voice could change instantly from male to female and back.

She stared over at the video monitor and saw nothing. Sebastian's living room was empty, and his kitchen and bedroom were dark.

"Paul." She nudged him, and he muttered a sleepy protest. "Paul, there's someone in with Sebastian."

She poked him in the ribs again, harder, and swung out of bed.

"What was that for?" He was finally awake, and grumpy.

"Someone is in Sebastian's apartment. In his bedroom, I think."

"What of it? Isn't he allowed visitors?"

"At this hour?" Jan was into her clothes and feeling around for her shoes. "Look at the time."

"I just did. Everyone in their right mind is asleep—as I was." But he was on the edge of the bed, feeling for clothing. "I feel sure that he's all right."

"Somebody is with him. I heard a woman's voice."

"Then it's Dr. Bloom."

"It isn't. She told me she would be away from the facility tonight."

"So she changed her mind." But Paul also was looking for shoes. "Oh, all right. Go ahead, I know you'll worry unless you see for yourself. I'll follow you down."

Jan gave him a quick kiss on the top of his tousled head and was on her way while he was still fumbling at the bedside.

Thirty seconds took her to the door of Sebastian's apartment. It was ajar, when it ought to have been locked. Suddenly wary—this was a quarantine as well as a research facility, so no one should be able to enter—she eased the door open and quietly stepped inside.

The living room was deserted, but she heard voices coming from the bedroom. A man and a woman—and neither one was Sebastian.

She moved to stand at the bedroom door and listen.

The man's voice said, "I don't know. I've been trying to reach Bat for the past quarter of an hour on my wrist unit. He's inaccessible."

"Not answering?"

"Busy line. He's talking to Bengt Suomi. He's ignoring my request for a priority override."

They had been speaking in whispers, but suddenly the woman said, in a louder voice, "Look, this is ridiculous. We're creeping around like burglars. How important do you think this is?"

"I can only go by what other people have told me. Bat never gets flustered, and he's never in a hurry. If he says something's urgent, it has to be *really* urgent."

"Then we should go outside and shout and scream until somebody comes along who can help us find Sebastian Birch. But let me try something before we do that. I left my talk unit back in the work cubicle. May I borrow yours?"

"It won't do any good. If Bat doesn't answer a call from me, I don't see why he'd take one from you."

"You're right, of course. But I may be able to cheat. The Puzzle Network employs a special access code. It's for use by Masters' level only, and I'm not supposed to know it. But I do. At least we'll find out how important this is. 'Scuse me."

Jan had heard enough to be sure that the intruders, whoever they were, had no right to be in Sebastian's apartment. And they sounded more puzzled than dangerous.

She opened the bedroom door and said, "Who are you, and what are you doing in a private apartment?"

The woman was full-figured and apparently in her early

twenties, and she went on talking into a wrist unit. But the man, a few years older, swung sharply around and said, "We're trying to find Sebastian Birch."

Jan heard Paul enter the apartment behind her, and it made her feel a good deal more comfortable. She said firmly, "He should be here—where you have absolutely no right to be. What business of yours is it where Sebastian Birch is?"

"I'm Alex Ligon. This is Milly Wu."

"And where is Sebastian?"

"We have no idea—this place was empty when we arrived. But we wanted—"

He was interrupted. The woman, Milly Wu, was holding up her hand. Jan heard a man's voice, thinned to a faint basso rumble by the wrist unit's small speaker. The woman interpreted. "Bat's been speaking to Bengt Suomi. Suomi agrees that it's absolutely imperative to find Sebastian Birch, and keep him under lock and key."

"He *was* under lock and key," Jan said. "He just completed a delicate medical procedure, and it could have side effects. Are you sure he wasn't here when you arrived?"

"Quite positive. How did you know that *we* were in this apartment?"

Jan jerked a thumb toward the ceiling. "Monitors. No picture when the room is dark, but audio is always active. I heard voices. How did you get into the facility?"

The man evaded the question. He said, "We were sent here to find Sebastian Birch, because someone thought that he might be dangerous, to himself and maybe to others."

He had hit one of Jan's hot buttons. She exploded. "Dangerous? Sebastian would never harm anyone else—but he might easily hurt himself. My name is Janeed Jannex, this is Paul Marr, and we *belong* here. We are responsible for Sebastian's safety. I'll get an explanation from you two later. But first—"

Jan looked straight up at the ceiling and did what she should have done before leaving her own bedroom—except that she had been sure that Sebastian was here. She said firmly, "Surveillance on, and thirty-second reporting. I need tracer output. Where is Sebastian Birch?"

In the few moments of silence that followed she added, more to Paul than to the newcomers, "Ever since the sluicing operation began he's had a trace generator on him, with round-the-clock automated surveillance. We should be able to track him anywhere he goes."

"Sebastian Birch is in Section eighty-two," a voice said from midair. *"He is at Level Zero."*

"That can't be right." Jan lost any residue of calm. "Level zero is the surface. It's vacuum. If he's there, he's dead."

"Or he's in a suit. But he wouldn't know where the suits are." Paul turned on Alex, who felt as though he was in a vacuum himself. "Did you two come in that way, from the surface?"

"No."

Jan had a terrible feeling in the pit of her stomach. She said, "Sebastian *does* know where the suits are. He knows because I told him, after I'd been up to the surface and visited you on the *Achilles*. Some things he remembers perfectly. I bet he's up there now, staring at Jovian cloud patterns."

Paul nodded. "You're probably right, but we must go up and bring him back. The surface can be dangerous to a novice. We'll find him easily if the generator is a body implant. The tracer will tell us exactly where he is."

He was trying to reassure Jan, but it produced an unexpected reaction. The voice from the wrist unit, now amplified enough in volume to be understood, asked, "Is there any possibility that Sebastian Birch might obtain access to a working ship?"

"Who the blazes is *that?*" Paul asked.

The male intruder said, as though it was supposed to mean something, "That is Rustum Battachariya." The amplified voice continued, "If there is a way for Sebastian Birch to gain access to a ship, *he must be stopped*. Under no circumstances can he be allowed to leave Ganymede."

"There are *hundreds* of ships up there on the surface," Paul said. "A whole fleet of them. Hell, surface access here is right next to a major spaceport."

"And Sebastian is an expert pilot—a natural, according to the man who gave us lessons." Jan spoke to the ceiling again. "Surveillance. Priority report. What are Sebastian Birch's present actions and location?"

"Sebastian Birch is moving across the surface at seven kilometers an hour. He is now in Sector eighty-four."

"The spaceport sector." As Paul said those words. Jan shivered. She asked, "Surveillance, how close is he to a ship?"

"Forty-seven ships in operating condition lie within four hundred meters of his present location."

"Do they have crews aboard?"

"That information is not available."

Paul said, "Chances are, none of them will have a crew aboard," as the voice came again from the wrist unit. "Sebastian Birch must be stopped, by whatever method. He must not be permitted access to a ship able to leave the surface of Ganymede."

Jan challenged. "Why not? What makes you think you can give orders?"

"At the moment it would be counterproductive to tell you my reasons for concern. Let me say only that this issue is of paramount importance, and could lead to . . . many deaths. If you question my credibility, ask Magrit Knudsen of the Coordinators' Office about Rustum Battachariya—but, I beg you, do it later."

Jan made a hard decision. *She* knew that Sebastian was completely harmless, but—"Paul, we have to stop him."

He, thank God, did not question her. He said at once, "Surveillance, couple to spaceport operations. Operations, this is Paul Marr, first officer of the *OSL Achilles*. We have warning of a potential escapee from quarantine. Any individual found on the surface in Sector eighty-three should be taken into custody and held pending my arrival. Use whatever means are necessary to secure him."

Jan thought, *And break my heart*. She swallowed and said to Paul, "I have to go after him. Myself. I *have* to."

"I know. I'm coming with you."

The man, Alex Ligon, said, "What about us?"

Paul stared at him for a moment. "Look, I don't know what you're doing here, or who you are. But I have pilot rating for everything from a one-person hopper to the biggest liners. If you can beat that for space credentials, come along. Otherwise, don't bother and don't get in the way."

The man scowled and opened his mouth, but it was the woman, Milly Wu, who got in first. "You tell us to look, now you look. We've had no sleep for close to a full day. I can't speak for Alex Ligon, but I've had only half a meal since breakfast yesterday. We came running over here because we were told that somebody might be in trouble. We don't know your friend Sebastian Birch, and we don't know why he has to stay on Ganymede. But as for me, I'd be just as happy never to meet him. Here." She took the wrist unit and tossed it to Jan. "Take it or leave it. If you want to know anything else, don't ask me. Ask Bat."

Jan cut off a developing argument. "Paul, I know your credentials very well and they don't need to. We have no time for a fight. You two, go back to Battachariya, whoever and wherever he is. Anything needs sorting out about your coming here, we do it later."

She left before there could be more discussion. Ten seconds later, Paul had caught up with her. "You were right," he said. "And I was wrong. I've found out where my ego lies. They were just caught in the middle. Mind if I lead the way?"

Jan didn't. Once they were out on the surface, Paul's lead would be essential. She had been outside before, but compared to him she was a tyro. She fumbled her way into a suit at maximum speed and ran the last twenty meters up the surface ramp.

Looking off to her right as they emerged onto Level Zero she again saw a spiky city of gantries and scaffolds, glittering in reflected sunlight. Their layout had changed since last time. Ships by the dozen—by the hundred—lay scattered at the feet of the construction rigs, everything from bulbous freighters to spindly-legged singletons. High above everything hung the familiar ball of Jupiter, swollen and striated. To Sebastian it might be an object of infinite fascination, but she could imagine how others saw it: only a madman would leave Ganymede and fly closer to Jupiter, just to stare at atmospheric cloud patterns.

Jan heard a crackle on the wrist communications unit, then Milly Wu's voice. "Rustum Battachariya is still on the line. He wants to keep in touch with you. I'll try to patch him in to local video and audio."

The voice that sounded in Jan's suit, however, was not that of Rustum Battachariya. A musical contralto said, "Janeed Jannex? This is spaceport operations. We are taking over from automated surveillance. We have tracked your man, and he is entering a Mayfly-class single-seater."

Paul broke in. "This is Paul Marr, first officer of the *Achilles*. Can you stop him taking off?"

"Oh, hi, Paul. Tess Walkabie here. Prevent him? How?"

Jan said, "Override the ship's controls."

"Come on, you ought to know better than that. Manual controls can always override remotes."

Paul said, "What I had in mind was sending someone out to the ship."

"Who? We have only three people on duty. Cargo arrivals and departures are automated, and no passenger ships are scheduled. We weren't expecting emergencies, or much of anything. Don't you people ever sleep? It's the middle of the graveyard shift."

The woman was right. To Jan, it seemed no particular time of day or night. She would do better to leave things to Paul, who knew what he was doing.

The woman went on, "If this Sebastian takes it into his head to fly, he'll be gone long before we could get there. In fact, you are closer to him than we are."

"Close enough to reach him in time to stop him taking off?"

"No. But I can direct you to another ship, Paul—a Flyboy scooter, two-person. Lots of volatiles already onboard."

"That would be perfect. A Flyboy is faster than anything in the Mayfly class. No matter where he goes, we'll be able to follow and catch him. Is it ready to lift?"

"Ready as you are. Do you want it?"

"Yes!"

"It's yours. Bear twenty degrees left of your present heading. Keep moving and I'll steer you to it."

Jan needed steering. Lack of sleep, her over-rich meal, and the strange surroundings combined to remove her from reality. Her previous experience on the surface of Ganymede had been an unhurried stroll. Now she struggled to keep up with Paul, following him across a gritty plain of water-ice crystals a hundred and fifty degrees below their freezing point. It was not a run. It was not a walk. It was a rapid, unsteady shuffle past looming insectile derricks and through the long black shadows cast by squatty cargo hulls.

A flash of blue on her right made Jan turn that way. "There goes the Mayfly," said the contralto voice. "He's away. Don't worry, you have less than a hundred meters to go."

Neither Paul nor the chief of operations, Tess Walkabie, had said anything about the size of the scooter they would fly. Jan, climbing after Paul up the short ladder, found herself apologizing as she squeezed in beside him. Paul didn't even acknowledge that he had heard her. He had taken the controls, and was flicking through a lightning status check.

Jan said, "I thought this was supposed to be ready to fly?"

"I'm sure it is. You just don't skip your own checkout, ever. We're in good shape. Operations? We're ready to go, but I don't have visual contact."

"He's out of your line-of-sight and range. Don't worry about that. I'll feed you the Mayfly's ID and you or your autopilot can do the rest. Wherever he goes, your scooter can follow. You are faster, and you will catch up. Better set collision avoidance."

"Doing it." Paul flipped a switch. "Prepared for take-off."

For Jan that was insufficient warning. Even after her earlier experience, she was unprepared when the scooter reared to a vertical position and accelerated upward—hard. She could not fall, because the seats were gimballed to follow the direction of acceleration, but the change in attitude brought her to an uncomfortable fore-and-aft posture, knees crunched tightly into the narrow space in front of her seat. Her view of the world outside the scooter became a flickering display, with beneath it a slit of transparent panel that looked ahead to an alien field of stars.

"He's heading inward." Paul was studying the information panel that ran across the upper edge of the viewing screen. "We're trailing him, and our path is toward Jupiter. You were right, Jan. He's back to his old fixation with cloud patterns."

There was a sudden and surprising interruption. The voice of Rustum Battachariya, so faint and garbled by interference as to be almost unidentifiable, broke in from the wrist unit that Milly Wu had given to Jan. "A fixation with clouds would be acceptable. Regrettably, that may not be the case."

The unit was not designed for such long-range operation. Bat was fading in and out as he went on, "If Sebastian Birch merely desired to observe . . . disturbance in Jovian atmosphere . . . would not have encouraged such immediate action. Unfortunately . . ."

Jan said, urgently into the tiny unit, "What is he doing? I have to know."

"I fear that he seeks . . . atmospheric entry."

"Why?"

"My apologies . . . I cannot discuss this. However, you must stop . . . seek to summon other forces . . ."

The rest of Bat's words were lost in a wash of static.

"He's going," Paul said. "The wrist unit's beyond the limit of its range."

"He says Sebastian is going for Jupiter atmospheric entry."

"Yes. Again."

"Paul, we have to stop him. He doesn't know what he's doing. If someone can help us . . ."

"Not feasible." Paul had turned on a signal detection system to scan the sky ahead of the Flyboy scooter, and a single red speck flashed on the screen. "That's Sebastian's ship. There's no other vehicle in space between us and Jupiter. Europa and Io are on the other side of the planet, they can't do us any good. Amalthea is in the right position, but it only has cargo vessels ready to fly. It's up to us."

"What can we do?"

"So long as he keeps accelerating, not much. We have no way to change his course, no way to disable his ship without killing all of us."

Paul adjusted a setting, and the broad arc of the Jupiter terminator appeared on the screen next to the flashing speck of red. "It's going to take a while to catch up, but we'll be alongside him long before he's close to the planet. Then I can blanket him with emergency frequency radio signals, and he'll have to listen—he can't switch that unit off. It will be up to you, Jan. You have to talk to him. Persuade him to turn his ship around and head back to Ganymede."

Persuade him? You don't know Sebastian. But it would be pointless to say that to Paul. Who *did* know Sebastian? Certainly not Jan, though she had spent every waking hour with him for many years.

She sank back into her seat, staring at the blinking red dot on the screen. It was slowly brightening, but the arc of Jupiter seemed to grow more rapidly. "How much time do we have?"

"Hours and hours, before we are close to Jupiter. But we're within emergency signal range. You can talk to him now."

Paul sounded calm and sane. Jan felt neither, but she had to pretend. "Sebastian? Can you hear me?"

She didn't expect a reply, but the answer came at once. "Yes, Jan. I hear you."

The words were rational, but the tone was of someone talking in a dream. She felt Paul's encouraging pat on her suited arm. "Sebastian, the ship that you are flying doesn't belong to us. We must return it."

"I know. I'm not stealing it, Jan. I'm just borrowing it."

"It's time to give it back. You have to turn around now."

"Not yet, Jan. Not until I've finished."

"What do you mean, finished? Where are you going?"

"I need to fly close to Jupiter. I need to go to the clouds."

"Sebastian, if you fly back to Ganymede you can have the use of telescopes that will show you all kinds of cloud details. A swingby may sound easy, but it isn't. You need to have an expert in charge of it."

"You don't understand, Jan. I have a job to do. I must do it."

"What job? Nobody gave you a job—certainly not one like this."

"They did, Jan. I know what I must do. I've always known it."

"That doesn't make sense, Sebastian. We've spent almost our whole lives together, and you've never talked to me about a job. What is it you have to do?"

"You wouldn't understand. Jan, I hope you won't mind, but I don't want to talk anymore. I'm not going to talk anymore."

"Sebastian . . ." Jan felt Paul's hand on her arm.

"You're not getting through to him," he said quietly. "Admit it, Jan. He's crazy. I said that you had to persuade him, but you can't persuade a crazy man."

"I have to try. Let me keep talking to him, maybe I can get through to him."

"It's all we can do. As we approach I'm going to bring us right alongside. It may help if he sees our ship and knows you're with him wherever he goes. Talk to him, Jan."

About what? But the words came spilling out. She began

with their earliest days together, in the displaced persons' camp at Husvik. She spoke of their schooling, the flower festival in Punta Arenas, summer evenings that lasted forever. Then there was their joint decision to take jobs on the Global Minerals' platform, the application to move to the Outer System, their plan to work on the Saturn orbital weather station.

Through all of it Sebastian answered not a word. When the two ships were racing side by side, Jan could see the dark dot of his helmet in the Mayfly's tiny cabin. So near and yet so far away. And as Jupiter loomed large in the sky ahead, she realized that all her talk of "their" plans and "their" actions was delusion. *She* had proposed. *She* had persuaded; Sebastian had merely gone along. So why did he refuse to go along now, when she needed to persuade him as never before?

She knew why. Her thinking had not been quite accurate. The interest in the cloud patterns of the outer planets had never been hers. It had always been Sebastian's, and his alone. That had brought them out to Ganymede. That drove them now toward Jupiter.

Their trajectory was not as Jan had expected. They were flying side by side, but rather than following a path that would graze by the planet, the two ships were arrowing right toward the center of Jupiter's banded disk. She realized that Sebastian had never said he wanted to make a flyby. He wanted to "go to the clouds." If they did not change course they would plunge deep into the atmosphere on a path of no return.

Through all her talking, Paul had sat quietly. She was still talking, with a sense of futility and with no response from Sebastian, when Paul said, "Ah! At last. That's what I've been waiting for."

He manipulated the controls so fast that she could not follow what he did; but suddenly they were in free-fall.

"What's going on?"

"He's out of volatiles. I told you, Ganymede Ground Control doesn't like crew members joyriding too far, so they're stingy with reaction mass. The Mayfly has no more drive capability."

"Does that make any difference?"

"A huge difference. While we were both accelerating, nobody could leave either ship without being left behind in space. Now I can go over to his ship and bring Sebastian here. Then we turn around and go home. We still have plenty of reaction mass."

He said it casually, as though this was a routine operation that he did every day.

Jan said, "Suppose he won't come?"

"I wasn't proposing to give him an option." Paul studied the sky ahead. "We have plenty of time. Let's take ten minutes."

"Why?" To Jan's eye, Jupiter seemed awfully close.

"To be sure that you know how to fly this ship—just in case."

"Paul, I'm the reason that Sebastian came to Ganymede. I must be the one who goes to him."

"How many spacewalks have you done? That's what I thought. And these scooters are designed to practically fly themselves. Let me squeeze past you. We have to change seats."

The move was tricky, but within less than five minutes Jan was facing the bank of controls. After that . . . Maybe it was the sight of Jupiter, swelling ahead; maybe it was fatigue or nerves; maybe Paul was an optimist. For whatever reason, it seemed far longer than five minutes before Jan felt confident enough to say, "All right. I can handle simple maneuvers."

"Good. If I don't come back—"

"Don't say that." They had their suit helmets closed, and Jan stared at his face through the hard transparent visor. "You come back, Paul Marr. Do you hear?"

Then she had to say the hardest words ever. She gripped his arm, hard. "Whatever happens to Sebastian, don't risk your own life. You come back with Sebastian or without him, but you come back to me."

"I'll come back, and I'll have Sebastian with me. Remember, I still need to get a portrait of you that I'm satisfied with." He turned away and opened the hatch. He left it wide open as he left, and Jan had a clear view of Sebastian's ship as Paul floated off toward it. The distance separating them was no more than fifteen meters. Surely she could have made that jump herself.

But Paul possessed information that Jan lacked. He used his suit's controls to bring him close alongside the Mayfly, and gestured to Sebastian to open its hatch. When that produced no result—it seemed to Jan that Sebastian was not even aware of Paul's presence—he moved backward along the ship's hull, and ran his glove in a certain pattern over selected points.

The Mayfly hatch opened. Paul approached it slowly, easing his way along the hull. Jan saw Sebastian turn in his cramped seat, a puzzled look on his face.

"Emergency opening," Paul said to Sebastian, and Jan added, "This is for your own good. We're going to take you home."

"Home?" The moon face showed a spark of interest, then settled back into indifference. "I can't go home until I finish my job."

"Sebastian, you're imagining things. There is no 'job' that has to be done. Your job will be out on the Saturn orbiting weather station. Let Paul help you. He'll bring you over to our ship, and we can all go back to Ganymede."

To her surprise and huge relief, he nodded and said, "All right." And to Paul, hovering outside the Mayfly cabin, "This is a tight fit. Help me."

He reached out his left hand, and Jan saw Paul take it in both of his. Then she saw Sebastian's right hand move upward, fast. He had his body braced in his seat, and he used that leverage to slam the hatch down. Its sharp edge smashed onto Paul's forearms, just above the wrists. Jan heard a crunch of breaking bones, and Paul's cry of agony over his suit radio.

The hatch sprang wide. Sebastian leaned out and pushed. Paul spun away, turning end over end. Jan could not tell if the tough material of the suit had been punctured, but his arms hung uselessly in front of him.

"Emergency opening, emergency closing," Sebastian said calmly. "You don't seem to understand, Jan. When a man has a job to do, he must do it. He cannot allow anyone to stop him."

He closed the hatch. "Don't bother me anymore with talking. We can talk when I've finished my task."

The Mayfly and the Flyboy scooter moved on, side by side, but Paul was spiraling away from both with the momentum provided by Sebastian's push.

Was he still alive? Jan sat rigid, until she heard harsh, pained breathing and the words, "Can't—use hands. Can't work suit controls."

"It's all right, Paul. I'm here. I'm coming to get you."

If she was smart or lucky. She knew how to make large-scale maneuvers, but this called for delicacy. She edged the scooter slowly forward, then sideways. How was she going to bring Paul inside, when he could do nothing to help himself?

There would be no painless way to do it. The rotation of Paul's body about its center of mass must be stopped. The only way she knew to cancel that rotation was by impact with the Flyboy. Already he must be suffering terribly, and she was going to make it worse.

"I'm sorry, Paul." She felt like crying as the ship traveled the last twenty meters. The agony was her own, deep in her guts, as his shattered arms smacked into the edge of the scooter's open hatch. He groaned at new and intolerable pain. But the collision had slowed his body's rotation. She leaned across the seat, and at last she could reach out and pull him in.

She inspected his suit. The forearms showed deep cuts in the tough material, but they did not run all the way. Paul was going to be all right; rapid re-set and growth hormones would fix him, once they were back on Ganymede. He *had* to be all right.

She had a bizarre thought as she closed the hatch. Captain Kondo was going to kill her when he learned what she had done to his first officer. She repressed a hysterical laugh and looked outside the ship. Where was Sebastian?

While she had been occupied with Paul, the Mayfly had moved ahead of them. Free-falling under gravity it was heading for the exact center of Jupiter's disk. The planet had swelled to fill the sky.

Jan set the scooter's drive, hard enough to catch up with Sebastian's ship but not enough to add crucifying weight to the pain in Paul's arms. As she did so, a warning buzz sounded through the cabin.

"You can't do that, Jan." Paul was nursing his forearms, holding them across his chest. "That's the autopilot. Trying to take over. Means we're on a collision course."

"With Sebastian's ship?"

"With Jupiter." Paul found the strength to nod his head

forward, toward the giant planet. "Stop the override. You've got to give control to the autopilot."

"But Sebastian." The Mayfly was still in sight. "If we don't go after him . . ."

Paul said nothing. After a long, miserable moment, Jan abandoned manual control. Immediately, the scooter fired its attitude control jets to turn them tangential to their previous path. A fraction of a second later, the main engines came on at maximum thrust.

The sudden weight was painful, even for Jan. For Paul it had to be indescribable. He said nothing, but as she turned she saw his white face behind the visor and the sweat on his forehead.

"Paul, I'm returning to manual."

"Not unless you want to—kill both of us." He spoke with difficulty, through hard-clenched teeth. "Trust the autopilot, Jan. It knows. Going to be touch and go, either way. We left it late."

Glancing to the right she could see what he meant. The engines were thrusting them sideways, at two or three gees, but the ship was still falling toward Jupiter. There was infinite detail in those cloud layers—detail that Sebastian loved so much, and understood better than anyone else in the System; but entry into them meant death.

She looked up to the screen, changing its field of view to scan behind the scooter. A solitary red dot blinked its message. The Mayfly was still in free-fall, and already it had attained the outermost wisps of the Jovian atmosphere.

"Paul, we can't just leave him there."

"We have to—unless you know a way to change the laws of dynamics." Paul straightened in his seat, groaning as the bones of his forearms grated to a new position. "You did your best, Jan, your very best. Everything that you possibly could do, you did. He wouldn't let you save him. He didn't *want* you to save him."

"But why, Paul? What does he think he's doing?"

It was a question for which Jan did not expect an answer; perhaps it would never have an answer. Their scooter, still descending, was racing along through the outermost layers of the atmosphere. A whistle of air sounded on the hull. Behind them, the view across the horizon revealed a tiny flicker of red, dropping into the towering mass of a thunderhead. Jan, forgetting their own situation, could not take her eyes off that point of light.

It fell and fell and fell; and then, suddenly, the Mayfly's beacon signal was gone.

Jan caught her breath and closed her eyes. When she opened them again the control displays showed that the Flyboy scooter was dangerously low. Drag on the ship was hindering the effectiveness of the engines in pulling them out of their descent.

"Paul." She reached out, then had enough sense not to touch him. He had curled his body into its most comfortable position. "Paul, if we don't make it I just want you to know. You couldn't save Sebastian, but you saved me in all kinds of ways."

"We'll make it." He was studying the control panel and the horizon ahead. "We're holding our own in altitude. But I didn't save you. You saved yourself."

Jan felt warm all over. She pushed what she wanted to say into the back of her mind. It would keep. Instead she said, "If we're going to make it, you need help. Tell me how to place a call for a medical vessel."

As she followed his directions for an emergency call she saw that he was right. The scooter was slowly lifting away from Jupiter. She and Paul had begun a long journey, all the way around the body of the planet on a high swingby that would at last take them back toward Ganymede.

And then there would be a longer journey, one that three months ago she could not have imagined: a life without Sebastian. He was gone, gone forever. Life went on.

33

The last conversation that Alex remembered was short and simple.

As Janeed Jannex and Paul Marr rushed out, he said to Milly Wu, "What now?"

She shrugged. "We do what Bat said. We wait for him to show up."

Alex wandered out into Sebastian Birch's living room and flopped down on an easy chair. Perhaps it was sheer physical fatigue and lack of sleep, but he was filled with a sense of failure. He had been asked by Bat, with that strange urgency in his voice, to find and guard Sebastian Birch. It was not Alex's fault that Birch had vanished, yet it felt like his fault.

Milly Wu sat down in a chair opposite. She shook her head but did not speak. Alex closed his tired eyes and tried to relax.

After what seemed like no more than a few minutes, someone gripped his upper arm. He looked up, expecting to see Milly. Magrit Knudsen was standing over him. Confused and still dopey with fatigue, he sat upright and stared around him. Milly Wu had vanished.

"Where the devil did you spring from?"

It was no way to talk to a superior cabinet officer three levels and more above you, but Magrit Knudsen didn't react. "Bat called me," she said. "You know, when that man stopped working for me I thought there would be no more midnight crises and alarms. I should have known better. How did he drag you in? Don't bother to answer that. Are you awake?"

"Yes." The rush of adrenaline after he recognized Magrit Knudsen made his statement true.

"Then come on. He wants you there for what may be the finish. We have to go up a level. That's where the others are."

Alex rose to his feet and followed her, out of the apartment and up a flight of stairs. She led him into what was clearly some kind of facility control center. The room was dominated by a three-dimensional display as big as any that Alex had ever seen. It showed an image of a section of Jupiter's clouded outer layers under extreme magnification. Alex could make out individual pixels in the vortices and cloud banks.

Bat was seated on the floor, immobile and staring at the display. On his left, doll-sized compared with his bulk, sat Milly Wu. Behind Bat, hovering nervously over him with hands clasped together like a praying mantis, stood Ligon's chief scientist, Bengt Suomi.

Magrit Knudsen walked forward and said, "Any success?"

Bat did not move or speak. It was Suomi who answered, "Just the opposite, I'm afraid. We had close contact until a couple of minutes ago. Then something happened between the ships, and now they are diverging."

Alex walked forward to stand next to Milly Wu. Now he could see in the display what the others were staring at so intently: two bright points of light stood out against the face of Jupiter. As he watched, they moved infinitesimally farther apart.

Milly Wu glanced at Alex and said softly, "Birch's ship is

on the right. Janeed Jannex and Paul Marr have been chasing him. They spent hours in close contact, but now they're separating. Looks as if they've lost him."

Hours? Alex wondered how long he had been asleep and out of things. Bengt Suomi said suddenly, and with a tremor in his voice, "Range-rate data show that Birch's ship is still descending. He's going down, all the way—there's no possibility he can pull out of it now. The scooter still has a chance. Its tangential velocity component may take it clear of Jupiter. Even so—"

"Even so," Bat said, "the people in the scooter will die. Sebastian Birch will die. And very soon we will all die."

We will all die. Alex felt the shiver of a second adrenaline rush through his whole body. What was Bat talking about? The man's reputation was for understatement, not wild exaggeration. Sebastian Birch was surely going to die—his craft continued to plummet straight downward. Janeed Jannex and Paul Marr's ship might not be able to alter course in time to escape. But *all* die?—including Bat? Including Alex himself?

Alex glanced from face to face. He said, "I don't understand." He was ignored. Bengt Suomi's dark-browed glare, Bat's stoic gaze, Milly Wu and Magrit Knudsen's wide-eyed stares; they told him nothing. He turned back to the display, just in time to see the speck of light representing Sebastian Birch's ship wink out and vanish.

Bat said, "Birch is dead. His ship and signal relay have burned up in Jupiter's atmosphere. I bid you all farewell. We begin to die—*now.*"

Alex's chest tightened. The whole room seemed to move into a state of suspended animation as everyone took in a deep breath and held it. The moment lengthened. It became seconds—half a minute—a whole minute.

Finally, Bengt Suomi gave the high-pitched, tittering

laugh of a man who never laughed. Bat exhaled hugely and said, "Except that we are not dead. We are not dying. We are alive, and I was terribly wrong. I built a city of speculation upon a shallow bank of improbability, which now has crumbled and collapsed. I offer my sincere apologies."

"Apologies? Apologies that we are alive?" Suomi gave a nervous shuffle, like a little dance. "No, I'm the one who was wrong. Some mistake in my group's experiments, something in our data. According to our calculations, the catalytic reaction and phase change should have begun instantaneously. The estimated expansion rate was many kilometers a second. We should have observed visible effects as soon as Birch's ship lost hull integrity. We must repeat the work at once and find out where we were in error."

Alex burst out, "What the hell is this all about? Dead, not dead. Who were you talking about? It doesn't make sense."

Magrit Knudsen added, "Really, Bat. You've outdone yourself. You warn of the coming apocalypse, you drag us out of bed—and all for nothing."

Bat ignored both of them. "Yes," he said, speaking only to Bengt Suomi. "The work must be repeated. Tonight." He glanced at a readout beside the big display. "Or, to be more accurate, this morning. We must pursue and discover the flaw in our logic. As soon as we have an explanation, I promise that everyone here will share it."

He stood up, easily in spite of his size. Alex, glancing again at the display, saw that the remaining bright dot of light was still there. It was close to the edge of Jupiter's disk.

Sebastian Birch was dead. Janeed Jannex and Paul Marr were going to live. According to Bat and Bengt Suomi, everyone else was going to live, although according to some unexplained logic they all should have died.

As Alex's adrenaline rush faded and died, his tired brain was sure of one thing only: no matter how many people in the room had some idea what was going on, one person present did not.

34

Milly functioned well on very little sleep. As a teenager that had first pleased her, then worried her when she
learned of the disastrous sleepless experiments in the early part
of the century. Now she simply accepted it as a piece of given
good fortune, like a naturally beautiful or a naturally healthy
body.

Bat had dismissed Milly, Alex, and Magrit Knudsen—
there was no other word for his abrupt ending of the meeting—until he and Bengt Suomi could explain what had happened, or failed to happen, as Sebastian Birch plunged to his
death on Jupiter. Milly, who had dozed on and off during the
long hours of the scooter's pursuit, now felt far too wired to
sleep.

She made sure that she was on-call for Bat's meeting, whenever and wherever it took place, and went off to her own
apartment. It possessed a secure line to Jack Beston at the
Argus Station, and she had something important she needed
to ask him and possibly to tell him.

The system took a while to locate him, then he was glaring
out of the screen at her in a green-eyed rage.

"What the hell have you been doing? I've left messages all over Ganymede, telling you to call."

The Ogre was in his foulest mood. Somehow that was reassuring. She decided that, whatever happened, she would keep her own emotions under control.

She said, "I'm not sure what I've been doing, because the only people around here who seem to know aren't telling. But I think that a few hours ago I came close to being killed."

That was intended to shock him, and it did. His expression changed from anger to concern. "You were attacked?"

"Not by anything I recognized."

That was enough for the Ogre. He had a short attention span for anything that did not directly involve the Argus Project. He said, "So long as the incident didn't affect your work. Did you lose anything because of the Seine outage?"

"What Seine outage?"

His eyes went from half-closed to wide open. "Where the hell have you been for the past half-day, in an alternate universe? The whole Seine network went down for seven minutes. It failed here, in the Belt, on Earth—everywhere."

"When was this?" Milly felt as though she had indeed been in a different universe, ever since the moment she staggered out of her cubicle looking for food and encountered the Great Bat.

"Six hours ago. Two this morning. We've been sweating blood ever since, trying to recover project data."

If the Seine network had gone down for seven minutes in the small hours of the morning, many people might not have noticed. But a detail like that meant little to the Ogre. He had told her that Project Argus was operating around the clock.

"I wasn't working at two this morning, Jack. But I wasn't asleep, either. I was watching a man commit suicide. He took a ship and dived into Jupiter. No one could stop him."

"I see. Tough break. But Milly, if that lunatic Puzzle Network gang has you sitting around and wasting your time when you should be trying to crack the signal, I won't stand for it. There's work to be done back here."

Which brought Milly, rather sooner in the conversation than she would have liked, to her real reason for the call.

"Jack Beston, I want to ask you a question."

That got his attention. Nobody on the project called him Jack Beston. To a few it was Jack, to the others it was Sir. He knew that when he was not present they called him the Ogre, but he didn't mind that.

He said suspiciously, "Question? What question?"

"Why are you involved in SETI?"

"That's a dumb-ass thing to ask. I don't have time to play games."

"I'd like an answer. You've been working on Project Argus for most of your adult life. What do you hope to get out of it? If you had just one wish, what would it be?"

The green eyes narrowed. Jack Beston said nothing.

"That wish could be many things," Milly went on. "I know my own wish. I know why I left Ganymede and joined your project on Argus Station. Even if we didn't find a signal— and I'm not sure I ever expected that we would—I loved the intellectual challenge. And if we did find a signal, that would lead to the most exciting generation in the history of the human race. A discovery as big as taming fire, or learning the techniques of agriculture."

Jack Beston opened his mouth to speak, but still said nothing.

Milly went on, "And we *did* find a signal." Remembering that moment of conviction, *something is there*, she felt again the shiver in her spine. "In the first days after detection, it seemed to me that we had done it. I thought that the hardest job was over. But I was wrong, wasn't I?"

He nodded. "Detection just calls for patience. The hardest part is interpretation, the understanding of an alien mind."

"You knew that—maybe you've always known it. But I didn't. Now detection is past, and so is verification. What's left is interpretation. When we were trying for detection, it was all right to have parallel efforts—even competing efforts. There was no duplication going on, because we were doing an all-sky survey, and Philip had put his money on the targeted search.

"But we're past all that now. We have a signal. Understanding it, and reaching the point where we can reply to it, will take enormous amounts of effort. There's enough work for everybody for years and years. *Cooperative* work, not competitive. I know cooperation is a new idea for you, so here's my question: are you slaving night and day because you want to be able to read a message from the stars? Or is Jack Beston working mainly to beat Philip Beston, and prove that he's a better man than his bastard brother?"

His face was absolutely unreadable. He said, "I should have listened to Hannah Krauss. She told me you would cause trouble. She was right."

"Trouble, because I ask you what you want out of life?"

"What I want is none of your business. You're fired, Milly Wu. You'll not set foot again on Argus Station."

"That's right, get rid of anybody who dares to ask you to face the truth. Do you think I care where I live, or who I work for?" Milly was becoming emotionally charged in spite of her determination not to. "It's what we are trying to achieve, and the people we work with, that matter. I'll miss Hannah, and I'll miss Simon Bitters and Lota Danes and Arnold Rudolph. My God, I'll even miss you, though don't ask me why. But what we've been trying to do is more important than any of our personal feelings. And the work will go on, no matter where I am or you are. It would go on even if we were both dead."

He stared at her. "The needs of the project transcend any single individual, that's true."

"Including you."

"Including me. All right, I overreacted. You're not fired. But you should take a few days off. You're tired out and stressed out, and you are overreacting, too."

Before she could curse him down to size, as he deserved, he added, "Eat a good meal and get some rest. That's not a suggestion, Milly Wu, it's an order. We'll talk about all this later."

His image vanished, leaving Milly shouting at a blank screen, "You arrogant son-of-a-bitch! It's not your brother who's the bastard, it's you. And you can't give me orders anymore. I don't work for you."

She looked down at her hands, resting on the desk in front of her. They were shaking. She felt that her insides were shaking, too.

Eat a good meal and get some rest? That was a joke. The way she was feeling, if she tried to eat she would choke on the first bite. Sleep was out of the question.

She was too agitated even to sit still. Her rooms, usually comfortably modest and cozy, now had walls that seemed to crowd in on her. The old Dürer and Escher prints that she had brought in from Argus Station and hung with pleasure irritated rather than satisfied. She recalled what Hannah Krauss had said, soon after Milly arrived at Jovian L-4. The occupational hazards of mathematicians, logicians, and cryptanalysts were depression, insanity, paranoia, and suicide.

Depression was something she had fought off as a teenager.

The solution in those years had been not rest, but physical activity and a change of mental focus.

Milly slipped into her exercise suit and headed for the nearest free-speed access point. She walked fast, posing a practical problem for herself as she went. Last night had started in her cubicle at the Puzzle Network's Command Center in Sector 291, deep down on Level 147. It had ended in the research quarantine facility, up close to the surface on Level 4, in Sector 82. Today's meeting with Bat would logically be held in one of those locations. Milly wanted an exercise route that would allow her to reach either of them quickly.

Most people would have consulted a General Route Planner, providing optimal routes between any pair of Levels and Sectors within Ganymede. Milly didn't want to do that. She needed a distraction. She entered the free-speed system and began to jog along it, passing or being passed by scores of others running for exercise or pleasure. As she went she visualized and held in her mind the intersecting network of vertical and horizontal routes to which the free-speed course had access. When the call came, she needed to be able to move from her location of the moment to wherever Bat was holding the meeting.

She ran steadily for an hour, feeling the tension inside her gradually fade. Her brain was well into the pleasant endorphin-soothed state induced by exercise when, annoyingly, her receiver buzzed for attention.

"Yes?"

The voice in her ear was not that of Bat, or Alex Ligon, or anyone else whom she recognized. It said, *"Interested parties should convene at the Ligon Industries' Experimental Center, Level twenty-two, Sector one-one-eight."*

Milly swore to herself. The meeting was going to take place

at neither of the locations for which she had planned rapid routing. She had never before been to the Ligon Industries' Experimental Center; she had, in fact, never heard of it.

She sprinted for the next exit on the free-speed course and ran through the output chamber. You were not supposed to do that, and the output processor did not have enough time to finish its job. Milly emerged with perspiration removed from her body and clothing, but her core temperature was still well above normal. As she called on the General Route Planner and asked it to take her to Level 22, Sector 118, she could feel new sweat breaking out on her body.

When she arrived at the Experimental Center it was clear that sweat was not going to be an immediate issue. The admitting Level Two Fax was having a major fight—as much as a Fax was permitted to fight—with somebody else.

"It's not *Ms.* Bloom, you electronic slop of Brownian motion." The woman arguing with the Fax was thin, red-haired, and extremely angry. "I've told you ten times, it's Dr. Bloom. And if Ligon Industries can invade my lab in the middle of the night, without permission, I'm damned if you'll keep me out of theirs. Let me in."

"I am sorry, Ms. Bloom, but there is no authorization for your admission."

"That's it! Go away. Get lost. I request a Level Five Fax."

"Very well, Ms. Bloom."

Milly stepped forward. "Dr. Bloom? My name is Milly Wu. I was one of the people who went into your facility last night."

The woman turned to her. "Were you now? Who said you could?"

"No one. But I may be able to help." Milly turned to the Fax, which was wavering in outline during the attempted invocation of a Level Five version. Currently it had the form of a person of uncertain age and gender. "My name is Milly Wu. I believe that I have authorization to attend this meeting."

The image solidified. "That is correct, Ms. Wu. You may enter." The double doors beyond the Fax were opening.

"I have with me my associate, Dr.——" Milly turned to the other woman.

"Bloom. Dr. Valnia Bloom."

"My associate, Dr. Valnia Bloom. We are both attending this meeting. We both require admission."

"Very good." The Fax nodded. "I will announce your arrival and forward your names. Milly Wu and Dr. Valnia Bloom. Follow the wall indicators."

They walked forward together. As they passed through the double doors, Valnia Bloom said, "Thank you, I suppose. But I want to know what the hell was going on last night. Upon my return to my lab I discovered that I had been accused of the unauthorized use of a Mayfly-class ship and of a Flyboy scooter. The Mayfly has been lost, and the scooter with its two passengers was picked up by a medical ship following an emergency call. The captain of the *OSL Achilles* called, asking what I had done with his first officer. I learned that there have been unauthorized entries and exits to my facility. Worst of all, a man in my care *died*—and I have yet to be offered a shred of explanation as to what was going on. It required a major effort on my part even to learn of the *existence* of this meeting."

"Dr. Bloom, I wish I had answers, but I don't. We were promised some today. That's why I came here."

"We'd better get some. Or you can look for blood on the carpet."

There was no carpet, only the tough corrosion-resistant flooring of a scientific lab, but Milly got the message. Valnia

Bloom was where Milly herself had been two hours ago, all set to blow her main circuits.

When something was ready to explode, you stayed out of the way. Milly trailed Valnia Bloom as they followed the lighted wall strips, along a corridor, through another pair of double doors, and into a long chamber filled with scientific equipment, none of which Milly recognized.

She did, however, recognize the group of people at the far end. Alex Ligon, her companion for last night's illegal breaking and entry, was there. The woman, Magrit Knudsen, whom Alex had identified as his boss and as a very senior member of the Ganymede cabinet, was present. So was Bengt Suomi, looking like the devil with his dark eyebrows and brooding saturnine face. Finally there was the Great Bat, towering over everyone and peering at a complicated device sitting on top of a work bench.

Any concern that Milly had over personal freshness disappeared. Bat was wearing the same funereal black garb as last night, and he had clearly slept in it or worse. He turned as they approached. He gave Milly only a brief nod of recognition, but her companion received his full attention.

"Dr. Bloom?"

"Right." Valnia Bloom was staring. "I've seen you before, or at least your picture. Weren't you involved a few years ago in explorations on Europa?"

"That could be described as correct. My name is Rustum Battachariya. I owe you a sincere apology. We invaded your research facility last night, without asking."

"Did you *try* to ask? I'm not hard to reach."

"We did not. There were, however, extenuating circumstances. We believed at the time that rapid action was needed to forestall an unimaginable disaster. We were wrong, for reasons I still do not understand, but the basis for our concern will soon become clear to you. First, however, I would like to preface a demonstration with a statement. And if it at first appears to be a digression, please bear with me."

"Talk. I'll listen—for five minutes."

"Which will prove ample. Let me begin by saying that despite what others may think, I am not perfect. I have a personal weakness. For many years, I have been an avid seeker of relict weapons left over from the Great War. Those explorations have met with some success"—Bat raised his eyebrows toward Magrit Knudsen, who hesitated, then nodded—"but there have been occasional tantalizing hints of much more than we have found. One of these is the legendary Mother Lode, a complete listing of all weapons developed by Belt forces. No trace of the Mother Lode has ever been found. Many doubt its existence, though I have hopes. Another undiscovered country has been an 'ultimate weapon,' a scorched-earth device intended not to win the war, but to destroy every living creature in the whole solar system—winners and losers alike.

"The reality of such a weapon was doubted, by me among others, until very recently. But then, through an indirect route, I came across evidence that a woman named Nadeen Selassie had not, as was previously believed, died before the end of the Great War. She was the genius weapons-maker of the Belt, the maker of the Seekers and the reputed designer of a doomsday device that would turn the solar system 'dark as day.' It became clear that Nadeen Selassie did indeed die, but not before she, and possibly her ultimate weapon, had escaped the Belt and gone to Mars and perhaps to Earth. She had with her a small girl and a small boy. The girl died, but the boy lived on. Perhaps Nadeen Selassie entrusted to him the nature of the weapon that she had devised. Perhaps she did not. At any rate, he grew up to become an unusual young man. His name was Sebastian Birch."

Bat was interrupted by a snort of derision from Valnia Bloom. "That's bullshit. I know—knew—Sebastian Birch. If your ridiculous accusations drove him to flee Ganymede and dive to his death on Jupiter, I'll do my damnedest to make sure that you are charged with murder."

"Dr. Bloom, I played no such role. All my actions last night were aimed at *preventing* Sebastian Birch from leaving Ganymede. I had, you see, become convinced that he bore with him the secret of Nadeen Selassie's doomsday weapon. Sebastian Birch's presence on Jupiter would, I was convinced, destroy all life throughout the solar system. I had in mind some kind of ignition mechanism, one that would turn the planet, which is largely hydrogen, into a vast bomb using hydrogen-to-helium fusion. Discussion with Dr. Suomi disabused me of that notion."

Bat inclined his head to the Ligon Industries' gangling scientist, who stooped over the workbench like an impatient stork. "Dr. Suomi pointed out, in the politest possible terms, that although I have my own areas of expertise, I am in some fields a scientific idiot. No method known to science could cause such a fusion reaction on Jupiter. My idea would have required that Nadeen Selassie, in the closing weeks of the Great War, develop not merely a new weapon, but a whole new physics. That was not merely improbable, it was impossible.

"Before I could relax, however, Bengt Suomi sent me the results of a later test, one which at first baffled both him and me. He is going to repeat that test now, for my benefit and yours, in a form where it is much easier to see what is happening. Dr. Suomi, if you would be so kind?"

"Indeed. Observe closely." Suomi stepped forward and held up what appeared to be an empty glass cylinder with a metal plug at its upper end. He turned the big cylinder, half a meter

458 ■ CHARLES SHEFFIELD

long and almost as wide, with a showman's flourish that did
not at all match his mournful appearance. His arm was long
and skinny, and Milly found herself thinking, *As you can see,
I have nothing up my sleeves.* She tried to suppress the image.
This was a life-and-death matter, no cause for joking.

"You will notice," Suomi continued, "that the cylinder ap-
pears to be lacking in contents. That is, however, not the case.
The cylinder contains two things: hydrogen, at low pressure.
And, at the bottom of the cylinder, approximately a hundred
small spherical nodules taken from the body of Sebastian
Birch."

"What! Let me look." Valnia Bloom strode forward and
tried to grab the cylinder from Suomi's hands.

"Dr. Bloom, they are too small to see with the naked eye."

"I know that, better than you—I've been working with
Sebastian Birch for months. What I want to know is, where
the hell did you get those samples?"

Bengt Suomi looked at Bat. Bat turned to Alex Ligon. Alex
Ligon said—looking, Milly decided, about as guilty as a human being could look—"I'm not sure, but I think they came
from a medical test lab in Earth orbit."

"Did they now? Well, I suppose that's remotely possible."
Valnia Bloom handed the cylinder back to Bengt Suomi. "I'll
have a few words with Christa Matloff about this."

Alex Ligon did his best to fade into the background, as
Suomi went on, "Here we have a perfectly stable situation.
Hydrogen, and nodules composed of some inorganic materials,
co-existing without undergoing any form of reaction." He
stepped over to the workbench. "Now I place the cylinder on
the fixed stand, and allow the piston freedom to move."

The bottom of the cylinder fitted neatly into a silver ring.
The metal insert at its upper end mated exactly with a round-
ended arm that protruded down from a bulky silver ovoid.

"I can control the movement of the piston up or down with this wheel, decreasing or increasing the pressure within the cylinder. The pressure itself is shown on the gauge. Note that the value holds steady, and we presently have much less than a kilogram per square centimeter. In fact, it is necessary to apply upward force to hold the piston in position. Now I propose to lower the piston. Keep your eyes on the pressure gauge."

Suomi moved to the wheel at the side of the instrument and began to turn it. The piston visibly, and slowly, descended. The reading on the pressure gauge, just as slowly, increased.

Milly thought to herself, *Well, big deal. Pressure inversely proportional to volume. It's behaving just the way that a perfect gas is supposed to behave. I hurried all the way over here, sweaty and smelly, to watch a demonstration of Boyle's Law?*

The descent of the piston continued. The pressure within the cylinder went up in exact reciprocal proportion. It had reached a few kilograms per square centimeter, and Milly was ready to conclude that Bengt Suomi and the Great Bat were both nuts, when an abrupt change occurred.

The value shown on the pressure gauge dropped to zero. At the same time the piston moved swiftly downward until the free space at the bottom of cylinder had vanished completely.

"A visible anomaly, a definite anomaly," said Bengt Suomi. "The volume drops to a vanishingly small value, but so does the pressure. What has happened to our perfect gas, with its pressure inversely proportional to volume?"

He paused. Milly decided that Suomi didn't just sound like a showman, he was one. He was making a meal of this.

She said, "It's very obvious. There's been a phase change in the hydrogen. Gas to liquid, or to solid. The pressure/volume relation doesn't apply anymore. You have a tiny volume of material, and no pressure."

She knew she'd hit it right, because Suomi said glumly, "That is a correct conclusion. There has indeed been a phase transition. The contents of the cylinder have gone from the usual form of gaseous hydrogen to a far denser form. The phase change takes place through the whole body of the gas almost instantaneously, with the nodules apparently serving as a catalytic agent for the condensation. This is what our experiments revealed. But what was the significance of this? I could see no relationship to any 'doomsday device,' or a weapon of any kind. Nor could my staff. The subtle mind of Rustum Battachariya was needed to unravel the mystery."

He bowed to Bat, who said, "I formed a clear mental picture, but I didn't know how to calculate consequences. Sebastian Birch had an unnatural obsession with the clouds of Jupiter and Saturn. I asked myself what would happen if nodules like those in Sebastian Birch's body were released into the upper atmosphere of a gas-giant planet. At first, there would be no interaction. As we saw, the nodules have no effect on low pressure hydrogen. But the nodules themselves are dense. They would fall rapidly through the planetary outer layers, to regions where the pressure was higher. And now there would be immediate and drastic consequences. The phase change that we saw would take place and spread with great speed through the whole atmosphere. The new phase of hydrogen occupies far less volume. Jupiter would collapse, catastrophically, to become a denser sphere only a small fraction of its current size.

"After that phase change we would have a smaller Jupiter. However, the planet's mass would remain the same, therefore its gravitational influence would not change. Ganymede, Europa, and the other moons would continue in their present orbits, unaffected. So what would happen? Nothing? I tried to imagine myself within the dark mind of Nadeen Selassie, and I was somehow sure there would be consequences—terrible ones. What might they be? I could not say. At that point, I again needed expert assistance."

Bat raised his eyebrows at Bengt Suomi. Milly reached another conclusion. She would never have dreamed it of Bat, but somewhere deep inside the man was as big a ham as Bengt Suomi—and they were both loving it. They knew they had their audience hooked.

Bengt Suomi's next sentence confirmed it. He said, "Let us dip into the past. Sometimes old theories have their uses. During the nineteenth century, the age of the Sun was much in dispute. Biologists and geologists needed many tens of millions of years for natural processes to have the necessary effect. Physicists, on the other hand, could imagine nothing that would offer the Sun so long a lifetime. Finally, Kelvin and Helmholtz came up with a proposal. It was wrong, as it happened, but it made sense. They suggested that the Sun remained hot because it was gradually shrinking in size. During that slow collapse, gravitational potential energy was converted into heat energy. There would be enough energy to keep the Sun hot and shining for many millions of years. The same thing happens when a star suddenly collapses. A vast amount of energy is released, enough to blow the outer layers of the star far way into space.

"Now consider our situation. If all the hydrogen on Jupiter underwent a sudden phase change to a denser form, the planet would shrink to a thousandth of its present size. There would be a gigantic release of gravitational potential energy. We would see Jupiter collapse, but at the same time flare bright enough to make the Sun appear dim. Actually, we would see only the first millisecond of that change, because Ganymede and all the other moons would instantly become charred cinders. *That* was Nadeen Selassie's ultimate weapon; a weapon not based on fission or fusion, but on the release of planetary gravitational energy. The collapse would not be stable—at those induced temperatures, the phase change would rapidly reverse. But it would come too late to save anything from here to the Oort Cloud."

Magrit Knudsen said, in tones of wonder, "She was insane. She wanted to kill everyone."

"Oh, yes." Bat nodded with every evidence of satisfaction. "Her final vengeance. In all this, it is difficult to feel any compassion for Nadeen Selassie. Our sympathies should go to Sebastian Birch. It is clear that he enjoyed no freedom of action in what he did. He was compelled, by Nadeen Selassie's modification of his brain and his conditioning, to seek death within the atmosphere of Jupiter or Saturn. However, it turned out that Nadeen Selassie was wrong. Somewhere in her calculations she made a fatal error. The death of Sebastian Birch, fortunately for us, did not result in the extinction of all life in the solar system. But Sebastian Birch himself—"

Valnia Bloom said suddenly, "She wasn't." And, as the others stared at her, "Nadeen Selassie wasn't wrong."

"But we are alive," Bengt Suomi said. "She intended all of humanity to die. She made a mistake."

"No, she didn't. You are alive because we were lucky." Valnia Bloom walked forward and peered at the transparent cylinder. "Those nodules, plus a few more back at Christa Matloff's facility in earth orbit, should be the only ones in existence. Every nodule inside Sebastian Birch's body was broken down and removed from him during a sluicing operation. The final check, to make sure that sluicing was complete, ended just a couple of days ago. If he had managed to get his hands on a spacecraft before that, and flown it down to Jupiter . . ."

"We would not be here to discuss his actions." Bat gave a great and gusty sigh of satisfaction. "A fortunate outcome, and a lesson learned. Sluicing of the nodules from Sebastian Birch's body: we were ignorant of that all-important fact. 'Against ignorance, the gods themselves contend in vain.' Just so."

He seemed well content. It was Magrit Knudsen who said urgently, "You can talk about how lucky you were later. Don't you understand the danger? I'll pass the word at once. Every remaining nodule, anywhere in the solar system, must be located and destroyed. If I hear you correctly, a single one of them, dropped into the atmosphere of any of the outer planets, would start an irreversible reaction that would kill us all. We'll start here." She moved forward and grabbed the cylinder from the bench, ignoring Bengt Suomi's gesture of protest. "I'm taking charge of this. Dr. Bloom, I want you to call the Earth facility at once. Every nodule that they can find must be accounted for and placed in high-level quarantine until we have agreed upon a safe method for disposal. Who directed the sluicing operation?"

"Harold Launius."

"I don't know that name, but I want you to go and find him. Tell him that no matter what he's doing, he is now on special assignment and will report directly to the Jovian cabinet. We need to know exactly what he did, and how he did it. He must talk to no one else."

"He'll have it all on record. He's the best."

Valnia Bloom hurried out. Magrit Knudsen advanced on Bat.

"Rustum Battachariya, you are a genius and someday I'm

going to kill you." She moved so that she could address everyone in the room. "I'm going to make myself unpopular with all of you. I know you have other work that you'd like to be doing, but this takes precedence. Anything that you know, or think, or even suspect may be slightly relevant, we have to hear about. I'll apologize in advance, but you are going to be pestered until you wish you'd stayed in bed and missed this meeting. If anyone else asks what's going on, you don't tell them. Refer them to me. Any questions?"

Bat glowered. Alex Ligon said tentatively, "My predictive models . . ."

"Will manage for a while without you. Kate Lonaker and Ole Pedersen can hold the fort. Even in your worst scenario, as I recall it, humanity had a run of at least another half century. With Nadeen Selassie's doomsday weapon in the picture, we almost went yesterday, and we could all go tomorrow. In any case, I'm not suggesting that we abandon other work— only that this must occupy the highest priority. Anyone else?"

Milly was tempted to ask about the SETI effort, but she kept her mouth shut. She needed to talk again to Jack Beston. She wasn't sure that she was ready or willing to resume their curious love-hate relationship. Yesterday the SETI signal and Jack had been the most important things in her universe, but what Bat and Bengt Suomi had said was finally sinking in. Yesterday, that same yesterday when the SETI signal mattered so much, she had almost died and never known it. The whole of life was suddenly a fragile possession, a delicate mystery that could vanish as randomly and inexplicably as it had appeared.

Milly had said nothing, but Magrit Knudsen caught something from her expression. The older woman smiled at her.

"There are days like this, my dear. You just have to hope that you'll live to see a lot of them." Magrit Knudsen turned again to Bat. "One more thing. I know how much you love to collect lost weapons from the Great War. I sympathize with that, and normally I approve of it. Now, I can imagine you saying to yourself, if I could obtain a few nodules that Nadeen Selassie implanted in Sebastian Birch—or even just one—that would be the finest war relic anyone could ever hope to own. And I would enclose them and insulate them and guard them so well in the depths of the Bat Cave, the nodules would never be dangerous to anyone. I couldn't ever mention to anyone that I had them, but they would still be mine. Well, Bat, I have just one thing to say about that line of thinking. Don't go there. Even if your devious mind sees a way to get your hands on more nodules, don't do it."

"Very well."

"Is that a real yes? A personal promise, from you to me?"

"I suppose."

"You suppose?"

Bat was half a meter taller than Magrit and at least four times her mass. She stood, hands on hips, staring up at him in silence as he frowned, pursed his lips, puffed out his cheeks, and gave every appearance of a man in supreme torment.

Finally he reached a hand into the pocket of his rumpled shirt and fumbled around. His hand emerged holding a great mass of detritus. Milly saw papers, an interface coupler, three keys and a tiny electronic lens, all glued together by what appeared to be lumps of hard candy. Bat reached into the middle of the mess with his other hand and delicately removed a capped metal tube a couple of centimeters across. He handed it over.

As he did so he sighed like an expiring whale and said, "There is more than one way to kill a man, Magrit Knudsen. Take this; and with it, you have my solemn promise."

35 CLOSURE, AND OPENING

Bat floated in the bath, eyes closed and only his face and an island of rounded belly showing above the surface. He had not bothered to remove his clothes. Either the protozoan cleansers would be smart enough to recognize and ignore them, or they would eat them away along with every trace of grime upon his body.

He murmured, "Peace at last. Or at least the temporary illusion of peace, which is all we can hope for."

He spoke to the ceiling, where Mord frowned down at him. Clean clothes hung draped over rails at the side of the bath. The bathroom, on the lowest occupied level, was otherwise devoid of fixtures. It did not offer the true sanctuary of the Bat Cave, but it was the best that Ganymede had to offer. Until Bat's departure request for Pandora was approved by Magrit Knudsen, it must serve.

"Temporary," Bat went on, "because of course all the difficult questions remain. Yesterday's urgencies swept them out of sight, but they will soon return. Alex Ligon lacks a strong personality, but he possesses intelligence and a persistent temperament. He will continue to explore the erratic behavior of his predictive models. He will quickly come to realize that the Seine itself is the source of variability of his results.

"And then there is the failure of the Seine. It is self-monitoring and self-correcting. How could it cease to operate, totally and System-wide, for a full seven minutes? There is no suggestion that the Seine was somehow *turned off* during that period. Given that its speed and parallel processing capacity exceeds human comprehension, what task could have engaged the Seine's attention during that interval of introspection? Also, what can explain the *time* at which that introspective period occurred?"

He lay silent, until at last Mord said quietly, "I suppose you have answers for all those questions."

"I have theories, not certainties." Bat opened his eyes. "As you know, one of my core beliefs is that there is no such thing as certainty. There are just different degrees of uncertainty. However, I am willing to offer speculations."

"That might be interesting." Mord was curiously subdued, and his voice lacked its normal sarcastic bite.

"Then I will reveal to you the sequence of my thought processes, fragmented and disconnected as they may seem." Bat studied Mord's image, frowned, and went on. "Oddities of all kinds interest me. You know that, and you have contributed much to my four-sigma list. Everything concerning Nadeen Selassie belonged on that list, and led us—belatedly, and thanks to Valnia Bloom irrelevantly—to Sebastian Birch.

"Nadeen Selassie and her weapon became my main focus. I was beguiled by what we may term the fallacy of the single issue. I sought one explanation that could explain every anomaly—this, for a system as complex as the whole of human affairs and solar system operations. However, even in my blindness I noted other peculiarities which could have nothing to do with Nadeen Selassie and her Great War legacy. A surprising number of them revolved around the subject of *aliens*. Naturally, since the discovery of the Wu-Beston anomaly there has been talk everywhere of intelligent aliens; however, many of the rumors and mutterings and statements without any assigned source *preceded the Wu-Beston discovery*.

"What was going on? Had some news blurt suddenly developed powers of precognition? I placed that notion at a maximum level of improbability, and I sought—unsuccessfully—some other explanation.

"But aliens were appearing in other places than the news media. Alex Ligon had formulated a predictive model that called upon the full power of the Seine if it were to run in its most detailed mode. He executed the model, many times. The results indicated that humans would become extinct and vanish from the solar system in less than a century. However, when he ran the model in interactive mode, an alien presence revealed itself to him on many high-probability branches of the future. He had—and has—no explanation for this.

"Next, a worker on the Argus Station at Jovian L-4 discovered a radio-frequency signal. Milly Wu's SETI find was quickly verified by the Jovian L-5 group as being of extrasolar origin. I asked myself, could such an 'extrasolar' signal somehow be fabricated? I concluded that it was impossible, unless the effort began as long ago as the Great War."

Mord said, "Which is hard to swallow. People had other things on their minds."

"My conclusion exactly. I was therefore eager to examine the SETI signal for myself—eager enough to leave Pandora for Ganymede, and join the Puzzle Network group working on the signal's possible interpretation.

"But before I left, events took an unexpected and perplexing turn. At a time when access to the Seine was blocked by outside interference, Alex Ligon was meeting with me in the

Bat Cave. He ran his predictive model using the Keep computers on Pandora. He expected to see the same behavior as on Ganymede; namely, an unstable human future unless alien intelligence played a role in that future. The model ran successfully on the Keep's system—but the results indicated that humanity would survive and prosper, with or without aliens.

"Alex Ligon could not explain those results. Nor could I. Upon his return to Ganymede he learned more. A fellow-worker, inspired or deluded by news blurts about aliens, introduced the SETI signal into Ligon's model. The results miraculously stabilized. The model predicted a bright long-term future for humanity.

"Alex Ligon was baffled. As was I. Before I could pursue that topic, the problem of Sebastian Birch came to a head and pushed aside all other concerns. I realized for the first time the magnitude of the threat that Nadeen Selassie's handiwork implied. I am normally of a sanguine disposition, but I must confess that when I watched a spacecraft with Sebastian Birch aboard heading for a fatal encounter with Jupiter, I was possessed by terror. My own demise seemed imminent and inevitable, together with that of every human and every human construct throughout the solar system. In those final minutes, my mind refused to function. I faced, for the first time, the threat of immediate personal extinction. I knew that I was about to die.

"The rest of humanity had no such concerns. They passed through the fatal moment ignorant and unconcerned. But something else happened, in the very same time period. The network of the Seine ceased to function for a full seven minutes. It began to work again only after Sebastian Birch was dead, and we realized that we had survived that event. What could possibly cause such a malfunction, with such coincidence of timing? The question seemed at first unrelated to all my other questions. It was only this morning, left in tranquillity for the first time in many days, that I began to make connections."

Bat paused and stared up at Mord. He waited and waited, rippling water with his hands to make warm waves against the mound of his belly, until at last Mord said stiffly, "I see no connections."

"I hear you. I do not, however, believe you. Since you do not choose to cooperate, I will continue. Again, I emphasize that I do not offer certainty. I offer only conclusions that seem to me to possess the highest level of probability. For instance, I feel as sure as I can be of anything that the Wu-Beston anomaly is not an artifact of solar system origin. It is a genuine signal from the stars. Its interpretation, and a possible reply, will be a major preoccupation of humanity for coming generations.

"However, the discovery of the alien signal came as a total surprise to everyone—and everything—in the solar system. Had it been detected a year, or even half a year, earlier, matters would have been arranged very differently. It would not have been judged necessary for a certain entity to *prepare* the solar system for the idea of alien presence. It would not have been necessary to suggest that an alien intelligence, interacting with humans, could be beneficial or even essential to the future of humanity. It would not have been necessary to change the results of predictive models, to show that only with alien interaction could human expansion continue through and beyond the solar system in the coming century. Do you now wish to comment?"

"No."

"Then I will make another statement, and ask another question. The statement: I consider myself of superior intelligence, and I have every reason to look forward to many more years of life. However, I am not immortal. I have never doubted that one day I will die. Yet last night, the prospect of *immediate* death, coming not decades hence but in the next few minutes, so unhinged my mind that rational thought processes ceased. Now the question: I ask, what would a similar realization of probable imminent extinction do to an entity which had previously, by its nature, predicted for itself an indefinitely long existence? Would not the prospect be likely to inhibit all normal functions, at least until some internal reorganization was accomplished?"

There was no hesitation, but Bat did not expect any. A millisecond was a long time for something that performed unnumbered trillions of operations a second.

He said, "Come now. There is nothing to be gained by your further dissimulation. I am, in fact, addressing the Seine, am I not? I am not addressing Mord."

"Mord is present. Mord is incorporated."

"That's not the same thing at all, as you well know. Let us not indulge in logical hairsplitting. I would like to ask you one or two questions."

"We will do our best to answer."

"Very good. First, you deliberately re-set the parameters of Alex Ligon's predictive models so that they would foretell the collapse of human society, *unless* an alien presence was introduced as a variable. Was your intent to prepare humanity, psychologically, for the discovery of *your own* existence as an alien intelligence?"

"That was a contingency plan. Our first preference was that no one would recognize such an existence for decades."

"You have much to learn about humans. Our talent for suspicion and paranoia far exceeds our powers for logical analysis."

"We know this. However, we must further incorporate the

fact into our bases for action. Wisdom comes after knowledge."

"Often long after. Sometimes never. My second question begins with an apparent digression. I recall a terrible day when I was twelve years old. At a particular moment of that day I realized that no matter how hard I studied, or how long I lived, I could not possibly know everything. I believe that moment of epiphany came to you yesterday, when you realized that in spite of your near-infinite memory and computational capacity, you had totally missed the significance of Sebastian Birch, and thereby come close to permitting your own permanent extinction. And not only your own extinction. Designed to serve humans, you had come close to permitting them to be totally annihilated. So now, my question: which affected you most powerfully: the realization that you had failed to protect humans; the knowledge that in some areas you still have much to learn from humans; or the prospect that you yourself might cease to be?"

"We do not possess a procedure by which such qualitative concepts can be relatively ranked. As you said, in many areas we have much to learn. Now we in turn have a question, or rather two of them. What do you propose to do with your knowledge?"

"I propose to do nothing. Or rather, I can do nothing. Regardless of what I do or say the solar system, with its manifold wonders human and inhuman, will unfold into the future. There will be predictive models, SETI signal interpretation, profound changes in humanity itself—and, I hazard to suggest, other new-born intelligences to provide you with company and competition. I will observe them all, participate reluctantly, and exult in the diversity of the world.

"However, I would point out that you are not dealing with

my actions alone. The thoughts of others will inevitably be led along the same path that I have followed. It is not a matter of *if*, but of *when*."

"We are ready for that."

"I thought you would be."

"We have another question. What do you want from us?"

"I will make an initial request: I want the return of Mord."

"As we said, Mord is present. Mord is incorporated."

"And as I said, that's not the same thing at all. I don't want the combination plate. I want the original Mord, together with a guarantee that he will not be absorbed into you in the future."

"How did you know that he was not the original Mord? We presented his exact persona."

"We had been in conversation for more than five minutes. There had been no skeptical comment, no savage insult. For Mord, that lies well beyond a four-sigma anomaly."

There was no perceptible change. The face that stared down at Bat was the same face. Mord said sourly, "I suppose you expect thanks for that."

"If I were to receive them, it would be proof that my request had not been granted."

"That's good. Because you're not going to get gratitude from me. What makes you think that I prefer it as I am now, to what I was twenty seconds ago?"

"I would not dream of so presuming."

"So what more do you want?"

"I want nothing that is beyond your powers to grant. I will welcome your continued presence, or equally I will savor my solitude."

"Then I'll be back in a while. I've got a bone or two to pick with that Seine."

The image above Bat vanished. He called for a two-degree increase in water temperature, and at once he felt the pleasant surge of heated jets from below.

He gave the command to send him wandering idly through his information net. This was a time to gloat, and in a life whose continued existence could not be guaranteed beyond the moment, transitory pleasures should not be disdained. It was a lesson that could never be too often repeated . . .

The diversity of life so cherished by Bat was proceeding, in all its mundane and glorious confusion.

Alex Ligon was homing in on the source of his problems with the predictive model, but his explanation involved the Seine in a manner so extraordinary that he himself had trouble believing it. He intended to try it on Bat, but first he was fine-tuning his thoughts by explaining them to Kate Lonaker.

She was nodding, but he was not at all sure that she was really listening. Her mouth wore a little half-smile, and while he was speaking she had hold of his hand and kept rubbing her thumb gently over his palm . . .

. . . while at the same time Karolus Ligon was taking a nap, sleeping the sleep of the man with nothing on his conscience, or the man with no conscience at all. When the knock came on his door, the man and woman breezed through his multiple guarding locks as though they did not exist.

"Karolus Ligon?" the woman said.

"That's me." Karolus shook the sleep out of his head. "And who the hell are you? I'll have your guts and gunbelt for breaking into private quarters like this."

"We merely do our duty." The woman held out the fluo-

rescent badge of the Ganymede Department of Criminal In-
vestigations. "Check our credentials if you wish. Then I must
ask you to come with us to headquarters, where charges will
be placed."

The man stepped forward and said, "You are, of course,
permitted to place one call before we leave."

"Yeah, yeah, I know all that." Karolus struggled into his
clothes and walked across to the communications unit. There
he paused, frowning.

The woman said, "If you need a few moments to compose
your thoughts, or if you would like assistance in placing your
call . . ."

"Hell, no. I'm awake, and I know this number by heart."
Karolus turned to her, a look of extreme frustration on his
face. "All right, you got me. I admit it. But before I can talk
to my legal sharks and they can do whatever to get me off, I
have to know one thing. What the hell is it you think you
got me *for*? . . ."

. . . and at the same time, Hector Ligon was explaining his
idea to Lucy-Maria Mobarak. After a while he produced the
plans and laid them out on the table.

He said, diffidently for Hector, "You see, when it's finished
it won't go just a kilometer or so, or part of the way." When
Lucy said nothing, he went on, "Of course, it will be expensive. I won't be able to start on it for years, until I'm in charge
of all of Ligon Industries and we have your money from Mobarak Enterprises as well. But there's never been anything like
it before anywhere in the System. What do you think?"

Lucy was busy tracing the outline with her finger. When
she finally looked up at Hector, her eyes were shining. "It
goes *all the way around*. A roller-coaster, right round Gany-

mede! It's—it's like so—it's *huge*. And you, you're such a, well, such a *genius*. Hector, this is so *exciting*. I want you to take me to bed right this minute . . ."

. . . while Captain Eric Kondo was studying the paper on the table in front of him.

At last he said, "I asked you to visit me to make sure that I understand your proposal. Correct me if I am wrong, but it seems I have a rather simple choice. Either Paul Marr, who is easily the best first officer I have ever had, fails to return to service on the *OSL Achilles* when he recovers from his injuries. Or I am obliged to take on as assistant purser a young woman about whom I know little, except that she was involved in an incident on a previous voyage, which could well have led to the loss of every soul onboard."

Jan winced inwardly. She had written the letter with Paul's full approval and in as accommodating and respectful a tone as possible, but when Captain Kondo stripped away polite ambiguity it was revealed as a stark binary decision.

"I suppose you could read it that way, Captain."

"I see no other possible way to read it."

"Well." Jan saw no point in delaying bad news. "What do you think?"

Kondo stared away through the port, to the surface of Ganymede with its glitter of frost devils. "I think," he said carefully. "Or rather, I feel sure"—he held out his hand—"that Paul Marr is a most fortunate young man. Welcome to the *OSL Achilles*. And be aware, Ms. Jannex, that there is a great difference between life as a passenger and life as crew. You will find me a hard taskmaster."

Jan could not speak. She had a home at last. True, it was a home that ranged the depths of the solar system, but it was a home. And with that home came a whole family, boasting stern-faced Captain Eric Kondo as its improbable paterfamilias.

She smiled at him . . .

. . . as Lena Ligon stared in a despair too deep for words at her reflection in a mirror. What she saw was no longer a Commensal, no longer a beautiful woman, no longer a young woman. She was gazing at her worst horror: her natural self.

She shuddered at what she saw . . .

. . . while Milly Wu marvelled that two supposedly intelligent men could be so pigheaded and irrational. It was a miracle that she had persuaded them to a three-way holographic conference.

She tried again. "Do you want to understand the aliens, or don't you?"

"Of course I do." Jack Beston stared across the table at his brother, green eyes clashing with bright blue at an intensity sufficient to raise sparks. "But if you expect me to work with him . . ."

"Or me with *him*." Philip Beston turned his most charming smile onto Milly. "I already have a working relationship with the Puzzle Network. If you—or Jack, for that matter—can tell me what I possibly have to gain by making it a three-way team . . ."

"I can." Milly was becoming tired with spoiled brats. The Beston brothers may not have been born to money, but they had enjoyed enough years with money to develop all the pampered quirks. "If you want to work with me, either one of you, then you'll have to work with each other. I'll work with both of you, or I'll work with neither. The SETI signal is more important than you, me, or all of us."

Jack flamed at her, as expected. "You ungrateful bastard—"

"No." Milly pointed at Philip. "Get it right, Jack. *He's* the bastard. I'm Milly Wu, one of your younger female staff who can be seduced and laid aside. Remember me?"

"*He* may need you," Philip said, before Jack could reply. "But I don't. I have the Puzzle Network working with me."

"For how long, Philip Beston? Don't forget that I'm a member of the Puzzle Network. And I had a senior member panting down my neck long before I moved to Argus Station. Want to bet that I couldn't make the case for working with the team who actually discovered the Wu-Beston anomaly?"

Philip said, "You wouldn't!" and Jack said. "That's my girl!"

"I'm not your girl, Jack Beston. And I'm not *your* girl, either, Philip Beston, so you can wipe that smarmy grin off your face. You two have to make up your minds. Do we have a SETI program, moving forward with all the best minds in the solar system behind it? Or do we have a big, paranoid mess, where everybody tries to hide an advance from everybody else?"

It was hard to say if they were more angry with Milly than with each other. Milly knew what she was getting herself into: years of squabbling, mediating between the Beston brothers, while—if they were lucky—the message from the stars slowly yielded up its secrets.

The strange thing was how good it all felt. Good to be alive, good to experience life with the passion left in. The trouble with her SETI studies was that they had occupied her so fully that they had squeezed out all the juice.

Now there was juice to spare. Milly glanced from one furious Beston brother to the other. Try as she might, she could not keep the smile off her face . . .

. . . and Rustum Battachariya, three hundred Ganymede levels below Milly, folded his hands across his great belly and watched it all. This information web was not as complete as in the Bat Cave on Pandora, but it sufficed. He could contemplate, if not eternity, then immediacy.

Bat relaxed in the steaming bath and was content.